TROLL LOTTA LOVE

THE HIPPOSYNC ARCHIVES
BOOK 5

DC FARMER

WYRMWOOD
BOOKS

COPYRIGHT

This edition published by Wyrmwood Books 2025

A CIP catalogue record for this book is available from the British Library

eBook ISBN - 978-1-915185-36-5
Print ISBN - 978-1-915185-37-2

Published by Wyrmwood Books.
An imprint of Wyrmwood Media.

EXCLUSIVE OFFER

WOULD YOU LIKE A FREE NOVELLA

Please look out for the link near the end of the book for your chance to sign up to the no-spam-guaranteed Readers Club and receive a FREE DC Farmer novella as well as news of upcoming releases. HERE ARE THE BOOKS!

FIENDS IN HIGH PLACES
THE GHOUL ON THE HILL
BLAME IT ON THE BOGEY (MAN)
CAN'T BUY ME BLOOD
Coming soon
SOMEWHERE OGRE THE RAINBOW

PART 1

CHAPTER ONE

NEW THAMESWICK, THE FAE WORLD

WIMBUSH the alchemical herbologist stood opposite the New Thameswick pub known as Withersporks, watching the punters skip in and roll, or get thrown, out. He'd been skulking in a doorway on the other side of the street for twenty minutes, preparing what he had to say. He was already two hours late for his soon-to-be brother-in-law's stag do. Truth be told, he did not want to be there at all. He had no time for such frippery. And spending a whole Saturday afternoon and evening getting drunk fell very much into the frippery bracket in Wimbush's estimation.

He would have cried off were it not for the fact that he had something to tell Jac, and even in Wimbush's preoccupied, self-absorbed mind, he'd felt that perhaps it was best if he delivered the information in person.

Gritting his teeth, he stepped out from the doorway onto the pavement, waited for a couple of driverless horse-drawn carriages to trundle past and hopped over a couple of mounds of steaming horse manure to the other side of the road. He pushed open the creaking front door and peered into the gloomy, smoke-filled interior. It was difficult to see anyone, but not difficult to find Jac's party. All Wimbush had to do was follow the voices singing the chorus of 'The Wizard's Shiny Wand'.

'Kenwyn,' cried Jac Logsdon as soon as Wimbush entered

the dingy back room they occupied. A dozen of them were seated around a table: four had no shirts on, two wore constabulary helmets and Jac, who immediately stood and ambled across to greet Wimbush, was wearing a pink tutu over striped underpants and safety boots. Jac was a big man, a blacksmith by trade, and his clamping embrace of Wimbush was enough to drive all the air out of the alchemist's lungs.

'I thought you weren't coming, Kenwyn,' Jac said. 'I am soooo glad you could make it.'

Over Jac's shoulder Wimbush quickly counted thirty-five tankards on the table, as well as a couple of bottles of Dragon's Breath whisky and a dozen voices belting out the song. Wimbush thought it silly, irksome and bawdy. But the singers were clearly having a wonderful time.

You can wash it with dishcloth…

'Having a good time, Jac?' Wimbush asked.

Jac released him and stood back. 'Let me get you a drink.'

You can dip it in a pond…

'No, Jac, listen. I need to tell you something.'

'Okay.' Jac swayed in front of Wimbush, his eyebrows arched inquisitively over a very red face. 'Remember I told you and Selma—'

You can polish it till it glistens…

'I'm marrying her, did you know that?' Jac's face bloomed into a wide grin. 'Your sister.'

'Yes, I did know. Well, remember I told you I had this project I wanted to do in the north?'

'Somink about flowers?'

The wizard's shiny wand.

'Yes, a very special flower. Silver wolfsbane. Well, the chancellor of the Polyalchemic managed to get me a spot on a mining expedition leaving on Friday.'

'Wow, thassgreat. So long as you're back on the twennieth.' Jac belched.

Wimbush inhaled a waft of cheese, onion and beer thick enough to stir with a spoon.

'Me an' Selma are geddin….geddin married on the twennieth.'

'Yes,' said Wimbush. 'That's what I came to say. I won't be able to make it.'

Jac frowned and blinked. 'Whaaat? But Selma'll be gutted. You're her only bruv, Kenwyn.'

'I know, but this is a golden opportunity for me. A chance to get my thesis finished. If I can pull this off…' Wimbush's eyes had drifted out of focus, but now they zeroed in on Jac in front of him. 'I'll be away for several weeks.'

'But there'll be other,' Jac burped again, 'other,' he swayed, this time alarmingly, '…other speditions.'

'Possibly. But who knows when. And my work is very important to me, Jac.'

Oooohhh, yeeew can point it at a donkey…

'Know that. You keep telling us that. But izzit more important than your only sister's weddin'?'

'I can't think of it in those simple binary terms, Jac. It's vital work. So, I'm sorry. I won't be there.' He handed Jac a note. 'I'll be at the port in Sampton from tonight. I'll send you and Selma a card.'

Or wave it at a blonde…

'But Kenwyn,' said Jac, 'she's your only sister, mate. An'…an' she told me she had this bridesmaid friend who quite fancies you.'

'Yes, well. Needs must.'

It's hard as wood and knobbly…

'She's going to be gutted, is Selma. Aren't you going to tell her yourself?'

Wimbush cleared his throat. Twice. 'No, have to go. Transport to Sampton is at four today and she is not at home. So, best of luck to you both.' Wimbush held out his hand.

'Stay for a drink at leasst,' said Jac.

'Not possible. The world is waiting for Kenwyn Wimbush, Jac.'

The wizard's shiny wand. Hey!

With that, Wimbush turned on his heel and left the pub, pushing all thoughts of his sister's crushing disappointment from his head. There was important work to do. He'd done his duty by telling Jac. That was all there was to it.

CHAPTER TWO

SPIV, THE FAE WORLD

When her brother did not return to the cabin at his usual time, Nadia was not worried. Sometimes Kasimir liked to visit with Yana, but it was never for very long and Nadia didn't mind. She liked Yana, too. Not in quite the same way as her brother, obviously, but with all that golden hair and her wide, welcoming smile, Yana was very likeable. Such a contrast to Kasimir's dark features, though his smile could be just as winning. Nadia often wondered how things would be if ever Kasimir and Yana married. She'd probably have to live with them unless she found a partner of her own.

She made a noise like a horse sputtering. There was no one amongst the puerile village boys that she wanted to spend three minutes with, let alone a lifetime. Most of them moved their lips when they thought. Which meant that there was not much silent lip movement at all in Spiv.

Nadia the gooseberry it was, then.

She squeezed her eyes shut. These thoughts were as stale as last week's bread, and twice as unpalatable.

Sighing, Nadia padded over to the window and peered out.

Darkness was approaching at speed. Nadia knew it represented nothing more than the sun's descent beyond the mountainous horizon, and that all the bits that were visible in the world in daylight were still there if you knew where to look. But, for the other inhabitants of Spiv, the night's arrival also brought a whole host of things that only ever existed in the absence of light. Things that weren't visible, other than in the odeon of the imagination; to wit all that was supernatural, unfathomable and altogether terrifying.

The dark was the mother of all intangible fears when it came to the unfettered ignorance that passed as the village's superstitious belief system. Nadia knew how to voice the protective charms Kasimir had taught her, yet she toyed, as she often did as the light leached away from the sky, with not performing them. Embraced, for a moment, the thrill of wondering just exactly what would happen if she didn't cast the praesidiom. What if she simply sat in in the dark and awaited…events. But she knew Kasimir would ask her as soon as he came through the door if everything was done. Had she swept the room? Placed the stones? Secured the chimney? More often than not he'd repeat one or two of the rituals just to be sure. Kasimir, being older, was insistent.

Of course, they had to perform the sacred enchantments.

Everyone did, and woe betide the person that failed to. Didn't she know that not hexing the chimney could let in a lepertroll? Didn't she realise she had to lock the door and be inside once the sun set because to be caught outside in the dark put you at the mercy of the dreaded capcaun? And that, Kasimir would say with rolling eyes, could only mean abduction and a horrible death.

Kasimir did a lot of eye-rolling when he was with Nadia.

'But how do you know that? How do you *know*?' she'd asked when she'd been nothing but a curious child.

'Because the elders say so, and they are wise and wish to ensure we come to no harm,' he'd explain, exasperation turning his statement into an incredulous laugh that implied how ridiculous and infantile it was she needed to ask. 'Why would you even risk finding out otherwise? You know the story of Gorik the Blind, who wandered out into the night and was never seen again. Taken by the witch—'

'Babramic Jaggr.'

The look of horror on Kasimir's face when she said this had startled her. But not half as much as the way he immediately shut his eyes and hopped on one foot in an anti-clockwise circle three times before touching both eyelids and the tip of his nose with his thumb. She'd managed not to laugh on seeing the relief register when he'd opened his eyes and realised nothing had changed.

'You said her name without holding a warding stone,' he'd whispered, genuinely horrified as he reached into his pocket to retrieve a hollowed-out pebble to press into her hand. 'Promise me you will never do that again.'

She'd nodded, feeling as if she might burn up in the intensity of his impeaching and zealous gaze.

But of course, being Nadia, she did speak the name of the forest witch out loud to herself many times without the warding stone, though she was careful to do it out of anyone else's earshot so as to avoid anyone screwing themselves into the ground by accident. She spoke it just to see what might happen.

Nothing ever did.

Not once in the hundreds of times she'd dared herself to do so.

The wind didn't howl, or the clouds darken, or the earth tremble, or the air fill with a hail of snakes like it was meant to.

Still, Kasimir had made her promise.

Sighing, she took some masoma dust—a foul-smelling concoction of powdered roots, dried garlic and goat dung—from the jar in the cupboard and sprinkled a tiny amount onto the floor of their living room-cum-kitchen. Then she took the corkscrew hazel broom and swept the dust outwards in increasing circles until she got to the front and back doors of their small cabin. She knocked twice on the inside of the door and, satisfied that no one answered, opened each in turn and swept the dust out into the cool evening air. Air that carried the fresh smell of pine and far away on its breath.

The elders said the masoma would keep the strigoi away.

Next, she prised up the flagstone from under the sink and removed a toad from the moist spot beneath. It croaked in remonstration, but Nadia soothed it with some soft words.

She fetched three flat pebbles from a bowl and rubbed each in turn against the toad's skin before returning the amphibian to its home. She took the three stones and placed one carefully on a tiny shelf above each of their three windows.

The elders said the stones protected the house from lelele. 'Let this stone be a wall against the prying eyes of the demons of the night,' she said, trying to sound as if she meant it, as she recited the charm three times.

She turned back to the table and lit the lamp before fetching a battered handwritten book passed down from generation to generation in each family. It was full of cramped, flowery writing outlining the history and deeds of her forebears. It was the elders' role to meticulously copy the words into new tomes to replace those that were lost or so faded as to be illegible. In the book was the history of how once the people of Spiv and the surrounding lands of Steppeinit once lived peacefully as hunter gatherers until the evil one, Babramic Jaggr, cast her shadow over the land.

In one night, according to legend, she transformed the forest into a place of horror and death.

It was said she lived in a house made of bones guarded by two-headed pricolici and commanded an army of monsters. The subsequent war between the humans and terrifying supernatural foes was more a case of battling for survival than anything else. It was said Babramic Jaggr laid waste to vast tracts of land leading to the mountains and it was only Spiv's relative isolation that saved it from the worst of her excesses. Even so, the attrition rate was high. The monstrous abominations that emerged from the forest to kill and feast terrorised the villagers. And yet, as with all the best stories, there came a hero. Everyone knew about Grigori, the one who came forth and discovered the sacred berries that forced the witch into accepting an uneasy truce. In was into this time of peace that Kasimir and Nadia were born. Yet it was a peace dearly bought.

Nadia didn't open the book. She knew the story. She'd heard it a thousand times and though some people read it religiously every night, that was not the reason why she drew the book towards her now and looked longingly at its dog-eared corners and the faded, threadbare spine. She ran her fingers over the title and felt the depression where the leather had been worked.

The Chronicles of Spiv

.   .   .

NOT THE MOST inspiring of titles. Yet she could only thank the elder who'd rewritten this copy and repaired the pages with thick white thread. It was clear to Nadia that the book had been damaged at one time. Dropped, perhaps, when its owner was forced to flee, into something fluid that ruined many of the pages. The repairs resulted in a thicker copy than was usual. But it also meant that some of the newer inlaid pages were inserted with the facing page blank. And it was that simple fact that filled Nadia's heart with joy. Using the tip of Kasimir's hunting knife, she trimmed the blank pages and thinned out the remaining frill of paper so it would stick easily to the page beneath with sugar water. The net result was a complete book devoid of empty pages…and lots of blank sheets upon which she could write. The elder scribes—her betters—wrote using oak gall and fine quills. Nadia made do with crushed blackberries sieved through muslin, mixed with vinegar, water and salt, and a quill fashioned from a crow's feather.

But the words remained on the page where she put them and that was all that mattered. Because Nadia was blessed, or cursed, with an imagination. She placed the book on the table and worked her finger under the spine to loosen the thread she'd sewn it back with. It opened as a flap. From there she could access the pages she carefully hid in the space between the leather cover and the thicker board of the book itself. Out of habit, she then turned her copy of the *Chronicles* over and opened the pages, laying the spare sheets onto its spread surface so that to anyone watching it would appear that she was reading the good book full of the words of truth.

Except these weren't the book's words. These were simpler words, crafted with wonder and, worst of all, imagination.

These were Nadia's words.

CHAPTER THREE

Once, in a country not too far away, there lived a family of farmers. They worked the land, grew vegetables and tended goats. The farmers had a daughter called Lilith who did many chores and milked the goats and weeded the vegetable patch. But when the weather was fine and warm, and her chores were done, Lilith would go for long walks through the meadows and across the stream until she came to the old wood. There she would stand and inhale the wood's breath sharp with the tang of pine, sometimes musty with the damp odour of mushrooms and dead leaves. These smells would call to her and she would follow along the paths taken by the animals under the green canopy of leaves sheltering her from the bright sun. Lilith would pick berries and sit on the fallen trunks and watch badgers and foxes play. Sometimes she would climb the trees and look out across the land to the mountains beyond, and dream of snow and ice. Sometimes she would wake up at night and walk through the meadows under a sky glittering with a million stars. Lilith loved the land and the land loved Lilith.

THERE WERE OTHER WORDS, too. Other tales of animals and Lilith's adventures. Simple stories in simple prose. But in Spiv, these innocuous words in these innocent stories were dangerous beyond measure.

No witches, nor pricolici, nor capcaun, nor strigoi.

The truth, for the occupants of Spiv, was that the world was full of such dangers, whereas Nadia's world contained none of them. Her stories were full of the smell of flowers and the noise of burbling streams and glimpses of young animals play-fighting. Her stories, therefore, were full of lies.

Nothing but seditious, blaspheming nonsense.

Nadia knew what would happen if the elders found out and so she hid her words in the book. Kept them secret. Even from Kasimir. But what she loved more than anything, except Kasimir, was to make up her stories, write them down and then read them back to herself, allowing her imagination to soar. She could lose herself for hours after only a paragraph or two. As she did now on this tangy spring evening with the nightjar's gruff warbling fading as dusk eased into the darkness of night.

Time slipped away like water through a cracked stone. When she heard the knock on the door, for a moment Nadia had no idea what time it was. She glanced at the clock: it was well after nine.

The knock came again. Urgent, insistent.

'Nadia, do not be afraid. It is I, Dalibor. No ghoul or spirit lurks without.'

Panic flared in Nadia. She gathered up her loose notes and stuffed them back between the pages of the *Chronicles*. She was flustered. Dalibor was not only an elder, but a portreeve: the head of the council.

'How do I know you are Dalibor?' she said to buy some time as she shut the book and turned to face the door.

'Good, Nadia. Well done. It is well to be wary. Ask me a question.'

Nadia hesitated. 'If eight goats wander off the pasture and three come back, how many are there left when there were fourteen to begin with?'

There was a pause before Dalibor said, 'The wind howls. I have difficulty hearing.'

'If eight goats—'

'Still I cannot hear you.'

'IF EIGHT GOATS—'

She heard a sound like a forehead press against the door and a low whisper. 'Ask me something not involving numbers. Mona. Ask me about Mona.'

Nadia sighed. 'Mona fell and hurt herself last week. How was she hurt?'

'My clumsy daughter broke her thumb,' Dalibor said.

Nadia undid the bolts and lifted the latch. Light from inside the room spilled out to illuminate Dalibor's long dark beard and intense gaze. Two others were with him: Radomil, a boy the same age as Kasimir; and Mrena, the mother of Tasia, a girl of Nadia's age whom she had once called a friend.

'May we come in, Nadia?' asked Dalibor.

Nadia nodded. 'Of course.'

It was only when they were inside that Nadia saw the gravity of Dalibor's expression, how Radomil wouldn't look her in the eye and how Mrena's lips were thin and bloodless.

'Can I offer you—'

Dalibor cut Nadia off. 'We have grave news.'

'What?' Nadia asked.

'Kasimir. There has been an accident at the Gathering.'

Nadia's breath caught in her throat. 'An accident. Is Kasimir hurt?'

Radomil, who'd looked up when Nadia spoke, slid his eyes away like startled lizards scampering off a rock when her frantic gaze met his.

'He fell into a nest. His rope snagged on a sharp rock and he undid his harness.' Dalibor's face was granite. 'It was quick. He did not suffer.'

The room swam in front of Nadia's eyes. At once Mrena's hands were on her elbows, guiding her to a chair.

Kasimir. Her Kasimir…dead?

Nausea gripped her, and she felt her head forced down between her knees.

'Breathe, Nadia. Breathe,' Mrena said.

'We share your pain, Nadia,' Dalibor murmured.

'I couldn't reach him. I tried, but…' Radomil's words choked off.

Nadia's mind whirled. Death was no stranger to Spiv, especially at the Gathering. But Nadia knew Kasimir was careful. Always so careful.

He fell into a nest. That could only mean a rjeper's nest. She'd never seen one but Kasimir had and he'd described the vicious, agile, sharp-toothed predators well. As large as wildcats but more a belligerent cross between a mink and a clawed badger. Their fur as pale as milk and their disposition rapacious beyond measure.

'Did he suffer?' Nadia asked.

Radomil winced but shook his head. 'He was at the top. He fell almost ninety feet. He did not move once he had fallen. He did not move when the rjepers…' The words trailed off into nothing.

'Let the tears come,' Mrena said, squeezing Nadia's shoulder.

But no tears came. Not with all three of them watching. Especially not with all three of them watching. For some reason, despite the pain of inexplicable loss that churned her gut and made it difficult to breathe, Nadia decided she did not want to give them the satisfaction. Stubborn and deep would have been her mother's description of her character. The more generous people of the village called it contrary. Most simply defaulted to weird.

'Because there is no body, we cannot cremate. But we will hold a remembrance meeting tomorrow. Kasimir was strong and respectful. He will be missed.' Dalibor's words were tender, but their meaning felt like a sharp spike in Nadia's spine. 'As is the custom, Mrena will stay with you tonight. An hour before dawn, she will light the lamps and assist you in assembling Kasimir's possessions for distribution to the rest of the community. You may keep three small items for sentimental purposes. This house will be reallocated to a different family and we will find you suitable accommodation. Tomorrow, it will be expected of you to take Kasimir's place at the Gathering. You know one member of each family must do his or her duty to appease Babramic Jaggr.'

Mrena spoke up. 'But portreeve, she is not suitable for such work. We have discussed this several times at council and—'

Dalibor held up a hand to stem the woman's words. 'It is the law. We must not make exceptions. Families who refuse to partake in the Gathering do not survive. Do you not remember the Yanachs? Conscientious objectors. Visited in the night by some entity that killed without mark to make then permanently unconscious objectors. I do not want such a fate to befall Nadia. We have no choice.'

This was a threat, Nadia knew it. But then threat was a watchword in Spiv. The village's whole existence was predicated on threat. The families farmed, grew vegetables and tended animals but it was mandatory that one member attend to the Gathering; the tall chambers under the earth where the dread rjepers lived in the caves by day and hunted in the forest by night. The Gathering had been arranged at the behest of the witch and signed in blood a decade ago.

The Spivs laboured to set up wide shelves of oak to capture the guano deposited by the vast colonies of bats that nested in the caves. In the Gathering the young people of the village toiled to remove the filth by the hundredweight and throw it into the deep gorge where Babramic Jaggr magically disposed of it. All so as to protect the rjepers, whom the witch saw as pets. But it was dirty and dangerous work high up on ropes in the darkness of the caves. And, of course, Nadia constantly pointed out the folly of it all to Kasimir. The rjepers had occupied the caves for centuries before the Gathering came along. So had the bats and both had existed perfectly well and shared the environment without coming to any harm.

But such talk was slapped down.

A deal with the witch had been struck and the forest, though dangerous, was no longer the deadly threat it had once been. This was the contract that allowed Spiv to live in her shadow and not to perish. Or so it was said.

'But she is not like the others,' hissed Mrena with a nod to Nadia. 'She is a dreamer. She talks to herself. She—'

'Enough. You will stay with her. Prepare her and clear the house before dawn.' Dalibor looked around at the small cabin. His eyes alighted on the copy of the *Chronicles* on the table and he smiled. 'I see that you have been reading your *Chronicles*, Nadia. Good. You will find solace in these words.' He reached for the book and picked it up. 'Well worn, I see. The spine is almost severed. You must let me take it to the scribes. They will make good this copy.'

'No,' wailed Nadia. She sprang up and snatched the book out of Dalibor's hands but succeeded only in slapping it to the floor, where it clattered, the spine flapping open like a gutted fish.

'I will return it,' said Dalibor in reprimand. 'Radomil, pick it up.'

Radomil obliged. 'It's coming apart,' he said, retrieving the loose pages that fell from the book.

'Well, it is certainly now in much need of repair. Let me see.' Dalibor took the book and the pages and held them under a lamp, his tall figure stooped as he assessed the damage. Silence filled the cabin as the portreeve read. Mrena exchanged a questioning glance with Radomil. But all the boy could do was frown and shake his head.

Dalibor remained still and silent for long seconds.

When, finally, the portreeve looked up, the blazing anger in his eyes made both Radomil and Nadia flinch.

'What is it?' Mrena asked.

But Dalibor's eyes fixed on Nadia. 'Who wrote these words?' he croaked.

Nadia didn't reply.

'Who wrote these words?' The voice rose to a rumble of thunder. 'Was is Kasimir? Was it your brother?'

'No,' yelled Nadia in defiance. 'Kasimir didn't write anything. I did. And they're just words. Nothing but scratches on the paper.'

'They are much more than scratches on paper, girl. These words are redolent with sacrilege and profanity. They defy all our teachings. All our beliefs. Even to think these thoughts is to incur the wrath of the witch. To commit such thoughts to paper is…' Dalibor's face was blotched purple with rage. He turned away and began pacing. 'You look like your brother, but he was true and honourable. You…' He shook his head. 'This changes everything. I must summon the aldermen.' He turned to Mrena. 'Do not let her out of your sight. Radomil, stay here and guard the door. No one and nothing is to be let in except me. Do you understand?'

Radomil nodded, his face white with shock.

With that, Dalibor swept from the room. Radomil bolted the door. Nadia watched, her insides now as hollow as the cave that had stolen her brother's life.

'What did you write on that paper?' Mrena asked, her voice stern.

'Words. I wrote words.'

'I have never seen the portreeve so angry. What did you write?'

'Did you call the witch names?' Radomil whispered. 'Did you?'

'I didn't call the witch anything. I simply…I wrote how I wished things were. No witches, no monsters, no haunted forest, no Gathering. Just us and the land and the sun and the wind soughing, though I admit soughing was a bit over the top—'

Mrena let out a moan. 'Blasphemy.'

'Kasimir said you were different,' Radomil said, his back to the door. 'He said you needed watching. I was going to—'

'Quiet, boy,' Mrena ordered. 'There will be no more talk of this. We remain in silence until the aldermen return.'

And so Nadia sat, mired in her own dark, miserable thoughts. She knew she would not sleep. There was too much pain in her heart, but it was the pain of loss, not of fear for herself. And so she sat alone, while Mrena watched and Radomil slumbered. Sat alone and grieved for her wonderful, strong brother and awaited her fate.

CHAPTER FOUR

THE NORTHERN SARMATIC FOREST OF
STEPPEINIT, THE FAE WORLD

WIMBUSH THE ALCHEMIST sat up in his tent and rubbed his eyes.
Grey dawn light filtered through the thin canvas onto a
haphazard arrangement of portable equipment scattered about
the interior. He could hear voices and the crackle of a fire in the
early morning stillness.

Another day, another opportunity. He reached for his leather-
bound journal, put on his glasses and began to write.

DAY 17

*Having pushed east yesterday, we are now near the banks of a great
river. Our guide, Steffan, calls it the Uuze. The miners seemed very discour-
aged in their twig analysis. They say there is no trace of silver, though the
geology would suggest rich mineral deposits should abound. I, on the other
hand, have found three new species of beetlewort. As yet, no sign of the
wolfsbane, but I remain hopeful. We are all vigilant after our discovery of
the bodies of some prospectors three days ago. Their blood was still fresh
when they were found. I know that Riggon had wanted to spare me the sight,
but it is clear that evil stalks these forests.*

Otherwise, the day looks promising.

. . .

He closed the journal and stretched before climbing out of the fur covers. Quickly, he slid on his coat and wrapped a scarf around his neck. His bladder, like an insistent three-year-old, was demanding attention. He stuck his head, covered by a striped nightcap, through the tent flap and spotted Steffan feeding the fire.

'Morning,' called Wimbush, clambering out.

'Mornink,' Steffan growled.

'Is it safe to…you know what?' Wimbush asked. The cold was triggering some uncomfortable spasms below his umbilicus and he did a little dance outside the tent with a rictus smile.

'You know what?'

'I need to…empty myself.'

'Ah.' Steffan nodded. 'I have asked all the bears and they are happy for you to empty anywhere except east of the camp. They would not want you to empty there. East is their, how you say, toilet place.'

A second man came out of the trees carrying a bucket. Square and solid, Riggon's craggy features gave little away. He walked into the clearing and began to pour water into a pot.

After a significant pause, Wimbush asked, 'So bears use the woods as toilets?'

This caused Riggon to pause in mid-pour. He looked up at Wimbush, frowned like a man who had been confronted with situations like this several times already over the past twenty-seven days and had given up trying to rationalise how anyone could be so astonishingly bright on the one hand, and so hope-lessly naive on the other. Turning back to his pot he said, simply, 'They do indeed, Wimbush. So go south. Safe there.'

Riggon shot Steffan a look. The guide shrugged and grinned.

'South it is,' said Wimbush. 'I shall whistle. If I stop whistling, you will know that I have encountered a problem as per the agreed protocol.'

'Right,' said Riggon, still pouring. 'The agreed whistling protocol.'

Wimbush, his nightshirt ending halfway down his shin to leave a small but significant gap before woollen socks and boots began, looked up at the sky and turned south. Whistling loudly, he headed out of the camp. After fifteen paces there was no sign of the tents, but thankfully the smoke from the fire was visible above the dense canopy of trees. He continued to whistle while he emptied, nervous eyes scanning the forest, and watched the steam rise gratifyingly from around the base of a target tree. Finished, he turned back and retraced his steps.

The remaining two of the five-man expedition had risen and were busy making breakfast. The taller and thinner of the two went by the name of Kebbers, had hands like shovels and face like a hatchet. The other was Ozil, older and smaller with a morning rattle and wheeze on his chest that spoke of a two-ounce-a-day pipe-smoking habit compounded by a working life spent underground in all kinds of dust.

But then, Wimbush reminded himself, this was a mining expedition. He knew little about mining. Though being a well-read academic alchemical herbologist, he knew a great deal more than most. His presence on the recce was purely a working arrangement. Riggon had agreed to let him come—for a signifi-cant, some might say extortionate fee—on the basis that he stay out of their way. The West Thameswick Polyalchemic, where Wimbush normally lectured in arcane herbology, had granted him a six-month sabbatical to allow further pursuit of his interest in the extremely rare silver wolfsbane, *aconitum argentum*. In sabbatical terms, he was eligible for twelve months, but Wimbush, being the diligent, thorough and conscientious soul that he was, did not like to leave his students for any longer than three.

They, on the other hand, would have been quite happy for him to have taken the full year.

Several, even.

Wimbush's lectures were well researched, packed full of information and topped the list of the most boring in the whole of the Polyalchemic. But he, possessing an outlook as narrow as a gnat's whisker, remained blissfully unaware of his droning unpopularity. And though he might have walked into MENSA with his eyes shut, it is likely he would have done so with one hand over his ears to blot out the intrusive chamber orchestra playing on the stage, forget to shake hands with the nice man offering the certificate and not laugh at the, 'Wimbush, that's a great name for a botanist,' quip, no matter how many times he heard it.

'Bacon, doc?' asked Ozil, laying rashers in a pan.

'Ah, no. I will prepare some porridge as usual, but thank you for the offer, Mr Ozil.' Wimbush went back into his tent and emerged with a canvas sack from which he took a small saucepan. Filling this with water that he measured in a tin flask, he then added two and a bit spoonfuls of oats, taking at least five minutes with the 'bit' by counting out the ingredients individually—fifty oats, twenty dried fruits and forty grains of salt—before adding these to the mixture and setting it to simmer on the fire.

'Kwafe?' Steffan asked.

'Who?' Wimbush asked.

'Kwafe. Boiled kwafe beans.' Steffan threw him a small red cherry-shaped bean. 'They grow wild in the forest.'

'Ah, *rubiaceae*. How does it taste?'

Kebbers nodded. 'Not bad. Bitter, but if you add some honey it has a kick.'

Steffan held out a battered tin mug. Wimbush took it and sipped. 'Hmm. Aromatic, but too acrid for me, I'm afraid.' The mug had a logo. 'Stirbacks? Who or what are they?'

Steffan shrugged and took back the mug. 'Kwafe shop in Kansk. You get many refills and, if you can drink ten cups, a free mug.'

'Is it good?'

'Is run by vampires.' Steffan made a face. 'Also bearpiss'.

'Is it that bad?' Wimbush frowned.

'Bearpiss. The kwafe at Stirbacks gives me bearpiss.' Steffan thumped his chest and belched.

Wimbush blinked and let his mind consider the logistics of how one would go about collecting the urinary output of what was a highly dangerous mammal when a cog shifted. 'You mean burps?'

'Yes. Bearpiss.' Steffan belched again.

'But you still drank ten mugfuls?'

'Of course. You get free mug.' Steffan opened his hands in a gesture of obviousness.

Ozil snorted and poked at the sizzling bacon.

'Mr Riggon, the plan for today is to head north, yes?' Wimbush asked, deciding that he'd heard more than enough about bearpiss for one day.

'It is. We move away from the river towards the higher ground.'

Wimbush paused to stir his nicely bubbling porridge. 'My offer still stands, gentlemen. I would be happy to use the dousing—'

Riggon cut him short. 'No, thank you, Mr Wimbush. We don't believe in wands or wonderworking when we prospect. Taints the ore. Never been a good lode found using wonderworking. We have our own methods.'

Ozil nodded and Kebbers grunted in agreement.

Wimbush shrugged. 'Have you though that perhaps your method of testing twigs for traces may be faulty? I am no geologist, but these forests indicate young mountains and the dousing technique—'

'Thanks for the offer, but, like I say, we have our own methods.'

'Obviously.' Wimbush stirred his pot, pondering. 'However, where there is more than one method it makes sense to try a different one if—'

'We've been through this,' Riggon said with a touch of irritation.

'Indeed.' Wimbush nodded. 'But your response to my offer lacks a certain logic and—'

'Just leave it, doc,' Kebbers said, and there was far less subtlety in his voice. It was a warning, just loud and growly enough to get through even Wimbush's thick skin.

Wimbush looked up into the tall man's scowling face. 'Well, the offer is there if you change your minds.'

Riggon nodded, took a last sip of kwafe and threw the rest onto the ground. As he stood up he hesitated and reached into an inside pocket. 'Almost forgot.' He pulled out a folded piece of paper with rough cut edges. 'I found this just outside your tent. Near where you'd been writing in that journal of yours. I didn't know what it was, so I had to read it. Apologies for that. It's from your sister.'

Wimbush got up quickly and took the letter from Riggon. 'Must have fallen out from between the pages,' he muttered.

'It's none of my business, but you gave up being at your sister's wedding to come on this expedition?'

'It is none of your business, but yes, I did.'

'Pity. Was she upset that you missed the wedding?'

'She will get over it.'

'Will she, though? You're her only living relative and were meant to give her away. You could still turn back now, you know. It wouldn't take you long to get back to the last lumber camp. Couple of days at most. From there it would be a few days by boat.'

'It's just a wedding. I do not see what the big fuss is all about.'

'No, you don't, do you?'

Wimbush stared. 'Why would I go back?'

Riggon shrugged. 'You did read that last paragraph, didn't you? The one about her putting the wedding off because you weren't there. That there's more to life than getting on at the Polyalchemic?'

'My sister is—'

'Very sensible, it strikes me. And she's worried about you. Flowers won't keep you warm at night, Wimbush. Even very important ones like your wolfsbane.'

'I have a duty to my work.'

Riggon's mouth turned down at the corners. 'Some might say that your first duty should be to those close to you, bugger the flowers.'

Wimbush's mouth formed a mirthless smile. 'I'm sorry, but you, like so many others, simply do not understand.'

Riggon spat into the dirt. 'I don't think it's me that's having trouble understanding.'

It was another beautiful day. Above them, the sky stretched from one side of the clearing to the other an unblemished blue, and the sun was already warming the air. They ate their breakfast, packed up the camp and set off, Steffan in the lead, Kebbers and Ozil behind him, then Wimbush, who had replaced the nightcap with a wide-brimmed hat in West Thameswick Polyalchemic colours. From the brim a transparent gauze hung down to protect his face from the bugs that buzzed busily in the still forest air. Behind him walked Riggon, silent and watchful. Every time Wimbush stopped and stooped to check on some alpine flower blooming on a rock, Riggon would pause and wait, ever patient.

CHAPTER FIVE

SILVER.

That was the expedition's theme. Riggon and his men were interested only in the metal. Wimbush was passionate only about the wolfsbane with silver as its prefix. Yet it was that prefix that made all the difference. This rare plant bore the adjective because of the way its light grey leaves glistened in the dewy dawn and its pale flowers lit up a glade in the moonlight. But it was sought after not only for its colour but because of its rarity and for the particular extramundane properties it possessed. Its cousins, the variously coloured or quirkily named plants who were also members of the family *aconitum*, were all uniformly poisonous and deadly with spiked leaves that could graze a leg and paralyse its owner faster than you could say, 'Ow, my le—'

But silver wolfsbane was different. Though equally lethal in large doses, smaller distillations, properly prepared through the correct alchemical processes, had proven extremely useful in the treatment of lycanthropy, dancing legs syndrome, globe artichoke haemorrhoids, intractable nightmares and, worst of all, the red death.

Wimbush, as a young apprentice, had travelled to Fitsot to observe. There, he'd seen the red death first hand. An illness that began with a high fever and severe aches, soon giving way to an eruption of painful pus-filled blisters covering the skin. The blisters then burst and scabbed over, leaving deep scars, while the afflicted suffered from intense exhaustion and delirium. It had a profound effect on him. And the only thing that had helped the terrible suffering had been extract of silver wolfsbane. And this had all been through research based on the dried root supplied from rare shipments from Steppeinit's Malkovitch monks.

No one had ever successfully brought back a living plant.

Not yet.

———

A MILE in from the river, the land began to ascend. They followed a stream and half a mile later, Kebbers put up a hand and grunted a halt. He and Ozil were pointing to the rocks that formed a jagged wall parallel to the trail they were following, alongside a small dry wash leading into a narrow channel.

'We'll try here.' Kebbers turned back to speak to Riggon.

Ozil walked off the trail and gave a sudden excited shout. 'Hey doc, is this what you're looking for?'

Wimbush followed the miner to stare down a bank. There, a crop of erect yellow flowers with deep green palmate leaves grew in a patch of dappled shade. Wimbush stepped down and knelt to examine the flowers.

'Ah, sadly no. What you observe here is the witches' cowl, *aconitum venefica*. Particularly deadly. Touch the plant and then pick your nose at any time within the following six hours and it will induce raging diarrhoea, vomiting, paralysis and death before the day is out. That, Mr Ozil, is not the silver wolfsbane, but it was a nice try.'

'Got any more funny stories, doc?' asked Ozil as the herbologist stepped back to the path, whistling cheerfully.

Wimbush inclined his head. 'I am surprised that you found that story amusing. After all, the effect of the plant is hardly funny for the victim.'

'Gods,' Ozil said, with eyes to the heavens.

Frowning, Wimbush left the miners to it. He wandered off, absorbed by the wonderful alpine flowers he found, watching rabbits scamper away and listening to the birds chatter in the canopy above. Half an hour later, he heard Riggon shout his name.

'Any good, gentlemen?' asked Wimbush as he rejoined the men.

'No. Nothing here,' said Riggon with his usual sanguine expression. 'We press on.'

And press on they did. They stopped at one more likely spot where the miners looked for placer deposits and studied the trees and foliage, occasionally snapping off a twig or a stem and mixing it in a small flask with some fluid that Kebbers carried in his shoulder pack. The lack of any sort of reaction from either the miners or the flask told Wimbush that their search had not ended and would continue.

They climbed steadily as the afternoon wore on, the air getting cooler as the sun dipped ever lower. Sometime in the early evening, with the light beginning to die, they emerged into a clearing. What struck Wimbush most was how incongruous it felt, this open space on a domed meadow in the middle of the forest. There seemed no obvious reason as to why no trees grew here, and yet the space marked a rough oval amidst the beech and pine.

'We camp here,' said Riggon.

Steffan, in the lead and already having crossed the clearing, turned back. 'I would not recommend here, Mr Riggon. This is not good place.'

Riggon frowned. 'It's a perfect place. The ground is dry, there's running water not a hundred yards back on the trail. What's not good about it?'

Steffan walked back quickly to close the gap between him and Riggon and spoke in a low voice so as not to be overheard. When he'd finished, Riggon shook his head but seemed at least in part resigned to whatever message the guide had conveyed.

'We'll have two-hour watches, but I see no reason to go any further. This spot is ideal. We make camp here.'

Steffan looked like he was about to protest again, but Riggon's expression brooked no argument and, with a deep breath, Steffan nodded reluctantly and set about finding the best spot. The last climb up had been hard going, alternating between dense forest and rocky, sometimes precarious paths. Every member of the team was only too glad to pitch their tent, eat and rest.

They soon had a fire lit and Steffan, a skilled hunter, quickly procured a couple of rabbits for a stew. An hour after sunset, Ozil announced that he was turning in.

Riggon spoke. 'I'll take the first watch, two hours, then Steffan, Wimbush, Ozil and Kebbers.'

There were a couple of groans, but it was Wimbush who asked what they were all thinking.

'A watch? May I ask why now, since we have had no watches for the last twenty-seven nights?'

Riggon started banking the fire. 'I'd better let Steffan answer that one.'

The guide shot Riggon a look that was a troubled mix of anger and anxiety. 'It is only that these spaces in the forest have a name. The locals call them cicataria. They believe that cicataria are where spirits of the forest, not all of them friendly, come to rest at night so they may look at the stars.'

'Them's just stories,' Ozil said. 'And even if they weren't, we aren't doing anything to stop 'em.'

'It is said that the witch haunts these forests,' Steffan said in a low voice that ticked with fear. 'That is why it remains a wilderness.'

Ozil hawked up something viscous and spat. Then he pulled a small amulet from around his neck and kissed it before returning it to his chest. 'Good thing I ain't superstitious, then.'

'May I contribute?'

They all turned to look at Wimbush, his face glowing in the firelight.

'Glades such as these are generally the result of some natural and local causation. For example, an avalanche may have come through here and laid waste to the trees. Or there may have been a lightning strike with local fire damage. Occasionally, poor soil, too thin to support trees, might be the reason.'

'Or the spirits banish the trees to give themselves an, how you say…arena to lie and look at the stars,' said Steffan.

'Yes, but arcane tree-banishing seems the more unlikely explanation of the two, wouldn't you agree?'

Riggon spoke again before either Wimbush or Steffan could continue. 'Whatever the reason, these glades attract wildlife to feed on the grasses. Deer and elk attract predators. So we will keep watch. Anyone object?'

No one did.

CHAPTER SIX

SPIV

THEY CAME for Nadia at 1.00 am, the pit of night. A firm knock on the door startled Radomil awake. Mrena, who had been waiting, opened it a crack, spoke some hushed words and then pulled the door fully open.

Dalibor, on the threshold, looked in but said nothing. Nadia stood and looked up into his expressionless face before peering out into the dark night beyond, towards the figures waiting there. They stood in a half circle, the aldermen, all masked, torches flickering in their hands. Dalibor stood aside and Nadia walked out, her few possessions in a cloth sack slung around her shoulder. Walked away from the small cabin she'd called home and out into the cool, sharp night air. At the steps leading down to the communal yard, she felt a hand on her arm. Turning, she saw Mrena holding out a coat. She stood while it was draped over her shoulders. When Nadia caught Mrena's eye, she read sympathy and dread in equal measure.

The aldermen stepped back to make space for her and she crossed the grass, the coat draped like a cape on her back, the men marching in two lines, one on either side of her, like an execution squad. They advanced towards the forest, its jagged silhouette dark against the starlit sky. She crossed the dirt path, the grassy area where the children played, the scrubby land where the horses grazed during daylight hours. These were places she was familiar with and a sudden pang of fear and longing gripped her. Was this the last time she would ever smell the grass or hear the horses whinny?

She looked around. The aldermen were watching her progress, fearful, perhaps, that she might decide to run; ready to join arms to prevent her escape. When they were no more than twenty yards from the wooden fence marking the village boundary, the procession stopped in response to Dalibor's order. Nadia stopped too, wondering what was going to happen now. A crude ladder was set against the fence. The aldermen formed a loose semicircle into which Dalibor stepped.

'Nadia Komangetme,' Dalibor boomed, and Nadia heard the faint emphasis she always heard whenever someone spoke her full name. The villagers had difficulty pronouncing it because it was foreign to their native tongue. She knew why.

Her grandfather was not from these mountains. He was a hunter, found severely injured in the woods and rescued—or so the story went. A bear attack, her grandmother told her. And she knew, since it had been her who had nursed Arne Komangetme back to health. When he'd recovered, he knew a good thing when he saw it and decided to stay. A decision that had everything to do with her grandmother and nothing to do with Spiv, or so Nadia's mother used to tell her with a knowing smile.

'The council of aldermen have met to consider your fate.' Dalibor's voice broke in on Nadia's ruminations. 'You are charged with seditious and blasphemous acts, namely the denial of the existence of the witch. The evidence for this is written here.' He held out his hands containing the pages. 'Do you plead guilty?'

'I wrote the words,' Nadia said, 'but I don't think I'm guilty of anything.'

Dalibor nodded. 'It is not your place to decide what constitutes wrongdoing, girl. The laws are clear. You are a transgressor. The punishment for such an act is that you will be banished from the village and cast out into the forest for the witch to deal with as she sees fit.'

All around her, the circle of aldermen began chanting. This was an unfamiliar incantation that rose and fell, more like a moan than a spell.

Dalibor fell to his knees. 'Babramic Jaggr, who haunts the forests and mountains, accept this woman as a transgressor and teach her the folly of her beliefs. Be assured that we, your servants, wish to cast out her thoughts from our midst and cleanse our minds of her poison. Oh, Babramic Jaggr, conductor of the rivers, guardian of the rocks, let this girl learn of your power.'

The chanting stopped. Between where Nadia stood and the forest, the ring of aldermen stood back to widen the gap.

'Go now, blasphemer. Your fate awaits you.'

'What if I don't want to go?' Nadia said.

The ring of aldermen murmured their disapproval. Dalibor drew out a hunting knife from his belt. 'You have no choice.'

Nadia turned towards the dark forest, a looming black wall outside the light of the flickering torches. She took four steps and balanced on top of the ladder before looking back at the strange little gathering of men.

'But what if there really isn't a witch?' she said.

The aldermen gasped.

'What if all there is are trees and foxes and rabbits and badgers and the odd bear—'

'Silence,' boomed Dalibor. He turned to the entourage. 'Cover your ears so as not to hear these wicked words.'

'Wicked words?' Nadia said. 'You're the ones being wicked by throwing me out. What if something else steals the chickens and paints ugly faces on the sides of the cabins at night besides witches and orcs?'

The aldermen immediately put their hands over their ears and began moving their tongues back and forth between their lips whilst singing a single note.

Nadia sighed. 'Okay, okay. I'll go. But you all look really stupid.'

Hands fell away from ears.

'I promise I won't say anything else,' Nadia said and stepped down off the fence onto the forest side. 'Except…No witch!'

Two score hands flew back up in horror and the ululations began again to blank out the blaspheming words. Dalibor, enraged, ran forward, knife held in his outstretched arm. Nadia didn't move. When Dalibor got to the wall, his arm rebounded back before it could cross the threshold.

Nadia shook her head. Her mother told her how her grand-father would tease her grandmother by dismantling the totems she'd carefully constructed to ward off the terrors and deliber-ately messed up his charms just to see her reaction. Nadia had spent a lot of time with her grandfather.

'Leave now, woman. Do not torment us anymore with your foul words.'

'All I'm saying is that someone should take a step back and think about—'

'LEAVE!' screamed Dalibor.

Trembling despite, or perhaps because of, her bravado, Nadia turned and stepped into the haunted forest. She was tired, she was distraught about Kasimir, but most of all she was angry. The anger gave her strength. She walked, letting her eyes adjust to the dim light through the trees above, welcoming the moon when it appeared. She didn't look back and so she did not see the aldermen remove their masks to better watch her departure. Did not see the abject terror and horror displayed in their faces. This, for them, was like watching a lamb stroll innocently into the middle of a pack of dozing wolves. They watched and waited for something dreadful to happen. When, finally, Nadia's pale form disappeared from view, they turned and hurried back to the warmth of their cabins, satisfied with their night's work. Justice had prevailed. The forest had her now. Let it do with her what it would. And secretly, of course, the aldermen all hoped it would do something awful because then they might find a jot of solace in the harrowing justice they'd just meted out on a woman a few months short of her twenty-third birthday, but who looked much closer to seventeen. And most of them needed that jot because their own existence—in thrall to a supernatural being that none of them had ever seen—was not one overburdened with fun and frivolity. A bit of proof now and again would come in handy.

Unfortunately, not one of them had any idea that Nadia already knew the paths and trails within the forest better than anyone alive because, while they turned their faces away in superstitious fear, she'd dared the witch to prove her existence.

As yet, such proof had not been forthcoming.

But it was cold and dark in the forest, and Nadia was very much alone. Later, in a clearing, she cried tears of grief. She cried for almost an hour for her brother and the sheer waste of his life. She cried because she hadn't said goodbye to him properly that morning because she'd stayed in bed. She cried because her world was one riven by superstitious nonsense.

But when she had cried enough she stopped, stood up, wiped her face clean of salt, set it into the faint breeze and walked on.

CHAPTER SEVEN

THE NORTHERN SARMATIC FOREST OF STEPPEINIT

WIMBUSH FELL ASLEEP the moment he laid his head down. A minute later, or so it seemed, Steffan shook him awake.

'Your watch,' he said.

Wimbush knuckled the sleep from his eyes and climbed out of the tent. The glade was now bathed in wonderful silver light from the bright moon directly above.

'Anything to report?' he asked the guide.

'No,' came the terse reply. 'But be wary.' His eyes swept the treeline.

'Of course. That is the definition of watch, is it not?'

Steffan hurried towards his tent with a shake of the head and an unintelligible grumble, leaving Wimbush to tend the fire. The botanist threw on a few logs and sat with a blanket over his shoulders, stretching out the lethargic stiffness that lingered in his limbs. He yawned widely and blinked. There was barely any wind. The glade sat in complete silence apart from the hoot of an owl somewhere in the forest. It was breathtakingly beautiful and easy to see how the ignorant might indeed consider this an arena where supernatural beings might come to observe the stars. Wimbush craned his neck to look up. A cloud drifted over the moon and suddenly they were all there. The constellations.

Professor Bitumen, his old astronomy master, used to say that all the answers to life's mysteries were in the glittering stars. You only needed to know what questions to ask and have patience for the answers to come. And come they would. Even if you'd be a pile of dust under a stone that read, *Ask and it shall be granted…but not in this lifetime* when they arrived.

Sometimes Wimbush would sit on the roof of the boarding house where he rented a room and look up at the sky on starlit nights. Occasionally, the New Thameswick smog cleared enough for a man to catch a glimpse. But it was never like this. Never had Wimbush seen this many stars on display. Bitumen had been right. Such cosmic secrets demanded answers.

Like when, if ever, he was going to find his silver wolfsbane.

Or when, if ever, he was going to be offered tenure at the Polyalchemic.

And when, if ever, he might find the time to seek the companionship of someone of the opposite sex.

Oh dear. Where on earth, or the cosmos, did that question spring from?

Oh, there had been female companionship over the years. One or two had shown an interest in him. But always some paper or other had needed finishing, or an exam loomed and somehow, when next he looked, the girl had gone, leaving behind nothing but a tantalising waft of perfume entitled *opportunité manquée*. But of late, the feeling that he might be missing out on some aspect of his life kept nagging. His mother, may she rest in peace, had always told him not to bother with girls and to stick to books. Being a solitary child, Wimbush had been happy to do just that. And solitude was a place he never balked at visiting. Though, of late, the road to solitude had sometimes forked off to lonely street.

And there was no denying that the majority of his associates —there were few actual friends—all seemed to be finding partners and getting married.

Now, staring up at the stars, Wimbush promised himself that after this trip he would make a conscious effort. Perhaps buy some new clothes. Or visit a barber and get his beard shaved off. Even have a bath once a week. He'd read that physical attraction played a significant part in establishing a relationship, so he ought to look into that side of things.

A sudden movement on the far side of the glade drew his attention. Some shift amongst the darker shadows. A low shape slinking across the treeline.

Wimbush's pulse ticked into a canter and he sat up, squinting into the night. An animal of some kind, there was no doubt. But its movements were swift and jerky. He'd familiarised himself with both the fauna and flora of the forest before joining the expedition, but he could not recall anything that moved like this. Not with rear limbs longer than the front. There was something very disturbing and simian about the shape as it paused and turned its head up to the air. Wimbush knew that the thing was sensing him. He held his breath, waiting to see what might happen. But the creature remained static for long seconds, and when it did finally move, it slid silently into the undergrowth behind. His first instinct was to go to the fire and fetch a brand, but one glance told him that his good night vision would be lost if he did that and though it was not clear, he could just about see the moving shadow in intermittent glimpses. Better he stay dark-adapted for the moment.

Now the thing was no longer static, arcing around, stopping intermittently, and when it did, Wimbush became convinced that it was watching him. He stood, legs creaking from the move-ment, and moved to put the fire and its light behind him so as to allow a better view of the forest edge. The moon emerged once more and shone angular beams into the foliage.

It was then that he saw them. There, in a patch of illumina-tion near to where he'd last glimpsed the creature, something shone. Something small reflecting the moonlight, gleaming like a string of lights a few inches off the ground.

Wimbush's insides swooped. He forgot about the moving shadowy creature, and his legs, as if under their own autonomous power, began to walk towards the glittering silver string. Could it be that for once the folk tales were true? That something in a flower's structure might fluoresce in certain light or reflect a particular wavelength so that they became illumi-nated just like…He'd gone ten paces when another inconvenient cloud passed over the moon and the tiny beacons he was following faded into nothing.

'No,' he moaned through gritted teeth. 'No, no, no.'

He lunged forward, knowing that he was on the right trajectory, and stopped within an arm's length of the forest wall. Desperately, he peered into the darkness beyond and saw nothing while the moon was hidden. It didn't matter. He'd wait. He'd stand there and wait until the moon reappeared. He risked an upwards glance. The edge of the cloud was just visible, a paler grey diffracting the moonlight. It shouldn't take more than a minute or two until the light re-emerged. He snapped his head back around to where the glittering string had been and saw instead two yellow eyes staring back at him.

Wimbush barely had time to let out a muffled cry of surprise when the face containing those yellow eyes accelerated towards him with an open jaw and a large number of teeth and a deadly mouth through which emerged an unholy screech.

Surprise is what saved Wimbush. His reaction to the snarling thing that lunged at him was to fall backwards from his crouched position, rotating his knees upwards to engage with the shadowy beast and propel it several feet over his head into the glade behind. Above him, the stars whirled in the firmament as his back thumped the ground, sending the air hissing from his lungs and his glasses arcing up and away. Half blind, Wimbush spun onto his belly and clambered onto all fours, staring in the direction that the beast had been catapulted. It was there, righting itself, its eyes and teeth the only pale items in a jet-black shape. At last Wimbush realised his predicament and did the only thing he could do.

'RIGGON! HELP!'

The beast flew forwards. Wimbush clamped his hands over his head and made himself as small a target as he possibly could, waiting for those sharp teeth to find flesh. But even as he prepared for the worst, he heard a rustling in the forest to his left and turned to see a bush on legs brandish a stout stick that whistled through the air to meet the black shape in mid-flight.

There was a yelp of pain, then another unearthly screech. The bush bustled forwards, wielding the stick with practised ease and catching the beast several telling blows on its body and head.

Vicious though the beast might have been, stupid it wasn't. With a final look at Wimbush, the beast let out another screech and turned tail for the forest.

There were voices now. And the ringing sound of knives and a machete being unsheathed. The bush turned to run but, as

Wimbush watched, it was yanked backwards and fell to the ground as a loop of rawhide tightened around its middle.

The bush squealed. Wimbush barely had time to register this before a hand grabbed him and sat him up.

'Glasses,' he muttered.

Ozil handed them to him and Wimbush put them on. The world swam back into focus.

On his left, the bush was being dismantled.

Bits of twig and branch were roughly stripped away by Kebbers and Steffan while Riggon stood on one side with machete raised. The defoliation soon revealed a remarkably human shape beneath the camouflage just as the moon decided to show its face once again.

What the moonlight revealed was a woman, small and lithe like a girl, dark hair matted, her faced dull with streaked dark mud so that it appeared almost featureless apart from the peculiarly opalescent eyes that shone in the moonlight.

'You okay, doc? Did she do any damage?'

'What?' Wimbush said.

Steffan grabbed the girl's hair and yanked the head back. 'Did she bite you?'

The woman let out a yelp of pain.

'No, she did not bite me—'

'Good. She has a witch's eyes. See how they glitter in the moonlight? Better we slit her throat now and let her blood seep into the earth.' Steffan slid the knife forward.

'No,' Wimbush cried and pushed the knife away. 'What are you talking about? It wasn't she who attacked. There was a creature. Something dark with yellow eyes. Something halfway between a monkey and a dog, I'd say.'

Steffan threw him a terrified glance, his knife still at the girl's throat. 'What noise did it make?'

'Didn't you hear it? It screeched loud enough to wake the dead.'

'Do not speak of such things in jest,' hissed Steffan.

Riggon grabbed the guide's arm. 'You know what this creature is?'

'I have heard tell of such things. Mabocawl, the forest people call them. No one knows where they come from. It is said they only appear at the witch's behest when she wishes to avenge herself and inflict a slow and horrible death. They track their prey, sometimes for days. Half ape, half cat. An abomination.'

As he spoke, Steffan's pressure eased on the woman's hair and she muttered hoarsely, 'Mabocawl.'

Steffan jerked the head back again.

'Stop,' ordered Wimbush in alarm. 'She came out of the forest and attacked this, this mabocawl. She has knowledge.'

'How do we know that they aren't in cahoots, this woman and this creature?' Ozil said.

'Nonsense. I saw what I saw, heard what I heard.' Wimbush's voice was strident. He had recovered enough to be angered by the fact that they weren't believing him. 'Stop doing that. You're hurting her.' He stood on shaky feet and grabbed Steffan's forearm to ease the pressure on the woman's hair.

'I tell you this was not safe place to camp,' said the guide, his face full of dread.

'I vote we slit her throat and be done with it,' Kebbers seethed.

Wimbush shook his head. 'I will not be a party to murder. Let us at least find out why she is here.'

Steffan stood the woman up and tied her hands. They walked back to the centre of the glade and the fire. Steffan did the talking, the young woman answering in a local dialect that sounded, to Wimbush, as impenetrable as the dark forest.

'She says that her brother died in accident and she ran away from her village. She saw the mabocawl heading for us. She tracked it here.'

'Likely story,' muttered Ozil.

'Why did she follow it?' asked Riggon.

'Because it is the first time she has seen any sign of…evil, "despite what the elders preach". Her words.'

'Lies,' said Kebbers, his face half in shadow. 'She probably saw her chance and set her dogs on you. I vote we slit her throat and let her rot.'

'With all due respect, Mr Kebbers, you were not the one attacked.' Wimbush glared at the taller man. 'I know what I saw and this person saved me from whatever it was. She certainly does not deserve to have her throat cut, nor her hair yanked. Besides, if she is from this area, she may well be able to assist me in finding the wolfsbane.'

'Give me strength,' muttered Kebbers.

'And what exactly does she mean by evil?' Wimbush asked, glancing at Steffan.

Once again, there was an exchange of words between the guide and the woman. It went on for some time until, eventually, Steffan swung back to Wimbush. 'In her village they believe that the forest is haunted by a witch and that bad things roam the mountains. She has been alone in the woods and has seen nothing. Except for tonight.'

'So, she does not believe the forest is haunted?'

Steffan shook his head. 'She does not believe in the witch, but tonight she believes that something evil is abroad.'

'Or maybe she is the witch, trying to trick us into giving her sympathy,' Ozil said. 'Maybe we should stick her head in a bucket and see if she drowns. We'd know then.'

Wimbush shook his head, brow furrowed in disgust. 'Forgive me if I have a little difficulty following that flawed logic.'

'S'well known. If she drowns, she ain't a witch. If she turns into a fish or a bird and flies off, she is.'

'And how in all that is sane does that help the poor victim who is innocent but now dead?' Wimbush asked.

'At least she'd die innocent,' Ozil argued.

'Not while I am here,' Wimbush said.

Riggon spoke. 'We need to continue this in the morning. The witch stays tied to a tree. Wimbush, get some rest. Ozil, your watch.'

Wimbush supervised the binding and made sure the knots were not too tight. He also stopped them from gagging her. 'If Mr Ozil suddenly decides to test his witch theory, I want her to be able to let us know,' he said and, before turning back to his tent, asked Steffan one final question. 'Does she have a name?'

Steffan spoke once more to the woman and she answered defiantly.

'Nadia.'

CHAPTER EIGHT

WIMBUSH AWOKE SLOWLY. For a blissful moment in that strange land between wakefulness and sleep he believed he was still in his room in New Thameswick's Pegville district. As a student, he'd first rented some cheap digs on Mephitis Lane. But as his finances gradually improved, he'd moved a couple of streets away from the pall of the methane gasworks to the relative sweetness of Stench Avenue where he had his breakfast and dinner prepared for him by Mrs Mbata, who ran a very orderly boarding house, thanks to her charm, six-foot-three frame and her tendency to carry an assegai strapped to her back. In a minute he'd get up and have a quick wash and brush up, and then go down and have a big bowl of mieliepap porridge with honey and...it was at that point that Wimbush turned over and wished he hadn't, as a sharp pain shot through his left hip into his back, inducing an involuntary grunt.

Memory didn't so much flood as avalanche down upon him like a two-foot accumulation of snow on a porch roof disturbed by an absent-minded slam of the front door.

Mabocawl.

He tried to sit up, stopped in mid-rise as his back twinged again, and tentatively inched the rest of the way up into a sitting position.

Groaning and stiff, Wimbush poked his head out of the tent flap. The world was grey. A thick mist hung over the glade. He could hear a fire crackling and disembodied morning-gruff voices, but there was no sign of anyone. Stiffly, he donned coat and boots and dragged himself out of the tent, knowing that all his aches and pains were a testament to his escapades of the night before. That meant they were real and not a dream. Realisation sent him a shiver that had nothing to do with the temperature. Outside, the mist was a chilly one. Wimbush felt it seep through his thin nightgown and inch its way up towards his thighs and anatomical areas further north that rarely saw the light of day, felt the warmth of the sun or the tingling caress of frost. The tingling caress of anything, if truth be told. He crossed his legs in the hope that doing so might delay the cold's progress, knowing that the sensible thing to do was to dress properly.

But not yet. He needed to check on something first.

Steffan and Ozil were sitting by the fire, both sipping from tin mugs and picking bits of charred pork from their teeth.

'Mornink,' said Steffan. 'How are you?'

'Aching,' Wimbush replied. 'Nadia, where is she?'

'She is still tied to that tree,' Ozil said.

'Kwafe?' Steffan proffered a cup.

Despite not being enamoured by the flavour, Wimbush accepted it, shivering. Hot liquid of any kind was welcome this freezing morning.

'Is cold, yes? But sun will burn away fog in one hour,' Steffan said.

'Good to hear.' Wimbush walked away from the fire to where Nadia had been tethered. What he found was a curled-up vaguely human shape under a ragged blanket. He knelt and asked, 'Nadia? Are you awake?'

Nadia's hands were tied together by a thick rope, which had been looped through the knot and around the trunk of a tree. Wimbush waited while she pushed her face up from behind the blanket. Instantly, his breath seized in his throat.

It was the eyes that did it.

Nadia's face was grubby from the mud, her hair matted and studded with dried leaves and pine needles, but her irises were a deep shade of cobalt blue, set in the most remarkable canvas of almost turquoise sclerae.

She stared back at him defiantly. It took a full thirty seconds before Wimbush managed to say, 'Good morning. Are you okay?'

Though she obviously did not understand his words, she dropped her chin, and blinked slowly while pursing her lips. A little pointed triptych that said, 'What do you think?' in any language.

'Ah, yes, not an ideal situation. Let me see what I can do.'

Wimbush retreated towards the fire, where Riggon had joined the other two.

'About the woman, could we untie her?'

'Out of the question,' said Riggon.

'I appreciate your concern, Riggon, but if she is anything like me in the mornings, she probably needs to perform some kind of bodily function.'

'She can go behind the tree,' Ozil said.

Wimbush considered this. 'Right, yes, that is a viable option, but what about later, when we move on?'

'We could hang her from the same tree,' Ozil suggested.

Steffan snorted.

Wimbush frowned. 'I have to say I find your attempts at humour not always in the best taste, Mr Ozil.'

'Wasn't joking,' muttered Ozil. 'Can't trust these indigenes. Slit your throat soon as look at you.'

'Since you're the one who's insisting on her being alive and here with us, when we leave, she will be your responsibility,' Riggon said with a pointed look at Wimbush. 'She stays tied to you.'

'To me? I…right, that might not be very convenient.' Wimbush noticed that all the men had turned away from him and that his protests were not so much falling as plummeting on deaf ears. He went back to Nadia to find she was standing up now. She was short and slender, with sinewy arms toned from outdoor work, her face streaked with dirt, the features fine and full of defiance. 'I'm afraid they won't let me untie you. But if you want to, erm, relieve yourself, then I'd suggest behind the tree.'

Nadia frowned, and Wimbush blushed deeply as he tried to mime pee by squatting and waving his fingers down towards the ground.

Nadia nodded and pointed to Wimbush. She then jutted her chin towards the fire and the men around it.

'Oh, you want me to stand guard? Yes, right, I, um, I can do that.' He turned his back and started to whistle tunelessly while some rustling took place behind him followed by a watery tinkling. A few moments later, when he turned back, Nadia was standing in front of him. He smiled and offered her his cup.

'Kwafe?'

She looked at him curiously and sniffed the cup. The reaction that followed was both surprising and vehement. She shrank back, staring in horror at the cup and then at Wimbush's mouth with the other.

'No? You don't like it?'

Nadia shook her head, staring wide-eyed and with what could only be described as disgust at Wimbush.

'Tell you the truth, neither do I.' Wimbush emptied the kwafe onto the ground. 'How about I get you some water once I've, um…' he made a feeble waving motion with his fingers at waist level, 'whistled too?'

CHAPTER NINE

It was a subdued breakfast that morning. Kebbers and Ozil said nothing, but their furtive glances towards Nadia spoke clearly of their suspicions. When the others had eaten, Wimbush, with Riggon in attendance, untied Nadia and looped the rope that had connected her to the tree around his own waist. The girl ate some of the honey-sweetened mieliepap porridge Wimbush made with her fingers but refused anything other than water to drink.

'She's your responsibility,' Riggon warned with a meaningful scowl as he walked away to fetch his kit. 'Don't make me regret this.'

Steffan's forecast held true and an hour after he'd got up, Wimbush felt the welcome caress of the sun on his face as it burned through to the glade. They broke camp and doused the fire.

Riggon said, 'We go north for another five miles. Real wilderness but at least it's flatter, so the going should be better than yesterday.'

'Oh, good. I don't think that I could—' Wimbush froze in mid-sentence.

He remembered.

He remembered the little silver string just on the edge of the forest where the mabocawl had hidden.

The silver wolfsbane.

Without thinking, Wimbush turned and marched off towards

the spot, completely forgetting his companions and, more importantly, the girl now tethered to him.

'Hey, what's the problem?' Riggon called after him.

But Wimbush had begun to trot, mumbling as he did, 'Moonlight…last night…glittering…'

Beside him, a confused Nadia trotted, too.

He arrived at the very spot, marked by a flattening of the grass where he'd fallen on his back. He stood and peered, pulling back the foliage to get a better view. This was where he'd seen it, he was sure. Just next to a large beech…

He let out a cry. What should have been triumphant, was full of anguish. He'd found them. Silver wolfsbane in a small crop of perhaps half a dozen plants. These were what he'd seen the night before. Delicate flowers reflecting the moonlight just as they had been described. Only now, they were reflecting nothing and would not ever again because the mabocawl, in its frenzy, had trampled the whole lot into a barely recognisable mush.

Tears of frustration and regret coursed down Wimbush's face. Next to him, Nadia looked on in bemusement. Behind him, Kebbers was staring in derision. Ozil made a circular motion with an index finger just above his left ear.

'Have you seen something?' Riggon asked.

'Yes,' wailed Wimbush. 'Wanton destruction. They're here. *Aconitum argentum*, the plant I've been searching for. Ruined. Dead.'

Steffan stepped forward. 'Perhaps you could press between pages of book.' He leaned forward to pick up the battered remnants.

'NO!' screamed Wimbush.

Steffan jerked back as if the plants had become vipers.

'Touching those mashed plants with bare skin is definitely not a good idea,' Wimbush said, 'unless you want to be vomiting up your own liver in a couple of hours' time.'

Riggon stepped closer to look. 'If they're so poisonous, why do you want to find them?'

'Because, Mr Riggon, if you want to cure someone from a deadly snakebite, you first need to know the snake. By modifying the extract there is a potential for some excellent medicines from this plant. The werewolf community in particular will benefit immensely from a long-lasting potion. And all those poor people in Rainever who suffer the red death? Just think of what might be achieved if we could cultivate the plant.' He stared again at the mess on the forest floor. 'So close,' he whispered. 'So close.'

'Come on,' said Riggon. 'We need to move.'

Reluctantly, Wimbush turned from his one and only glimpse of living silver wolfsbane and trudged after Ozil. He kept his head down and didn't see the quizzical frown on Nadia's face. They marched onwards through the woods for several hours and if Wimbush was aware of the way Kebbers kept glancing at him and Nadia, he showed no sign of it, mired as he was in wolfsbane misery.

They stopped mid-afternoon at another dry stream bed running off into the forest to the east.

'We'll follow this in for a quarter of a mile. I spotted it from down below.' Riggon turned to Wimbush. 'Stay here and we'll be back in an hour.'

He led his men off and Wimbush found a stone to sit on, not bothering to remove his heavy backpack. Nadia, still tethered, sat nearby. He offered her some water from his canteen. She drank thirstily.

'I know you can't understand a word I say, but seeing the wolfsbane so cruelly macerated…It hit me hard.' He sniffed.

Nadia looked back at him. Did she understand? She handed back the canteen, plucked a fern leaf, threw it on the ground and trampled it with her foot.

'Yes.' Wimbush nodded, suddenly animated. 'You've got it in one. My beautiful silver wolfsbane, mulched.'

Nadia frowned and then stood abruptly and beckoned to Wimbush to follow.

'Oh, do you want to…empty?' He mimicked a squat.

Nadia dropped her chin again and shook her head. She pointed to the fern and said, 'Lujuk, lujuk.'

'I hope that doesn't mean something more…substantial on the ablutionary front, does it?'

Nadia beckoned again, more urgently this time. Wimbush looked up. The miners and Steffan were already out of sight. He shrugged and let Nadia lead him on through the woods. She seemed to find her way through the trees remarkably easily as she wound in a loop away from the stream bed towards higher ground. They emerged onto a rocky outcrop some fifty feet above where Riggon and crew were working. By some quirk of rocky acoustics, their voices carried clearly through the air.

'…far enough of the main trails…' Riggon's voice.

'…start digging…' Kebber's.

Looking down from above, Wimbush wanted to wave at them but some strange instinct stopped him with his hand already chest height. He stood, poised, until another tug on the rope snagged his attention and he turned to follow Nadia another dozen yards towards the edge of a small clearing.

He froze.

There, in front of him, grew a carpet of silver wolfsbane.

He turned towards the waiting girl, who had a questioning look on her face as if to ask, is this what you're after?

'How…what…but…' Wimbush spluttered, his eyes never leaving the plants. He stepped closer and knelt to examine the curved hood-shaped flowers and the silvery-grey palmate leaves. 'It is, he whispered. 'It's *aconitum argentum*.' He turned back to Nadia, who was leaning forwards, hands on her knees. In one move Wimbush stood and clasped her in a huge, air-expelling hug. 'You've found them, you've found them! You wonderful, wonderful…forest person.'

Nadia struggled and pushed him away. To his horror, Wimbush saw that she looked frightened.

'Oh no, please, I'm not…I mean…' He held out his hand.

Nadia considered it before slowly reaching out her own hand. She stood, bemused, as a beaming Wimbush pumped it vigorously.

'Right, I am not letting this opportunity slip away,' he said, and unslung his pack. He took out gloves, the specially designed specimen jars and a neat foldable trowel, and carefully began to transplant half a dozen of the flowers, whistling softly and adding a generous splash of water to each.

Nadia stood by and watched.

'Just wait until I tell Riggon the news. He's not going to believe it, and neither are those doubters at the Polyalchemic. Imagine finding a crop like this. You're a genius, did I tell you that?' He grinned over his shoulder at Nadia. 'I expect those miners will be highly disgruntled to hear that I've struck silver and they haven't. In fact…'

He broke off from his work and walked back to the point at

which he could see and hear the other party. Kebbers and Ozil were the closest, busy digging. If it struck Wimbush that it was an odd departure from the norm—previously they'd looked for placer deposits on the surface, not buried in the soil—he brushed it aside. They knew what they were doing. Steffan and Riggon were further away and seemed to be having an animated conversation. Wimbush walked forward to get a little nearer.

'…what you were brought up here to do,' Riggon said. It sounded like a command.

'Getting rid of competition is one thing,' Steffan grumbled. 'Finding and eliminating interfering prospectors, okay, I see that, but Wimbush is harmless—'

'Is he? He's from the Polyalchemic. In case you haven't noticed, he's looking for silver wolfsbane. A plant found near silver lode. Imagine we rock back, telling everyone we've found none. He goes back with a bagful of the plant. Who are they going to believe? Before you know it, this neck of the woods will be crawling with people staking claims. And the people who pay our wages will not like that. The mabocawl was supposed to get him but it didn't, so now it's up to us to finish the job.'

'People will ask kvestions. You should never have let him come.'

'I'll handle the questions. Kebbers and Ozil will do the needful…'

They moved on, out of earshot.

Wimbush thought about hailing them, but then thought again. There was something about their conversation that triggered an itch inside his head, and shouting to them now wouldn't scratch it.

Forty yards further back, Ozil and Kebbers were still digging. Wimbush, with Nadia in tow, crept back until he was above them.

'How deep did he say?' Ozil asked.

Kebbers grunted a reply. 'Four feet. Doesn't want the animals to dig 'em up.'

'Don't see why we don't wait for that mabocawl thing to come back tonight and do it all for us,' Ozil muttered.

'But they only put the mabcurse on Wimbush, didn't they? That means we've got to do the female. Might as well be hung for a sheep as for a lamb. I'm with the boss on that. Sooner the better. Though we could have a bit of fun with her first, eh? What Riggon doesn't know won't hurt him, which is more than could be said for her.' The Kebbers chuckle that followed sent an icy trickle down Wimbush's spine. 'Then we can inspect the village and piss off out of here. Tell everyone there's no silver up here and that there are bandits and worse in the woods, picking off innocent prospectors. That should shut the buggers up for another year or two.'

Ozil responded with a laugh that caught in his chest and rumbled into a hawking cough.

Wimbush had forgotten to breathe and now took in a huge gulp of air. They were discussing the mabocawl as if they knew all about it. And the cheerful way they dismissed those poor prospectors didn't sound right, somehow. In fact, it sounded cold and crowing, almost as if…No, surely not? And why were they digging? Why two trenches four feet deep? And why would animals want to dig up rock samples…

The triumph and jubilation from the wolfsbane discovery that had suffused his heart sputtered and died. He was not an overly suspicious man, but you didn't spend your nights walking through the streets of Pegville without learning to spot danger on every corner. And though he didn't want to believe them, Wimbush's instincts told him that the miners weren't discussing geology here. They were discussing something else altogether. Something heinous and terrible. And they weren't digging up samples.

They were digging holes in which to bury something.

Or someone.

Wimbush took another deep breath that shuddered on the way in and even more on the way out. He'd been naive and stupid and blinkered. Three things that should never appear on a survivalist's checklist.

He turned to see Nadia at the end of the rope five yards behind him. She stared at him with a troubled look in those incredible eyes. But Wimbush ran past her, back to his jars neatly arranged on the forest floor. With trembling hands, he finished the transfer of the last one into his bespoke backpack before sliding it over his shoulders.

He toyed with trying to explain in words but then reverted to charades.

He pointed to himself and then to her.

Then he pointed back towards Riggon and his party.

Then he drew his finger across his throat and mimed digging.

Then he pointed to Nadia and himself again and let his fingers do the walking off into the distance.

Nadia's expression, initially mildly confused, morphed into wide-eyed horror as she grasped what was being explained to her. She walked back to look down at where the men were working and then nodded, turned and began to walk quickly off into the forest. Wimbush stood until the rope yanked him into action, then did his best to follow and fend off low branches. They'd travelled almost a mile when they heard the first shout.

'Hello? Wimbush? Hello? Time to leave, yes?' Steffan's voice. It sounded far away. But the look on Nadia's face echoed Wimbush's thought.

Not far enough.

Nadia and Wimbush stopped and listened, trying to pinpoint a direction. Nadia tilted her head and pointed. Wimbush nodded. They set off in the opposite direction, Wimbush whispering away, knowing full well that she did not understand, but whispering anyway, running through the exit strategy his brain had suddenly come up with.

When they paused for breath, he pointed at the sun and arced his finger to the west. As usual, it produced nothing but a frown from Nadia. 'If we can get to sunset, then I think I have a plan.'

Nadia blinked.

'You don't understand a word I'm saying, do you?'

Nadia blinked again.

Wimbush sighed and waved her forward with his hands. But Nadia didn't move. Instead, she tilted her head, narrowed her eyes and let them drop to the rope still tied between them.

'You're right. You should not be tied to me or to anything that I want to do. They'll be tracking me, not you.' He walked towards her and undid the knots that held the rope to her waist and then undid her hands. She rubbed her wrists and, without a word, turned and ran into the woods.

Wimbush watched her go with sense of desperation mingled with…what, regret? He'd started to like her. She had not complained once. Not that she could have, since she didn't speak gabble, New Thameswick's language. But he also sensed that, even if she could, she would not have. Nadia, he surmised, was not the complaining type. She was the doing type. And right now, what she was doing was running away from here and him as fast as she could. But she had helped him find the silver wolfsbane and saved him from the mabocawl. For that, Wimbush had no regrets about freeing her.

He started to make his way towards the trees. Yes, silent, uncomplaining and brave, that was Nadia. He quite liked that in a person since, in his experience, people talked far too much for no other reason than liking the sound of their own jolly, raucous voices. And they were always saying things they didn't mean just for effect, or an attempt at humour, and he never found that either understandable or funny. But he could hardly expect a captured villager to want to help him, Kenwyn K Wimbush, avoid a pack of murderous—

A figure emerged from the dense patch of trees she'd disappeared into and beckoned to him impatiently.

Nadia.

Wimbush immediately rephrased his last thought and joyfully replaced 'hardly expect' with a much more truthful 'still desperately hope'.

Grinning with relief, Wimbush jogged towards the girl.

CHAPTER TEN

THEY WALKED. Quickly. Nadia read the terrain without difficulty. And while Wimbush managed to snag endless bits of twig in his hat, or trip over the tortuous and tangled roots of trees, she seemed totally at ease as she sought out animal trails and even a bridleway. She was a skilled forager and they ate berries as they walked and found clear streams to drink from. But they never stopped for more than a few minutes, and then only if they ascended or found a suitable patch in which to rest.

And listen for the sound of pursuit.

Once, as they followed a tiny stream, they heard voices carried up through the natural acoustics of a narrow canyon. A cough followed.

Ozil.

Nadia immediately took a perpendicular route away from the stream and headed into the forest once more. But as the afternoon wore on, Wimbush's stamina started to flag. Almost three weeks' worth of trekking was taking its toll on his feet. He now had blisters on his blisters. When, in the late afternoon, the noise of cascading water reached his ears, he called to Nadia and they followed their ears to a ravine, at the head of which was a waterfall. Negotiating their way across a steep slope to its base, they found a clear, deep pool. There, Wimbush sat and bathed his aching feet, while Nadia scavenged for more food.

Wimbush watched her as his feet gently cooled. She didn't look in the slightest bit tired and he wondered where she got her energy from. But then, he reasoned—so as to make his own pathetic lassitude more acceptable—some people were built that way. Mrs Mbata's cousin Kwasi, straw thin and with a smile that was visible from space, could run fifty miles per bowl of mieliepap porridge with ease.

Wimbush wiggled his toes. They looked pale in the water. He knew they couldn't stay long, but the spot they'd found was astonishingly beautiful with dappled shade and huge ferns growing in the moist air. The water, too, was cool and fresh on his skin. Under different circumstances he would have loved sketching this spot, capturing the foliage in all its glory, but now was most definitely not the time. Above them the sun was well past its high point. Another three hours or so until sunset, he esti-mated. And then…

And then what exactly? His hand strayed to the inside of his many pocketed jacket. Just as well Nadia couldn't understand him because as plans for when sunset arrived went, his was a cross between his socks and a good mountain cheese in terms of how many holes it contained. He felt in his inside pocket for a small parcel no bigger than a matchbox, and drew it out. It was wrapped in brown paper and tied with a blue ribbon. This was his travelling gift from Great Aunt Hester, whom he'd gone to visit just before leaving on the expedition. She, an adventurer of considerable fame, looked him in the eye and pressed the little parcel into his hand before closing his fingers around it.

'A goojl, in case of real emergencies,' she'd breathed, her head nodding constantly with the tremor that had arrived with her ninetieth birthday. She was almost a hundred now, but still as bright as a new farthing. 'Cook 'em up meself from a recipe a shaman in Kang taught me. Brilliant pyromancer. Got me out of a scrape or two, did goojls, I can tell you. 'Specially in Kang. Sometimes we'd get marauding packs of leopard men. Always came at night, sly so and so's. So I always had one standing by. Only for dire emergencies, mind, when all else fails and it looks as it everything's gone bosoms up. But it only works at sunset, which is generally when bosoms are up the most in Kang.'

Some people might have considered this so much rambling nonsense from a centenarian, but this was Great Aunt Hester who was speaking, and she knew exactly what she was talking about. Wimbush's family were pretty ordinary. His father worked as a printer, his mother stayed at home and raised Wimbush and his two sisters, and cooked meals for his father. And they'd followed the pattern set by their own parents and siblings. As such, no one in his direct family quite knew where Wimbush's career choice came from. No one else in the family was in the slightest alchemically minded. But then, no one else in the family was like Wimbush except, perhaps Great Aunt Hester and her twin, Great Uncle Helmut.

'He could draw anything perfectly after just looking at it,' Great Aunt Hester had once explained. 'Trouble was, he had a compulsion to eat whatever he drew. We never found out if it was because he was hungry, since he only ever answered questions with numbers. One of the clever coves at the university said somethin' about a speck drum. My old mum looked everywhere but never managed to get one. If we had, it might have made a difference for old Helmut.'

Obviously, that side of the family was were the non-conformists lay. Great Aunt Hester was a prime example, since she was about as conventional as strawberries with mayonnaise. Eschewing the normal life of a schoolgirl, Hester had studied and learned and gone on her first archaeological dig when she was seventeen. She'd opened tombs, incurred curses, dug up civilisations and notably discovered the Egit's scrolls, now ensconced in New Thameswick's Museum of Dubious Artefacts, having been 'liberated' from a Kang temple by Hester the Relic Hunter, as she was known by her contemporaries in the Society of Archaeology, and Hester the Grave-Robbing Cow by most everyone else who had the misfortune of being visited by her. The 'Dubious' label as per the museum applied to both the artefacts' power in terms of dark wonderworking and the legitimacy of their ownership, hotly contested by Kang's newly elected president, but resisted by the museum on the basis of the YTYEOTB (you took your eye off the ball) rule of international theft.

Great Aunt Hester was one of those people who'd been everywhere and seen everything and had the mementos to prove it. She delighted in the knowledge that Wimbush, in his own very small way, was following in her footsteps and had insisted on the goojl present. Wimbush, being both a sceptic and naturally wary of anything shaman-related, had been loath to accept. But now that he found himself running and in trouble, he was secretly

relieved at his foresight in having let it be thrust upon him. Even
if the truth was that he'd been too scared of Hester to say no.

He removed the parcel and read the tiny words written on
the paper between the strips of ribbon.

SIC TRANSIT GOOJL

INSTRUCTIONS
Place on flat surface
Undo ribbon
Unwrap parcel
Light blue touch paper
Stand within three feet
Caution: Use only at sunset. Speak Clearly. Do not eat within two hours
of expected use. Does not work under water.

WIMBUSH SHOOK HIS HEAD. Having to light anything was, in his
experience, always a risky thing. Having to light anything that
Great Aunt Hester had made under the tutelage of a shaman
was tantamount to risking permanent injury. But needs must.
And he'd had to ask what goojl meant, fully expecting it to be
some sort of ancient curse. When someone had explained that it
was an acronym for Get Out Of Jail (without the 'Free' because
in Hester's world, nothing in this life was for free), he'd laughed
in a shrill giggle bordering on hysteria.

Nadia returned to the pool and splashed water on to her
face. The mud ran and she wiped it off with her sleeve.
Wimbush saw a creamy complexion appear under the smudges
and those amazing irises. Her eyes really were remarkable.

Nadia caught him looking, frowned and then yanked on his
sleeve.

'Yes, yes, all right. I'm coming.'

Wimbush removed his feet from the water, dried them in a
shirt from his backpack and put on his boots. Five minutes later,
they were deep in the forest once more.

CHAPTER ELEVEN

THEY WALKED ON, heads down, constantly on the move. Wimbush realised that Steffan was probably tracking them, but there was nothing they could do about that other than to follow the bed of any stream they came across for at least a couple of hundred yards before accessing the opposite bank to try and throw him off the scent.

That had all been Nadia's idea.

They'd climbed steadily through the afternoon and were now emerging onto more open spaces where the trees thinned out as even they gave up the effort of trying to survive at this temperature, and at this elevation.

The views were magnificent. To the west, a huge plain extended towards snow-capped mountains. To the east, the hills reached ever upwards. But at least here, if they kept going south, they could keep an eye on the sun. Wimbush resisted Nadia's desire to head back into the trees and insisted on staying at the edge so he could watch the sun's descent. When the rim of the golden disk finally met with the dark mountain ridges on the horizon, Wimbush stopped. They'd reached an outcrop twenty yards from the tree line and he walked out onto it. Nadia, frowning, beckoned for him to come back under cover, but he shook his head. He was well and truly done for. He did not want to walk any further, especially now that the light was fading.

Time to see if Great Aunt Hester was worth her salt, pepper, vinegar and brown sauce.

He went back and held the girl's wrist gently, smiling as he did so. Behind them, in the deepening shadows of the woods, came the sound of a branch snapping and, somewhere to the north of that, a screech: half cat and half something else much bigger.

'Mabocawl,' said Nadia, her eyes wide.

'I know,' Wimbush said. 'But it's okay, really. I have a plan.'

Cringing at his own words and Nadia's sceptical frown, he returned to the outcrop, bringing Nadia with him. At its edge, the world dropped away to the valley floor a long way below. This is where their journey was to end, one way or another. Wimbush found a flat rock where he could set the goojl down out of the cooling breeze. As the daylight turned the mountain range behind a dull orange, he undid the ribbon and unfolded the brown wrapping. Inside was a rectangle with a twist of blue paper extending from the top. On the side of the rectangle were shapes and squiggles, the like of which Wimbush had never seen before.

Another branch snapped behind them. Much closer than before.

'Krisis, krisis,' urged Nadia, pointing down the slope.

Wimbush grabbed both her arms and shook his head. 'No, no. It's okay. This, no krisis.' He pointed at the blue touch paper and made a flat scissoring movement with his hands, all the while keeping his face positive with a fixed smile as he struggled to find some matches. Nadia's extraordinary eyes were now huge orbs of fear. After three shaky attempts, Wimbish managed to light a match and held it to the blue paper which, after several stubborn seconds, glowed a dull magenta.

It was then they heard the shout behind them.

'Here! I see them, Riggon.' Steffan walked out of the woods. He had a machete in his hand.

Wimbush put Nadia behind him, took out a large hunting knife and stood in front of the glowing goojl, watching as Riggon, Ozil and Kebbers joined the guide.

'Well, well, doc. Had a nice walk, have we?'

'We no longer want to be a part of your expedition, Riggon. You've had your money. We wish to leave.'

'Oh, do you now? Well, that's okay, then. We'll just turn

around and go back the way we came.' Riggon spoke without mirth, though Ozil let out a wheezy chuckle.

'I would appreciate that,' said Wimbush.

'I'm sure you would. The problem I have is that we can't let your little girlfriend go back with you.'

'She is not my—' He told himself to shut up and added instead, 'Why? She has done you no harm.'

'True, it's just that she has those funny eyes. If we let her go, people will ask all sorts of questions as to where she got those eyes from. And now that you've seen those eyes, we can't let you go back either.'

'What are you talking about?' Wimbush was genuinely puzzled. 'What is so important about her eyes?'

'The most important thing in the world. Money. We're here to make sure that the source of that money stays secure. Which means no one needs to know about your wolfsbane, or her eyes, geddit?'

Wimbush shook his head. 'I am aware that some people worship that god. But I am not one of them. I have no knowledge of the source of any money other than your search for silver. I am sad that you have not been successful. However, your words imply something other than silver lode as your purpose here.'

Riggon nodded sadly. 'You're right. We're here not just for silver. In fact, not for silver at all. And you knowing that makes you expendable. Just like her.'

Behind Wimbush, the goojl started to fizz. *Come on Hester*, he urged with clamped-together teeth. 'I can assure you that Nadia is no threat to you,' he said aloud.

'Just another girl with turquoise eyes, right?' Ozil said. Wimbush did not like the way he licked his lips.

Riggon sighed. 'Hand her over and I promise I'll make it quick. You know you're going to lose any fight. And besides, I think you'll want to let us finish you off nice and smooth, too. Because you have a friend coming for you, and I don't think he's choosy.'

As if on cue, another screech met their ears a hundred yards to the north.

Wimbush tried to swallow, but his mouth was as dry as the

riverbeds Ozil and Kebbers had pretended to prospect. 'No,' he said.

A shadow burst from the trees to the north. Wimbush's scalp contracted at the sight. It moved with great agility and speed on all fours. There was something abominable about it because it had the wrong shape for a living creature, with oddly large front limbs and shorter back legs. But it didn't waver as it headed at speed down the slope towards them.

'This I have to see.' Kebbers' grin was sickly.

Wimbush stood, rooted to the spot. The knife shook in his hand as he readied himself for what was to come. When he glanced at the men in front of him, they wore the expressions of voyeurs at a freak show.

Behind him, he heard a louder fizz as, at last, the goojl sparked into life and sent up a shower of silver sparks into the air, illuminating Wimbush and Nadia from behind. But at the sight of the lightshow, the approaching mabocawl skidded to a halt.

'Fireworks, too? This is going to be good,' Ozil said.

The mabocawl, its macabre, baboon-like head low down between its shoulders, crept forward, confused by the pyrotechnics, but ready to leap.

Wimbush felt Nadia's grip tighten around his waist. She was frightened. He was frightened. 'Oh, manure,' he said.

Ozil and Kebbers sniggered.

The mabocawl inched closer.

What a way to go. Wimbush was sure that this was not what Great Aunt Hester'd had in mind. But perhaps he'd made the cardinal error of assuming that she'd had a mind when she gave the blasted goojl to him in the first place. Ah well, fireworks alone it would be, then.

The goojl erupted behind him and the silver sparks became a thick fountain of golden streaks that enveloped Wimbush and Nadia just as the mabocawl made its leap. There was a sound a bit like a mosquito hitting the side of a hot lamp and the smell of singed fur.

Wimbush could just about see Riggon and his crew through the golden curtain. He heard Riggon curse and use a word much worse than manure. He saw Kebbers and Ozil draw knives and throw them. He tensed and turned in preparation for the thud of the blades, but all that happened was the sound of steel meeting steel and a woman's voice that sounded an awful lot like Great Aunt Hester's, ask, 'Destination?'

'Pegville!' yelled Wimbush.

The world fell away from his feet and the dark forest melted into nothingness. He could feel Nadia's arms still clinging to his waist, but he couldn't breathe, and his ears rang with the sudden absence of noise. He could see nothing but had the sense that something was whirling about him. And then there was solid ground beneath him and the unmistakable smell of methane. Someone bumped into him and he stumbled.

'Oi, mate, watch where you're goin'.'

Wimbush opened his eyes. He was in a gaslit street. It was cold, and it was wet. A hooded shape, young and male, stood nearby, eyeing him with a look a crocodile might give a wayward flamingo at a watering hole.

'So sorry,' said Wimbush.

'Yeah? You will be—'

It was then that Nadia fell out of the goojl-induced rip, directly onto the head of the hapless onlooker/potential robber. They fell together. Nadia rolled away, unscathed. *There is something of the cat about her*, thought Wimbush. The would-be mugger scrambled to his knees and stared at the woman who'd materialised out of nowhere and almost knocked him out. Stared at the way her eyes glittered unnaturally in the gaslight.

The sound of rapidly retreating feet reverberated down the cobbled street to the accompaniment of a foot-sore alchemist and a forest girl laughing hysterically in the way of people who had, by the skin of their goojl, avoided catastrophe.

PART 2

CHAPTER TWELVE

MERTHYR TYDFIL, WALES, THE HUMAN WORLD

NATURE HAS a way of reminding man that, though he thinks of himself as the dominant species, there is a long way to go before he understands all her little quirks. One only has to look at a duck-billed platypus to realise that. An egg-laying mammal with a venomous spur is not easy to explain, even in a country where death by arachnid, reptile or cartilaginous fish is a daily possibility. Of course, death by falling out of bed is twenty times more likely in Australia, even if it sells less newspapers. And noticing a funnel web on the duvet when you wake up half drunk on a Sydney stag weekend only qualifies as a contributory factor if you snuff it by slipping on the lethal empty beer bottle when you leap out of bed screaming, 'Spider!'

Yet even on the opposite side of the world in Britain, where the only animal likely to kill you on a Friday night is an undercooked leg from Chicken AsYouLikeIt, nature could show her claws in the weirdest of ways. Take creating a big empty space where there should have been rock and earth, for example. If you didn't have the geological inside info on sinkholes or know any better, such happenings could easily be misconstrued as almost, well, magical.

SEVERAL WEEKS after Wimbush lit the blue touch paper of his goojl, Captain Kylah Porter stood at the edge of a crumbling pavement and stared into the depths of the chasm stretching across what had once been Tripoli Avenue in Merthyr Tydfil.

From somewhere she heard the clash of iron on iron and the whinny of a horse and caught a whiff of acrid woodsmoke. She shook her head to clear it. There was nothing within the vicinity that could provide any such noise or smell or impression.

Except the chasm. And she knew that was impossible. No battle raged at the bottom of this hole. No undead walkers, white or otherwise, were clamouring to get out. But she also knew what she just heard. She squeezed her gold-flecked eyes shut in frustration and forced her mind to concentrate, because she was convinced she'd heard that noise and smelled that smell somewhere before. Her recollection was a gossamer-thin perception that danced away whenever she reached out to it. Like a maddening final crossword clue, it remained elusive no matter how many times she looked at it. And now was not the time to get distracted by such thoughts.

Because now there was business to attend to.

Next to her, Roberta 'Bobby' Miracle, shivering in the bitter wind despite a full-length cape with lined hood over her black leather maxi dress, said the obvious. 'Right, definitely a big hole in the ground, then. What are we supposed to do now? Throw in a coin and make a wish?'

'You can if you like,' Kylah said arching one eyebrow, 'so long as you give me time enough to get a long way away before you do.'

'Ah,' Bobby said, accepting the mild tone of rebuke in the spirit with which it was intended. 'So, this is not your run-of-the-mill sinkhole then, I take it?'

Kylah didn't answer. Instead she popped her index finger into her mouth and held it up. Satisfied, she turned, lifted up the police tape guarding the circumference of the huge hole and stepped outside. 'We need to get downwind,' she explained. They crossed the road and walked twenty yards before Kylah stopped and lifted her head to sample the air. 'There, smell it?'

Bobby sniffed and made a face. 'Sulphur and blocked drains?'

'What else?'

'A kind of wet, burnt smell. Like damp ashes.'

'No woodsmoke, is there?'

Bobby sniffed again. 'No, definitely no woodsmoke.'

Must have been my imagination, then. Kylah filed away her thoughts and said, 'Yup. Brimstone. All the rest might be accounted for by fractured sewerage pipes, but that burnt smell is classic. The unmistakable odour of dark wonderworking at play.'

'I suppose you're going to tell me next that we're going to have to go down there.'

Kylah quirked an eyebrow. 'It's what we get paid the big scruples for, Bobby.'

'I must have misread that page of the contract.'

'I'll speak to the local plod and get the area properly sealed off. Best not let any more engineers or council workers near the place until we find out what's really going on.'

Bobby nodded.

That sounded like a good idea since the last three workers had run screaming from the vicinity, convinced that something down there had been stalking them. And this had not been a pride-of-lions-versus-wildebeest kind of running away, either. This was more an unless-we-get-out-of-here-now-something-is-going-to-tear-our-souls-from-their-moorings kind of sprint. One of the workers had heard moaning, another screams; a third was convinced his long-dead aunt, who'd died in a fire, had come back to say hello. All of them had scrambled for the ladders and all of them were in hospital being treated for 'shock'; that catch-all diagnosis doctors used when they had no idea what the hell else to call it. Someone had eventually suggested they'd come across a pocket of trapped gas that had induced hallucinations and, for now at least, the press and bewildered authorities seemed happy to run with that.

Kylah Porter, an expert in all things arcane, suspected otherwise.

She caught the question in Bobby's glance and answered it. 'And yes, we will need to interview them at the hospital.'

'Just interview?'

'Followed by a bad-dreamectomy if needed. If there is something other than marsh gas down there, it had no right to give three innocent workers the heebie-jeebies, and we can definitely do something about that, can't we?'

'Yes, we can. What do you want me to do?'

Kylah smiled. One of the many things she liked about Bobby was her ability to roll up her sleeves and get on with things. 'You get back to Hipposync and brief Sergeants Keemoch and Birrik. We will certainly need security backup. Meanwhile, I will talk to our local police colleagues.'

Bobby chuckled. 'That should be fun.'

It was still early. This part of town, known as Dowlais had yet to wake up properly. As a reminder that it was to be yet another miserable end of winter's day, a fresh gust of wind whistled down from west of the Black Mountains and spat a squall of rain at the two Department of Fimmigration officers.

'Shall I bring back coffee?' Bobby asked, pulling up the hood of her anorak.

'No, I'll be back later. Once I've visited the hospital.'

Bobby nodded, and Kylah watched her hurry towards the nearest house, where she did not bother knocking on the door. Instead she attached a small purple and green opalescent knob to the hinge side, pushed it open and stepped through. That door, as would any fitted with the Aperio, would then take her not to the cosy hallway of the house, but to a canal-side property in Oxford, England, which was the headquarters of the Department of Fimmigration; the official government-sanctioned organisation where they both worked.

Kylah made her way carefully around the perimeter of the collapsed road and when she got to the safety of the opposite pavement, raised a hand. The lights of a police squad car flashed once.

'Fun indeed,' she muttered and walked towards it.

That was the trouble with trying to conduct a DOF investigation in the full glare of the public eye. Someone high up had seen the sense of bringing them in early, but it was always done on the understanding that the police officers on the ground were on a need-to-know basis only. Because it was deemed prudent that people, local plod included, were better off not knowing that there was a DOF in the first place. Much easier to sleep under a duvet in blissful ignorance of the fact that there were things that went bump in the night and that funny noise in the wardrobe at 3.30 in the morning could actually be a ghoul trying to get out. By and large it never happened because the DOF were there to prevent such transgressions. But now and again, things did go wrong, and a sinkhole appearing in the street of an ex-mining village in a Welsh valley was enough of a story without the added frisson of something very unseemly and highly unnatural, not to say supernatural, lurking at its bottom. Not only lurking but possibly even the cause of the geological disruption in the first place.

So, Kylah and Bobby had badges. And when most people, including the local police, saw them and ran checks through the system, what came up was a classified National Security Organisation with restricted access to the enquirer. It was all most people needed. And deity alone knew that in this day and age there was reason enough for the existence of such organisations. Security had become a word that covered just about everything. Usually something foul-smelling and fetid.

Kylah got to the car and the window wound down. A waft of stale policeman and fried food emerged. The driver, a constable with a jolly red face who made the BMW's front seat look like it was designed for a toddler, broke into a grin.

'So, what we going to need, ma'am? Canaries or ghost-busters?'

Next to him, his partner almost choked on an egg sandwich.

'I usually like champagne with my cabaret, Constable Doyle, so show me the Moët or belt up. For now, I'd like a lift to the hospital. And we need to extend the perimeter around this thing in case someone falls in. Unfortunately, I suspect we'll probably need a permanent presence.'

Doyle switched on the ignition. 'Oh, we do good permanent presence here in Wales, ma'am. We'll get Sid Mackeson on the case. He's been known to stand stock still for two hours at a time. He can lean for even longer. Been known to make twenty quid in coins on a quiet Sunday in town from people thinking he's an installation. He'd be a shoo-in for one of those mimes who paint themselves grey and pretend to be statues. He'll love this.'

'Is he any good with the press?'

'Loves 'em. But he can never eat a whole one.'

Kylah sat in the back and watched the damp early morning streets roll by. She could have taken the same thaumaturgical route as Bobby to the hospital and been there in a minute had she ever been there before, but without memory of the venue, it was difficult. It could be done with photographs illustrating the point of entry, but best to play it straight for now. There were appearances to keep up here. Neither of the policemen had enquired about Bobby entering the house, assuming, quite wrongly, that the DOF had set up a forward security post there. So, silent police car ride to the hospital it was. She only hoped that the smell of eggs permeating the space was pre-digestion sandwich-related and not the result of rapid intestinal transit.

Oh, the glamour of it all.

Still, it was a necessary evil, which was more than could be said for what might be lurking at the bottom of the hole in Tripoli Avenue. She let a small sigh escape and allowed her mind to drift. As always, it drifted towards Matt Danmor, the man who had been her partner on such cases for several years and with whom she shared her life, now seconded to the Bureau of Demonology in New Thameswick; a place as far away from Tripoli Avenue as it was possible to be, since it was in a different country in a different world in a different dimension. She'd often wondered about that straightforward, concise description of their relationship. Partner sounded simple. Whereas, in truth, it was unbelievably complicated. Unbelievably being the operative word.

Matt Danmor was the only man she'd ever considered spending the rest of her life with. He'd saved that life once, together with his world—the world of Tripoli Avenue—and hers at the same time. He was a man with a thin, hard body and soft eyes who loved silly puns, fart noises, dogs and any film featuring the much missed Alan Rickman. And she had neither seen nor touched him in almost a week.

And whose fault is that exactly? asked her annoyingly self-critical inner imp.

Mine. All mine.

And that was, in part, true. It was, after all, she who had suggested his transfer to the Bureau of Demonology based at New Thameswick. She'd done so in order to try and salvage their relationship. She cringed at the image of her fingers making airy quotation marks around that phrase. Yet she knew, deep down, that no matter how trite it sounded, it was the truth and made absolute sense. After working together in the DOF, she as the security chief and Matt as a 'consultant'—there were those annoying quotation marks again—it had become pretty obvious to Kylah that working with someone you shared a bed with wasn't ideal. In fact, working with someone whose working premise was to literally trust in luck had begun to drive her up the wall.

But there was little she could do to change Matt's MO. His valuable and innate talent was a rare gift whereby he stacked the what ifs up in a scatter gun and fired them off, trusting that somehow those what ifs took all the luck, for want of a better word, in the vicinity and made the strangest things happen. It meant that on assignment, plans were necessarily vague. And Matt's phenomenal abilities only required that he tap into his trigger. Anger helped, or anything involving criminal, unpleasant, or, most potently, evil behaviour. 'Gits and git-related,' in other words, as described so eloquently by Matt.

Whereas Matt's modus operandi was the definition of winging it, Kylah's work relied on investigation, planning, critical analysis and execution. Matt's inability to take anything too seriously was just the last bit of grit in the ointment that had driven a wedge between them. A spot of retraining at the BOD had suited them both, especially since Matt's partner and mentor there was Asher Lodge. Someone Kylah, who rarely trusted anyone or anything unless it was inanimate and rendered so by her, trusted without qualms and who also happened to be Bobby Miracle's significant other. The trouble was that the BOD was in New Thameswick, a city in the Fae world—her world—whereas Hipposync Enterprises, where Bobby was hopefully briefing the two Special Elf Service officers permanently garrisoned there and making a bucket of hot coffee, was very much a part of the non-Fae world.

As a cover for the DOF, Hipposync, dealers in rare books, worked perfectly. The trouble was that Krudian physics—the physical and thaumaturgical laws that allowed both worlds to exist in parallel—held sway. And at present they had swayed towards a most inhospitable twelve-hour difference based on interdimensional saving time, which developed slowly over a four-year period. It would all snap back at the spring equinox, and that was only a few days away, but it would get worse before it did. So, Matt and Kylah's lives were twelve hours out of sync. When she slept he worked, and vice versa. It was less disruptive to both of their schedules that Matt lodged in New Thameswick for the working week. On weekends they tried to catch up… sleepily.

Kylah knew she had no right to complain and she was not alone. Bobby was in exactly the same boat. But she was a trainee witch with just a few months left of her accelerated course. And being a witch, Kylah knew she'd find a way around the time difference with Lodge. Perhaps she ought to have a chat with Miss Miracle. See if she had a potion or two that might help.

CHAPTER THIRTEEN

PRINCE CHARLES HOSPITAL, MERTHYR TYDFIL, WALES

THE HOSPITAL WAS full of sickly, miserable people. And that was just the staff, weighed down by responsibility, crap wages and an NHS lumbering along on two crutches.

Both the evacuated council workers and the engineer were housed in a four-bed unit on a general medical ward whilst the medics decided what to do with them. A psychiatric transfer was on the cards, or so the charge nurse that accompanied Kylah along the ward explained.

'I think a decision will be made on today's ward round. We've kept them away from the other patients, but the fact is that physically there's little to find and we need the beds desperately, especially with the flu that's going around—' The sound of running feet interrupted the charge nurse and both he and Kylah spun around to see nurses and doctors sprinting towards the far end of the ward.

'That'll be Mr Winterbottom again,' said the charge nurse, already hurrying away. 'Should be on CCU but they're rammed. You'll have to excuse me…' His voice rose as his trot became a canter.

Kylah didn't object. Better she did this alone.

The three men lay in bed. Two had blankets pulled up to

their ears and had turned, in foetal position, with their backs to the ward entrance. The third lay on his back and strained to lift his head off the pillow and stare at Kylah as she entered. She smiled and picked up the chart from the end of the bed.

'Mr Hagley?'

The man, pale-faced and grey-bearded, nodded warily. Kylah saw him glance towards the curtained-off fourth bed with a look of barely disguised terror.

'Mr Hagley. My name is Porter and I am helping the police—'

'We're not making it up, you know,' Hagley butted in. 'None of us. It happened. It really happened.'

'I believe you, Mr Hagley. I've just come from the site.'

Hagley started, the whites of his eyes instantly visible. Only they weren't white. They appeared to be a subtle blue-grey. Easy to see why the establishment had thought that gas was involved. Something that might have tainted their haemoglobin, or perhaps their livers.

'Did you see…' his whispered words were dread-laden.

'I haven't been down to the bottom. I wanted to talk to you first. What exactly—'

'It's not here, is it?' He swallowed. 'Tell me it's not here.' His eyes darted once more towards the curtained-off bed. One of the other men whimpered softly.

Kylah glanced across and then walked over to the fourth bed, pulled back an edge of curtain and peered inside. The bed was unoccupied. However, someone had placed a sphygmo-manometer and a box of cardboard vomit bowls on its made-up surface. Probably left there by someone too busy to put things away. Troubling, no doubt, for anyone with a hospital phobia but hardly demonic in any sense of the word.

'It said it was going to follow us wherever we went,' Hagley croaked from behind her. 'Find us and tear us apart.'

Quickly, Kylah pulled back the curtains to show Hagley what was on the bed. His craning neck flopped back down in relief.

Kylah pulled up a chair and sat next to Hagley's bed. 'Tell me exactly what happened.'

The sinkhole had appeared, as sinkholes do, overnight. Given the area's industrial heritage, old coal mine workings and erosions coalescing into a hole big enough to swallow subsoil and street was top of the list. Hagley and co-workers had been sent to inspect the damage caused to cables and pipework. The geologists had already declared the walls relatively stable, and ladders and ropes were placed. By the time everyone involved in health and safety had given the all clear, it was late afternoon. Hagley and the others had descended as dusk fell, equipped with lights driven by generators. For some reason that was difficult to explain, the lights seemed to lose their effectiveness some ten feet from the bottom.

'We thought it was some kind of local phenomenon,' Hagley explained. 'Water vapour in a temperature gradient inducing a sort of localised fog or mist. At least, that was what they kept telling us.'

Outside in the corridor, someone shouted. Probably in relation to Mr Winterbottom, but Hagley flinched visibly, and his eyes flew to the source. There was nothing to see.

'Tell me what you saw,' Kylah urged.

'I was inspecting the pipes. We have a sewerage main running down both sides of this street. One was intact, but the other had clearly fractured. It was Saturday, the day after takeaway Friday. Handle a lot of volume on a Saturday, do those pipes. A four-foot section had fallen away completely. It was about eight feet above where I was standing. Quite a bit of seepage. The smell was…' Hagley hesitated.

Kylah waited.

'I'm used to bad smells. I'm in sanitation, so I should be. I was on the team that dealt with that slurry accident in 2010, up Brecon way. But this was much worse than anything I'd smelled before.' Hagley's eyes clamped shut and he forced a swallow.

'Take your time,' Kylah said.

'Then I saw…her. Her face in…in the open end of the sewerage pipe. My aunt, Sister Connie.'

Kylah guessed that Hagley must have been early fifties. That would more than likely give him a blood relative in her seventies if not older.

'She was looking right at me, nun's veil and all. Looking at me and saying, 'Nice to see you, William. Nice of you to drop in.' Her face was covered in…' The effort of recall was suddenly too much for Hagley. He fell back on to his pillow and turned his head away.

Kylah wondered if he was crying. 'Who is your Aunt Connie?' she asked gently.

Hagley kept his head turned. 'My mother's eldest sister. She was a nun. Taught in a convent school. She was a tartar. We used to hate visiting her. She'd sit us on a sofa and dare us to speak or move. I was terrified of her. God knows what she did to those poor kids at the school.' He sniffed. 'She died in a fire ten years ago. There was a suspicion of arson. My dad said it might have been spontaneous combustions from both her legs rubbing together in bed at night…'

Kylah smiled. It took courage to find the humour in terrifying situations. She liked Hagley already. 'Did she say anything else?'

It took a good half minute before Hagley spoke again. He turned back to look at Kylah and said in a desperate whisper, 'She said she was glad that I'd found her after all these years. And now that I had she would come and visit me, too.'

In the other bed, one of the council workers let out a convulsive sob.

'Tommy heard his old English teacher calling to him from behind the wall,' Hagley continued. 'He hated that bloke. And poor Janick was at the deepest point. There's a much deeper fissure in the limestone. He was shining his light into that when he saw a face in the rock. A *baboshkack*, he called it. Some kind of monster from folk lore. He's Hungarian and has a body like a truck, but he screamed like a child. They're telling us it was some sort of gas, but—'

'Okay, I think I've heard enough,' Kylah said. She stood up and went to the doorless opening in the wall that led out into the corridor beyond. There was no one there. Mr Winterbottom was proving to be a handful, obviously. She took a small stoppered bottle from her coat pocket, poured out a measure of powder into her palm and threw it into the space. Instantly, a shimmering, transparent curtain appeared. Anyone looking in from the corridor would now see three peacefully sleeping occupants and no Kylah.

Quickly, she turned her attention back to Hagley.

'This has been a terrible ordeal for you all. I need to do a quick scan using this portable device.' She reached into her satchel and took out a headband with a green stone at its centre.

She placed it gently around Hagley's forehead. 'This might make you feel a little tired afterwards, but it is completely painless.'

Tommy and Janick turned to watch. The green stone at the centre of the Pentrievant began to glow. Hagley's lined expression gave way to a wide smile and droopy eyelids. He yawned and lay back, watching Kylah with a pleasantly bewildered expression.

She quickly repeated the 'scan' on Tommy and Janick, and ended the camouflage charm without being disturbed. But, as she stepped out into the corridor, she was met by a flustered-looking charge nurse.

'Sorry about that,' he said, looking into the four bedder. 'Oh dear, are they still sleeping?'

'Yes. I managed to have a few words with Mr Hagley, though. He seemed a lot brighter than I expected from your description.'

'Really?' The charge nurse frowned. 'That does surprise me. He's been jumpy and agitated all the while he's been with us.'

'Oh well, perhaps the effect of the gas is wearing off.'

'I hope so. Dr Santana can be a bit of a tyrant when it comes to discharges.'

'I am quietly confident that psychiatric services will not be required,' said Kylah before adding drily, 'given that I am not medical and know nothing at all about it.'

The charge nurse shrugged. 'I don't think even the cleverest doctor here has any real idea. I wonder what really went on at the bottom of that sinkhole.'

Kylah thanked him and left the hospital, sure that Hagley and the others were about to confound the medical profession with a complete and rapid recovery from whatever it was they'd encountered. But though she was happy to have helped, it was a tainted satisfaction because now she was certain that something was very definitely not right here.

This case had DOF written all over it.

CHAPTER FOURTEEN

NEW THAMESWICK

As KYLAH's sense of foreboding burgeoned and she tried to not let thoughts of Matt Danmor intrude, the man himself was trying not to think at all. Far away on the other side of the Krudian fence in New Thameswick, it was 8.30 on a Friday night at the Ancient Dog Botherer. A place that was raucous at the best of times, and doubly so on the evening of the last working day of the week. The laughter, hoots, carousing and occasional screams emanating from New Thameswick's revellers fired up on cocktails and BOGOF deals meant that hearing yourself speak was out of the question. It was only a short step to not hearing yourself think, but it was a step Matt was prepared to take to avoid thoughts of what he might be treading in, judging by the way his soles squelched on the soggy carpet beneath his feet.

To his credit, Matt was not voluntarily partaking of the merriment. He, like Asher Lodge, was there in an official capacity searching for a ne'er-do-well by the name of Haggis Len; a name earned from the hagfish of almost the same name famed for being able to produce up to 20 litres of slime and free themselves from pursuers and predators by tying themselves in knots. Hagfish was the more accurate epithet. However, since Leonard Cork (real name) spent most of his time in establishments like the Ancient Dog Botherer amongst people whose ability to pronounce anything properly after three rounds of Botherer Bombs was negligible, Hagfish had morphed into Haggis and stuck—like so many other inexplicable bits of underworld mythology—onto the wall of common street parlance upon which it had been thrown.

A known dealer in illegal philtres, unlicensed hexes and dubious potions, so long as the thing was not kosher and likely dangerous in a mind-altering sense, Haggis Len could get you it. Big on enthusiasm but microscopic on detail, utilising Haggis's services was very much a game of Krudian roulette. He'd once procured a bad batch of love potion with a misspelled incantation that, once spoken, propelled the hapless user to a place between worlds where one was compelled to stand knee deep in effluent as a demon's plaything. Not exactly the valentine's gift that had been hoped for. Especially when thrice-an-hour headstands were mandatory.

Matt took a sip from his non-alcoholic chestnut juice, stared about him and considered the tortuous route that had brought them to this nefarious nightspot.

He and Asher were obviously not interested in love potions. Hawkshaw Crouch, one of New Thameswick Constabulary's finest, had contacted Asher through the Bureau of Demonology. A spate of supposed suicides had rippled through the city. The most recent involved three previously young fit men, migrant workers, all of whom had previously shown no sign of any depressive tendency, according to their landlady, Mrs Canticle. Her boarding house on Marinade Avenue was somewhere both Matt and Asher had visited on more than one occasion since it appeared to be the honeypot around which every lowlife bee buzzed. Crouch preferred a slightly more scatological analogy involving flies and something far less agreeable than honey, but the general principle applied in both instances.

But as with all things New Thameswick-related, knowing where to get information on criminal activity came with complications. For example, any and all conversations with Mrs Canticle were complicated by her conviction that:

A) Her husband, a sailor continuously at sea for at least twenty-five years, was about to return at any moment, and,

B) That he would find her the irresistible thirtysomething

that she might have been a quarter of a century, and counting, before.

To that end, Mrs Canticle, now the size and shape of two one hundredweight sacks of potatoes, felt obliged to warn men against any type of romantic advance. The fact that any man with a functioning sense of smell and even half of one good seeing eye would rather swallow a slug smoothy than make any type of advance was beside the point. Mrs Canticle remained convinced by a delusion of such staggering proportions that Matt, on his first encounter, had wondered if she was either mad or a candidate for comedianof the year. Crouch, however, had put him straight.

'Yeah, it's pretty hysterical but ignore it at your peril. One day Mrs Canticle is going to realise that Mr Canticle is shacked up on some island in Fitsot with three wives and a penis gourd, and will declare herself available. I wouldn't want to be the bloke who says, "Hello Mrs Canticle," and have that interpreted as, "How's about a quick knee-trembler up against that tree?" Because believe you me, twenty-five years, seven months, fifteen days and deity knows how many hours of enforced celibacy— her words—and pent-up frustration is going to make much more than some poor bloke's knee tremble. I don't think much of the tree's chances either.'

Mrs Canticle, welcoming Matt, Asher and Crouch back like old friends with her usual trait of lifting her larger left bosom up to meet its fellow in the straining arrangement of wire and straps she wore to contain these dirigibles, was as effusive as ever in her description of what happened on her top floor when they had visited to take a statement a few days before.

'Them Easties from Crowshee?' She shook her head. 'Got loads of 'em. Good workers, but boy, do they know how to enjoy theyselves.' She tutted before turning and pointing a wagging finger at Matt. 'But I has rules. No one in a bath towel on the landing after 7 pm except me. No strumpets, and lights out at 10.30 sharp. These were nice boys. Polite and quiet, though two of them kept giving me the eye. Understandable, o'course. Any man might feel an urge when faced with womanly charms like what I got.'

Matt threw Asher a look. The Bureau of Demonology officer did not look out of place here. Pale and thin, he could have walked off the pages of a New Romantic fan magazine from the eighties with a high-collared coat and eyelashes that Kylah termed 'just plain unfair'. Now, he wore the fixed expression of someone who'd just noticed that the brown thing under the door everyone had assumed was a draft excluder had just flicked out its tongue in search of dinner.

'But this noise I heard was definitely not your usual rowdy card game noise,' Mrs Canticle went on. 'This was…unnatural, if you get my drift.'

They all did. Carrying a whiff of unwashed clothes and stale sweat peppered with smoke from whatever herbs Mrs Canticle stuffed into her pipe. But underneath all that, her drift was tinged with typical Mrs Canticle wisdom. She had, after all, seen most things any living person was capable of in this boarding house, and quite a few things they were not.

'So what did you do, Mrs Canticle?' Crouch asked.

'I went up, keys a-janglin. That gives 'em warning, that does. S'enough to quieten 'em down, usually. But not this time. Made no difference no matter how hard I jangled.' She chuckled. 'Mr Canticle used to say I could jangle harder than most.'

Matt dared not look at Asher.

'So I marches up to the top and knocks. The noise, by this time, was awful. Like a pig with a thorn in its arse. But worse was this laughin'…' She shook her head and her non-seeing left eye wandered disconcertingly further towards the far wall. 'I knows what real laughter is. Mr Canticle used to really laugh when I slipped off me nighty. But this wasn't like that. Not ecstatic in any way.' She smacked her lips together as a distant memory wriggled out from a dusty drawer, but with alarming speed that same wandering eye flicked back to fix on Crouch. 'This laughin' was somethin' else altogether. So I knocks again and again no one answers. Then I unlocks the door.'

Mrs Canticle hesitated at this point. Under the layers of grime on her face, it looked suspiciously like she'd blanched. Even Crouch, one of only a handful of shapeshifters in New Thameswick's law enforcement agency, was taken aback.

'I'll never forget what I saw,' Mrs Canticle whispered. Something ticked obligingly in the rafters and her wall eye wobbled off on its own again as she lifted her chin in acknowledgement. 'Yeah, even this old house agrees with me. When I opened the door, it was freezin', for a start. The window was wide open, and it shouldn't have been because it was a wiccan's mammary of a night. But it was open 'cos one o' them Easties was crouched like a bird on the sill. He had the silliest grin on his face. I could tell they'd been smokin' some waccyweed, but this wasn't the usual blue smoke on the ceiling. This was yellow and sickly, and the smell whiffed of damp fur and rotten egg. And then I saw that the bloke on the sill wasn't seein' me at all. He was smilin' at the other two.'

Mrs Canticle paused and removed a grubby handkerchief from her apron pocket and blew her nose. She inspected the result, nodded her approval and replaced the handkerchief.

'One of his mates was squattin' on the bed. He was tryin' to cut his own throat with a bit of glass and he was doin' a grand job of it, too. He was the one squealin'. The third one, he was the one laughin', though he had no cause to, seein' as he had a huge knife in his chest. At first, I thought he was trying to pull it out, but then I saw that what he was doin' was pushin' it further in. Then the bloke in the window cawed once and jumped out. The worst thing of all was that I'm sure I saw him fly past that window twice before he dropped like a stone. Though that could have been the effect of all the waccyweed floatin' about that room, I admit. But it was their eyes…that's what did it for me. They'd all gone that funny colour blue.' Mrs Canticle made a face, which, on top of the face she already had, was pretty dreadful. 'They was completely off their heads.'

Crouch could not have agreed more. An 'eruption', he called it. Waccyweed laced with lava juice. And it was this particular brand of lava juice that seemed to be causing the problem. You couldn't get arrested for using waccyweed, but lava juice was a banned substance that could masquerade quite easily as demonic possession. In fact, Crouch had used that very argument to recruit Asher and Matt from the BOD. Asher, a necreddo who could talk to the dead, was also a skilled investigator who'd suffered for his labours when he'd worked for the constabulary. The newly established necro squad had paid the price of major teething troubles that had resulted in Asher's brother, also a necreddo, dying and Asher suffering a meltdown. As for Matt, he had skills no one knew how to describe and so everyone had given up trying. Suffice to say if luck was a lady, she'd be stuck like a Siamese twin to his hip.

Though lava juice had been around for years, it was difficult to get hold of. So, its emergence on the streets of New Thameswick and with such devastating effect had prompted a full-scale investigation. Crouch wanted to know if it was a new source, or just old stuff tainted with a hex…or something worse. Asher had tried communicating with the three dead Crow-sheeites, but whatever it was they'd taken resulted in such a profound paranoia that it had accompanied them to the other side. Post-mortem confusion states were unusual since murder victims were usually highly miffed and only too willing to tell their story. In time, it was probable that acceptance and realisation would kick in, but given the language difficulties, Asher feared that by the time the victims' riven souls understood what had happened to them, it might be too late for a whole host of other unfortunates. Whatever was in this lava juice was pretty potent when it came to scrambling brains.

Even the brains of the dead.

CHAPTER FIFTEEN

AND SO, on a Friday night in the war zone that was New Thameswick's Claret area (the whole of New Thameswick was a red-light district, but where the real fun happened, it was even darker red), Matt found himself half listening to a girl from Splosh tell him that he had lovely skin and she'd be happy to massage a particular bit of it for just ten scruples a throw, whilst sipping a dandelion spritzer and searching the Botherer's crowd for Haggis Len.

Thankfully, Asher nudged his elbow before the girl could get any further. Matt turned and looked in the direction of Asher's nod. Some bright young things were at a corner table making a lot of noise, the majority of it very silly. They looked, and acted, like they'd come straight from Lucre Street, New Thameswick's financial sector. Asher had spotted them the moment he'd walked in, but he hadn't noticed the girl climbing onto the table until now.

She did so almost languorously; sinuous movements in time with the music coming from the four-piece band bravely trying to make themselves heard in the other corner. They were banging out that old favourite, 'Molasses Myrtle', and the girl's friends were now encouraging her with hoots and claps. She was tall and wearing a velvet dress with a slit up the side, which showed quite a lot of a slender leg as she started gyrating on the table top. She smiled at her companions, but Matt got the distinct impression that she was smiling at something else. Something only she could see or hear as she lost herself in the music, arms outstretched, neck extended. Then her head fell forward, and she gazed into the eyes of one of the men at the table with a look of melodramatic lust so smoky it made the man half stand. But all the girl wanted was his scarf, which she whipped off before running long painted fingernails up the man's throat and teasing him with an almost kiss.

Her table went wild. The man kept standing, unwilling to give up the invite.

She began twirling the scarf above her head, pulling it taut between both hands to rub against her face and neck. And she was good, this girl. Her movements were fluid and seductive. But Matt couldn't help noticing the little curl of yellow smoke that hung unmoving on the ceiling above her. There was a lot of smoke everywhere else, too, but it was a standard grey-blue. Only near the girl's table was it a sickly yellow. He was about to bring this to Asher's attention when it happened.

The Ancient Dog Botherer was an old pub with low beams and not much ventilation. The girl's arms, when stretched above her head, could reach the cross-beams. She did that now, walking along the table in time with her arms straight up, as if she was holding up the building. A different man made a lunge for her, but she stepped away and, laughing, picked up a bottle of beer and tilted it neck first towards him.

He grinned. Perhaps he was her significant other. Perhaps they'd only just met. Perhaps he thought that she'd picked him out and he was in with a chance.

If so, he was about to be sadly and brutally disappointed.

Still swinging her hips, the girl tilted the bottle back towards her lips, took a swig and smashed it into the man's face.

The table erupted in horror as chairs scraped back and the unfortunate man collapsed, blood spurting from his torn and bleeding flesh.

For a moment, all eyes turned to the victim. No one looked at the girl. When they did, they recoiled in horror. Something had happened to her pretty face. A rictus grin seemed to make her mouth bigger than it should have been. And there was enough light to see that the whites of her eyes were no longer white. They'd darkened to a turquoise blue. She grabbed the cross-beam and, with surprising agility, hauled herself up to stand upon it, surveying the chaos below. It was then she started to really laugh. A shrill, unpleasant, almost unearthly sound. She was still laughing as she looped the scarf into a smaller crosspiece of the oak A-frame truss she was standing on. Her hands worked confidently as if sure of their task, unwavering and deft as they formed a short, tight loop in the material of the scarf. She looked at the crowd, laughed again and stepped forward off the beam as if she was about to set off on a country stroll, thrusting her head through the makeshift noose in one, still smiling, movement.

Even above the screams and shouts, Matt heard her neck snap.

He stood, paralysed by the horror of it all. But then he felt Asher's hand on his arm and saw his pointing finger. There. Near the back door. The man they were after.

Asher was already moving. But so was half the pub. People wanted out while some of the girl's friends were trying to stand on each other's shoulders to get to her.

'Shouldn't we…?' Matt said, his eyes on the girl.

'Too late for her. But not for him.' Asher dived towards a squat, well-fed, red-faced man in a green coat desperately squeezing himself through the crowd towards the exit.

'Haggis Len?' Matt asked.

Before Asher could answer, another scream drew their attention back to the girl. Her friends had grabbed hold of her but the precarious arrangement of one man on another's shoulders collapsed, yanking the girl loose from the scarf to crumple onto the table beneath. It was a harrowing sight. When Matt drew his eyes back to the exit, there was no sign of the red-faced man.

'He's gone,' Matt said.

'Well named, is Haggis,' said a grim-faced Asher. 'But don't worry. All we need to do is follow the trail of slime he leaves behind. Come on.'

They pushed through the crowd into the cold March night, their breath pluming out in great furls of steam. Constabulary officers blowing whistles were heading to the Ancient Dog Botherer, much to the derision of the crowd, who were noticeably agitated and understandably so. Partly by the suicide, but mostly by an awareness of all those half-finished drinks on the tables.

The Botherer did not have many rules, but one that did exist was the two-minute rule. Any drink left unattended for any longer than that became fair game. It made going to the toilet a sprint. It also made for some interesting watery patterns on the fronts of men's trousers. At the beginning of the evening this could be explained away by the hurried splash of water onto hands from the one pump the toilets contained for washing. A couple of hours later, it was far more likely to be a result of a hurried putting away of equipment before completion. The usual two shakes and a pull lost you vital seconds in the rugby scrum that involved getting back in time to make sure your drink was still there.

You wore dark trousers to the Botherer. Always.

The streets teemed with people…well, some people and some not people, but it teemed nonetheless as the Friday night crowd hurried to their destinations. Asher thought he caught a glimpse of something green disappearing down an alley, but it was too late. They'd never catch him in this mob.

'Right,' he said. 'We'll round up the victim's friends and take them down to the guardhouse. Perhaps they can help us.'

'You think Haggis Len had something to do with what happened?'

'I am not a betting man, Matt, but I think the answer to that is what is known as a dead cert.'

CHAPTER SIXTEEN

The constabulary's city centre headquarters, affectionately known by the population of New Thameswick as The Foot on account of it being at the bottom of Leggit Lane, buzzed with activity. It was, after all, a Friday night. The scarf-wearing man from the table of revellers at which the dead girl had been sitting was slumped on a hard chair in a state of white-faced disbelief. Around him, drunks leaned against walls or sung songs whose words they knew vaguely, if at all. Ladies of the night, as inappropriately dressed for the weather as their work demanded, protested their innocence. A wedding party, clothes torn and faces bruised, glowered across the room at a comparably motley crew. From the similarity of their facial features and the drooping carnations in their lapels, it was clear that they were all related.

All in all, The Foot was not a place to grieve quietly.

Matt and Asher walked in to the sight of one of The Foot's duty sergeants holding court over the queue of people waiting to complain, hurl abuse or be banged up. A line of yowling, swaying or furtively glancing beings stood in front of the desk, behind which stood Sergeant Colm E Maardam, aka 'Sergeant Smiler' on account of his inability to arrange his lips into anything other than a scowl when someone drew attention to the obvious comic value of his name. His colleagues, blessed with healthy survival instincts, had wisely opted for a less contentious, but nicely ironic, nickname. The person currently engaged in conversation with Smiler was a cocky, well-built young fellow, probably in town for a boys' night out, judging by the ridiculous party hat he was wearing.

'Name?' asked Smiler.

'Ivor,' said the kid, beaming and hanging on to the wooden desk for support.

'Ivor what?'

'Ivor got a luvverly bunch of coconuts.'

Sergeant Smiler, glasses perched on a large and bulbous nose, put down his pen and studied the specimen in front of him.

'Taken a funny pill, have we, son?'

'Got to keep me spirits up,' said the boy.

'Difficult to do when you're chained to the dog kennels out back on a night like this.'

The boy's smirk slipped a notch. 'All I done was take a pie. I was gonna pay for it, like.'

Smiler nodded. 'Not how it works here in New Thameswick, son. We have this old and venerable tradition whereby people pay for the goods before they walk off and consume them, not after.'

'S'only a pie.'

'Only a pie? ONLY A PIE? What you snaffled was not only a pie, my misguided young friend. This was one of Thai Me Down Bundit's curried cormorant pies. World famous, they are.'

'I didn't know that. Tasted nice, though.' He rubbed his stomach defiantly.

'Ate it all then, did you?'

'Every last crumb.'

'Shame that, because it means we'll have to put you out with the dogs now because in about four hours' time you are going to have a visitor.'

'Oh, yeah, who?' The boy drew himself up to his full gym-rat height. Physically, he was a match for any of the coppers standing in wary anticipation around the room, nightsticks in hand.

'Bundit's revenge, aka the krut. That's what's coming your way,' Smiler said, without any hint of a smile.

'What's the krut?'

Several of the surrounding coppers inhaled through pursed lips, causing the boy to look around, confused.

'Bundit's curried cormorant pies carry a health warning which you clearly did not read, did you?'

'No.' The boy was wary now, his bravado losing a bit of its sheen. Whether it was the word 'krut' or 'reading' that carried the most power to disquiet was hard to tell.

'Do not consume in one sitting, it says. Take test dose first, it says. In pretty big print. And not in joined-up letters, either.'

'Why?' asked the already regretful thief.

'Because it'll give you the krut as soon as giblets. So, my lad, you are in for an interesting night. And, if you want access to a WC and good supply of paper, you'd better start playing ball. Otherwise you're in with Balthasar and Beelzebub, our Alsatians, and they do not take kindly to nasty smells and rumblings when they're trying to kip. And nasty smells and rumblings, as well as quite possibly a return visit of the majority of what you've consumed in the last forty-eight hours, is exactly what you are facing, or if you're lucky and quick, not facing, if you get my drift.'

'Micah,' wailed the boy, his face now a sickly yellow. 'That's my name. Micah.'

Sergeant Smiler wetted the tip of his pencil with his tongue and wrote. A muscle twitched at the corner of one eye. To those that knew him well, it meant that Sergeant Smiler was enjoying himself.

Asher walked over to where the scarf-wearing man was sitting. He was much younger than he first appeared, perhaps twenty, if that, head down and trembling. His two companions, a man and a woman of about the same age, sat in shock, their arms folded, hunched in on their own thoughts.

Asher pulled up a chair. 'We saw what happened in the pub.'

The young man glanced up. He looked like someone who'd seen a ghost. Or at least seen a ghost freshly made. 'Is that why you're here? Witnesses?'

'No. We're on official business.' Asher took out a wallet and flashed a BOD ID.

Matt didn't bother; he simply stood watching the young man's face as memory of what had happened not half an hour before swirled around in his head.

'What's your name?' Asher asked.

'Barney.'

'And the girl?' Matt asked.

'Libby. She wasn't just a girl, she was my—' the last word died on a choked sob.

'Your girlfriend?' Asher asked.

Barney nodded. His two friends looked on with anguish, angling their eyes and mouths downwards.

'What was the occasion?' Matt asked.

'A birthday. One of the other girls.'

'You knew that Libby was smoking lava juice?'

Barney nodded and squeezed his eyes shut as a short-lived mental battle ensued. Saying yes was self-incriminating, but saying no was to throw Libby to the wolves. Barney knew he'd lost either way. In the end, he opted for the truth which, given that he was sitting in a place full of liars, thieves and miscreants, was going to give him no end of a leg-up in officialdom's eyes. 'No. Just some waccyweed. Someone on the table said it would be a laugh and Libby said she knew where she could get some.'

'How?'

Barney shook his head. 'That was Libby all over. Just leapt right in. I asked her the exact same question and she just said that in a place like The Botherer, there was always someone selling it. She excused herself and I saw her walking around the room, smiling and asking questions. That was the thing about her, you could never say no to her. She had this smile that…'

Asher waited while Barney let his thoughts stray off before he reeled him back in again. 'Who was she talking to?'

'I don't know. I've only been to the Botherer a couple of times before. It's too manic for me. I prefer somewhere you can at least hear yourself shout.'

Matt pressed him. 'Describe what you saw.'

Barney looked up into Matt's face and nodded. 'She was over by the WC and this bloke was leaning against the wall. Squat, short sort of bloke with a red face and a green coat. She kept smiling. She was so happy when she came back to the table. Well pleased with herself. She had a little purple bottle, the usual sort of thing. She borrowed my pipe and stoked it with waccyweed and then poured on some drops of this purple stuff and took a long toke. I could see something was wrong right away. It was her eyes. The white…it changed in an instant. Went a funny colour blue. And then she went wild. Dancing, kicking off her shoes, getting onto the table. I tried to stop her getting up there, but she wouldn't listen. She was just smiling all the time. But it wasn't like her. I mean, it was like she wasn't there anymore. Then she reached for my scarf and…'

'We know. We were there,' Matt said.

'Then you tell me what happened,' he wailed. 'Why did she do that? I mean, we were…she was….'

'I don't suppose you have any of the lava juice with you?'

'I didn't touch it. Must be still in her coat pocket.'

'Okay, thanks. We'll…' Matt felt a hand on his arm and caught himself. He was about to say 'pick it up at the morgue', but Asher's hand stayed him.

'I'm sorry for your loss, Barney,' Asher said.

Barney could only nod and study his shoes.

'If it's any consolation, she says she's sorry that she messed things up.' Asher's voice remained neutral.

'Wha…what?'

Asher nodded. 'I'm a necreddo. I've spoken to her. Wasn't easy. Even in death the lava juice, or at least this lava juice, is very potent. Luckily, she didn't take much. She was confused and—'

'Frightened? Was she frightened? I'd hate it if she was—' Barney's voice squeaked with emotion.

Asher cut him off before he became desperate. 'She wasn't frightened. They seldom are. Confused at first, but death always brings with it a kind of peace.'

Barney shook his head. 'I told her not to mess about with that stuff. But I couldn't stop her. She was so headstrong and… What else did she say?'

Asher hesitated. 'Nothing else. She told me to say sorry…and that she'd always love you.'

Barney's face crumpled, and he dropped his head into his hands.

'Ah, the dynamic two-oh,' said a voice from somewhere in the crowd. Matt looked up to see Crouch hailing them. He thought about correcting the hawkshaw, telling him that the better term was dynamic duo, but he knew well enough that DC comic tropes meant nothing at all in New Thameswick.

And Matt also knew that if you travelled far enough in this world, you'd find much stranger things than men who thought they were spiders or dressed up in capes and masks. One glance around The Foot's Friday night clientele confirmed that in a trice.

They crossed the room to where Crouch was standing near a stone statue. Or rather was transforming from being that large statue. Being a shapeshifter had its advantages when it came to unobtrusive observation of the criminal classes and when there was little or no space. Where Crouch manifested was just about the only unoccupied part of the reception area.

'You here for the hanging?' Crouch asked with his usual diplomacy.

'We had front-row seats. Haggis appears up to his neck in it, if you'll excuse the pun,' Asher explained.

Crouch nodded. In his semi-human form, he was the whole constabulary shebang. Bowler hat, long black coat, cane, moustache and a dusky skin that shifted in colour, just like his currently hazel eyes, depending on his mood. 'I'm supposed to ask that kid some questions. Is it worth it?'

Matt shook his head. 'He's distraught. One minute, his girlfriend's the life and soul. The next, she's—'

'Just soul,' said Crouch with his usual tact.

'But he did manage to implicate Haggis,' Matt said.

Crouch nodded approvingly. 'I'd better take a statement, then. Was he using lava juice too?'

'Didn't get the chance,' Matt said. 'He isn't the culprit here.'

'Know anything about eyes turning blue?' asked Asher.

Crouch's lip curled up at the edge. 'Do I look like an optimystic?'

'You mean optometrist,' Asher said.

'That's what I said. Why?'

'Barney reported that the whites of Libby's eyes turned an odd blue shade just before—'

'What did you just say?'

The all turned at once. The question, in a voice that probably had its own cake stand at a country fair, came from the woman currently the lucky recipient of Sergeant Smiler's not-so-unbridled attention.

'Sorry?' said Asher.

'About the eyes. Did you say odd blue shade?' The questioner, headscarf tied tightly around a thin, pinched face in the

middle of which was a mouth with lips you could open an envelope with, glared defiantly at Asher. Horsey was the adjective
that struck Matt. She looked like the sort of woman who'd
ridden horses, bred them and might even get mistaken for one in
a certain light.

'Sorry, we're not at liberty to—' Matt began.

'It's exactly what I'm trying to tell this…this miserable, crude
specimen, except that he refuses to listen.'

Sergeant Smiler looked up, eyes narrowing at the sound of
'specimen'. It was impossible to offend the desk sergeant
anymore, though many had, and still did, try their best. Most of
the people in the station couldn't help themselves since 'F', 'B'
and 'C' were about as much of the alphabet most of them knew,
and so words beginning with these letters and seldom containing
more than three more, made up their lexicon. Occasionally, if
they were posh and had waded the shallows of New Thameswick
to find themselves treading the very deep waters of The Foot,
Smiler was willing to make an exception. But if you'd had an
education and therefore practised being ungracious, and even
knew what the word meant, there were no excuses.

The sergeant leaned forward. 'Madam, the wrong colour of
eyes does not constitute an offence.'

'Of course it doesn't and I'll thank you not to suggest that
I'm suggesting they do. But you're not listening, are you? Your
body posture may imply that you are listening, but your expression tells a very different story, Sergeant Maardam. And these
eyes that I am reporting are not merely different, they are posi-
tively offensive.' The woman wagged a finger at Smiler, who
calmly put down his pencil and tilted his head. He'd heard most
of everything before but was always game for something new
with which to entertain his mates at the annual sergeants'
gurning night.

Matt pushed through the crowd to the desk. 'What exactly do
you mean?'

'Well, just look at him,' the woman insisted. 'I have a statue
at home that's more cheerful. You know, one of those men with a
protruding thingy to hang your hat on. Well, the one I have lets
you hang your hat and a couple of scarves and a handbag—'

Matt shook his head. 'I don't mean Smiler, sorry, Sergeant

Maardam. I meant the eyes. What exactly do you mean by the "offensive" eyes?'

Under the headscarf a strand of greying hair lay like a dead bird's wing over the woman's forehead. Her upper lip hardly moved when she spoke, and she held a battered leather handbag in both hands very primly. Matt was prepared to bet it had been used more than once as a weapon. 'One of the gels in my charge. That's whom I'm here to report. It is she who possesses the eyes.'

Behind the desk, Smiler, always keen to delegate and get one of the great unwashed that sullied The Foot's reception area off his radar, turned to Crouch. 'Sounds like,' he pushed his glasses up his nose and consulted his notes, 'Miss Hoare here has something you want to hear, eh, Crouch?' Having taken extra care to pronounce her name with double the volume he would normally use, the Smiler's frown slid into…slightly less of a frown.

Crouch threw him a look and turned back to the now named, Miss Hoare. Her tweed skirt looked as if it had at least three years' worth of cat hair stuck to it, but her brogues, paradoxically, shone. He sighed in defeat. 'Go on, then. Let's go to the interview room.'

'Next,' yelled Smiler.

CHAPTER SEVENTEEN

CROUCH LED the way through the door he'd just emerged from. The interview room was tiled in white; a legacy of The Foot's previous incarnation as a sanatorium. A couple of high windows let in draughty air, but a fire had been lit and there was a kettle to hand. Asher pulled out a chair for the interviewee.

'Tea?' Matt asked as Miss Hoare settled herself on a rickety chair.

'Four sugars and just a splish of milk,' said Miss Hoare, who was clearly pleased at having been listened to at last. 'Am I now having special treatment?'

Asher smiled. 'Indeed you are, Miss Hoare. Mr Crouch reserves this room for our VIPs .'

Miss Hoare shifted her neck and sat up straighter.

'Now,' said Crouch. 'Tell us about this girl.'

While Matt made the tea, they listened to Miss Hoare explain that she was the proprietor of a rooming house for young women. The sole proprietor now that her father, a pastor, had passed away. Many came to New Thameswick to seek work, others to escape situations of repression or abuse, and Miss Hoare provided a safe and male-free environment. And occasionally there were those for whom society had no real place and to this end, Miss Hoare was also able to be of assistance. She drew a line at the mad, but she did have one or two 'square pegs' that had found their way under her caring, charitable wing. It was with regard to one such unusual client that she felt obliged to turn to the constabulary that evening.

Asher handed Miss Hoare a mug of builder's tea. She clutched it in hands wearing fingerless woollen gloves.

'What can you tell us about this "unusual client" of yours?'

And so, in clipped tones, Miss Hoare did just that. 'There's not much to tell other than her rent is being paid for by a young gentleman. An alchemist, and pleasant enough young man, if a little lacking in social graces. Works at the Polyalchemic. One of their boffins. Herbologist of some kind, always off on some expedition or other. Goes by the name of Wimbush and looks to have about as much common sense as a broad bean.' Miss Hoare rolled her eyes. 'Anyway, he came to me a few weeks ago, asking if I could take in a young gel. A refugee, he called her. Didn't speak a word of gabble, but she was apparently a fast learner.' Miss Hoare leaned in and dropped her voice. 'He explained to me that she'd escaped from the forests up in Steppeinit and that she needed somewhere safe to stay while he worked out how best to help her.' She paused to slurp some tea with her right pinkie pointed before continuing, 'One of them thin-but-strong gels. Long dark hair that needed a good wash. At first, I thought she was blind because she wore these really dark specs. Never saw her without them…until this morning.'

Miss Hoare shook her head and took another healthy slurp.

'Her name is Nadia and Mr Wimbush used to call regularly…at first. Every day he'd climb the stairs and sit with her to teach her some gabble. It was all very respectable and proper. I approved. But lately he hasn't called so much, though he still pays the rent on time. Always on time. Anyway, Nadia keeps herself to herself. Never goes out, happy to sit in her room and read—except when the gels had their self-defence lessons with Miss Nigishi. And she is a big reader, is Nadia. Newspapers, books, anything she can get her hands on. Of course, some of the other gels, being gels, almost died of curiosity. But I warned them to stay away. And mostly they did. Until today.'

Another loud slurp followed.

'What happened today, Miss Hoare?' Asher asked.

'Bathroom incident,' Miss Hoare explained. 'There are always problems with the bathrooms. Gels and bathrooms are a logistical nightmare. They'd spend hours in there if they could.

If it was up to them, they'd each have a bathroom of their own.'
Miss Hoare snorted. 'Imagine. I have strict rules, ten minutes
each in the morning and twenty in the evenings on bath nights.
I'm in and out of there in five, of course. I fail to see the attraction. I'm a great believer in the three Fs. Face, feet and fa——'

'What was different about today?' Matt broke in with a
timely question.

'Madrigal. That is what was different. She's one of my gels
from Cobb, and you know them. Never backwards in coming
forwards. Works at the brewery and has boys outside the
windows every weekend, drooling like dogs scenting heat.
Anyway, I was coddling an egg for my breakfast when I heard
Madrigal scream. It wasn't her turn in the bathroom, but she's
always chancing it, just to get one last look, see if her earrings
are dangling properly, or that her lipstick's the right shade.
Anyway, it was supposed to be Nadia's ten minutes. It's all
written on the rota. She must have gone in and come out but left
her dark glasses on the washbasin. Maybe she'd gone back into
her room to fetch something, I don't know. Anyway, Madrigal
snuck in and found the glasses and decided to take them to
Nadia's room. "Trying to be helpful," she said. I suspect that it
was more outright nosiness. But, as she got to Nadia's door, the
gel herself was coming back out to go back to the bathroom, so
Madrigal gets the one good look at Nadia's face that we'd all
been waiting for. That was when she screamed.'

'What did she see?' Crouch asked.

'Nadia's eyes, that's what she saw.'

'And?'

'Madrigal came galloping down the stairs. "Oh, it's horrible,
Miss Hoare, it's horrible. Her eyes, they're, like, sooo disgusting."'
Miss Hoare's Madrigal impression came with fluttering eyes and
hand movements. 'So, I investigated. Of course, Nadia had her
glasses back on but I made her take them off, and there they
were. Blue as a robin's egg.'

'She has blue eyes, so what?' Matt said.

'They're not just blue, they're *all* blue. No white bits at all,'
Miss Hoare explained. 'I do wish you'd listen. That's exactly
what I was trying to tell that horrible man on the desk. Not just
her irises. I mean the whole thing, even where the white bit
should be?'

'Sclera,' said Asher.

'Funny thing is, I don't think we did,' Miss Hoare said.

'Did what?' Asher asked.

'Scare her. She's tough, that one. She just shrugged it off, said, "Satisfied now?" in perfect gabble, and went back into her room.'

Crouch nodded slowly. 'So why are you here?'

'Well, I've been busy, you know, shopping and the like. Current, the baker's boy, he told me that having eyes like that is a sign either of demonic possession or of a lava juicer. I won't have any of that nonsense in my house. I came here to report it and have her removed.'

Asher, Crouch and Matt exchanged glances. They were all thinking the same thing. Up until that evening they would have laughed Miss Hoare out of the building. You couldn't arrest anyone for being or looking different. Certainly not in New Thameswick. If you did, the jails would be full to bursting within the hour. But they'd just seen a juicer throttle herself and saw the whites of her eyes turn blue in front of their own.

And so, much to Miss Hoare's unmitigated delight, Crouch said, 'I think we'd better pay Nadia a visit, don't you?'

CHAPTER EIGHTEEN

Miss Hoare's establishment was a crumbling pile in a part of New Thameswick that was on the gentrification list. Currently, however, it was very much hoy polloi territory. The grand buildings that had once been family homes had been carved up into apartments and rooming houses. Dun Roomin needed a lick of paint to remind everyone that its colour was actually white as opposed to the dirty yellow it had become thanks to years of horse manure and urine fumes drifting up from the street. Great for keeping the moths off your clothes, but a bugger when it came to depigmentation. Inside, it was shabby but clean.

'Room number six,' said Miss Hoare and pointed up the stairs. 'Second floor.'

'Aren't you coming up with us?' Crouch asked.

'I've done my duty as a good citizen in reporting the situation to you, Mr Crouch. Now I'll leave it in the hands of the professionals. Plus, I know what these lava juicers can do. Read it in the news. Go berserk, some of them. And there's always the teeniest possibility that she's not a juicer but possessed by something or other. I'll stay here and contact the exorcist if she is. Besides, the cats need feeding.'

'How many do you have, Miss Hoare?' Matt wanted to put everyone out of their misery.

'Just the ten.'

Crouch led the way to the second floor and a narrow, cramped landing. To the left were three doors, two to the right.

Number six was far left. Crouch knocked, while Matt and Asher hung back on the landing.

No answer.

Crouch knocked again and said, 'Constabulary. Open up please, miss.'

They all heard the faint metallic scrape of metal as the cover of the peephole slid aside, followed by a key turning in a lock. The door opened just enough to reveal a girl's face. It was difficult to comment on the features since they were mostly hidden behind a sizeable pair of round and very dark glasses. But what was visible looked lean and pale.

'How can I help?' said the girl in an accent that marked her as originating somewhere to the east of the Bleak mountains. The delivery was flat, the voice surprisingly deep for her size, which was bordering on the elfin. It had a raspy, gravelly texture that gave it maturity and depth, and a certain allure.

'Just making some enquiries, Miss.' Crouch showed her his badge. 'Wondered if we could have a few words.'

Nadia looked past Crouch to the two men loitering on the landing. 'They are constabulary, too?'

'Ah, no. They're…consultants, helping me with the case I'm investigating.'

'What case?'

The unmistakable noise of a door clicking open below met their ears.

'I think it might be better if we continued this conversation inside. Unless you'd like to come down to the station…'

'It's all right, dear,' called Miss Hoare from below in a syrupy voice of staggering duplicitousness, 'I've checked their bona fides and they are all in good working order. They are who they say they are. But if you need anything, anything at all, just shout and I'll be up in a jiffy.'

Matt and Asher exchanged incredulous looks.

But then Miss Hoare stage-whispered with one hand cupped around her mouth, 'Keeping her off guard. The exorcist is on his way.'

Nadia rolled her eyes and opened the door wide. She turned her back on the men and walked across the tiny room to sit on the edge of the bed. Crouch, Asher and Matt trooped in after her. Cheerless was quite a generous adjective when describing the stark little room. Nails glistened where the floorboards had worn through, the rug was threadbare and the curtain over the window resembled a muslin rag. But Matt could see not a scrap of dust or dirt anywhere. Nadia looked like the sort of person who made the most of things, even when those things were bordering on the worthless.

'Right, well, Miss…'

'Nadia.'

'Okay, Nadia it is,' said Crouch.

It was then that Matt noticed the shoes. A pair of old but highly polished ankle-length boots sat on a newspaper on the table next to an empty vase. 'Why do you keep your shoes on the table? Isn't that supposed to be bad luck?'

Nadia lowered her chin and peered at Matt. 'I do not believe in superstitious nonsense.'

'Right,' said Matt in the airy way someone does when they realise a pas has just been faux'd.

Asher stepped forward. 'We're investigating a spate of deaths linked to corrupted lava juice. Know anything about it?'

Crouch shook his head and muttered, 'And I thought I was the unsubtle one.'

'Lava juice? What is lava juice?'

'It's a kind of drug,' explained Matt. 'Recreational…people take it for fun. It makes them feel happy. But we think a bad batch has reached the city. And that bad batch is making people very unhappy.'

'So unhappy they top themselves,' Crouch said, drawing a finger across his throat with a click of his tongue

'And one of the side effects of this new lava juice is to make the whites of the user's eyes go blue,' Asher explained.

Nadia listened, nodding slowly. 'I see. And how does this involve me?'

'A little bird told us that you have blue eyes.'

'So do you,' said Nadia, staring at Matt.

'Not just blue, *blue*,' said Crouch.

'What is blue, *blue*?'

Asher took a step forward. 'Would you please take off your glasses.'

'No,' said Nadia.

'Why not?'

'Because light hurts my eyes.'

'Okay, then we'll draw the curtains for you.' Crouch nodded to Matt, who did the needful.

Nadia watched, but didn't move.

'There, nice and not so bright,' Crouch said.

'This is in-fringe-ment of rights,' Nadia said, working hard on her pronunciation.

'You're absolutely right,' Crouch said. 'Silly me. What we'll do is go away and persuade a magistrate to issue a summons for the glasses. We'll take them to the station instead. How about that?'

Nadia sat, weighing up this statement. 'That would be silly.'

'Yes, it would,' agreed Crouch. 'About as silly as you not agreeing to take them off for us. Now, please will you remove your glasses.'

Slowly, Nadia slid off the dark glasses, keeping her eyes slitted.

'Now open your eyes wide,' Asher said.

'I cannot. This is why I wear the dark glasses. I am photo-phob-ic.'

'Shame. It makes you look like a constipated owl,' Matt said.

In response, Nadia threw him a full, wide-eyed glare and everyone's breath stopped. Her eyes really were blue, *blue*. Deep cobalt irises surrounded the pupils but where the whites of her eyes should have been were sclerae the colour of a shallow coral sea.

'Ye gods,' said Crouch.

'Remarkable,' Asher added.

'Blue, *blue*,' confirmed Matt.

'Now do I look like constipated owl?' Nadia asked.

She was feisty, this one. 'No, you don't,' Matt said. 'I apologise. However, telling you that you did seemed to do the trick.' He grinned.

Nadia frowned.

'So, Miss…Nadia.' Crouch cleared his throat. 'Have you always looked like this?'

'Where I am from, everyone looks like this. Except babies. Babies have white …*biddas*…what is the word?'

'Sclerae,' said Asher.

Nadia nodded. 'Sclerae.'

'And where is it you come from?'

Nadia began to explain, but her geography wasn't up to much and after five minutes of place names that sounded more like she was reading a poem backwards than actual language, Crouch put up his hand for her to stop.

'Right, we know it's called Spiv and it's somewhere up in Steppeinit, but where exactly remains a mystery. What about the bloke, the alchemist? He'd know, surely,' Matt said.

Crouch agreed. 'Yes, your friend the alchemist. How do we get in touch with him?'

Nadia shrugged. 'Friend? Perhaps he is my…friend. But I do not know where he lives. He may call, he may not. I have not been invited to his…abode.'

'Okay then, forget his abode, what's his name again?'

'I only have one name for him. Wimbush,' said Nadia.

'Great, thank you.' Crouch got up to leave.

'When you find him, tell him I am waiting for his call,' Nadia said. It was a simple enough statement, but obvious to all who heard that it carried with it a forklift truckload of heavy baggage.

CHAPTER NINETEEN

OXFORD, ENGLAND

It was coffee time in the Department of Fimmigration garrison. It was also a Wednesday. That meant a team briefing in the office of the chief, Mr Ernest Porter. These meetings were supposed to function as a link between the work the DOF did in monitoring and policing the activities of the Fae in the human world, and news of nefarious activities in the Fae world, in order to cross-check between the two. All in all, a pretty good idea, were it not for the fact that Mr Porter's concentration span was that of a forgetful goldfish and the meetings inevitably ended up being little more than discussions about the quality of the homemade biscuits that accompanied the coffee.

Today, however, Mr Porter was away visiting relatives in New Thameswick, and so the garrison convened in his niece Kylah's room; a neat and tidy office full of pale, bleached furniture and steel filing cabinets and a small fridge filled with bottles of Slavabadrian spring water.

Kylah had briefed everyone on the sinkhole situation by the time coffee was delivered by Mrs Hoblip, a Bwbach who looked after Mr Porter and whose culinary skills were to die for, but only if you insulted her very badly. Kylah enquired politely about her son, George, who'd been spending quite a lot of time lately with his girlfriend, Lulem, in a far-flung corner of the universe, or at least the corner of a universe. Mrs Hoblip's face, pumpkin-shaped and covered in tight orange curls, had beamed and explained that he was coming home for Easter. She'd backed out, as she always did, on curly-toed slippers, gurgling a polite enquiry as to whether anyone would be there for lunch.

'I don't think so, Mrs Hoblip. I suspect we'll be in the field.'

Mrs Hoblip smiled and nodded, shutting the door behind her.

'What field?' asked Sergeant Keemoch, one of the two special elf service members co-opted to the garrison. Both he and Sergeant Birrik were Sith Fand: tall, long-limbed creatures trained in all sorts of unarmed combat as well as experts on a variety of arcane weaponry.

'Well not exactly a field, more a hole in the ground.'

'Sounds fun,' Birrik said as he dunked a biscuit.

'Or you could stay here and do paperwork…' Kylah allowed the suggestion to permeate the air like a bad smell.

'Holes in the ground are one of my favourite things, Captain,' said Keemoch.

'Next to raindrops on roses,' agreed Birrik, his mouth half full of dunked biscuit.

'I bet.' Kylah shook her head.

The door opened, and Bobby came in waving a bit of paper. 'Okay, I've just got off the phone with the local council in Wales. They've called in some heavy civil engineering help and their tests show no gas leak of any kind. They're diverting the sewerage temporarily and plan on starting repairs immediately.'

'That's one holiday cottage we won't be renting, then,' Birrik said.

'And how do they do that?' Keemoch asked. 'Repair a great big hole, I mean?'

'Lots of dirt,' Bobby said, helping herself to coffee. 'They pour concrete in to plug the bottom and then fill it with truck-loads of sand and clay and wait to see if it behaves.'

Kylah nodded. 'I thought they might want to start the process sooner rather than later. But from what I've seen this morning, this is not just a big hole in the limestone.' She explained about her hospital visit.

'What do you think is down there, Captain?' Birrik asked.

'I don't know, but I think we need to find out before they plug it just in case whatever it is objects and makes things a hundred times worse.' There were all sorts of glowing blips on Kylah's radar regarding this so-called sinkhole. The trouble was there was no way of knowing whether they were torpedoes capable of mass destruction or just a few errant dolphins up for a bit of acrobatic ebullience. Only one way to find out.

'What do you suggest?' Bobby said.

'We go in as environmental officers. Hazmat suits, the works.'

'And what exactly are we looking for?'

Kylah shrugged. 'We'll know that when we find it.'

Keemoch grinned. 'That's what I like. Precision planning.'

Kylah ignored the barb. 'You two kit us out with suits and gear. Bobby, you warn the council that we'll be there later.' She almost added, *I, meanwhile, am going to consult a higher source*, but wisely kept it as part of her internal dialogue instead.

Birrik drained his coffee and got up. 'I'm on it.'

When everyone had dispersed to get on with their tasks, Kylah turned to a locked cabinet bolted to one of the walls. There was no key. Instead, she moved her hand in a practised configuration and said 'Agora'. The door clicked open, and though there appeared to be just the one lock, the accompanying noises of cogs turning and bolts sliding indicated that this was no ordinary cupboard and the locks were no ordinary locks. Eventually, Kylah opened the door to reveal neat shelves of books, vials and muslin bags labelled in strange writing. Ignoring all of this, she waved her hand again and once more spoke the word, 'Agora.'

This time the shelving appeared to slide down into a space in the ground that wasn't there a moment before to reveal a much larger room beyond. It bore little resemblance to the cupboard, or indeed to the Hipposync building in Oxford. Hardly surprising, since this room was neither in the building, nor in Oxford. The DOF had few properties, but the room in which Kylah now stood existed in the basement of a building that had been there for more years than anyone could really remember, not even her uncle. It was unoccupied, hidden from the eyes of passing strangers, or even those who tried to seek it out for a variety of criminal purposes by camouflage charms and hexes. She had begged her uncle to let her stand outside it once, just to see what it really looked like, and had been granted that wish. She could still remember walking out through a huge oak door, three times the height of a man, to look back at a turret building built of opalescent stone with a blue-grey slate roof and twelve crenelated parapets reaching skywards.

'The Sith Fand call it Elerelon. I prefer bolthole,' Mr Porter had said, with a trademark chuckle.

Although Kylah had not been down into the sinkhole herself, what she'd heard from the engineers that morning had spoken of something old and deeply unpleasant. And usually, such things needed old wonderworking in order to quell them. And then there was that odd conviction she'd had of hearing the sound of a battle.

Kylah was no stranger to the bizarre and unnatural. Yet horrors that could manifest in mud and earth were odd to say the least. Something about those descriptions rang a deep and insistent alarm. Yet try as she might, she could not think why. It was more a tingling awareness that she should be worried by them, rather than a memory of having confronted something like this before, that set her teeth on edge.

On a table near the window where the curtains remained constantly drawn, sat a carved artefact in soapstone. It resembled something vaguely fish-like but with a head not like any fish that had ever swam under the water. Many arcane lines were etched into its surface and its battered and crumbling edges hinted at its ancient history.

It was to this strange carving that Kylah went. She picked it up, weighing it in her hand as she stared at it. It felt cool, and yet thrummed with some inner power. She closed her hand around it and instantly it changed into a metal key no more than three inches long but etched with identical marks to those on the soapstone. The table upon which it had rested metamorphosed into a narrow wooden chest, taller than it was long. It, too, bore similar markings.

Kylah inserted the key and the lock opened smoothly. Inside, on a velvet cushion, sat a large stone egg as black as obsidian but shot through with gold. Kylah moved a lever and the egg slid smoothly up so that it sat proud on the surface of the chest.

Vidom's oracle was ancient, and this was old magic. Unruly magic. She had been drawn to it by a conviction that what had frightened the men in the sinkhole was old, too. She could not explain why, and she knew better than to try. Aspects of her training and her skills were not open to logistical analysis. Awareness and instinct played as much part in her CSI as fingerprints and DNA analysis in the human world. But accessing the oracle was never done lightly. Like cleaning the cupboards under the stairs, it was occasionally a necessity, but you were never quite sure what you might find. This was not the first time she had used it and she knew its value. Yet it was a value that was never easy to interpret.

Vidom's power had once held sway over an empire that controlled half of Kylah's world. Yet the one thing Vidom could not control was time and its inexorable effects on his physical state. Even a wizard as powerful as he knew that eventually he must succumb. And so, in an attempt at immortality fuelled by the haughty belief that the world could not do without him, he arranged at the last for his soul, or that part of his soul that was his intellect, to occupy the egg. The gem was shaped from a source obtained from the deepest part of the oldest seas, unsullied by exposure to light and the weather, the purest that was possible.

Yet, Vidom's success was also his downfall. Despite years of meditation in preparation for the final spell, he badly underestimated the lack of sentience. The egg became less a depository of wisdom than his eternal prison. A cold, hard place from which he could never escape. The result was a bitterness and longing that tinged all his answers with a cryptic vitriol. In short, Vidom had become the miserable old git he was always meant to be.

So yes, consulting Vidom's oracle was, what Matt might term, a 'trip'.

Kylah performed the incantation. The egg glowed silver and then projected an image of itself five times that of the original into a black bowl that sat atop the velvet cushion.

'Tell me about the things in the sinkhole,' Kylah asked.

A voice, cracked and ancient, oozed out of the bowl. 'You must answer three riddles in order to access—'

Kylah cut across the voice. 'Please, can we just forget all the drama for once.'

'Insolence!' screamed the oracle. 'Once, such behaviour would have cost you your tongue.'

'Yes, I know. You would have attached it to a vice and hung

me from the ceiling until it was pulled from my throat.' Kylah sighed.

'Then be afraid, questioner. Be afraid.'

'I am afraid. Afraid that I'm finally going to drop your egg on the floor and watch it smash into a hundred pieces.'

Several seconds of silence followed.

'You would not dare,' croaked the oracle.

'Accidents can happen.'

More silence.

'If it smashed, I would be free of this cold, heartless prison,' mused the oracle.

'You put yourself in there.'

'Only in the hope that one day a great mage might allow me to return into a living form that would act as my vessel. Has that day not yet arrived?'

'They're busy working on it,' said Kylah, who knew that it was well within the brightest and best at the university's capability to restore Vidom. She also knew that if it ever happened he would face at least a hundred lifetimes banished to some dimensional twilight zone for all the war crimes he'd committed. Zones that would make the egg seem like a penthouse apartment complete with butler, dedicated lift and bonkubines, which were like concubines, only better trained.

'But they are still researching?'

'Every day. Now, about the sinkhole?'

'You see,' said the oracle bitterly, 'once again you do nothing but use me as a tool for your needs.'

'Isn't that why you did all this?'

Another silence.

Reluctantly, 'Perhaps.'

'No perhaps about it. Definition of oracle: a priest or priestess acting as a medium through whom advice or prophecy was sought.'

'Will you polish me?'

'What?'

'Afterwards, will you polish me?'

Kylah squeezed her eyes shut. The thought of polishing anything that pertained to this obnoxious voice brought a little bit of vomit to the back of her throat. 'Maybe.'

'That would please me to know. Even though I will not be

able to feel your fingers, the thought that they might succour my pain brings a certain—'

'Right. So, the sinkhole.' She proceeded to explain, ending up with the question she wanted to ask. 'Why is it that I feel I know something about this and yet that's impossible because I also know that this is the first time I have come across it?'

She could almost hear the sly pleasure in the oracle's voice. 'All memory comes from previous experience. Yet the past is a country with a vast and open shore upon which the mind can be easily shipwrecked.'

'Brilliant. What does that actually mean, if it means anything at all?'

'Perhaps you have a memory of events that are yet to manifest.'

'Then that's a premonition, isn't it?'

'Not if the events are yet to manifest.'

'You've already said that once. How can a memory be something that is yet to happen?'

In the small silence that followed, Kylah imagined Vidom smiling. 'Think of it as throwing a stick that has yet to return.'

'A stick that has…you mean a boomerang?'

'If a boomerang is a stick that when thrown returns, then yes.'

'This feeling I have is a boomerang? I know I shouldn't have bothered to ask. Why can't you give me a straight answer?'

'Your memory is a function of time. Ontologically speaking, one could consider that all points in time are valid and real, both past and future. Think of your…recollection…as a boomerang. It is curved, and its shape lends it the ability to slice through the air or, as in this instance, time. Perhaps your…sinkhole represents the position of your boomerang at this moment. Depending on whether you've thrown it into the future or the past will define memory or premonition or rarely, both.'

'Wonderful,' said Kylah, shaking her head. She let the air hiss out from her lungs. 'Can you now tell me in English?'

'You are remembering something that is yet to happen.'

'That's not memory. That's premonition.'

'Not if it will happen anyway. Boomerang.'

'Wonderful.' Kylah rolled her gold-flecked eyes.

'It is my pleasure to give assistance. Now the polish.'

'But you haven't—'

The black bowl shape diminished into the egg. It pulsed twice and then returned to its dense black-and-gold colour.

'Boomerang my foot. I should have known better,' muttered Kylah.

She started to close the lid only to hear a bleated, 'Polish!'

She let out a groan of disgust and looked around the room. A prickly wool blanket on the back of a rocking chair caught her eye. She grabbed it and, using it as a barrier between her hands and the egg, picked it up and quickly wiped the egg. When, after a few seconds, she thought she heard a moan, she dropped the egg onto its velvet cushion, slammed the lid shut and locked it.

'Boomerang,' she muttered as she retraced her steps back into her office at Hipposync with a burning desire to wash her hands in disinfectant.

CHAPTER TWENTY

THEY RECONVENED AT 11PM. The bio suits that Keemoch and Birrik turned up with were grey with sealed faceplates and breathing filters incorporated into the hood. The Sith Fand had already morphed into their human disguises: the giant and bearded Alf and the wiry and much smaller Dwayne, in case anyone looked into what was behind the mask. When Bobby picked up a suit, Kylah stopped her.

'Don't you have a class to go to?'

'Yes, there is a lecture after lunch, but—'

'No buts. You get to the Le Fey. Besides, I want you to catch up with Asher and Matt. They ought to be briefed on this since we'll be out of the garrison for most of today. You can join us afterwards.'

'I could easily swing by. Since they're twelve hours behind they'll probably be on the way to lunch in the pub.'

Birrik sniffed. 'Lucky b—'

'Thank you, Sergeant,' Kylah raised a warning finger before turning back to Bobby. 'This time difference is driving me nuts.'

'It'll all snap back in a few days' time at the spring equinox.'

'I know, but still.'

'I'll make sure Matt and Asher know what's going on.'

Kylah zipped up her suit. Her voice now sounded like it was coming from inside a goldfish bowl. Which, of course, it was. 'You first, Keemoch. No one's going to challenge a six-foot four spaceman walking down the street.'

Their wellington boots squelched as they made their way to the blue room.

'Dare I ask where you got these from?' Kylah was already getting warm inside the plastic.

'Got a friend in Porton Down. These have only been used once.'

'Oh good. That's all right, then. What was it, anthrax, sarin gas?'

'No.' Keemoch sounded offended. 'Blocked drain.'

In the blue room, Kylah attached the Aperio to a door that usually opened onto a brick wall and stood aside to let Keemoch through. He emerged onto the garden path of the nearest house to the sinkhole. Birrik followed, then Kylah exited last of all and turned to wave.

'Have fun,' said Bobby.

No one challenged the three suited-up DOF agents as they hurried along the road towards the sinkhole. Groups of hard-hatted men in suits under Hi-Viz gilets were writing things on clipboards on both sides of the street. Kylah ignored them and followed Keemoch to the ladders. Once they'd gone down thirty feet, she reached into her pocket and drew out some sandy granules that she threw up into the air. The granules defied gravity and kept going up until they were level with tarmac. There, they started to spin. Kylah watched and then spoke several words in a low whisper. Above her, a low bloom of light flashed between the granules as the shield charm kicked in. Kylah recommenced her descent. When they were all on the bottom, she turned to the other two. 'Right, I want a detailed search. Anything unusual, I want to know.'

CHAPTER TWENTY-ONE

NEW THAMESWICK

THE FOLLOWING MORNING, with Crouch following up a lead on Haggis Len in the Claret area, Matt and Asher tracked Wimbush down to a small fenced-off woodland some three hundred yards to the rear of the Polyalchemy.

He was the only person there.

Having said that, it would not have been difficult to pick him out in a crowd, since it was a miserably cold and drab not-quite-yet-spring day and he was the only person in the whole of New Thameswick dressed in shorts and oversized walking boots. Admittedly, he'd made a bit of an effort by wearing a woolly jumper and a scarf but spoiled the warming effect by having both sleeves rolled up. He was squatting on his haunches, peering intently at a patch of earth, when Matt and Asher caught up to him. Wimbush looked up, nodded, and then went back to peering.

'Hello?' said Matt after several long seconds of silence.

Wimbush sent them a second, this time irritated glance. 'Oh, um, could you come back later? Only I'm a little busy.'

Asher looked around at the woodland and then at Matt. 'Kenwyn Wimbush?' he said.

'Hmm?'

'Is that your name?

'My name? Yes, of course it's my name. Who else's name would it be?'

Asher and Matt exchanged 'we've got a right one here' looks before Asher moved to step in front of the alchemist, who immediately let out a scream and rugby tackled him to the ground.

Matt dragged him off whilst Asher regained his footing.

'Vandals! Vandals!' yelled Wimbush. 'I'll have the constabulary on to you. This is private Polyalchemy property.'

'And you are a certifiable menace,' said Asher, brushing leaves from his trousers.

'Who've you been talking to?' said Wimbush, shrugging off Matt's restraining arms.

'I would advise caution, Mr Wimbush,' said Matt. 'Assaulting an officer of the Bureau of Demonology is a serious offence.'

'Bureau of Demonology?' Wimbush forced a theatrical laugh. 'You've obviously made a serious error. I am an alchemical herbologist. Different department altogether. Also, I'm a very busy man in case you hadn't noticed. Even if I knew anything about them, I would not have the time to talk to you about demons. You'll have to ask someone else to lecture—'

Asher shook his head and took out his badge. 'We are not here about a lecture. We are here to ask you some questions.'

Wimbush's momentary bonhomie evaporated in an instant. 'Oh, and stepping on my propagation experiment is part of that questioning, is it, eh?'

Matt, eyebrows raised, went back to the spot where Wimbush had been peering and knelt. There was dirt and dried leaves, but no sign of any propagation activity as far as he could see.

'You might have ruined months of work,' growled Wimbush, eyes flashing.

'These invisible plants, then, are they?' Matt asked.

'Of course not,' snapped Wimbush.

Asher joined Matt. 'There is nothing here.'

Wimbush's face flushed purple. 'Oh, I see. Experts in this field, obviously. There is nothing there because this is a failed experiment. That is the nature of experimental work. You attempt something and then wait to see if said effort succeeds or…fails.'

Matt stood and nodded. 'And how many failed experiments have there been, Mr Wimbush?'

Unable to help himself, the alchemist glanced around at the woodland in many directions. 'A…few. But then *aconitum argentum* is a notoriously fickle plant. There are a great many variables one needs to consider. Experiments can be long and complicated when one small aspect of soil, or light, or watering is modified in order that—'

'Right. And I'm sure they'll fail just as well without you staring at them for a few minutes.'

'I really don't know if I can—'

'Either here or at the BOD, sir, it's your choice,' said Asher.

'Oh, very well. I can spare a few moments, I suppose. This is all highly inconvenient. But let us talk in a safe spot.' Wimbush walked ten yards to his right to a spot which looked identical to all the other spots in the woods. 'Here will do. Now, as you will see, I am very busy—'

'Staring at the ground,' interjected Matt.

'Studying my experiments.' Wimbush affected a tone halfway between irate and entreaty. 'And I cannot, for the life of me, think of anything that could possibly justify interruption of this work.'

Asher looked at him. 'No, I don't think you can, can you?'

'How about murder?' Matt said.

'Murder?' Wimbush said, aghast. 'I have no idea what you're talking about.'

'No, you don't. That's why we need to have this little chat.' Asher pulled an imp-pression from his pocket and showed it to Wimbush. 'Know this girl?'

Wimbush stared at the morgue imprint of the dead Libby and swallowed loudly. 'Why does her face look so swollen and—'

'That's what throttling yourself does to you,' Asher explained.

Wimbush shook his head vigorously. 'No, I have never seen her before.'

'Good. Didn't think you had. But this girl died as a result of smoking a drug called lava juice. Ever heard of that?'

'Of course. One doesn't teach undergraduate alchemical herbology without picking up a degree of street language. It's a distillation of the crushed leaves of the Hyco plant. Found in the great forests of the east.'

'Exactly. Trouble is, New Thameswick's been hit with a bad

batch. And one of the side effects is that it makes people's eyes go blue.'

'Their eyes?'

'He means their sclerae,' said Matt.

'And I think you know someone with very blue sclerae, don't you, Mr Wimbush?'

The alchemist's cheeks flushed a bright pink once more. 'I… I…'

'Nadia sends her regards and wonders why you haven't called,' Asher said.

'I…I…'

Matt stopped the stuttering. 'Yes, I think that's the trouble, isn't it, Mr Wimbush? "I." You strike me as a man who has great difficulty thinking about anything or anyone other than yourself.'

'I'm not sure I—'

'The thing is, Nadia isn't a juicer and yet she has sclerae that look like a pair of bluebells. What we want to know is why that might be?'

'I have no idea. It's possible that there is some genetic trait.'

'She tells us that where she comes from babies don't look like that,' prompted Matt. 'Scuppers the genetic theory.'

'Then there might be an environmental element.'

Asher nodded. 'Exactly. And this is where you might help. Nadia, the girl you seemed to have abandoned—'

'I—'

Asher placed an index finger across his lips to stop the alchemist's interruption. '—is not very forthcoming when it comes to geography. We need more detail of the location.'

'I have no idea. We found her in the forest.'

'We?'

Wimbush sighed. He explained about the mining expedition and his idea of latching on to the prospectors. He told them everything, including about Great Aunt Hester's goojl. He had to wait three times during the telling while Matt recovered from a bout of what appeared to be violent coughing, but which was in actual fact an almost apoplectic response to hearing Wimbush say 'lit the end of Great Aunt Hester's goojl' several times.

When Wimbush finally finished with a brief account of his dealings with Miss Hoare, Asher said, 'We need to go back.'

'Pardon?'

'We need to take Nadia back to where she's from to find out if there is any link between her and the lava juice.'

'Right.' Wimbush nodded. 'Well, best of luck with that.' He started to walk away only to be met by Asher's arm stretching across his path.

'Thing is, you are the only one with any real memory of where you were.'

'How does that help?'

Matt frowned at Asher. 'Exactly. You need a door to use the Aperio.'

'True. That is the safe way. But there is someone at the BOD who's been experimenting with free-fall peregrination. He apparently can make a door open into a space four square metres within the vicinity of any coordinates.'

'How do we get those coordinates?'

'Mr Wimbush's memory.'

'I beg your pardon?' Wimbush dragged his chin back into his chest and blinked several times.

'If you could spare a little time, it would be the quickest way.'

Wimbush laughed again. This time a genuine response to someone suggesting the completely ridiculous. 'A little time? These last ten minutes have been an extravagance I can ill afford. As you are well aware, I'm sure, I will never get those ten minutes back. Gentlemen, you will have to excuse me.'

'Nadia would like you to come along,' Matt said.

Again, Wimbush blushed. 'Nadia is a…she has…I've been meaning to…'

Mat waited in vain for one of these statements to cross the finishing line while Wimbush's face performed an excerpt from *Internal Turmoil*, the movie.

Eventually, beetroot red from having the unpalatable truth force-fed to him, the alchemist said crossly, 'I'm sorry, but it's quite impossible. As you can see, I am extremely busy.'

Asher and Matt looked across at the patch of bare earth Wimbush had been staring at again and then, slowly, back to Wimbush.

'We could arrange for a court order,' Asher said.

'Or get the constabulary to arrest you for illegally displaying those knees,' Matt looked pointedly at Wimbush's shorts.

Wimbush placed a hand on each side of his head and grabbed a hunk of hair in each fist before growling.

The last time Matt had seen anyone do that was at his cousin Rupert's eighth birthday party.

'How long will this take?' wailed Wimbush.

'Half a day at the most.'

'Three. Three hours is what I can give you, though it is under protest. I will do it. But it is under protest.'

'I am sure the victims will be very grateful,' Matt said.

'So, what now?' Wimbush asked.

'Now we go to the BOD and collect Nadia.'

CHAPTER TWENTY-TWO

In the end, Asher accompanied a reluctant Wimbush who insisted on going back to his laboratory to write up his thoughts after his morning's 'peering'. Matt picked up Nadia and went directly to Asher's office at the BOD. There, Nadia perched on a chair, staring with wary curiosity at the floor-to-ceiling shelving that covered the back wall that Asher had populated with books and a sizeable collection of totems and miscellaneous flotsam collected over his time at the Bureau. A shrunken head that insisted on telling the time every fifteen minutes seemed to particularly fascinate her. She sat with sunglasses off; dispelling the lie of her photophobia and confirming that she wore them only to avoid accusatory stares from others.

When Asher arrived, it was with a flustered Wimbush in tow. The alchemist had not bothered to change but had embellished his eclectic wardrobe with his wide-brimmed Polyalchemic hat and a backpack featuring more straps than an octopus's straight jacket.

Matt watched as Wimbush's eyes met Nadia's. He wore the expression of someone who was trying to smile whilst swallowing an earthworm.

'Hello, Nadia.'

'You did not call like you promised.' Nadia's face was granite.

'I know. I've been snowed under at work. Spring term is always a bugger. And my propagation research—'

'As in staring at the ground where things don't grow,' Matt muttered.

'—has taken all my time.' Wimbush sent him a withering glance.

'You promised,' Nadia repeated.

'Did I?' Wimbush's eyes looked everywhere except at Nadia, searching, it seemed, for an appropriate crack in the universe into which he could fall. 'It's just that they've recently appointed a new catering manager and I don't really know her well enough to ask if they were taking on new staff. But I will get to her, see if there are any openings. I really will.'

It struck Matt that Wimbush was a wheedler.

Nadia kept him in her sights for several more disbelieving seconds before saying once again, this time more quietly but with a hundredweight more feeling, 'You *promised*,' before letting her gaze drop.

'Right, good to see you two are getting on,' Asher said. 'Now, I've asked Magoose to meet us here at ten.' The sound of a rattling trolley reached them from the corridor. 'Oh good, that'll be the post.'

A face appeared around the door. Ned the stamp retained an adolescent gawkiness beneath a visage that was yet to suffer the ravages of a razor blade. His big blue eyes looked on expectantly.

'Can I do you anything', Mr Asher?'

Asher turned to his audience. 'Victoria sponge or a gypsy cream, anyone?'

'Oh, an' I got a special on Welsh cakes,' Ned added. 'Got a Druid conference up on the fourth floor. Managed to pick up some surplus.'

'Go on, then,' said Matt. 'Half a dozen Welsh cakes.'

'Make it a dozen and we'll call it a scruple,' said Ned.

Wimbush stood watching this transaction with his arms folded in disapproval. When Matt took a bite and offered one to him, the alchemist finally snapped. 'Is this why I've been dragged away from what is vital work? To sample pastries?'

'There's Victoria sponge if you want it,' Ned said.

'I do not,' said Wimbush. 'And besides, why is the mail boy delivering pastries?'

'We like to multitask here at the BOD,' said Asher. 'And please don't make the mistake of thinking of Ned in anything other than on equal terms to the rest of us here. His knowledge of the workings of this building and the people in it is unsurpassed.'

'Thanks, Asher.' Ned beamed a boyish grin as he passed over a sealed envelope. 'Prof Llewyn sent this down. Says she's a bit tied up in meetin's, but will catch you laters.'

Ned exited. Matt took a bite from the offered Welsh cake and let out a little moan of pleasure. 'These are delicious. I can hear male voice choirs, and feel rain on my face, and smell...yes, acorns.'

Asher looked at the packet and nodded. 'These are from Gragg's. No wonder they're good. I'll have one later. Nadia, can we tempt you?'

'I will try one.' She took one bite and looked slightly concerned. 'I too hear music. Who is Delilah?'

Matt grinned. Wimbush continued to scowl. God, he was a miserable bugger.

'Right,' said Asher as he read the note from Duana Llewyn, a pale blonde ice queen who was also a professor of demonology and their boss at the BOD. Asher frowned and then looked up. 'Suddenly, this has all become a bit official. The constabulary managed to confiscate some of the bad lava juice from a few of the punters stupid enough to have bought from Haggis Len. They've run it through a thaumaturgy scan and there is undoubtedly something dark about it. Very dark indeed, it seems. It's cursed, but not by anything that's in the database.' He waved the letter. 'We have the mandate to investigate.'

'Good,' said Wimbush. 'Then can we please get on with it? My plants need me.'

Nadia frowned at hearing this. 'Is it still silver wolfsbane you are having trouble with?'

Wimbush's eyebrows shot up in annoyance, as if he were about to challenge her for daring to stray conversationally into herbal alchemy territory. But he immediately seemed to think better of it.

Nadia took another bite of Welsh cake and chewed.

Doesn't give much away, does this one, thought Matt.

Thankfully, Wimbush's impatience was relieved by another knock on the door. Asher opened it and let in a small man with jet black hair, thick-lensed glasses and a slight stoop.

'This is Magoose. He has a first name, but it is so unpronounceable that no one bothers. Magoose heads up our experimental transportation section.' Asher handed round some earplugs. 'You will need to wear one of these. He does not speak any gabble, so you'll need a linguaplug.'

Matt inserted an earplug. Everything went dull on his right side but when Magoose spoke, though it sounded as if he were speaking from a cavern, his words were understandable.

'I am pleased to be able to make your acquaintance,' said Magoose with a little bow.

This attracted a variety of nods and hellos in response.

'Mr Asher has explained to you my work?'

They exchanged nonplussed glances that followed brought forth a grin of resignation from Magoose. He walked over to the middle of the room and took a notepad from his pocket. He flipped open the cover and it immediately expanded to a full-size flip chart. He then wrote *PEREGRINATION* in capitals on the top of the page and started to draw arrows.

'Normally, movement using peregrination depends upon user visualising or knowledge of destination and proximity of an appropriate entrance. Solid doors are needed. This places severe limitations, particularly in outdoor or wilderness environments where such doors do not exist. The complex thaumaturgical equations upon which peregrination is based were originally designed by Lee the Indolent during his employment as Emperor Stan's chief architect during the Fling dynasty. Lee first invented Infinite Palace with an infinite number of rooms. Many, many people got lost, never to be found again. Lee was ordered to find a way to get from room to room without walking, regardless of that room's position relative to another. Using Krudian shift, Lee developed a new field of wonderworking, namely Krudian Wave and Neospatial Teleportation via Unified Matrix, or Kwantum. What we have been working on is using a memory probe to elicit a three-dimensional image of doorless coordinate and applying this to Kwantum theory.'

'Does it work?' Matt asked.

Magoose bowed again and smiled. 'We think so.'

'Think?' said Wimbush. 'Don't you know?'

'Animal experiments in the laboratory have gone well. Unfortunately, our choice of animal, the bounding mouse, means that animal runs off after arriving at its destination in field trials. There is also a coordinate drift of approximately twelve feet.'

'Why a bounding mouse, dare I ask?' said Asher.

'The Kwantum bubble produced has a diameter of ten feet, therefore we have to use an animal capable of surviving a ten-foot drop if it manifests at the top of the bubble.'

'Really,' Asher said, smiling.

'I have tried myself and only broken a foot.' Magoose grinned.

'Oh, that's all right then,' said Wimbush, with an open-mouthed stare. 'I mean, the one place I can remember is the point from which we escaped. A rocky outcrop on top of a precipitous drop.'

'Thank you, thank you,' said Magoose.

Wimbush shook his head.

'How many people can appear in this bubble at one time?' Matt asked.

'Four is maximum.' Magoose smiled, eyes crinkling.

'Okay,' Asher said. 'I don't see we have much choice. It's either weeks of trekking through the mountains or Magoose's Kwantum bubble using Wimbush's memory.'

'Why don't you use Nadia's memory?' Wimbush asked.

'I am tempted,' said Asher. 'But we do not want to appear in the middle of her village unannounced. We need to see what's going on first. Lay of the land and all that.'

Matt and Magoose nodded.

'Is it only me that sees the many fatal flaws in this plan?' Wimbush said, exasperated.

'I am listening,' Asher said.

'One, it might be a ten-foot drop. Two, it's inaccurate by twelve feet. Either way, we might end up in mid-air over a three-thousand-foot drop. No, thank you. I don't think I'll take the risk. Easier I take up crocodile dentistry.'

Asher smiled a stretched smile, and Matt sensed that Wimbush's constant negativity and wheedling had finally struck home. 'Excellent points, Mr Wimbush. Sensible that we should abandon the Kwantum bubble. Therefore, it has to be the long trek through the forest for us. I must say, I am surprised. I thought you might want to limit your time away from your work.'

'Away from my work?' said Wimbush with another dismissive laugh. 'I don't know what you mean by that. I am going straight back the Polyalchemy now.'

'On the contrary.' Asher's voice was reasonableness incarnate. He glanced down at Duana Llewyn's note and then back up again. 'You, sir, are a material witness in a murder investigation. And one with possible demonic intent to boot. Under city state law, you can be compelled to cooperate in our investigation. And that investigation leads us back to Nadia's village. Whereas we might be able to reach it within hours via Magoose's Kwantum bubble, an expedition on foot will take considerably, and I mean considerably, longer.'

'But…' Wimbush had suddenly paled. 'My plants.'

'Will undoubtedly continue not to grow without you,' Matt said.

Asher turned to Magoose. 'Thank you, Magoose. Very educational.'

Magoose bowed, folded up his flip-chart and turned to leave.

Wimbush, meanwhile, looked like a man handcuffed to a briefcase watching his hand being sawn off and knowing there was nothing he could do about it. Except, save a lot of effort and blood by giving up the combination on the lock.

'Wait,' he cried, as Magoose reached the door. 'I want it known as a matter of record that I object. I object most strongly.'

'Why do you object when people are being murdered?' Nadia said in that deceptively deep voice of hers, so at odds with Wimbush's high-pitched whining. Everyone, Magoose included, paused to listen.

Matt smiled again, much amused. She might not say much but when she did it was worth listening. He liked this girl.

'What has that got to do with me?' Wimbush said.

'Perhaps nothing. But you are the link. It is your duty to help.'

'My duty? What a load of total—'

'Yes, your duty. To those others who might suffer.'

'My duty is to my work and—'

'Yourself.' Nadia had her cobalt-and-turquoise eyes on Wimbush. 'Which is all that you think about.'

Matt glanced at Asher and neither of them said anything.

But from the look on Asher's faces it was clear he was thinking exactly what Matt was thinking. This little exchange was well worth the entrance fee.

Wimbush wilted under Nadia's fierce gaze. 'Let's just get on with it, shall we?'

'Does that mean you will cooperate?' Asher asked.

Sighing, Wimbush nodded.

'Good. Then Magoose here will take you and start the preparation. It should take about an hour to get the probe done, is that right, Magoose?'

'One hour, yes?' Magoose grinned and bobbed, while Wimbush mouthed anxiously, '*Probe?*'

'Excellent,' Asher said. 'In the meantime, Mr Danmor and I will pay a quick visit to Blechern Holdings, the mining company whose employees were such good companions on your last trip. And I think we're going to take Nadia with us. How do you feel about that, Nadia?'

Nadia nodded. '*I* will help in any way *I* can.' She looked pointedly at Wimbush while ladling so much emphasis on the personal pronouns that it was a miracle they didn't snap in two.

Matt smiled and got one in return from Asher. It was clear that Nadia was their type of émigré. One who took no prisoners.

CHAPTER TWENTY-THREE

BLECHERN HOLDINGS HAD offices in the middle of the financial district. A pickaxe and barrow in shiny silver hung above the impressive front doors. The troll doorman opened the heavy entrance delicately with one axe handle finger and smiled. Matt was suddenly glad he hadn't eaten lunch yet.

They were met in a plush reception area, all tubular steel and leather, by a young woman in a spray-on dress who took them up to the fourth floor where the carpet was so thick it hoovered up the noise of their footfalls and encouraged only whispered conversation. They were offered seats in a stylish lobby with expensive-looking paintings on the walls.

'This is nice,' said Matt.

'Yes, it is. If you like that sort of thing,' Asher said.

'You don't approve?'

'Blechern do not have the best of reputations when it comes to looking after the environment, their workers or those unfortunates in far-flung corners of this world whose land it is they mine. Not so many years ago they were under threat because the price of silver declined dramatically after the market was flooded. But somehow, they managed to come through. This vulgar display does not speak to me of a company on its last legs.'

Matt looked around. Blechern certainly knew how to put the 'Oh' in opulence. 'Agreed. So how did they survive?'

'They cut costs. Culled their workforce, which means tried to get even more out of fewer employees. Their Chief Executive is a remarkable…man.'

Matt thought about asking Asher about the momentary hesitation but the idea stuttered and died when the door was opened by another girl with hair like snow in another spray-on dress so short it was more like a swimsuit. This one was made of even thinner paint, which probably would have made it flow through water with less resistance were it not for the already inflated flotation devices it contained. The girl ushered them into the room with a brilliant smile.

As offices went it would have made an excellent football field. At the far end stood a huge desk of rich dark wood and behind it sat an enormous being. The nameplate on the desk read *Oslo Elkson*. Ash blond with eyebrows to match and a face almost as long as a horse's, Elkson unfolded himself from behind the desk to stand at almost eight feet to greet his guests. Matt did his best to mask his surprise with a smile of greeting, but knew he was struggling. He had heard of the Northern Wights but had never met one.

Elkson's voice was surprisingly high and lilting, as if he was speaking through a larynx attached to a see-saw. 'Good morning. Very nice to meet you. Please have a seat.'

Leather chairs appeared and travelled across the floor of their own volition to positions behind Asher, Matt and Nadia. They all sat, staring up at the giant pale man like five-year-olds on their first day at school.

'Refreshments?' asked Elkson.

'No, thank you,' Asher said. 'We're a bit pushed for time.'

Elkson nodded and sat in an enormous chair behind his enormous desk. 'Then business it is.' He smiled, showing huge white incisors, then sat forward, hands clasped together on the desk in front of him. 'After your beemail yesterday, I immediately instigated an investigation into our last expedition into the northern forest. Of course, Mr Wimbush also reported the incident to us and we were relieved to hear that Miss Komangetme and Mr Wimbush were able to get to safety. However, our own men did not return.'

'It's been three months.'

Elkson nodded. 'The forest region they found themselves in is full of bandits and wild animals, not to mention talk of a witch.'

'What happened to them?' Asher asked.

'We do not know. We do know from what Miss Komangetme was able to tell us that there was a mabocawl at large.'

Nadia nodded.

'Generally speaking, mabocawl are fixation hunters. It appears that this one had Mr Wimbush in its sights,' Asher said. 'Why would it do that?'

Elkson opened out both hands in a gesture of shared and sympathetic ignorance.

'Have you any idea why your men might want to dispose of Nadia and Wimbush?' Matt asked. 'Why they gave chase?'

'In truth, we have no idea what happened. Our rescue teams have returned home after several weeks of searching. However, I was very disturbed to learn that the behaviour of this crew was less than professional. Clearly, we would have liked the opportunity to interview them. To understand this misunderstanding. But in the absence of that opportunity, we must accept what has been said to us.'

Matt shifted in his chair, letting Elkson's words sink in. He was a slimy one, all right.

Elkson turned his huge face to Nadia. 'Once again, may I reiterate that Blechern Holdings apologises unreservedly for your troubles. I can only think that perhaps our men thought you might have been some kind of shapeshifting threat sent by the witch.'

'There is no witch,' Nadia said.

Elkson blinked at her. 'That is not what we understand.'

'There is no witch,' repeated Nadia.

Elkson smiled and turned back towards Asher. 'The forest is a strange place, Mr Lodge. Who knows what tricks such conditions might play on a man's mind.'

Matt felt a mirthless smile crinkle his lips. *You slippery bastard.*

'So, are you likely to be prospecting in that area again soon?' Asher asked.

'Early reports indicated that there was little evidence of ore. Mr Wimbush will corroborate that finding. I think we will avoid it for the near future.' Elkson smiled again. 'We would not want anyone else to come to harm.'

'Will you go back there eventually?'

'I cannot rule that out,' Elkson said.

'But as of this moment,' Matt pressed him, 'you have no employees on the ground there?'

Elkson's smile remained, but his tone changed to mild annoyance. 'May I ask why you are so interested in this place? It is very far away and, as we have heard, a hostile environment.'

'We need to visit the area. It would have been useful to have someone who knew the terrain.'

'I see,' said Elkson. 'Then I am sorry, but I cannot help you.' The toothsome smile returned. 'Are you certain I can't offer you some refreshments?'

Asher declined the offer and Matt was glad he did. He wasn't sure if it was the man's size but there was something about being in Elkson's presence that made him very uncomfortable.

'Didn't give much away, did he?' said Matt as they walked down the stairs into the lobby on their way out. 'But I'm not too fussed. He gave me the creeps.'

Asher nodded. 'Even after all this time, the Northern Wights find it difficult to suppress their arrogance.'

'After all this time?'

Asher nodded. 'They were once the sworn enemies of men. Delusions of grandeur. Master race and all that. But that was all a couple of wars ago. Now they've turned their sights on winning the battle for superiority in business. Can't help themselves. Though, something about their manner makes you want to punch them in the face just to wipe that look off it. I don't suppose you've had to deal with that sort of thing in human history, have you?'

'Oh, we've had our moments,' Matt said and was about to launch into one of many examples when Nadia's voice stopped both men in their tracks.

'He lied.'

They turned to look at her. She stood above them in the stairwell, her expression unreadable, but her body tensed as if for a fight.

'About what?'

'Everything. I could smell it.'

Matt said, 'We'd need a bit more than that to—'

'Nadia's right,' said Asher. 'I sensed it too.'

'What do you think is going on?' Matt asked.

Nadia spoke, though it was not in answer to Matt's question.

Not directly. 'In my village, we call them leaf-skimmers. There were rumours that they worked with the witch. There were rumours that they hunted in the mountains. Only it was not animals they hunted.'

'I didn't know that Wights lived in Steppeinit?' Asher said.

'They do not. Neither do they belong there. Just as they do not belong here.'

Matt and Asher exchanged glances. 'More bloody questions than answers yet again.' Matt voiced what they were both thinking.

'Then let us hope Wimbush is able to cooperate and furnish Magoose with the information he requires.' Asher started back down the stairs.

'Why does that thought not fill me with confidence?' Matt muttered and followed him with Nadia bringing up the rear.

———

IT WAS ALMOST 1 pm when they got back to the BOD. Nadia excused herself and Asher led her towards a loo. A chaperoning necessity in a building where one wrong turn could lead to all sorts of surprises that rendered the need for a loo largely redundant, though the paper and the drier often came in handy in the immediate aftermath.

Matt headed for Asher's office, where there was someone already waiting for them. Bobby Miracle looked tired, though with the goth make-up and her dark clothes, it was sometimes difficult to tell. But her lids looked heavy with fatigue and Matt told her so the minute he clapped eyes on her.

She tilted her head with a resigned expression. 'It's not helping that I'm flitting back and forth across a twelve-hour time difference.'

'It is a nuisance.'

'Half the time I don't know whether I'm coming or going. Still, the equinox is almost here and then we'll all be back to normal.'

'Looks like you could do with a coffee.'

Asher entered the room and the tiredness instantly evaporated from Bobby's face.

Matt, with admirable diplomacy, left them to it and went in

search of warm brown liquid. He found some in a tearoom at the end of the corridor where there were ceramic cups and a self-replenishing pot. When he got back to the office, the conversation had not moved much further forward.

'In the meantime you burn the candle at both ends,' Asher said with a dollop of disapproval.

'Needs must, Asher.'

Matt handed round the mugs.

The door opened, and Nadia entered. Bobby pushed herself away from the desk she was leaning on, 'Hi, you must be…' Bobby's words tailed off as her eyes took in Nadia's startling appearance. 'OMG, your eyes.'

Nadia blinked at her with a frown.

'Sorry, I don't mean to be rude. It's just that I get like this when I've been hit on the head by the rubber coincidence hammer.'

Asher's eyes narrowed. 'What's going on, Bobby?'

'The unbelievable, that's what. I was on the way to the Fey for a lecture and Kylah wanted me to drop by to say hello and fill you in, but now…' She took a sip of coffee, her brows furrowing before she recovered enough to remember her manners and held out her hand to Nadia. 'Bobby Miracle.'

'Nadia Komangetme.'

Bobby glanced over at Asher. 'Okay. I'll go first.' Quickly, she filled them in on the sinkhole and what Kylah and the Sith Fand were doing at that very moment. 'But it's what happened to the council workers that's really weird. They were frightened. I mean, really frightened by something at the bottom of that sinkhole. And when Kylah went to see them at the hospital, something had happened to the whites of their eyes.'

'Don't tell me they'd gone blue?' Matt said.

Bobby nodded.

Matt turned to Asher, whose expression was a mirror image of his own bewilderment.

'I think this makes our trip to Spiv even more important,' Asher said. 'Like Bobby, I am not a great believer in coincidence. We need intelligence.'

'We will not need Wimbush for expedition?' Nadia said.

Once again, they all turned to look at her, Matt not even

trying to fight the smile that spread over his lips. This girl was sharp as well as feisty.

'Where's Spiv?' asked Bobby.

'Steppeinit. A mountainous, sparsely populated country in the north.'

'He means the back of beyond,' Matt mouthed from behind Nadia.

Asher quickly and concisely filled Bobby in on what they were about to do.

'Lava juice?' said Bobby when he'd finished. 'I've never heard of anything like that being used in Oxford or anywhere else in OW.' She used the 'Our World' acronym as agreed, not knowing how much Nadia knew about the DOF.

Asher nodded. 'No, I agree. There has been no record of human usage. And yet there must be a link.'

'Once your lecture is done, could you nip back and fill Kylah in on what's going on here?' Matt asked.

'That is, if you can stay awake,' Asher said, concern deepening his voice.

'I'm fine,' Bobby said, draining her coffee.

'Once we are back from Steppeinit we need to meet and seriously exchange information,' Asher said evenly, but his look suggested more than information might be exchanged at that meeting.

'I'll pass all that on.' Bobby, slightly flushed, got up from the chair, kissed Asher lightly on the cheek and waved at Matt. 'Kylah sends her love. She also says that come the equinox, you've got a lot of catching up to do. Apparently, there's a fire to light under Mount Slavabad. Mean anything to you?'

'It certainly does,' Matt said. The cabin that Kylah's family owned on the edge of a glacier was isolated and very private. There wasn't much to do there except light a wood fire, drink pure Slavabadrian water in between glasses of good champagne, and lie on the ethically sourced furs, letting the wind stoke the fire and the champagne stoke their passion. It had become their little retreat whenever their busy schedules allowed.

'You look sweet when you blush,' Bobby said.

Matt threw a wrapped falafel from Ned's trolley at her. Bobby watched it fly towards her and turn into a paper plane six inches from her face. The fighter soared back towards Matt, who had to duck to avoid it nosediving into his eye.

When she'd gone, Nadia said, 'She is a very pretty witch.'

'She's a very tired pretty witch,' Asher said.

'And who is Kylah?' Nadia tilted her head.

'Matt's boss, better half by far and a woman never to be messed with. She would like you a lot,' Asher said.

Nadia seemed pleased by this. 'What do we now do?'

'We eat lunch and get kitted out in cold weather gear and then we meet with Wimbush and Magoose again and hope they've ironed out the wrinkles.'

CHAPTER TWENTY-FOUR

MERTHYR, WALES

Bᴏʙʙʏ ᴇxɪᴛᴇᴅ through the front door of the same house she'd used previously, pocketed her Aperio, and stepped out through the gate onto the wet Welsh pavement. It had stopped raining, but the cold seeped into her and she tugged her coat about her as protection. It struck her then that this was an unnatural cold; a dank, miserable cold that somehow brought to mind unpalatable muddy water at the bottom of a filthy ditch. Where such unpleasant imaginings had sprung from, she had no idea and yet her training told her that they must have sprung from somewhere within the atmosphere or surroundings, and that meant the great big hole in the ground nearby. A small Portakabin at the far end of the street spilled yellow light into the roadway. She made her way towards it along the edge of the sinkhole. Looking down into the depths, she could see ghostly lights moving in the misty murk of the pit and was struck by the fact that even floodlights couldn't penetrate to the very bottom.

She knocked on the cabin door and was met by a rotund policeman who introduced himself as Sergeant Mackeson. She showed her badge and was let into a stiflingly hot room. A small portable TV was showing a Champions league game. The weather looked much better in Italy.

'Cup of tea?'

'Love one,' said Bobby. 'I need to speak to Captain Porter. Are there any comms set up?'

'Supposed to be but they're bloody useless, Miss. I got plenty of static if it's static you want.'

Mackeson handed her a mug of ochre fluid. He'd not asked if she wanted milk or sugar but had added both. She sipped. It tasted wonderful. 'Rich tea?' he offered, thrusting a plate towards her.

Bobby shook her head and took another gulp. 'So, how am I supposed to get her a message?'

'Could try chucking it down. But if it hits her on the head, you'd be out of the will.' Mackeson delivered this with a cheerful grin. It was clear that he had lived all his life in and around the area. It tinkled out of every lilting vowel.

'Then…'

Mackeson nodded towards a couple of hazmat suits. 'The ladders are well tethered, or so I'm told.'

'*Scheißen*,' said Bobby.

'Finish your tea first, for God's sake,' Mackeson said and proffered a different plate. 'Hob nob?'

Bobby ate two. She was tired, but the sugar rush helped, as did Mackeson as she struggled into the grey plastic suit.

He stood back appraisingly when she was dressed. 'One small step and all that,' he said, grinning. 'Come on, I'll walk you out.'

It was a thirty-yard spacewalk to the ladders. Mackeson was right, they were firmly tethered with wide handrails and foot-plates attached to the walls by iron staples. 'Shall I order fish and chips for five in an hour then?' he yelled down at her.

She gave him a thumbs up.

She didn't know then that it would be the longest hour of her life.

———

THE FURTHER SHE DESCENDED, the colder and danker it became. Fifteen feet from the bottom, the mist hung like a horizontal curtain. When her leg pushed through, despite the plastic of the suit and her clothes beneath, it felt like stepping into cold water. Four rungs later, she almost lost it when she felt a hand on her ankle. She glanced down to see the light from Alf's helmet—she knew it was Alf as he was at least a head taller that the others—beaming up at her. Bobby stepped down onto squelchy mud and saw Alf lean in close. Through the helmet, she just about heard him say, 'Nice of you to join us.'

She held out both hands in a gesture of ignorance and asked, 'Why are you still Alf?'

'In case someone sees,' he said.

Bobby nodded. 'Where's Kylah?'

Alf pointed to the southern edge of the crater where Dwayne and Kylah were hunched over. It looked like they were digging. Bobby joined them. It was supposed to be warm inside the suit, but all she could feel was the sapping cold. Instinct kept telling her this was not your normal, miserable British cold. This was something else. Something about as natural as a reality TV relationship.

Kylah and Dwayne broke off from their task as she approached. Kylah picked up a wire attached to her helmet and plugged the end into a socket on Bobby's and Dwayne took the wire from Bobby's and plugged it into his. Alf joined them and soon they had a telephonic chain link set up.

'Radio's useless down here,' said Dwayne.

'There was no need for you to come down,' Kylah said.

Bobby could see that she was sweating behind her faceplate. 'There is. You need to hear this.' Quickly, she told them all about her meeting with Matt and Asher.

Kylah listened with an apprehensive frown. When Bobby had finished, she shook her head. 'Those blue sclerae must mean something.' She looked at Dwayne, who nodded, and Alf, who shrugged.

'What's going on here?' Bobby asked.

'Good question,' Dwayne answered. 'We think we've found where the engineers got the frighteners.' He pointed to the left, where the sheer sides of the sinkhole looked slightly smoother than the rest. 'Though it's solid rock, we think we've detected some sort of activity either within or behind it.'

'Activity?'

'Definitely wonderworking. If you get close, you begin to see things.'

'Like what?'

'Unpleasantness. Bad memories. Stuff you'd rather have forgotten.'

Bobby had known Dwayne aka Birrik for a long time, and she knew he was not easily troubled. But something in his voice told her not to press too hard for more information.

'And on this side,' Kylah said, 'there seems to be another chamber of sorts. It's not very big but there's some sort of lintel above it, suggesting a doorway. We were trying to clear away some of the rocks when you arrived. I'm sure I can see something beyond but there's too much debris.'

'We'll get some tools, ma'am,' Alf said.

'Good idea,' Kylah said. 'I'll show Bobby what we've found.' She unplugged and led the way to a pile of rubble, stretching up and pointing over a large boulder. 'There, see? Something glinting? If only we could move this boulder.'

'I could try a lightening charm,' Bobby suggested.

Kylah nodded. 'Worth a try.'

Bobby put both hands on the rock. Letting her mind form the image of paper and feathers, she moulded them into the shape of the boulder. A familiar tingle built at the back of her mind. She lifted her hands and the rock tumbled away like a papier mâché prop.

'That's what an education gets you. When do you graduate?' Kylah asked, grinning.

'Couple of months.'

'Very impor—' Kylah's words were cut off. She had turned to look beyond the boulder to where they'd seen the glint. And suddenly it was more than a glint. 'Is that a—'

'Sword,' Bobby finished the sentence. 'Yes, I think it is.'

They squeezed through the narrow gap between two more crags. The sword stood at an angle wedged by the rubble, its blade silvery in their helmet lights. 'Anything on the handle?'

Kylah brushed away dirt and squinted. 'Can't see. It's wedged against the wall behind.'

'Will it come loose?' Kylah tried but it did not budge.

'Hang on,' said Bobby, beginning to unclamp her helmet.

Kylah remonstrated. 'What are you doing?'

'Can't get close enough with this thing on. It'll only be for a minute or two. There.' With the helmet off, Bobby slid easily in to the gap. She could now turn to face Kylah. 'You hold the handle, I'll push up on the hilt.'

In the cramped space, both women had to hunch over but they managed to get reasonable grips. 'You know what this reminds me of?' Bobby said, as she steadied herself.

Kylah nodded. 'Sword in the stone. Great cartoon but too much music and the style wasn't great. They were still using xeroxing to transfer drawings to celluloid in the sixties. Just like they did on *Dalmatians*.'

Bobby couldn't hide her surprise. 'Wow, I didn't know you were a Disney fan?'

'Uncle Ernest has been an advisor on lots of films. Especially period dramas. Now, ready?' Kylah said as she braced herself.

'On three,' said Bobby with a grunt. 'One, two, three.'

The noise was almost musical, the ringing of steel against stone. It lasted for a few seconds only before a deep rumble followed and the ground shifted beneath Kylah and Bobby's feet. Shifted and turned and twisted and…

Disappeared.

CHAPTER TWENTY-FIVE

'What's happening?' screamed Bobby.

They were falling through a hole, and yet their feet did not leave the ground. The world whirled about them, shifting in a dizzying kaleidoscopic collage of light and dark, green and blue and brown. A thousand images came and went in ten, perhaps twelve, seconds until a blaze of light brought everything to a stop.

Bobby threw her hand up to cover her eyes. The light was almost painful after the dimness of the sinkhole. But then she blinked, and the world returned. In an instant she knew it was sunlight, low and bright, edged by a darker craggy frame. It resolved into an opening. An opening at the end of a tunnel or cave? She looked to her left and was relieved to find Kylah standing there, one hand up to shield her eyes, the other clutching the hilt of the broadsword.

'Bobby, are you all right?' Kylah still had her helmet on and her voice sounded muted and distant.

That was when Bobby realised she was still holding the sword's blade, now free of its enclosure. 'What just happened?' she shouted.

'I have no idea, but it feels…different. Everything feels different. It's not as cold, for a start.'

'The sun…'

'Exactly.'

'And the chanting.'

'What chanting?' Kylah inclined her head, shook it, and then removed her helmet. 'Oh, that chanting.'

It was coming from behind them. Repetitive, faintly Gregorian. Slowly, both women turned and froze. There, bathed in the reddish light of the low sun, knelt fifty or more knights in full armour, their broadswords vertical in front of them, tips on the ground, hilts in front of their faces as if in supplication. To their right knelt half a dozen monks in robes. The monks were doing the chanting. Three knights knelt in front of the others, and the one in the middle stood up.

He was not tall, but the crown on his head made him taller. 'You have come,' he said.

'Have we?' Kylah answered with an over-bright smile.

The man frowned. The knights watched in silence. The man with the crown nodded his approval.

'Welcome, maidens. We are well met. We are in need of guidance.' Bobby noticed instantly that his accent had the same lilting vowels as Mackeson's. 'We have been waiting,' the man added.

'For us?' Kylah asked. She still had the sword in her hands.

The man nodded. 'For something or someone. It is you who have appeared.'

'And who exactly are you?'

The man, or was he royalty—the crown lent him a degree of gravitas—knelt again and bowed his head. 'Your servant, Arthur Pendragon.'

Bobby didn't speak for a couple of seconds, but when she did, the words sneaked out like a burp at a posh meal. Nothing you can do to stop it and you can only hope that not everyone notices. 'The sword in the stone,' she whispered.

'Boomerang,' whispered Kylah by return, memory of her visit with Vidom surging through her mind. Of something she should, by rights, remember but could not.

Then they both said, 'Krudian.'

The two knights on either side of Arthur stood.

'These two stout fellows are Cei and Bedwyr, my lieutenants. The men behind are mine, all sworn to the cause. Let us away to our camp where refreshments await. Our sojourn has been long.'

Arthur turned to his men and they all stood. With a clanking of chain mail, they trooped past Bobby and Kylah, the monks following, until only Bedwyr and Cei remained behind.

'Lovely boys, lovely boys,' said Bedwyr with an admiring shake of his head as the last of the men marched past.

'Boys?' said Kylah.

'Salt of the earth, mun.' Bedwyr said. 'We're a team, see. We look out for each other.'

'Aye.' Cei nodded. 'Put their lives on the line a dozen times already, those boys.'

'Are you fighting, then?' Bobby asked.

'Fightin'?' Cei said. 'S'all we're bloody doin' is fightin'. Them bloody Saicsons with their marchin' and speechin'. We've 'ammered 'em a couple of times already, but they won't give up.'

'Yeah, and now they're startin' to play dirty, isn't it, Cei?'

'Dirty? Bloody filthy if you ask me. They're employin' dark tactics.'

Bedwyr nodded again, a shadow passing across his face. 'They got this necromancer, see.'

Something moaned in the darkness of the cave beyond. Cei responded by swivelling around and raising his huge sword.

'Probably not the best place to be discussin' this, to be honest,' Bedwyr said.

'Aye, come on. Let's get some grub. Bloody starvin', I am,' Cei said without turning around.

Bedwyr led them out from the cave with Cei at the rear, sword still raised. They emerged into late afternoon spring sunlight. From the lack of foliage on the huge oaks all around them, it was not yet summer, but the sun was pleasantly warm on their faces. Bedwyr sucked in a lungful of air.

'Oh, that's better, mun.'

It was the first time Bobby could make out the knight's features. Under his domed helmet the face was scarred and bearded, but the eyes danced with amusement. Cei joined them. He was taller with smooth features. A quarter of a mile to their left stood a clearing and some tents. From the largest flew a banner: a black dragon inside a green outlined shield on a red background. If there was any lingering doubt as to where they were, it evaporated on seeing that banner.

'Tell me,' Kylah said, in a voice that suggested she didn't necessarily want to know the answer, 'and I still don't know how it is you can tell me or how it is that I can tell you, but have the Romans left?'

'Aye,' said Bedwyr. 'Gone for good, they say.'

'So…?' Bobby's question was full of trepidation.

'Early fifth century,' Kylah whispered.

'Oh my God.'

In front of her, Bedwyr turned and smiled. 'A prayer, is it?'

'Not exactly.'

'No, I'm with you there. There's been times these last months when I think that our God has deserted us. Gone with the sandal-wearers back to Rome. If it wasn't for M and M comin' up with a plan, I don't know where we'd be.'

'M and M?' Kylah asked airily.

'Myrddin and Morgana. You'll meet them now. It's them who did the summonin'.'

Bobby's brain felt like she was watching two express trains plough into one another head-on. No sooner had she formalised one thought than another crashed into it, crushing it beyond recognition and leaving her floundering for answers.

'Morgana? As in Morgana Le Fey? But isn't she a sorceress?'

'Apprentice to Myrddin, that's right.'

There were things that Bobby wanted to say but didn't. She was, after all, a novice at the Le Fey academy. An establishment named after the very same Morgana Le Fey. But that was in New Thameswick. And in most human Arthurian legends Bobby had read, Morgana had been the epitome of an evil seductress, a sexual predator set on ruining Arthur and all he stood for. She made that train of thought pull into a siding before it derailed her brain completely.

Better not to think too much. Best to just go with the flow.

The fifth-century flow…

CHAPTER TWENTY-SIX

They reached the small camp and Bedwyr took them to a tent where, by consensus, they removed their hazmat suits. A table was laid with some food and drink.

'Should we?' Bobby said.

'I don't know,' said Kylah. 'I'm completely flummoxed. If we are where I think we are, whatever we've done so far here does not seem to have affected our survival, otherwise we would not be here.'

'That's probably true, but when you can translate it into English, let me know and I'll have another listen.'

'We ought to be careful.'

'What you're saying is that I might eat a hazelnut and just disappear?'

'Yes.'

'I think I'll leave it.' Bobby put the nut back down. Her hand was shaking. 'Kylah, is this real, or are we trapped inside some sort of shared dream induced by the hallucinogenic fug at the bottom of that sinkhole? I ask because, if we really are back in the fifth century, that's bad, really bad. But my brain is buzzing. It's almost as if I'm a little high.'

Kylah shook her head. 'That may be something to do with you taking off the helmet.' She peered into Bobby's eyes. 'Yup, I can detect a little greying of the white.'

'Really?'

Kylah nodded. 'I suppose we need to consider all possibilities, but if Uncle Ernest's good friend Occam were here, I know what he'd say.'

Bobby pondered this answer for a moment and it only made her brain hurt more. If Kylah was referring to the Franciscan friar William of Occam, then Bobby had first to accept the fact that Mr Porter might actually know him, as opposed to simply be aware of him, before going on any further. Kylah was not one to wax rhetorical in these circumstances and though, a year or two before, Bobby might have laughed at the joke until she saw that Kylah was serious, she had learned that astonishing things were the norm under the Hipposync franchise. And though she'd never had to believe six impossible things before breakfast, two or three were de rigueur. So, having accepted that a fourteenth-century philosopher might indeed be pals with her boss, Bobby then had to wrestle with working out which of the choices Kylah had given her to consider was the least improbable.

'What would Occam have said?'

'To look at things simply.'

'Right. So, do you have any kind of simple explanation?'

'Only the one that makes me sound like I've just left the asylum.'

'Which is?'

'That, at the bottom of that sinkhole, someone left an enchanted weapon that has transported us back to the fifth century.'

'I thought you might say that. Weirdly, I've just finished a module on artefact protection charms. But Arthur Pendragon? Come on. I though he was fictitious?'

'He was not. I could have told you that. Trouble is, record-keeping isn't exactly a precise science at this stage of history. They didn't call them the Dark Ages for nothing. Much was passed down orally and Chinese whispers have nothing on medieval British fibs.'

Bobby paused to take this in. 'So why do the knights sound like a Welsh rugby team?'

'Probably because old Welsh, or a variant of it, is what they spoke. Whatever is translating for us is adding in a bit of dialect and accent for effect. It was the language of Britain until the Saxons came.'

'Saicsons,' Bobby corrected her.

'It might also explain why the sinkhole appeared in the middle of West Wales. The engineers have been thinking old mines when we should have been thinking ancient kingdoms.'

Bobby was admittedly reeling with this information. And her head was quite literally buzzing. 'So where does that leave us?'

'In need of more information.' Kylah looked at the huge sword she was holding.

'Isn't that thing really heavy?'

'Surprisingly, no. It just feels hot in my hand.'

Bobby giggled. 'Woo-hoo, sister.'

Kylah stared at her.

Bobby swallowed. 'Oh my God, what is wrong with me? It's like I've been hit with a jester curse. And you don't feel any different?'

'No,' said Kylah, narrowing her eyes. 'But I'm wondering if I should put this down somewhere before I get the urge to put you out of your misery.'

Bobby stared at the sword. 'You think it's the portway?'

Kylah paused, thinking. 'Touching it did bring us here. So maybe we should hang on to it.' She laid the sword down on a straw bed.

They didn't eat but they did drink some water. It tasted cool and clean and neither of them faded into nothingness. After ten minutes, Bedwyr returned and took them to the biggest tent under the dragon banner. Inside, Arthur sat next to an elegant woman in her early twenties with fair hair tied up in plaits. To his left, behind a trestle table covered with charts and parchments, stood two figures. One was a sprightly man with a shaved tonsure and straggly hair growing down at the back. The other was a lithe girl of perhaps eighteen with a circlet of silver around her forehead keeping her long auburn hair away from her eyes. They all looked up as Bobby and Kylah appeared through the tent flap.

'Ah, you have divested yourself of your strange garments,' Arthur observed.

'Only to dress yourself in stranger.' The woman next to him smiled and stood up. 'Gwenhwyfar,' she said, and held out a hand.

'I know your sister, what,' Bobby said and immediately put a hand over her mouth.

'Shut up,' Kylah hissed through her smile before stepping forward to shake the proffered hand, while Arthur looked on. Bobby did the same before realising that they were probably meant to have curtsied and kissed the hand, not shaken it, but she was too busy trying to stop herself from saying anything else stupid.

'And here are those responsible for bringing you here,' Arthur said. 'Our wise counsellor, Myrddin, and my sister, Morgana.'

Bobby tried to speak but the words took a wrong turn between brain and larynx and all she could do was grin vacuously.

Thankfully, Kylah had a bit more presence of mind. 'Kylah Porter,' she said, 'and this is my colleague, Bobby Miracle.'

Gwenhwyfar stood. 'Before I take my leave, for there is much for you to discuss, I wish to offer my gratitude for your sacrifice. The people of Bretain will not forget this.' Her accent was different: rolling and less lilting. She walked forward with poise, the cloth band around her forehead glittering before bowing to Kylah and then Bobby. She smelled of rose petals.

'We are at war,' Arthur said, watching his wife leave the tent. 'Gwenhwyfar tends to the sick and injured.'

'Saicson raiders?' Kylah asked.

'Indeed,' Arthur said. 'We have been taught a difficult and bloody lesson. Our small villages are easy prey for armies of a hundred or more. But we are learning. Such wanton destruction demands unification. We now have an army of our own. But the other enemy, the Nosdrwg, they are more difficult to overcome—'

Myrddin cleared his throat in a poorly disguised attempt at attracting the king's attention. His eyes remained wary as he regarded Bobby and Kylah, his voice as craggy as his features. 'Before we discuss the Saicson threat, we must assure ourselves that you are not our enemy.'

Morgana was staring at them intently.

She's looking to see if we'll flinch, thought Kylah. 'Though we have been brought here against our will, we intend no harm,' she said, leaving Bobby to wonder if this was a DOF-trained response. Page one of what to say if you're transported back fifteen hundred years and find yourself in a medieval court being questioned by the most famous sorcerer of all time. She ought to look up that manual when she had time.

'Then you will not object to an examination,' said Myrddin.

Kylah's eyes narrowed, but Myrddin did not allow her any time to respond.

'It is a simple enough test devised by my assistant, the lady Morgana.'

The woman in question came around from behind the table, her eyes never leaving the DOF agents' faces. Bobby had the distinct impression that this had happened before. Myrddin threw a chalky rope on the floor. It writhed briefly and then formed a circle around the feet of Kylah and Bobby.

'A containment charm,' Kylah said. 'You are very thorough.'

Myrddin picked up a staff with an oddly shaped head. Unsmiling, he said, 'You have nothing to fear if your hearts are true.'

Morgana spoke for the first time. Her accent was more like Cei and Bedwyr's. 'The test is simple. We want you to say the squire scolded the scampering squirrel.'

'The what?' Kylah asked.

Morgana took a pouch from the low-slung belt around her waist and removed a pinch of powder. She threw it high above Kylah and Bobby, where it hung like a powdery cloud. 'The squire scolded the scampering squirrel. In your own time.' Her words were calm, but her eyes lost none of their intensity. On the other side of the tent, Myrddin raised his staff so that the iron-shod end pointed at Kylah and Bobby.

'The squire scolded the scampering squirrel,' said Kylah.

'The squire scolded the scampering squirrel,' said Bobby.

The powdery cloud above their heads flashed a shimmering gold and then disappeared through a gap in the tent.

Morgana clapped her hands in delight. 'That's awesome, that is.'

Bobby had a moment to wonder at how anyone could spend so much time on the first syllable of the word 'awesome' without turning blue, before the snaky rope circle slithered away.

'We have yet to meet a Saicson spy who can pronounce that statement correctly,' Myrddin smiled.

'Squirrel is the word of power.'

'Funny that,' said Bobby. 'We have a very famous minstrel who said sorrel seems to be the hardest word.'

It earned her a sideways kick on the ankle from Kylah.

Morgana was beaming. 'Sorry about that, but we had to be certain.' She crossed the space between them with her arms open and three seconds later, Bobby found herself being hugged by the sorceress. She smelled of wild garlic and lavender.

'What was the powder?' Kylah asked when they'd extricated themselves.

Morgana kept her voice low. 'Hemlock rain. That was all Myrddin, mind. What it is, he's a bit careful when to comes to stuff like this. Don't blame him, I suppose. But I am sooo glad you are here. You've got no idea.'

'Morgana, we will have time for the diplomacy later.' Myrddin started gathering up charts.

'Just sayin' how glad I was that our summonin' worked, that's all.'

'So long as there's a reversal spell, eh?' Kylah's question cut through the air like a poisoned dart.

Morgana kept smiling.

Myrddin harrumphed. It sounded well practised. 'What's important now is that we get on with the task in hand. Then there will be time.'

'Task?' Kylah asked.

'Of course. The reason we summoned you here. To defeat the Nosdrwg.'

'Defeat the Nosdrwg?' Kylah repeated the statement with a little upwards slant on the last word, which implied that if there was a contract here, she had neither been given the opportunity to read it, nor show it to the lawyers.

'Our summoning requested a champion,' Myrddin explained. 'One from a time when the Nosdrwg were quelled. You must know that because only those exposed to the Nosdrwg can be summoned.'

Bobby was following Myrddin's argument with difficulty.

'But we have never seen the Nosdrwg—' Kylah began and then stopped. 'Tell us about them.'

Myrddin grimaced. 'They come at night. Slide into your dreams. We think they live in the caves. Inside the very stone.'

Morgana nodded. 'They are formless except in the dark. It's said that they do eat light. Once you acknowledge them, they are with you wherever a shadow lurks. Half of our company sleep while the other half keeps watch and keep fires and lights burning. The Nosdrwg are like nightmares, only much worse. They spin lies and squeeze out hope.'

'Sounds like the Eurovision Song Contest,' Bobby said. 'But if you say we're here because we have knowledge of them, I have no idea—'

'Sinkhole,' Kylah interrupted her.

'None taken,' Bobby said, wincing again at her inability to shut up and keeping her eyes straight ahead to avoid Kylah's warning glare.

'Listen.' Myrddin opened the tent entrance. Outside, the day was dying and its last rays bathed the tent in orange light as the sun's crescent dipped below the horizon. The second it was out of sight, a dreadful, mournful howling erupted from the direction of the cave Bobby and Kylah had appeared in.

'Are those the Nosdrwg?'

'They call to one another,' Myrddin said. 'Announcing their presence to all that fear them.'

'I'm glad we're in this nice tent, then,' Bobby said.

Morgana and Myrddin turned to look at her.

'Oh, don't say we're going to have to go back over there?'

'We must,' Myrddin said.

'But—'

Myrddin shook his head. 'You have been summoned. You will find the answer.'

Bobby shook her head. 'Really? Sorry to disappoint you, but I'm clueless. I have no idea how to fight shadow things that enjoy inflicting fear and sucking out joy. Okay, I have been out with a couple of blokes that fit that description but believe me, that was no fun.'

'We should probably take a look,' Kylah said, earning a stern glance from Bobby. Kylah shrugged. 'Know thine enemy and all that. Besides, I doubt we're going to get any help until we do.'

Myrddin nodded. 'Brave words, Kylah, But first I advise rest. It would be better that we confront the Nosdrwg nearer dawn as light approaches, when their power is diminished.'

Bobby sighed. 'Twenty minutes ago, I was drinking police-made builder's tea and feeling knackered and sorry for myself. Now, I wish I'd had that extra Hobnob. In fact, I wish I'd had two because I am hungry.'

'Me too. But let's just wait and see.'

Bobby nodded to the accompaniment of her stomach rumbling.

PART 3

CHAPTER TWENTY-SEVEN

NEW THAMESWICK

THE BOD CAFETERIA nestled in the basement of the building and was one of Matt's favourite places. The décor was a non-ironic, whimsical blend of Gothic charm and bureaucratic blandness, with flickering candlelit chandeliers and Formica tables. The day before, a geist had a fit over the soggy chips, sending trays flying and earning a stern lecture from the head chef, a grumpy Bwbach named Gareth. For security purposes they had in-house facilities with the sort of eclectic choices that would have made any self-respecting food fair seem like a school canteen. Nadia ate two portions of everything and in response to Asher's prod, Matt explained in a whisper, 'A hundred pounds soaking wet I reckon, but with that magic metabolism that lets marathon runners run a hundred miles. I reckon it wouldn't show on her if she ate a small horse twice a day.'

'Unlike Mobly the troll's,' Asher nodded in the direction of a corpulent being waddling towards a table with a tray so laden with food it seemed to sag in the middle. 'He was arrested for doing just that.'

At two, they found Ned, who took them down to Magoose's office. A journey involving at least five different staircases, three tunnels, a lift and a rope bridge across a yawning chasm deep under the building.

'Diamond mines,' Ned said as a throwaway comment. 'Abandoned, of course.'

He ushered the party into a small boat that moved under its own power through a series of lit caverns until they came to a small quay.

'Is there a reason why we're in the arse end of the earth?' Matt asked.

''Ealth an' safety, Mr D. If we get a Kwantum down 'ere, no one's any the wiser.'

'A Kwantum?'

'Yeah. As in Kwantum event. As in if one of Magoose's Kwantum bubbles explodes instead of implodes, you get my drift?'

'Explicitly,' muttered Matt.

Ned led the way along a passage that ended in an iron gate with a quite ordinary-looking white-painted corridor beyond.

'Third door on your right, Mr A,' Ned said, pushing open the gate.

The stencilled sign on the third door said, *EXPERIMENTAL TRANSPORTATION LAB*. Matt put in his linguaplug while Asher knocked.

Magoose opened the door and bowed, deferential as ever, welcoming them in. Runes and symbols covered three white-painted walls. The fourth, at the end of the lab, ended in a carved-out bowl in the rock. Seated in the centre of this bowl was Wimbush, wearing a helmet covered with an array of protruding rods of varying lengths. On a screen next to him a strange and constantly shifting image, more like an artist's impression than a real photograph, drifted in and out of view.

'Come in, come in,' Magoose said, even though they were already walking across the lab towards Wimbush. 'We are almost ready.'

Wimbush, distracted by the noise and movement, opened his eyes and the image became an artist's impression of the four of them walking towards Wimbush in a room filled with symbols and runes.

If ever there was an opportunity so say something pithy, seeing Wimbush with a ridiculous-looking hat on his head was it. But the sheer strangeness of the lab, the way the symbols seemed to shimmer and dance on the walls and the metallic tang of ozone in the air made even Matt, whose threshold for mockery was normally lower than a viper's undercarriage, keep his powder dry.

Magoose picked up a stick, which Matt assumed was probably a wand, pointed to three invisible spots above the helmet on Wimbush's head and instantly the image on the wall disappeared.

'Nice of you to join us,' Wimbush said.

'We brought you some lunch.' Matt held out a neatly wrapped parcel. 'Crayfish and rocket. Ned was out of chicken.'

'Good, I am hungry.' Wimbush ripped off the wrapping and took a healthy bite.

'So, how has your subject been behaving, Magoose?' Asher asked.

Magoose bobbed. 'Very good, very good. Easily distracted but highly skilled at imagining plants and trees.'

'But have we found a landing spot?'

'Yes. A rocky outcrop on top of a steep cliff. The only problem is that the last two feet of calculated bubble is overhanging.'

'Overhanging what?' Matt asked.

'A two thousand-foot drop,' Magoose said, smiling.

'Great,' Matt replied.

'I suggest tying everyone together with rope. If one falls, the others could save him.'

'Or the others could all be dragged down by one unlucky traveller,' Asher said.

'That's a lousy one-liner, Asher,' Matt said.

Asher shook his head. 'We stay separate. It's our best opportunity.'

'Very well,' Magoose said.

Wimbush finished his sandwich and they quickly kitted him out, including his favourite hat, which he now wore slung over his back to make room for the helmet.

'The window of opportunity will be small,' Magoose said. 'I will watch the screen and shout, "Jump!" when it is time.'

'Great,' Matt repeated. It was rapidly becoming his go-to word.

They lined up behind Wimbush who had both the helmet on his head and the Aperio in his hand.

'What about his hat?' Matt asked, standing at the rear behind Nadia, Asher and Wimbush.

Magoose grinned. 'The helmet will stay here. It is tethered to the wall and half a mile of rock above your head. Now, Wimbush. Imagine you are standing on the rocky outcrop. See the trees and the floor. Forget the cliff behind you.'

'Then don't keep mentioning the buggering thing,' Wimbush answered through gritted teeth as he concentrated with eyes squeezed shut.

Matt leaned forward, his scoffing mojo well and truly back, and whispered to Nadia. 'He looks like the front end of a pantomime porcupine.'

She half turned. 'What is pantomime?'

'Never mind.' Matt watched the screen where a collage of trees, cliff, sky, rocks, sky, trees, sky, rocks, valley floor, sky, trees, rocks, trees, rocks, sky, valley floor, rocks, trees, sky, trees—'

'Now!' Magoose yelled.

Matt felt the rush of cold mountain air on his face and a different wobbly horizon appeared in a gap in the air ahead. How it was possible to have a gap in air, he didn't know but his view see-sawed wildly between rocky floor and sky. And then he was jumping into the gap as it stretched to become as tall as he was, one hand on Nadia's shoulder as they fell forwards through the air.

He landed awkwardly, momentum carrying him sideways and he grabbed on to a rock just in time to see Nadia rolling the wrong way, backwards, away from the line of tress and towards the edge of the outcrop and ten seconds of emptiness before she crashed to the valley floor and certain death. Matt lunged for a flailing hand and missed. He had time to let out a groan of anguish before something moved quickly past him and grabbed on to the webbing of Nadia's backpack. Her legs were already dangling in fresh air before they were yanked back in violently by a red-faced and straining Wimbush.

He overdid it and sent her sprawling on the ground, but then a nuanced approach to pulling someone back from the edge of the abyss was not something one practised a great deal. Wimbush, meanwhile, fell back onto his backside, puffing like a steam train.

Asher, safe and well, was on his feet with his back to the line of trees. 'Excellent,' he said. 'And we now know that free-fall peregrination actually works. Magoose will go down in history.'

'Can he fetch my stomach while he's there?' Matt sucked in air in an attempt at forcing the horizon to settle into a solid line.

'Yes, we might suggest a travel sickness potion next time.'

'Great idea,' Matt said. Of all the things that were upsetting him at that moment, the words 'next time' uttered by Asher shot straight to the top of the list.

It took them a few minutes to recover, but recover they did. They had to. It was cold on the mountain. They knew it would be, but even so, Matt felt woefully ill-prepared for the biting wind and quickly took out scarf and gloves. It was meant to be spring, but in Steppeinit, spring had obviously not quite woken up yet, having decided to stay slumbering under winter's still snowy duvet. As if to prove a point, patches of the white stuff still lay thick in pockets where the spring sun could not reach.

'Let's get out of this wind,' Asher said.

No one argued, and they hurried towards the trees and shelter. Matt helped Nadia to her feet. She looked unscathed as she turned to a still puffing Wimbush.

'Thank you,' she said, her eyes almost silver in the flat reflected light. Wimbush looked momentarily startled.

'Oh, um, pleasure,' he said. 'Didn't really think about it. Instinct, you know.'

'I will think about it and remember,' she said and hurried after Asher.

'She's a strange one,' Wimbush whispered to Matt, hoping for a little conspiratorial confirmation. 'Forthright and a bit charmless.'

Kettle, pot, black.

'I'd prefer to use rare myself,' Matt said. 'As in raw and unrefined but still precious.'

Wimbush looked at him, eyes watering from the cold. 'I don't follow.'

'No, I don't suppose for one minute that you do. But then perhaps you've never come across a rough diamond.' He hiked up his pack and set off after Nadia, leaving Wimbush to stare after him, bemused.

CHAPTER TWENTY-EIGHT

THE NORTHERN SARMATIC FOREST OF STEPPEINIT

ASHER WAS RIGHT. It wasn't exactly warmer under the trees, but they did act as a screen against the wind, reducing the chill to a 'tic' less than arctic. Yet it was persistent, that wind, and capable of finding every nook and several crannies that their clothing didn't manage to protect. Wimbush, in his best inappropriate walking shorts, already had blue knees.

'We keep moving while it's still light,' Asher said. 'If we can descend from this high ground it should get a bit warmer.'

'What di…di…direction?' Wimbush asked, teeth chattering.

Asher looked at Nadia, who was looking up at the sun. She let her head drop and pointed towards a slope that would have made a good blue run on any European ski resort.

The going was tough to start with. Pockets of snow in drifts made Matt realise how much he wished he'd packed extra socks. Nadia seemed to walk right through them, but Wimbush cursed and grunted for a good two hours until they reached lower ground and a patch of scrub where the snow had all melted. They stopped, and Asher brought out a flask from his backpack and soon they were sipping hot tea and munching on biscuits.

'Ah, old school,' said Matt, accepting a digestive. 'Bobby bring these, did she? Mrs Hoblip's winter warmers. Mmm.'

'Do we have any idea how far this supposed village is?' Wimbush asked.

Asher looked at Nadia. 'Two days walking.'

'Two days?' Wimbush ejaculated. 'Argh!' The words spurted out unbidden, and half a mug of hot tea jerked from its receptacle as a result of Wimbush leaping up from a sitting position in horrified objection to the estimate of time. Said tea made its way, ironically, towards said holder's lap, causing him to run to the edge of the clearing emitting a strangled whimper and dousing the affected area in cooling snow. The others watched this little performance with astonishment. It was too cold to laugh. And deep down they all knew it was going to be a long two days if they made fun of every single one of Wimbush's eccentricities.

Nadia, by contrast, looked concerned. She hurried over and asked, 'Are you all right, Wimbush?'

Wimbush did not turn around. 'Fine, I'm fine. But two days? Honestly if I'd have known—'

'It would have made no difference since you'd have whined anyway,' Matt said loudly. 'Come on, have some more tea.'

Asher replenished everyone's cup and was screwing down the flask when the first of the crows appeared above them, cawing and circling the air above. The three men stared curiously; Nadia, however, let out a curse.

'Spies,' she said. 'Come. It was a mistake to stop. We must go. We head north for half a mile, then come back here to head south.'

'Why?' asked Wimbush, realising that this was going to add even more time to their journey.

'Because the crows will go back to whoever sent them and report. Let them believe that we run. Perhaps whoever sent them will run that way too.'

'But who? Who sent them?'

'The aldermen in the village would say it was the witch. I do not believe that.'

'Whoever it is, they know we're here. But Nadia is right. We need to distract them. Come on, north it is,' Asher said.

They walked for fifteen minutes into the forest. The crows followed at first, but then their caws became distant and intermittent as the density of the trees increased. In silence and at

Nadia's signal, they turned back to the clearing, waited under cover for clear skies and crossed to the other side.

'Now we must be careful. Watch and listen,' Nadia said.

'For what?' Wimbush asked as everyone knew he would.

'We will know when we see or hear it,' Nadia replied.

'Wonderful,' muttered Wimbush. 'Why do I let myself get talked into doing these damned things?'

'Because it is right thing to do.' Nadia surprised them all by answering Wimbush's rhetorical question out loud.

There was no reply. For once, the alchemist's retort reservoir was empty.

It was late into the afternoon when Asher brought them to another halt in a pass with views that would have made any self-respecting singing nun wet herself. However, Asher's face was anything but full of the sound of music. He crouched, head tilted.

Nadia caught his eyes and nodded. 'They have been following for half an hour.'

Asher nodded.

'Who have?' Wimbush's anxiety radar was up on maximum again.

'Good question,' Asher answered.

'Crows?' asked Matt.

Asher shook his head. 'Not this time. Let's keep going. We can continue for another couple of hours before making camp. I'll set up sentries then.'

'Where exactly is it we're heading for?' Wimbush asked like a grumpy six-year-old.

'There,' Nadia pointed to a small green patch in the far distance. 'To the left of the biggest mountain. My village.'

Matt nodded. 'It's still a good trek.'

'Then let's get going.' Asher moved off.

They walked through the late afternoon and into lengthening shadows. Finally, in a clearing at the base of steep incline, with the light now dimming, Asher stopped.

'Here is as good as anywhere,' he said and slung the back-pack off his shoulder. 'If we can find some firewood, that would be good. But do not stray beyond visual contact with someone else. Matt, you stay with me and set up. Nadia and Wimbush, you go for wood.'

Matt cleared a footprint of about forty square yards. The ground underfoot was mainly scrub and sparse grass, and the debris mainly branches. When he'd finished, he watched Asher extend a telescopic pole and stick it firmly in the ground before placing a tarpaulin-wrapped bundle next to it.

'Don't think that'll keep much snow off,' Matt said.

Asher threw him a look.

'You need help?'

'No. This is military issue. Ned managed to get this for us and curiously, I trust him.' Asher stood back and took out a small box from his coat pocket. He broke off a piece of what looked like yellow plasticine and rolled it into a ball between this thumb and index finger while he rehearsed the words written on an instruction sheet. After half a minute, he turned to Matt. 'I'd stand well back if I were you. Just in case.'

'Of what?' Matt asked but retreated anyway.

Asher grinned, lobbed the tiny ball of plasticine towards the upright pole and said, '*Aedifacarem.*'

With a crack and a loud bang, the bundle at the foot of the pole erupted and snapped open. The air filled with slaps and clangs as metal walls appeared and locked together, and wooden doors and windows thudded into place. Within ten seconds, their camp—a corrugated two-storey metal hut—was up and running.

'Whoa,' said Matt. 'That Ned knows his stuff.'

Inside they found a table and chairs, a galley with a wood stove, griddle and a ladder leading up to some cots.

'Home from effing home, as a vulture friend of mine might say.' Matt rapped on the table. It sounded and felt like solid wood.

Nadia and Wimbush appeared bearing bundles of wood. They let Nadia build the fire and while Matt prepared some food, Asher went out to set up a perimeter. He grabbed a couple of furry bundles as he exited.

'Howleyes. Should let us know if anything gets too close.' Outside, he threw the bundles us in the air and they flew towards the trees, emitting two identical hoots.

They ate well. Asher let Ned provide provisions and he had not skimped. 'You should upgrade Ned to quartermaster,' Matt said, as he helped himself to another spoonful of excellent stew.

'I'll speak to Duana,' Asher said. 'But between you and me,

Ned would rather keep a low profile. I suspect he functions better that way.'

Wimbush was silent and still wearing a sullen expression as he sat in his chair, scribbling in his journal and ignoring the others. He looked up, squinting in thought. 'This hut has a door, does it not?'

'I have to say not much gets past you, Wimbush,' Matt said.

Wimbush glowered. 'But if there is a door, why can't you use that aperitif thing to get us back to New Thameswick?'

Asher responded. 'A fair point, Mr Wimbush. Unfortunately, normal peregrination requires a fixed portal. This hut doesn't actually exist here, it's simply borrowed from another existence while no one wants it. That is how it is possible to carry a memory of it around in the tiny bundle that ended up being this construct. Only a fragment of it came with me, a ground-down powder from the walls trapped in yellow clay. If we tried to use the Aperio on this door, we would end up in a warehouse some-where, but not in New Thameswick. I believe that this is of dwarf construction, and so you could choose from one of their enclaves as a porting point.'

Satisfied, Wimbush turned back to his scribbling.

Tiredness followed food like night followed day.

'Should we set a watch?' Nadia asked.

'No need,' Asher said. 'The howleyes will wake us if anything approaches.'

Matt did not need an invitation to go to sleep. The hut was warm and cosy and it was difficult to believe that they were miles away from New Thameswick on the edge of Steppeinit. He dreamt of Kylah and of another hut, this one with log walls and with ethically sourced animal furs on the floor.

It was more a high-pitched yelp than a screech that jolted him abruptly awake at just after three in the morning. A repeti-tive, monotonous, piercing noise that dragged Matt out of his dreams like an icy hand around the nape of his neck. He sat up, saw Asher already on his feet and Nadia right behind him.

Before they could descend the ladder, the howleye warning cut out abruptly.

'Can they be harmed?' croaked Matt.

'Yes. But they can fly in the dark to escape if threatened,,' Asher said.

Matt clambered out of his bunk and shook Wimbush awake. How could he still be sleeping? And then Matt saw the moss stuffed into the alchemist's ears and pulled it out.

'Hey, who, wha…' Wimbush stared around in confusion.

Matt threw him his shorts. 'We have visitors.'

CHAPTER TWENTY-NINE

WIMBUSH WAS the last to arrive in the tiny galley.

'I knew this was a mistake. We're trapped like fish in a barrel. We're—'

'If you say "doomed", I swear I will punch you in the face,' Matt said.

'We are hidden. They cannot see us,' Asher said. 'I suggest we go outside and see what it is that disturbs our rest. So long as we stay within the camouflage perimeter, we can neither be seen nor heard.'

'What about weapons?' Wimbush asked.

'We will have no need of weapons—'

Wimbush rummaged in his backpack. 'I brought a miniature crossbow. Rapid loader. Fires five arrows a minute.'

Asher glowered at him. 'If we fire, it will give our position away. I suggest you leave it inside, Mr Wimbush.'

Wimbush shook his head. 'You're suggesting we go outside unarmed?'

'Not suggesting. Ordering.'

Wimbush gave Asher a look of pure disgust but leaned the crossbow against the table leg.

'Talk in whispers. Although the shield charm absorbs noise, it would be wise to remain stealthy. I will dim the lights so we can adapt to the darkness.' Asher blew out the lamp on the table and they were plunged into total darkness.

The door opened, and a cool wind rippled across Matt's skin

as a rectangle of silver light illuminated the exit. He inhaled and tasted the sharp tang of pine with a hint of far-off rain on its breath. Matt felt Wimbush knock his arm as the alchemist stumbled and kicked a chair leg with a loud scraping noise. He resisted the urge to chastise with great difficulty.

They stole across the cabin floor until they stood outside in dappled light. High above, the moon played hide-and-seek with fast-moving clouds. Asher had chosen well. From their vantage point they had a 180-degree view of the forest.

'Split up,' Asher ordered. 'Each of us takes a corner. Just observation. If you see anything, let the others know.'

Matt and Nadia took the rear of the cabin. From there the land rose on rocky ground. Squatting, Matt peered upwards to the dark outline of the hill against the sky. He supposed, later, that it was logical their followers might be using higher ground for its greater view, but it was on this irregular horizon that he spotted movement.

'Here,' he whispered. 'I think I see something.'

Asher was with him in a moment, with Nadia and then Wimbush close behind. Matt pointed, and they all looked. When the moon next appeared, Matt felt a numb horror grip him as the creature was revealed to them. It was too far away to make out any real detail, except for them all to know that it was not human. It squatted, its long snout pointing upwards, its horns sticking straight up from its head.

'What is that?' Wimbush hissed.

'Kulumkin,' Nadia said. 'Is kulumkin.'

'And what is a kulumkin?'

'A guardian of the forest spirits. He will move through you and make you evil. Or so they say.'

'Charming,' said Wimbush.

Above them, the horned beast turned its head this way and that, as if listening. And though the snout was long, Matt got the distinct impression that there was something faintly pig or bore-like about it.

'I do not believe in kulumkin,' said Nadia. Her voice sounded small in the darkness.

'Well, you'd better,' Wimbush said, 'since he's standing two hundred feet away.'

Nadia got up. 'All my life I have been told of such creatures. I am not afraid. I do not believe.'

Above them, the kulumkin stood on its back legs. It was tall, its legs and arms spindly, its head overlarge on its body. With practised ease, it began descending the slope.

'It's coming this way,' said Wimbush in a voice full, if not overflowing, with dread.

'Hold fast,' Asher said. 'Let it come.'

They watched the thing pick its way down the slope. Sure-footed between the rocks, it reached the base of the escarpment within a few minutes. It was now no more than thirty yards away.

'Let me get my crossbow,' Wimbush urged.

'It cannot see us,' said Asher.

The kulumkin raised its snout and tested the air. 'Maybe it can't see us or hear us, but can it smell us?' Matt asked.

'No.'

And then the thing raised its snout higher and let out a dreadful squeal, the like of which none of them had heard before. But even more terrifying was the distant screech that answered from somewhere deep in the forest.

'It is not alone,' said Wimbush.

'Really?' Matt said. 'Thanks for clarifying that because I might never have worked it out myself, given that the answering call came from the exact opposite bloody direction.'

Wimbush glared at him. But Matt's attention had never left the kulumkin. It was squatting, reaching out with its long arms, collecting what looked like branches.

'What's it doing?' Wimbush asked.

'Looks like it might be making a bonfire,' Matt said.

Within a few minutes the thing had amassed a reasonable collection of dead wood. They heard the crackle and spit before they saw the flame and the blue smoke rising into the cold night sky.

'Do kulumkin feel the cold?' Wimbush asked.

'They are meant to be supernatural beings,' Asher said. 'Cold will not affect them.'

'Then what's going on?'

The answer came quickly. The kulumkin stayed on its haunches, moving its arms in strange ways.

'The smoke,' said Asher.

They all saw it. The smoke was turning yellow and it was no longer rising but billowing out over the clearing, defying the light breeze that should be taking it away from them.

'This is dark wonderworking,' Nadia said.

The smoke rolled towards them over the ground, gathering speed.

'Is it poisonous?' Wimbush asked, his voice high with anxiety.

'I do not know,' Asher replied. 'But it cannot penetrate the shield charm.'

And it didn't. It struck the protective wall and curled around and over it.

'It's not meant to penetrate,' said Matt with grim realisation, already on his feet. 'It's a demarcation spell. It's showing them exactly where we are. We need to move, fast.'

Asher spoke loudly, '*Procido*!' and the cabin folded down and disappeared into its canvas bag. 'We go back into the woods,' he said. 'South to—'

But he never got to finish.

Nadia was already moving, running into the smoke.

'Nadia!' Asher yelled.

Matt tried to grab her, but she was too fast. He could see her legs under the smoke, pumping over the ground, and instinctively he followed. Nadia was a whippet. Matt heard shouts from behind and realised that Asher at least was following. He ran, horribly aware that at any moment he might trip and fall on a branch or a rock, his breath catching on the acrid smell of burning wood. Yet inside the smoke there seemed to be a sickly yellow glow as he desperately tried to follow Nadia. The glow, he realised was coming from the fire and it grew as they neared until without warning he emerged into cool clean air. The fire was to his left, popping and cracking some five yards away, but it wasn't the fire that drew Matt's incredulous eyes. It was the sight of Nadia wielding a thick branch and beating at a desperately backwards-scrambling kulumkin.

This was not a fair fight, for if the thing got to its feet it would tower over the girl. But she was strong and quick, had surprise on her side and had clearly taken it completely unaware. Its feet were huge and bare and definitely not trotter-like as they scrabbled back under Nadia's raining blows. Time after time she brought the branch down over the kulumkin's head and arm. Most of the blows were parried, but one slid past and struck the monster's head with a crunch. The snout bent sickeningly in response and the kulumkin shrieked in either pain or rage. It rolled out of range and started to rise. That was when Matt ran to the fire, plucked out a burning branch and stood shoulder to shoulder with Nadia, thrashing at the thing afresh.

It squealed again; a slaughterhouse screech. In the dancing light of the fire, its face was grotesque: small eyes, moss-covered horns and a hairy snout made uglier by the way it now tilted badly to the left. There were shouts from behind and Asher arrived, took one look and reached for a burning branch. It was too much for the kulumkin. It screamed again, turned on its front despite the blows, sprang upright and ran into the smoke.

Wimbush arrived just as the others were trying to recover their breath, hands on knees, barely able to speak.

'What did I miss?' Wimbush asked.

'Only everything,' panted Matt. He looked across at Nadia. 'What the hell possessed you do try such a bloody stupid—'

'I broke its snout with one blow. It makes fire. It is not a spirit.'

'What are you trying to say, Nadia?' Asher asked.

'A real kulumkin, it is said, could have turned me to dust with a look.'

'What exactly was that thing if it wasn't one?'

'Too tall to be a man,' Nadia said.

'But not too tall to be a Northern Wight,' Asher voiced what Matt was thinking.

'What's Northern Wight?' Wimbush asked.

'A tall, thin streak of urine,' Matt said.

'Urine can't walk or light a fire.'

'Figure of speech.'

Wimbush frowned while Asher took stock. 'We are now on the correct side of the clearing. It will be light in two hours. I suggest we ascend the escarpment, the way the kulumkin came. They will not expect us to continue in the dark.'

'And how are we supposed to navigate?' Wimbush asked.

Matt wanted to clout him one.

'From the way Nadia crossed that ground, I suspect she has excellent night vision, is that right?' Asher asked.

'In this moonlight, I can see very well.'

'Then you will be our guide. We stay close, within an arm's length. Nadia leads.'

'Sounds like a plan,' Matt said. What he didn't say as they set off was that he'd only ever met one Northern Wight in his life and meeting another one, if indeed that is what it was, in so short a time, could not have been mere chance.

On the other hand, there was another 'C' word that applied to both this situation, and, increasingly in Matt's head, to the one Wight they'd met at Blechern Holdings. But he was far too polite to say the word out loud even if it followed him all the way up the rocky climb to the top of the escarpment.

Once they reached the summit, a huge plain spread out before them. In the distance was the mountain Nadia had pointed out to them that morning, its snow-capped summit gleaming in the intermittent moonlight.

'It looks closer,' Asher said. 'How many miles?'

'No more than ten,' Nadia said.

'We could make that in a few hours,' Wimbush said.

'We could, but the safe way crosses two valleys. It is day and a half of walking.'

'What do you mean, the "safe way"?' Wimbush's radar was on full alert.

'There is another way. Across the roof of the valley in the barrels.'

'I don't think there is even one syllable of that sentence that I like,' Wimbush said.

'Shut up, Wimbush,' Matt said. 'Explain, Nadia.'

'We exchange goods across the valley. There are barrels that slide across the gorges. They are not meant to carry people.'

'There we are, then,' Wimbush said. 'That's a non-starter. And why are we standing here talking? We should be moving—'

'Do you think these barrels would take our weight, Nadia?'

'I have heard that sometimes a dog or once even an ass was transported.'

'In that case, there'll be no trouble sending Wimbush, will there,' Matt said.

Nadia looked at him and then smiled. 'You make joke?'

'Yes, I make joke,' Matt said.

'Which I did not find in the least bit amusing.' Wimbush scowled.

'No surprises there, then.'

Nadia giggled.

'Then it is the barrels for us,' Asher said. 'Nadia, will you take the lead again?'

'This is madness,' Wimbush said and stayed put.

'No, madness is trekking up and down two valleys while those kulumkin, or whatever they are, regroup and come after us. Because they will come after us. Now, are you coming, or would you like to stay here and be the welcoming party?'

Wimbush's expression was unreadable in the dark. Both Matt and Asher thought they heard a slight moan.

CHAPTER THIRTY

THEY'D BEEN WALKING for around an hour when Nadia came to an abrupt halt.

'Listen,' she said.

They all heard it. Carried on the wind, faint but unmistakable, the kulumkin's bestial screech somewhere behind them.

'They wish to let us know they are following,' Nadia said. 'They wish to frighten us.'

'They're doing a bloody good job,' Matt said.

For once, Wimbush stayed silent.

It got colder as they climbed. The previous day's downhill yomp had long been cancelled out as they wound along the foothills of the craggy range. Patchy snow soon gave way to swathes of white in the shadow of the taller crags and hollows where the sun could not breathe its warmth during daylight.

Nadia pushed them onwards and the men remained totally dependent on her as a guide. The wind had picked up as they ascended and now gusted around them, driving icy flakes of snow into their faces. At last, Nadia turned away from the open mountainside into a more sheltered narrow gap. There she paused and shouted above the wind. 'It will be even more exposed when we reach the landing stage. The wind will carry our voices. We must talk here.'

'Talk about what?' Matt asked.

'Who will go first to test the lines because I do not know when it was last used. It may be that this is the first time since winter. We will need to feed the first barrel across and then, once on the other side, that person can help.'

'The barrels are fixed on the rope that runs continuously through pulleys, is that how it works?' Matt asked.

'It is,' said Nadia.

'Cable car principle,' Matt nodded. 'I'll go first.'

Asher started to say something but one look from Matt cut the words off before they could gather speed.

'You need to stay here to supervise and I'm sure Wimbush won't volunteer.'

The alchemist looked at them both with dinner plate eyes.

'Nadia is the lightest,' Matt continued, 'but you're going to need her if anything should happen.'

The silence that followed was punctuated only by the wind howling through the crags, periodically rising to a high-pitched whistle like some demented football referee.

'Let's get on with it,' Asher said.

They climbed another thirty feet and emerged onto a stone ledge with a wooden gantry above and a deck below. The snow had blown clear of the decking beneath their feet. At the edge was a single post supporting a pulley and rope. Beyond that was only darkness and the impression of a very, very long drop beyond. The gantry looked solid enough: thick oak posts and purlins supporting an enclosed housing in which, Matt surmised, sat the large wheel. From the open side of this housing two ropes extended out into the darkness. Another rope, again a single loop crusted with ice, was tied to the largest oak beam at hip height. The barrels were stacked in a tidy pile behind another wooden barrier to their left.

Nadia took charge. She undid the thinner loop of rope and started pulling. Nothing happened. She called for help and Matt and Asher started yanking, too. After a couple of minutes' effort and with an unhealthy sound of ripping as the ice crust surrounding the wheel finally cracked, the wheel began to turn and the ropes extending from the wheel housing began to run.

'Let's hope that was just ice,' Asher said.

The barrels were reinforced by metal hoops, the uppermost forged to large clip hooks. Now that the rope had begun to move, Nadia kept pulling until a section of rope bearing two small nooses came into view. She clipped these loops to the barrel and looked up into Matt's face.

'How far to the other side?' he asked her.

'Three hundred yards,' Nadia said.

'When I'm on the other side and I can pull rope it all gets a bit quicker, right?'

Nadia nodded.

'But this first run will be slower. Let's see, one pull every five seconds. Two to three yards every pull. About fifteen minutes of pulling, I reckon.' Matt kept on talking as he manoeuvred the barrel to the edge of the platform and lifted up the barrier.

Asher offered his shoulder as support as Matt climbed into the barrel.

'This is madness,' Wimbush said from ten yards away.

'If you have any better ideas, we'd all be delighted to hear them,' Asher said. Matt couldn't tell if his teeth were clenched from anger or the cold.

Then he was in the barrel. It felt sturdy enough.

'All hands,' Asher called to Wimbush to assist with the hauling. It took one good pull and Matt felt the world sway drunkenly as his weight was taken by the rope and he swung free. Above him, the moon and clouds; below him, nothing. But the rope was holding.

'Go for it,' he yelled.

And then he was moving, lurching every five seconds into the darkness and the wind, feeling the weight sag on the line as gradually he moved further and further out. If he fell now…best not to think of it. He might be lucky and the rope might break on one side and he'd swing back against the rocks. Yeah, really lucky to have his bones crushed against the mountain rather than plummet all the way to the bottom. Of course, he might be really, really lucky and find a giant eagle under him to break the fall. But that sort of thing only happened in Middle Earth.

He tried to keep count of the lurching movements but gave up after seventy or so. Almost halfway across by his calculation. Probably the highest point, though he had no way of proving that. If he did fall, he wondered what Asher would say to Kylah.

Wondered how she'd react.

Would she insist on being brought here to this forsaken corner of beyond to see if she could resurrect his shattered bones? Would she try and get him mended so he could become a zombie shadow of himself? He'd heard about that sort of thing being done in this world. Done and always regretted.

He wouldn't want that.

The next time he saw her, he'd tell her that. He'd even try not to make a joke of it for once. But, if he fell, there would not be a next time.

He'd missed her since moving to New Thameswick and the realisation of that struck him now like a cold slap. It would not have been so bad except for this stupid time shift, which meant they basically only crossed on the stairs when he made it back to Oxford or she made the rare trips to New Thameswick. Mind you, they did try and cram quite a bit into those meetings on the stairs and it was surprising what use you could make of landings. It would all be so much better after the equinox.

The rope jerked and then became still for several seconds.

Wimbush needing a pee?

After a count of fifty, it started moving again and Matt got the impression that he was drifting up slightly. It was pure spatial awareness because the night rendered him blind unless…yes, unless that was a snow-covered crag he was seeing off to his right. Difficult to judge distances, but it was getting nearer. And then he could see it clearly. Not just a crag but a gantry and… yes, the landing platform. He had to lean over and undo the safety barrier and drag himself up the last foot or so because the weight of the barrel took it below the decking, but despite his freezing fingers, he succeeded, and the barrel scraped up and onto the platform, tilted and spilled him out.

He wanted to shout but he knew he could not be heard. He unclipped the barrel, unhooked the pull rope and hauled until the retaining loops had gone through the wheel. They surely would have felt the change in weight? He rehooked the barrel and placed a water bottle inside; their agreed signal for successful transit. Then he got on the rope again and began to haul. This time the barrel moved quickly. Ten minutes later, when he tried hauling, there was no weight at all. They'd obviously unhooked the barrel on the other side.

Matt waited and saw the running ropes sag a little. Someone else was coming. This time, when he pulled, the rope moved much more slowly. He realised that they could end up working

against one another and so he waited until there was no movement and then pulled. Soon they'd established a rhythm and,
some eight minutes later, the barrel appeared out of the darkness
with Wimbush, his face white with terror, clutching on to the
rims.

Nadia's passage was the easiest. Which left only Asher.

'We'll have him over in a jiffy,' Matt said as he helped
Nadia out.

'We must hurry. They are close. They call to us. Their cry is
aimed to terrify.'

There was no arguing with that. Matt got Wimbush on the
haul and they worked in tandem, pulling alternately. They'd
been working for almost twelve minutes when there was a
sudden resistance and the rope froze and alarmingly began to
move in the opposite direction.

'They've switched gears,' Matt said. 'Quick, there must be a
brake somewhere.' He ran to the edge of the platform and put
both hands around his mouth to shout. 'Asher, can you hear me?'

Asher's voice came back on the wind. 'I can't see you, but I
can hear you.'

'They've locked the runner. I don't know what they've got
planned, but I suggest you get out of the barrel and climb the
rest of the way.'

Silence.

'Asher?'

'I will do that.'

Above him, Matt saw the rope start to quiver. It reminded
him of a spider on its web waiting for the vibration that told it
prey was at hand. And then, even as he looked, a second sag in
the rope sent it down another couple of feet.

Nadia was at his side. 'What is that?' she asked, following his
gaze.

'If I were a betting man, I'd say someone else was on the
rope further across.'

The rope was dancing now, quivering violently.

'Asher, get a move on.'

'I am trying.' Asher's voice sounded strained.

Matt stood on the platform, peering into the darkness. Time
seemed to slow down. He stood there for many minutes until, at
last, a shape appeared. Dark at first and then settling into a pale

oval as Asher's upside-down body appeared, clambering hand over hand towards them. He'd sensibly tied a bit of rope around himself and the line for safety.

'Nice to see you,' Matt said, grinning when he was three yards away.

'Likewise,' said Asher.

Nadia looked from one to the other and shook her head. Matt reached forward and grabbed his friend's coat and pulled. A moment later he was standing on the platform, safe at last, but still with a rope around his waist and looped around the zip line. Asher's face shone with sweat in the moonlight.

'All that rope-climbing in the school gym finally paid off, eh?' Matt said.

'Indeed.' Asher leaned forward to catch his breath. 'I would not want to do that too many times.'

'The one and only, mate.' He turned to Nadia. 'Have to say this was a good call, Nad—'

The girl in question wasn't there. She was over on the gantry at the wheel housing, madly chopping at the exposed rope with an axe.

'What are you doing?' Matt cried.

'Arachghoul,' Nadia grunted.

Matt wheeled around and so did Asher. Neither of them said or did anything for several seconds as their minds tried to work out exactly what their eyes were seeing. It wasn't a spider, but neither was it a man. If anything, it had bent and angular limbs that had more in common with the kulumkin than anything, but it was the speed with which it travelled along the rope that momentarily paralysed both men. It sat on top, six limbs moving with practiced speed, gobbling up the distance. Nadia's chopping seemed to galvanise it and it screeched in anger. Its pale face upturned, its many eyes glinting in the moonlight.

Matt knew he should go and help Nadia but he couldn't move.

'Do not look at it!' Nadia yelled. 'Do not stare.'

But it was mesmerising. The movement so strange and powerful. Matt simply could not drag his eyes away.

Somewhere far away, Matt heard Nadia hit the rope with a huge grunt of effort. It was followed by an echoing thud and a long accelerating slithering sound. Next to him, Asher fell backwards as the heavy rope still looped through his temporary sling fell upon him like a writhing snake. Matt grabbed Asher's sling and tore it off as the rope rattled along the wooden platform, its weight dragging it down and out into blackness. He looked up in time to see the thing on the zip line leap. But it was still fifteen yards out over the chasm and already falling on the cut rope when it did. With a screech and a terrible flailing of limbs, it pivoted in the air and plummeted down into the darkness and the valley floor below.

When Matt looked up, Nadia was descending the gantry, axe in hand. Above her, Wimbush was also climbing down. He held a machete in his right hand.

Asher said, 'Thank you. Both of you.'

Matt shuddered. It was not from the cold. It was from his realisation of not having told Kylah just how much he missed her and the fear he had now of how close he'd come to not ever getting the chance to do just that. He hoped she was safe and cosy back in Oxford.

It would have been good to phone her, or text her, but there was no signal in New Thameswick. So, despite his swirling thoughts, all he managed say was, 'I'd like to get away from this place and never, ever come back here again.'

From the expressions he read on the others' faces, the feeling was mutual.

PART 4

CHAPTER THIRTY-ONE

MERTHYR, WALES, 500-ish AD

What sleep Kylah got was fitful and disturbed. She dreamt she was in the sinkhole alone in complete darkness. Yet somewhere, beyond sight, she could hear something moving. A quick, scurrying noise, the scrabbling of claws and sometimes what might have been a titter. She wanted to wake up, to welcome in the light, but exhaustion tethered her to unconsciousness. And so, she endured in the darkness, discomfited and fearful until the titter became louder and changed into the morning call of a jackdaw. When she opened her eyes, Bobby was already up.

'They brought us some fruit. I've washed it. The apples are really good.'

Stretching, Kylah got up, drank some water and contemplated the apple. There was some wisdom, conventional or otherwise, that suggested that if time travel were possible and the traveller did one small thing that changed the timeline, everything else would change from then on. She knew about this, it was a serious hypothesis. One that should have been termed something like the Armageddon scenario. The butterfly effect didn't quite hack it for Kylah. Theoretically, according to the boffins at the university, anyone caught in such a scenario should do nothing and wait to be rescued. But she was starving, and

Bobby had thrown caution to the wind and neither of them had disappeared as a result. So…

'Sod it,' Kylah said, and ate some apple. 'How did you sleep?'

'Weirdly. I slept well, but I had the most awful dreams.'

Kylah nodded. 'Me too. Do you think this is what their sleep's been like?'

'I asked the girl who brought the food. They call it cwsgddu, dark sleep. They've had it since the Nosdrwg infested the caves and pits.'

'What do you mean, infested?'

'They're everywhere, apparently. Anywhere there's shadow and no sun. And they bring bats with them. Big ugly things.'

'Lovely,' Kylah said. 'I love bats.'

'But only when they're deep fried with chips, I know.' Bobby grinned and then her expression froze as she realised what she'd just said.

'I don't suppose there's a loo, is there?'

'There's a hole in the ground at the back of the encampment. Take some lavender for your nose.' Bobby held up some dried flowers.

Cei and Bedwyr came for them a little while later.

'The king and his sister await us. Ready, are you?'

'As I'll ever be,' Kylah said.

They walked out into the grey morning. It was not raining but the bruised colour of the clouds in the west held little promise of improvement. Kylah was glad she'd worn layers as a chilly breeze followed them across the rough ground to the cave. Arthur, Morgana and Myrddin stood at the entrance. A posse of a dozen knights waited with wary expressions, watching everything.

'Well met,' Arthur said. 'I trust you rested?' The king drew himself up, but he, like his knights, had dark smudges under his eyes from exhaustion.

'I slept but my dreams were less than pleasant.'

'The cwsgddu is a treacherous respite, is it not? You will understand why we must get rid of its cause.'

Kylah nodded.

Myrddin stepped forward. 'When we enter the cave, we will

leave a portion unlit. No more than an arm-span wide. You can enter but do not do so for long. There will be people near at all times.'

'What could possibly go wrong,' Bobby said with a fixed grin.

'No need to be frightened, Bobby. I'll be there,' Morgana replied.

Bobby gave her a wan smile. 'I've just been comforted by the mother of all sorceresses.'

Morgana pointed to herself and mouthed, 'Me?'

Bobby nodded.

'Aww,' Morgana said.

Myrddin cleared his throat. 'Remember, what you will see and feel is not real. Time has no meaning. However, there are other creatures in the caves. The stlym sleep during the day, but if they are disturbed, they will leave.'

'You mean the bats?' Bobby asked.

Arthur nodded. 'We fear that their bite is poisonous. If, therefore, a disturbance occurs, we will leave immediately, understood?'

Both Kylah and Bobby nodded.

'Good,' Arthur said. 'Then we should commence.'

The knights went first, holding their smoking torches high for maximum light. They followed the path they'd taken the day before into the chamber where they'd both first encountered Arthur and his men. It was much darker this morning, with the sun barely up in the east, on the wrong side of the entrance.

There they stopped for Myrddin to whisper, 'From this point onward, we will be in Nosdrwg territory. We are here to allow our champions to understand the enemy. I will accompany Kylah, Morgana will accompany Bobby. We will be tethered with a rope leading back to this point anchored to our knights.'

Cei and Bedwyr raised a hand and brought forward ropes and tied tight knots around Kylah and Bobby's waists and gave the other ends to their chaperones.

'Morgana and I have protected ourselves against the worst of the Nosdrwg's evil. This will not be the case for you two. We will stay for but a short while. And though the king is with us, I have counselled against him entering the cave.'

Preparations made, Myrddin led Kylah into the cavern, away

from the group of anxious soldiers surrounding a tense-looking Arthur.

They turned a slight bend. 'This, I know, will be far enough. Now we must gain darkness,' Myrddin said.

A rancid ammoniacal smell hit Kylah's nostrils.

'Wait,' said Bobby. She took another half dozen steps, Morgana, also bearing a lamp, at her side. Bobby pointed up to the cavern roof. 'Are those the stlym?'

Morgana held up her lamp. Above them and halfway down one of the walls hundreds of bats hung from their nesting places, jostling and nudging one another in their sleep. Below them sat a small hill of guano.

Kylah shuddered. She knew well enough that they probably carried all sorts of diseases. Myrddin and Arthur had reason enough to consider their bites poisonous. What immediately sprang to Kylah's mind were those stalwarts of viral misery: rabies, Marburg and Ebola. She knew instantly, too, what Bobby would say if she spoke these thoughts out loud. Rabies, Marburg and Ebola; worst name for a law firm, ever.

She smiled. Gallows humour. She couldn't avoid it, not when she spent so much time with Matt and Bobby. It was the best form of release when you were in a tight spot; though release, when it came to thinking about gallows, might have a different connotation if you were the one standing on top of the trap door wearing a hemp cravat.

And then there was the other thing with the bats. These were not vampire bats but the association was hardwired in both women since they'd recently experienced a vampire encounter that had left them significantly traumatised. So seeing the stlym brought back some highly unwelcome recollections.

'You thinking what I'm thinking?' Bobby asked.

'Very probably.'

'Fangs for the memories, eh?'

Kylah had time to groan before Myrddin said, 'Steady your-selves. The darkness comes.'

He leaned in to the lamp and Kylah saw him blow. Morgana did the same.

The passage was plunged into total darkness. It might have been the loss of vision that made Kylah more aware, but suddenly it felt as if the temperature dropped a good ten degrees.

For several seconds, there was nothing to see or hear other than the absence of sight and sound. But then Kylah became aware of a faint stirring, a movement in the still air, a suggestion of sound far away. Her ears buzzed as if from straining to hear. She was on the point of turning to Myrddin, or at least where she though the mage might be because it was impossible to see him in this dense blackness, to say to him that nothing was happening, when a face appeared to her. It came slowly out of the darkness as if through a murky window. Recognition made her breath catch in her throat.

'Matt? Matt, is that you?'

And then she was seeing him with Asher and two other people she had never met atop some wild and windswept mountain. He was looking out and down into the void beyond an icy wooden platform.

Looking out towards her.

'Matt? Matt, can you hear me?'

But he showed no sign of knowing she was there. Kylah pondered what it was she was seeing. Something from Matt's past? But not if he was with Asher? Was this their here and now? Bobby had told her that the men had set off on some sort of expedition. A tiny bleat of astonishment escaped her throat as she blinked in befuddlement at how any of this was possible. Yet there was little solace to be found in Matt's white and strained face. This was not a nightmare. Okay, there was no communication, but seeing him alive and with Asher gave her a surge of hope. There was a moment to wonder at how Myrddin and Arthur had got things so wrong. Perhaps the Nosdrwg effect worked differently for some people. Perhaps—

Her analytical thoughts froze as the scene in front of her shifted and pulled back. Matt stood at the end of the wooden platform, his hands on the barriers. He turned and called something back to Asher who smiled and beckoned away towards some steps leading into the mountain. Matt turned to follow. He'd gone three yards when a monstrous leg, covered in bristling hairs and ending in razor-sharp claws, emerged from the abyss, its segmented joints clicking ominously as it reached out to ensnare the hapless Matt.

Kylah heard herself scream a pantomime warning. 'It's behind you!'

The appendage's movement was incisive and deliberate as it clamped powerfully around Matt's leg. He stumbled and fell to one knee, looking down in surprise. He had time only to call a warning to Asher before the appendage whipped him out and over the edge of the platform and into the dark void.

CHAPTER THIRTY-TWO

Kylah screamed and lurched forward, but instead, she stumbled as her movement reversed. She was being pulled backwards, her feet quick-stepping, while her arms flailed desperately forwards in a hopeless attempt at clutching at Matt in the image in front of her. And then there was light. Flickering yellow from torches and candles. Kylah blinked. She was outside the cave, and Cei and Myrddin had the rope in their hands.

'Are you back with us, Kylah?' King Arthur put a hand on her shoulder.

Tears streaming, Kylah nodded. She fumbled for a tissue, found none, and wiped her face in her sleeve.

'We will not ask you to share your experience. Your terror is your own,' Myrddin said.

'Tell me it isn't real?' Kylah grabbed Myrddin in a fierce grip.

'Some of it is real. The Nosdrwg can mould reality, show you things that seem impossible and so real that it is unnatural to think of it as anything other than the truth. But that is its power. Some of it is true. But all of it is not.'

Kylah sucked in air through her nostrils and squeezed her eyes shut to block out the image. A fresh scream made her snap them open again. Bedwyr was tugging hard on his rope. In the mouth of the cavern Morgana was fighting with a wild animal that had once been Bobby. Cei went to help her and they managed to subdue her struggles until Myrddin threw some powder under her nose and her eyes snapped open and she sucked in air in a huge gulp.

'Drowning, I was drowning. Black oil…the Sambolith in the cupboard.'

Her words made little sense to anyone except Kylah, who knew that this nightmare, too, had enough reality in it to make it a horror close to Bobby's bones, and therefore all the more terrifying. Kylah moved forward and held Bobby tight, finding as much comfort in the embrace as she hoped she might impart.

'It's okay. It's okay. It's gone.'

Bobby was shuddering, unable to speak.

'Come,' said Arthur. 'Let us away from this place of evil.'

They helped the women away from the entrance. As soon as the hazy sunlight hit her, Kylah felt the horror begin to lift. By the time they were back at the encampment, Bobby was able to walk without a supporting arm.

'Morgana has a potion that will help,' Arthur said. 'I will leave you for a while. I suggest we talk in an hour.'

Cei and Bedwyr stood guard at the door. It was all Kylah and Bobby could do to throw themselves on their straw beds and lie there until Morgana came back with two wooden cups full of a gently steaming greenish liquid. The sorceress sat on a stool and waited while the women sipped her potion. It tasted of blackberry and elderflower and cut grass, and once it hit her stomach, a great balloon of warmth began to spread out from Kylah's abdomen up into her chest and down her arms. It was like jumping into a cool lake on a hot day, but in reverse.

'I threw in a revivin' charm,' Morgana said as Kylah mumbled how good it was for the second time.

After half the cup had gone, Kylah felt strong enough to talk. 'That was the most horrible thing I have ever experienced.'

Morgana nodded. 'It hits some people so badly they never recover. Quite a few have given up. Hung themselves, thrown themselves in the lake. This Saicson necromancer is a real sod. Makes you believe that life is not worth living. That's what made me invent the reviver potion. It seems to help.'

Kylah looked at Bobby. They dropped their eyes at the same time. One day they might be able to talk about what they'd encountered in that cave. But that time wasn't now.

'Your potion is amazing,' Bobby said. 'You'll have to give me the recipe.'

Morgana beamed.

'But how do we even begin to stop these things?' Kylah asked. 'What do we actually know about them?'

'Myrddin has told me they were once a tribe, living people like us. It is said that they once were marauders who, staring defeat in the face, agreed terms of peace. But they broke their promise and lured the men away from a village, only to kill all the young and innocent women and children that remained. A mage, a predecessor of Myrddin's, punished the marauders by casting them into a twilight existence, locking them into the rock of the earth where they feed on fear and the droppings of the stlym.

'Wow, that's a mage you wouldn't want to cross,' Bobby said. She took another healthy swallow of Morgana's potion.

'Now the Saicson necromancer has woken them to haunt out dreams.'

'Dirty tactics,' Kylah said. 'So, do we try and fight these Nosdrwg or should we go after the necromancer?'

Neither of those options seemed to galvanize Morgana. 'We have no weapons against the Nosdrwg. They hide in the rock. They have no flesh. And the necromancer never appears in the flesh. He walks in places we could never travel. He summoned the Nosdrwg with the promise of fresh victims. They came unwillingly, but their anger is now aimed at their prey. Our people.'

'Perhaps we're thinking about this the wrong way,' Bobby said and earned identically quizzical looks from the other two women. 'Before the Samb…before they tapped into my worst nightmare, I saw something really weird,' Bobby said. 'I saw something collecting the droppings. A hand reaching out of the cave wall.'

'That's sickening,' Kylah said.

'Yes, it is,' she agreed. 'But if they really have been cursed to exist on bat poo, maybe we could make use of that?'

'I'm listening,' Kylah added warily. Some of Bobby's ideas since arriving in the fifth century had been so off the wall as to be on the ceiling.

'Well, the bats must eat something, right? Most bats eat

insects. These bats aren't native to this part of Britain, by the look of them. I mean, they're way too big. So they must forage.' She aimed a look squarely at Morgana. 'You have horses and horses make dung, right?'

'Every day,' Morgana agreed.

'And how are you on mushrooms? I presume you know about the good ones?'

Morgana dropped her chin and gave Bobby a look. '*Madarch hud*.'

'*Psilocybe cubensis*, aka magic mushrooms.'

'And in three different languages, too,' Kylah observed.

'Bear with,' Bobby said. 'Mushrooms like horse dung, especially mixed with a bit of straw for aeration.'

'How do you know—'

'That's how they do it commercially,' Bobby said. 'Don't you ever watch *Darkson's Farm?*'

'How is it that you know so much lore, Bobby?' Morgana stared at her, knowing nothing at all about *Darkson's Farm*.

'Okay, full disclosure. I once had a month's convalescence after severe tonsillitis, a very good broadband connection and a friend who wanted to go camping in the woods. Naturally, I did some research. The internet is a repository for all sorts, crap included.'

'Such a repository must smell very bad,' Morgana observed.

'Sometimes it stinks. Especially kitten videos.'

'I'll drink to that,' Kylah nodded.

'We also had a magic mushroom club in uni. If only I'd known then what I know now, we would have called it *madarch hud* and no one would have been any the wiser. Anyhoo, mushrooms like dung, and flies like dung. Bats feed on flies, especially juicy bluebottles who have a special thing for dung. So we find some *madarch hud*, mix it in with horse poo—and since mushrooms grow in dung it will not appear odd to the flies or to the bats—and pile it at the entrance to the cave near a warm brazier to help it…brew.'

Morgana and Kylah said nothing.

'Oh my God. Do the maths,' Bobby exclaimed. 'The flies will feast on the dung, load up on psilocybin and will be sluggish enough to get eaten by the bats who generally don't want to be chasing after stuff that's too quick. The bats' guano might then become very…interesting.'

'You think we can drug the Nosdrwg?' Kylah asked.

'I know how it sounds,' Bobby's voice went up a couple of notches. 'But, I mean, look around. Is it any stranger than,' she waved a hand, 'all this? I think it's worth a try. I mean, mushrooms and cow crap flavoured with added hallucinogenic. What's not to like?'

'I think I had some crisps with that flavour once. Somewhere that was a contender for most pretentious gastropub of the year,' Kylah said, the corner of her mouth twitching up. She was warming to Bobby's idea. Admittedly, it was largely because it was the only idea on the table, but it was so bizarre as to be almost brilliant.

'Yes.' Bobby was grinning. 'I like it because it'll literally send them bat-shit crazy. There is a precedent, of course. I mean, people say that civet coffee is the best in the world.'

'What is civet coffee?' Morgana asked.

'A drink made out of a bean that has been eaten by a cat,' Bobby said.

'Do they kill the cat to then get the bean?' Morgana asked.

'No,' Bobby said. 'They wait for nature to take its course and collect the beans in the droppings. Wash it, roast it and then grind it up and drink it.'

'Has this tribe been cursed, too?' Morgana asked.

'Only by decadence and too much disposable income,' Bobby said with a fixed grin.

Morgana grinned. 'You are well versed in the cunning, Bobby.'

Bobby shrugged.

'Whatever was in that sinkhole seems to have sent your brain into hyperdrive,' Kylah said.

'Will you teach me more of this natural science, Bobby?' Morgana asked.

'Of course, I will,' Bobby gushed.

'I definitely think your magic mushroom plan is worth a try,' Kylah said. 'If we can get these Nosdrwg to mellow out, they may forget to be such utter bastards.'

'Then I will get Cei and Bedwyr on dung duty and *madarch hud* collection.' Morgana grinned. 'They'll hate it.'

By late morning, they had a plan. The knights were sent in with blazing torches to shovel out the existing guano and wake up the stlym. The dung/mushrooms mulch was piled at the cave entrance and a fire lit to heat up the space and encourage bluebottles. By the time it was all done, it was early evening.

Kylah was glad of all the activity because it meant there had been moments when she had not had to think of that terrible image of Matt being dragged off the mountain by some awful… thing. Now, when she did think of it, it was with the knowledge that it had the quality of a nightmare rather than the truth, though it took a great deal of effort to convince herself of that fact.

It was all she could do while she waited for the onset of night.

CHAPTER THIRTY-THREE

THE NORTHERN SARMATIC FOREST OF STEPPEINIT

THE DESCENT from the barrel line tower was hard going, but knowing that they were not being followed, at least not directly, brought a welcome sense of relief to Matt. As dawn broke, they dipped back into the tree line again and followed Nadia as she led them through the arboreal labyrinth. The forest was a sea of green, the huge trees rendering the landscape featureless. The scent of pine was strong and had spawned a small cottage industry for the people in the slightly more populated areas of Steppeinit. Young branches were often snipped to form minia-ture three-inch-tall Yuletide tree shapes and attached to piece of string so as to dangle upright and provide wafts of scent in outhouses or carriages. The success of these fresheners resulted in a whole slew of alternatives such as Orange Zest from Fitsot and Freshly Laundered Linen from Tings. Less successful was the heritage range from a New Thameswick apiary who decided to try and bottle their pollen range. Unfortunately for them, Bee Eau de Toilette proved not to be a huge seller.

Wimbush, however, seemed in his element, stopping occa-sionally to fondle a fern or stare at a fungus. And although they sounded like they should be, neither of those activities were arrestable offences, which was more than could be said for his hat.

At last, pine gave way to deciduous forest.

It was too early in the season for foliage and the dark branches were stark against the pale sky, while the footfall crunch of the previous autumn's desiccated leaf fall added a weird percussion to their travels. They stopped only to drink, but when they did Nadia seemed uneasy and unwilling to tarry, constantly glancing the way they had come; a guileless barometer of their group anxiety.

The sun stayed hidden, the temperature cold. Everyone was hungry and exhausted. When Nadia called a halt at last, Matt was walking on autopilot and was startled to see that before them stood a wooden fence.

'Beyond is village,' Nadia said and began gathering branches and constructing a makeshift ladder.

'Is there no doorway or gate?' Asher asked.

Nadia shook her head. 'No need for gate. No one leaves or enters.'

Asher frowned but didn't comment.

Matt volunteered to go first and as his head crested the rough wooden barrier, he paused to look at what they had come all this way to find. It was hardly inspiring. The village was a cluster of dirt streets radiating out from a central square. The buildings, too, were simple. Single story, some of whitewashed stone, others of uneven clapperboard. All had small windows with shutters. Goats wandered across the meadow that surrounded the village like a flattened lake of green. Beyond, in every direction, were the woods. The dense, imposing, unwelcoming woods.

But to the north leading out of the village stretched a wide path.

'Where does that go?' Asher asked.

'That is road to Gathering,' Nadia answered.

'Gathering? What's Gathering?' Wimbush frowned.

'It is our duty,' Nadia said.

There was no opportunity to ask her anything else because a shout rang out from where the goats were being herded. A boy, perhaps no more than eleven, looked across and immediately began to yell and bang on the door of the nearest house.

'What's he doing?' Matt asked.

'Sounding alarm,' said Nadia simply. 'We are danger.'

'Indeed,' said Asher. 'Then let us be dangerous together. Come Nadia, follow Matt.'

As if in response, doors opened in at least half a dozen of the little houses and out poured men. One ran to a bell tower and, in the stillness of the early afternoon, sonorous tones began to ring out. More men appeared. Some of them clutched farming implements as weapons. There were scythes, pitchforks, even shovels. All of them looked capable of inflicting injury. All of the men looked scared.

They stood in a huddled group while some sort of activity took place behind the leading line. And then a gap appeared and through it walked men in dark cassocks, all wearing strange expressionless masks on their faces. The little procession came towards the expedition who, with Asher in the lead, walked slowly forwards to meet them.

'Who are the blokes with the masks?' Matt asked Nadia.

'Aldermen.'

'Surely not. I can see a few others without masks in the background.'

This caused Nadia to halt and look at Matt with a pained expression. 'You make funny joke?'

'That's questionable,' muttered Asher.

Matt gave Nadia a lopsided grin. 'Puns are one of my specialties.'

'Could have fooled me,' Wimbush sighed.

Nadia, though, had not moved. 'Why you make joke? Aldermen are very serious.'

'Jokes about being serious are usually the best kind. Nothing like seeing people with no sense of humour struggling to come to terms with having the air taken out of their tyres.' Matt turned and grinned at Wimbush, who simply frowned, as if he'd been given an imponderable problem to ponder.

Nadia nodded. 'Aldermen,' she repeated. A smile flickered into existence.

'Don't encourage him,' Asher said.

Their little pause had given time for the village procession to arrive at a spot some twenty yards from where they stood, farm implements at the ready. A man stepped forward. Nadia acted as translator.

'What business do you have here?' Dalibor asked.

Asher smiled. 'The business of coming to see you. We have a guide, one of your own.' He motioned towards Nadia.

'This woman is no longer a member of our village. She has been cast out.'

'Bit harsh,' Matt said.

Once Nadia had delivered Matt's criticism, Dalibor threw him a glance that might have been angry, or even scathing, but behind the mask it was impossible to tell. 'You have no business here. Leave and you will come to no harm.'

'I'm afraid that will not be possible,' Asher said, squaring his shoulders. 'Not until we have answers to certain questions.'

'What is it you seek? Are you spies from Butholenbittsch? We will never give up our recipe for the best goat cheese in the mountains. Never! Or do you wish to steal from us the secret ingredient we add to water buffalo yoghurt? Or perhaps you would like to pilfer the best way to keep wolves from depositing on the cabbages? Many have tried to wrestle these secrets from us, but none have succeeded.'

'Did he really say "depositing on the cabbages"?' Matt whispered to Nadia.

'Very well,' Asher said. 'Tell him none of the above. Tell him we have been chased all over the mountains, we are tired and hungry, and we will pay for food and shelter.'

Nadia told Dalibor all of that and a bit more. The aldermen stayed resolute.

She turned and translated for Asher: 'We may not enter.'

'But we already have,' Matt said.

'We must go back into the woods.'

Matt shook his head and addressed Dalibor directly. 'Oh dear. Did you know that where we are from, refusing entry to weary backpackers and sending them back into the woods is considered extremely poor form and likely to bring the very worst kind of bad luck on the banisher?'

Nadia translated. On hearing the words 'bad luck', the aldermen turned to look at one another.

'In fact,' Matt went on, 'keeping them waiting whilst they're thirsty and footsore usually results in at least a pestilence.'

The aldermen murmured.

'And woe betide not offering them fresh water and some

goat's cheese. That's avalanche and landslide territory if ever there was one.'

Dalibor turned to his expressionless little gaggle and conferred before speaking.

'Nadia Komangetme may not enter the village. She has already cursed us with her blasphemy,' Nadia said.

'Ah, but refusing entry to an interpreter trumps blasphemy by a plague of frogs.' Matt was on a roll.

Nadia coughed to smother the laugh that threatened and delivered the message.

Dalibor started. Once again, the aldermen conferred. 'Very well,' he said finally through Nadia. 'But I may not talk to a goat, pick a flower with my left hand, laugh at a pregnant woman or lift my sleeve with my index finger.'

Asher turned to Nadia. 'Think you can manage that?'

Nadia nodded.

'Then we're all set.'

Dalibor nodded and spoke again to Nadia in serious tones. She translated. 'He says we are to follow in single file and we are not to speak. He will take us to the meeting house where we must sit without crossing our legs and eat only with a spoon given to us by a girl.'

'What happens if we don't?' Wimbush asked.

Nadia conveyed the question.

Dalibor answered, Nadia interpreted. 'Then the witch will skin you alive for disobeying her.'

'I think I am in a waking nightmare,' said Wimbush with weary resignation.

CHAPTER THIRTY-FOUR

SPIV

THEY FOLLOWED Dalibor and the other aldermen to the meeting house: a long low building with chairs in rows and a table at the front. They threw off their packs and sat. Wimbush attempted a leg cross, remembered just in time and ended up doing an air scissors which almost sent him toppling. Some village girls appeared with water, soup and bread. The soup had nothing but long strings of cabbage in it, but it was hot and peppery, and they all ate with gusto. The white-aproned girls, every one of them with astonishingly blue scle-rae, sent Matt and Asher shy glances and Nadia the odd hostile glare.

Half an hour later, several men appeared, this time without masks. Nadia introduced the bearded Dalibor, who addressed them, once again using Nadia as interpreter.

But Asher held up his hand to stop him and burrowed into his backpack. 'Linguaplugs,' he said, handing them around to everyone including Dalibor, who eyed it suspiciously before finally fitting it to his ear.

'This way at least we can talk face to face,' Asher said.

Dalibor flinched. 'Face to face risks incurring the wrath of the Wereboar. We should stand at least a foot to the left of each other during any conversation.'

'It's just an express…Never mind. I speak for my friends when I say that we are grateful for your hospitality.'

'We offer it so as not to incur the misfortune that not offering it might cause.'

'Right,' said Asher with the kind of smile he reserved for the terminally convoluted. 'We are grateful nevertheless. We have travelled far for this meeting and it has not been easy, what with being chased by Wights.'

'Wights?' hissed Dalibor in consternation. He turned to the assembled aldermen and uttered a word that was three times as long but had exactly the same dismaying effect on the assembly. The collective intake of breath from the villagers was enough to suck most of the oxygen from the room. When Dalibor turned back, his expression was graver. A significant feat in itself since happy-go-lucky had hardly applied before. 'Wild Wights have never been seen this far south. You must have been most unfortunate to have encountered them.'

'Misfortune has nothing to do with it,' Matt said.

'I agree,' Asher nodded. 'They knew where we were. They were hunting us.'

Dalibor threw his hands up in the air, let out an ululation and pivoted on the spot three times.

'Wow, the foxtrot has changed,' Matt muttered.

'It is to ward off evil,' Nadia explained.

'We are here,' Asher said, wanting to get on with things, 'because of Nadia and her eyes.'

Dalibor's eyebrows crawled towards one another. Quickly, Asher explained about the connection between bad lava juice and blue sclerae. Dalibor listened, Wimbush fidgeted. When Asher had finished, Dalibor's eyebrows were almost touching.

'But, as Nadia has explained, all are born with white *biddas*. They become blue within a few weeks.'

'Have you any idea why?' Asher asked.

'No. But those of us that attend the Gathering have eyes that are the darkest blue.'

Asher sat up. 'Can you show us?'

Dalibor turned and talked to the aldermen. One of them left the meeting house.

Wimbush leaned in and motioned to Asher and Lodge. 'Interesting as all of this is, I feel that I have contributed more than enough in getting you to this picturesque spot. I would now like to go home.'

'And how do you propose to do that?' Asher asked. 'Are you able to conjure up wings?'

'You have tools. I have seen you use the Aperio. There are many doors in this village. You could easily send me back. What you do is up to you, but I need to get to my plants.'

'Your invisible plants,' Matt muttered.

Wimbush rounded on him. 'They are experiments!'

Asher sighed. 'Obviously, you did not hear the conversation I had earlier with Nadia. Every door in this village has been charmed until its latches rattle. And I mean every door, down to the last cupboard. Years of protection against wonderworking so as to prevent the witch and her minions gaining egress. I'm afraid the Aperio will not work here. If it did I'd have had reinforcements here an hour ago.'

'But you cannot expect me to stay here any longer,' Wimbush pleaded.

'Look, we don't want to hang about either,' Matt said. 'The plan is that we could maybe build a door. Unfortunately, having a door on its own is useless. It has to open into a functional room or space. That's one of the laws of peregrination. And I should know because I work with someone who wrote the rules. And we don't have Magoose here to try the freestyle variety. So, for the moment, we're stuck here.'

Irritated, Wimbush said, 'Then let us get on with door construction without delay.'

'I don't think it's going to quite as easy as that. You see how paranoid and superstitious they are here. They're hardly likely to just let us build a door. Even if they did, they'd charm the hinges off it. So, we thought that we'd utilise your botanical expertise and let you go off on a bit of an expedition which might involve constructing a hide with a working door.' By now Matt had taken out the linguaplug so Dalibor couldn't hear.

'A hide?' Wimbush asked.

'Yes, a hide, as used by a watcher of birds,' Asher explained.

'I am neither a twatter nor a carpenter,' Wimbush said, embracing the idea with his usual degree of abject negativity.

'It's twitcher,' Matt said, 'but in your case twatter will do nicely.'

'We are not expecting you to construct a large building,' Asher explained. 'Simply four walls and a door. Nadia will help you. I think the sooner she is out of here the better, considering the hostile looks she is getting.'

'Nadia?' Wimbush said, as if he'd never heard the word before.

'Yes, Nadia,' Matt said. 'You know, the girl that saved your skin and ours more than once.'

'But my work is important. I need to reassess the spagyric potential of the wolfsbane, perhaps recalculate the fermentation rate under different lunar saturation concentrations.'

Asher shook his head. 'You can be an insufferable clever Dick.'

'Less of the clever, if you ask me,' Matt muttered.

'There are many interesting plants in the woods,' Nadia said.

'Are there really?' Wimbush said in tones of sodden sarcasm. Nadia deflated.

Matt sent Wimbush a flinty glare. 'If I didn't think that you were at least three-quarters of the way along the spectrum, I'd happily break your nose here and now.'

'What spectrum?' Wimbush asked.

Matt glared at him. 'The one that allows for you to have got where you are with zero people skills and a double-digit negative score on the emotional intelligence scale. In other words, I honestly don't think it's your fault, but you need a little insight because you can, and should, work at it. We need neurodiverse of the XY variety, otherwise we'd never have computers or ham radios or sheds. But if someone like Nadia is willing to help you, I would grab hold of that offer with both hands and never let go because, and I speak with some authority having spent much more time with you than I would have chosen to by dint of need, it ain't going to happen too often, pal.'

Wimbush opened his mouth to speak, but though his lips formed the shape of 'computer' the words evaporated before they were spoken.

Matt made more staring eyes and nodded towards Nadia, who had started collecting their bowls.

'I…' began Wimbush

'Oh, forget it,' Matt said. 'But if you want out of here, then you are going to have to muck in. If you build it, they will come.'

'That is profound, Matt,' Asher said. 'Are you quoting someone?'

'Kevin Costner.'

'Is he a great philosopher in the human world?'

'Big time. He can dance with wolves, steal from the rich to give to the poor, rescue people from raging seas and is an astoundingly loyal bodyguard.'

'Truly a wondrous man,' Nadia marvelled.

Matt's face stayed as straight as it could for all of twenty seconds.

'Are you being cynical again, Matt?' Asher asked.

'I am,' grinned Matt. 'But only so that I don't have to punch Wimbush.'

The door to the meeting house opened and the alderman who'd previously left came in with a younger man in tow. The boy was late teens, lean and pale. But the whites of his eyes were the deep blue of ink, making it difficult to demarcate the sclerae from his slightly darker irises.

'This is Iohan. He is one of our gatherers.'

Matt and Wimbush couldn't help but stare. Asher stood and shook the young man's hand. When he let go, there was panic in the youngster's face.

'You shook an even number of times,' said Dalibor urgently. 'Greetings should be odd. Even greetings incur the wrath of—'

'The witch, yes, I understand,' Asher said.

'Now you must touch each other's left shoulder with your right hand and then shake again an odd number of times.'

Asher glanced at Matt, whose eyes were already rolling, but he did as instructed and saw Iohan relax.

'Tell me,' Asher asked, 'what is it that you do at the Gathering?'

'It is forbidden to speak of such things.'

'Forbidden, I see. Okay, then how long was it after the Gathering that your eyes turned this darker blue?'

'A week, perhaps less.'

'Thank you.'

Iohan, relieved, took his leave.

'Does that satisfy your quest for knowledge?' Dalibor asked.

'For now.'

'Then you no longer have a reason to stay?'

'No. I don't suppose we do.' Asher smiled. 'But it is getting late and we would appreciate the opportunity to rest here tonight. I promise that we will leave first thing in the morning.'

'That can be arranged. I will send some spellcasters to make safe the room against the witch. Please do not talk to the spellcasters, or touch the air within three feet of their passing.'

Within half an hour, seats had been rearranged and straw beds laid for four. By the time the spellcasters had been and done their thing—spraying water from a strange rattle-like container with holes at the end, chanting and moaning the spells while ignoring the four travellers completely—exhaustion was setting in. At last, as lamps were lit and darkness fell, they were alone.

Matt said, 'I'd like it noted that these people are completely mad. I coughed earlier, and I swear that one of the spellcasters did five press-ups and a burpee.'

'Warding off bronchial demon,' Nadia explained.

'Bronchial demon, my arse. It was just a stray crumb from this dry bread.' He knocked a crust on the seat of a chair. It made a noise like an iron bracelet against a coffin.

Asher collected up the linguaplugs and stored them away. 'It appears that the villagers are in thrall to the witch and have learned, or have been taught, that obedience and ritual is the only way to avoid her wrath.'

'But they literally cannot sneeze without doing some sort of penance or stupid OCD count.' Matt shook his head.

'It is the way.' Nadia shrugged. 'They know nothing better. Now that I know different, it seems…strange.'

'It seems totally bloody mad,' Matt said. 'Why doesn't someone question it?'

'If they do, they are banished.' Nadia let her chin fall.

'Ah.' Matt nodded thoughtfully. 'So that's what happened to you, is it? Good old put up or shut up?'

'Yes.'

'But we are here now, and we must work with what we have.' Asher turned to Nadia. 'What time do the villagers set off for the Gathering?'

'An hour after dawn.'

'Why an hour after dawn?' Matt asked. 'Surely that means that they leave much later in winter?'

'That is true.'

'Is there a reason?'

'The bats will be roosting. They are less likely to die if the bats are roosting.' Nadia's answer was blunt.

Wimbush stared at her. 'Die? How?'

'The Gathering is a dangerous place,' she said. 'The gatherers never talk about it. They are sworn to secrecy. I only know what Radomil told Dalibor when Kasimir, my brother, died. He slipped. Fell from his harness.'

'They work on high ground?' Matt asked.

Nadia shook her head. 'It is not the height they fear. It is the ground and what lives upon it.'

These were enigmatic words, but Nadia would say no more on the subject and no one quizzed her. They were all too exhausted to enter into any more discussion. What lay in wait would be there still the following day.

CHAPTER THIRTY-FIVE

MERTHYR, WALES, 500 AD

THE LONG DARK night wore on. There was little to do but wait until the bats had roosted again. Kylah tried to rest and make up for the previous night's fitful sleep, but Bobby's restlessness was palpable and infectious and worried at her like an unreachable itch, or worse, an itch that is reachable but not one you'd want to scratch in polite company.

Neither of them slept because they were scared of what sleep would bring with it. Kylah had no intention of experiencing that scooped-out desperation she'd felt on seeing an insectoid arm clamp on to Matt's foot ever again if she could help it. A part of her, the logical, reassuring part, knew it was nothing but a trick, a fear that these Nosdrwg had sensed, buffed up and represented in inglorious technicolour. But the image had been vivid and horrific, and she'd had to use all her willpower to convince herself that it was a nasty Nosdrwg trick. Even so, if something unpleasant leaps out at you from inside a dark cupboard, only an idiot would go back to that cupboard a second time. And Arthur's men were not idiots.

Neither was Kylah.

She couldn't help but wonder why everyone was so exhausted. Attrition by sleep deprivation. A stealth weapon if ever there was one.

When grey light finally began to filter through a gap in the tent, Bobby sat up on her straw bed. 'I can't stay here any longer. There must be something else we can do. Let's find Myrddin and make him tell us how they set up the sword as a portway in the first place.'

Kylah turned and rested on one elbow, smoothing down the back of her hair where it had flattened from the pillow. Bobby looked wide awake, whereas Kylah felt the horrible exhaustion like cotton wool pushing out from inside her brain. 'Agreed. At the very least they should be able to tell us what incantations they used. If there was a specific sequence or protocol for the wonder-working, we might be able to reverse engineer.'

Get the boomerang to come back, even.

They got up and opened the tent flap. The morning was cool and overcast and their guard was nowhere to be seen. But somewhere off to the left they heard shouting in the distance.

'What's that?' Kylah asked.

Bobby shrugged. Another shout was followed by the sound of something metallic hitting something else metallic.

'Blacksmith?' Bobby offered.

'Maybe,' Kylah said. But something bothered her about the noises. Forges, in her experience, emitted regular noises like the rhythmic sound of metal being beaten, bellows pumping, and the occasional crisp hiss of singed eyebrows as an apprentice leaned a little too close to the fire. What they were hearing now were much more sporadic noises. Suddenly, a scream erupted above the muffled shouts. Long and agonising, it cut through the air and twisted Kylah's gut into an anxious knot. 'It's a fight,' she said.

They followed the noises. Their path took them away from the caves, down across a broad slope and through a copse onto a small plateau. A smattering of rough cruck-built wooden buildings sat clustered around a central coral in which some goats and a couple of cows looked up curiously as they neared. The looks on the faces of the knot of women and children huddled inside one of the buildings was almost as bovine: grey with exhaustion and hopelessness. The women were lean and hard-faced with rough hands; the children mud-streaked. They stared with wide-eyed, wary expressions as the two women approached.

'They've accepted their lot, haven't they?' Bobby said.

Kylah didn't answer, but Bobby was right. You could find the same expression in any number of refugee camps or those tent cities where famine stalked the land. Something had taken the essential spark from these people. They were alive, but they weren't living. They were merely existing. And barely, at that.

The Nosdrwg were winning.

Kylah was about to ask if they were okay when another shout, this one louder and away to their left, caused them both to swivel their heads.

Kylah pointed. 'There.'

They turned and entered the trees bordering the hamlet at a trot, the noises getting louder and mingling with grunts and yells and curses. Definitely fighting.

They'd gone twenty yards when a sudden and inexplicable smell, rank and full of decay, brought them to an abrupt halt.

'Wow,' Bobby said. 'Someone light a match.'

'Are we near the ocean?' Kylah asked. 'We must be.' Because it was definitely the sea they smelled. Or at least the reek, salty and ripe, of mudflats after the tide has gone out. Yet even as she spoke, the suggestion struck Kylah as being more than odd since she had assumed they were well inland. An assumption fed by the absence of any coastline anywhere in the vicinity.

They walked on, more slowly now because of the all-pervading stench. The path led to a gap in the trees where the land fell away. Somewhere ahead and out of sight, they could hear the noise of rushing water.

'Sounds more like a river than the s—' Bobby didn't finish the sentence because something had appeared on the path in front of them. A thing, or what had once been a person, stood dressed in a rusting chain mail tunic baring a battered shield in one hand and a war hatchet in the other. The clue was in the way it stood.

Something alive wouldn't lean drunkenly to the left like that since it'd probably have had a foot at the end of its leg instead of just a bit of pale bone. The thing looked at them through the eyeholes of an elaborately worked faceplate. Though looking was stretching things a bit because looking required organs capable of seeing, whereas this specimen seemed to have nothing but dark spaces where there should have been eyes. Instead, it swivelled its head from side to side, trying to locate them. Sensing

Kylah and Bobby, it lurched forwards with a sickening off-kilter gait, arm and hatchet upraised like a bad extra at a historical re-enactment museum.

But whatever was behind that faceplate wasn't a tour guide.

'Kylah,' Bobby yelled.

Kylah fell into a crouch, slipping one of the knives from her belt to her hand. 'Stand your ground,' she ordered. 'We are not your enemy.'

'Wiiiccccaaah,' the thing grunted in a horrible bubbly voice and kept coming.

Kylah assessed its armour. Its chain mail fell to below its knees. There wasn't much, if any, exposed flesh. The closer it got, the clearer it became that there wasn't much flesh full stop. Whatever this thing was, it did not look at all healthy. She was pondering whether to go straight for the eyeholes when she heard Bobby shout the spell. Instantly, the ground between her and the monstrosity erupted in a mini tornado of dirt and leaves that caused the thing to skid to a halt and throw up a protective hand.

'Dervish dirt,' Bobby explained.

'Thanks,' Kylah said as they retreated quickly back along the path.

But their respite was short-lived. Groaning, head bent, the ghoulish warrior stepped through the dust storm and bounded, or rather hopped, after them.

'Doesn't look very friendly,' Bobby said.

'Doesn't look very alive,' Kylah added.

'Think it was on its way to the village?'

'I wouldn't be surprised,' Kylah replied grimly. 'We need better weapons.' She stooped to pick up a sturdy branch, but it stayed glued to the ground as, a yard to her left, a booted foot stepped out of the trees and stood on it. She jumped back, knife ready and stared up into Bedwyr's grinning, helmet-less face.

'No need. This bugger's mine.'

He slid on his helmet, hefted his heavy sword and ran towards the oncoming warrior with a roar. Steel met steel with a clang. The figure pivoted, unbalanced by Bedwyr's ferocity and more agile movement. Once past, Bedwyr shifted his sword grip to his left hand and made a fist with his right. He held this out in front of him, said something incomprehensible and opened his hand.

Kylah saw nothing physical leave Bedwyr's palm, but the moment he opened it, his opponent froze. A second later its arms and legs flew forward as if it had been hit by an invisible battering ram. The heavy sword clattered to the floor as it collapsed onto its back. Instantly, its clothes and skin began to crumple and curl, drying up and flaking away in the thin breeze. Bones and fluid became a decaying dust that was taken up by the wind and blown away, leaving nothing but a slight stain on the ground.

'Needs to change its moisturiser,' said Bobby.

Kylah caught her breath. 'What was that, if you don't mind me asking?'

'Scum,' said the knight. 'This bloody Saicson necromancer uses the undead. Morgana trains us in battlefield wonderworking to combat them. Good at it, too, she is.'

'What about the villagers? Are there more of these undead about?'

'We patrol,' Bedwyr said. 'But the villagers are easy prey, see. Many of the men have been killed or taken by Saicson raiders. The women and children…they're exhausted by their dreams.'

'The Nosdrwg,' said Bobby.

Bedwyr nodded. 'That is why we must defeat them. Otherwise our people will be wiped out.'

Another waft of rotten kelp-stained air struck them.

'Are we near the sea?' Bobby asked, wrinkling her nose.

Bedwyr shook his head. 'The ocean is leagues away to the west.'

'Then what is that smell?'

Bedwyr's expression hardened. 'The necromancer uses water as a tool. Black rain that scorches the earth. Today he's brought a couple of guests to the fight. Lucky we've got Myrddin and Morgana to do battle for us. Without them, we'd have no hope.'

'Are they near?'

Bedwyr nodded.

'Can we see them?'

This time there was definite hesitation in the knight's reply. 'Of course. But I must warn you that what you will see not many have witnessed. The villagers who first saw…some of them have lost their reason.'

'We are trained to expect the unexpected,' Kylah said.

Bedwyr regarded them for a moment before acquiescing. 'Then follow me. But stay close, mind. There will be more undead, no doubt.'

He led the way along the path, explaining about how they patrolled the woods in daylight and set guards during the long night. Above them, the sky was lowering, the clouds thickening. The stench of decaying fish grew with every step now, as did the sound of rushing water. At the end of the path the terrain became rougher as the ground rose and the noise of water soon became a roar. Finally, they crested a small hill and stopped.

Kylah, already weakened from lack of sleep, felt the world not so much tilt as bounce up and down twice, do a headstand and finish off with a Māori kapa haka.

The river, winding and swift after recent rain, snaked along a valley floor, woods reaching to the edge of the gentle banks. But what might have been a fisherman's dream was now every man's nightmare. Fifty yards downstream from where they stood something had happened, was still happening, to the waterway. Abruptly, and in mind-boggling defiance of the laws of nature, the water was running upwards in a thick sheet for some fifty feet, where it spilled over the jagged rim of a huge rent in the air.

Kylah gaped in disbelief. Hovering in the sky was a ragged slash some forty feet tall and thirty feet wide. The roaring river was falling through this gap, down—if perpendicular could be called down—into a great body of dark, roiling water. But it was not only water that sat at the bottom of this great hole in the air. Creatures moved within it too. Some with huge wafting tentacles, others with claws at the ends of thin arms, their misshapen heads staring up and out into the world of men. Beneath the water swam creatures with reptilian jaws snapping and gnashing. Kylah felt a chilling conviction that they were waiting, like animals in a cage, for their food.

'Crumbs,' Bobby said. 'It's like Dalí on acid.'

Kylah gagged. The stench here was truly awful. But it was the sight of it that had the worst effect. Its terrifying wrongness sent shudders through both women. This was powerful wonder-working. They were staring at a hellish gateway to another place, a slash into another dimension. These creatures gathered in the depths were not from any world Kylah was familiar with. And then her eyes drifted to the figures on the bank in front of where nature itself was being defiled. Myrddin and Morgana, impossibly small against the huge body of water, had their hands reaching up, shaping the air, moulding the dark matter that all of wonderworking was made of. It was clear they were trying to counteract and contain this calamity, this heinous rent in the fabric of the world. And the thing about any rent was that unless you sorted it out, all it did was got bigger and bigger until the bailiffs came. And these bailiffs, judging by the look of them, weren't going to knock politely and ask to be let in. They looked far too hungry for that.

Kylah's eyes darted around the bank. There was no sign of any armed men. But with the great maw of horror sucking in the world, who needed soldiers.

'What the hell is that?' she finally said.

'No idea,' Bobby breathed beside her. 'But it's bad. Very bad.'

Bedwyr's voice was tight. 'As you can see, Morgana and Myrddin are busy.'

Kylah let out a thin laugh. Bedwyr gave great understatement.

'Maybe I could help,' Bobby said.

Kylah shot her a glance. All trace of tiredness had left Bobby's face. She looked like a racehorse in the starting gate desperate to be off. 'Do you think you can? Do you think you should?'

Both questions were loaded and primed. Bobby had not yet completed her conversion course, though both women knew that it was nothing but a formality. Bobby would graduate summa cum laude. But the second question was the more urgent. They were in the past and the past was an unforgiving creature. How much, if any, interference should they risk? And yet Kylah knew that this enemy was powerful and had to be dealt with. Otherwise, the dark ages were going to be truly dark. Dark enough perhaps to snuff out the enlightenment.

'Last term we covered accidental extra-dimensional infringements,' Bobby said, holding Kylah's gaze.

'I hope you took notes.' Kylah could see a fire in Bobby's

eyes. Was this an effect of whatever it was that had turned her sclerae that pale blue? She knew the risk. If they did nothing and the Saicson necromancer changed the world here and now, this world might take a different path. One where Bobby and Kylah might never have existed. On the other hand, helping might have exactly the same effect. But doing nothing in the face of such a horror was impossible.

'Go,' Kylah said. 'Do what you can.'

CHAPTER THIRTY-SIX

BOBBY RAN down the slope towards the river. Towards the insanely roaring, backward-flowing waterfall. Towards the cunning man and the cunning woman frantically casting and shaping the raw dark matter into containment charms. Neither Myrddin nor Morgana turned to look around, but she knew they saw her.

Her warlock professor at the Le Fey, the one who was an expert in dimensional infringement, had come with his own unique accent. 'Nature', he'd insisted, 'vos your strongest ally because it belonked in zee von and only place and had no business in any ozer.'

Nature resisted change at anything other than millennial pace. It abhorred transgression. It was, contrary to all those documentaries about extreme weather, generally on your side and gave you fair warning if it was upset. If you built a house on the side of a volcano, there was no point complaining or expecting sympathy if you woke up one morning to a mouthful of pyroclastic flow.

Bobby had a good memory. No, a great memory. She remembered listening in the lecture theatre as the warlock whispered the words of power, felt the rock a hundred feet beneath her feet twitching as he uttered it. But there was more to it than simply words. There was belief and character and guts.

She recalled exactly the word and the inflection and the

control in the warlock's eyes. This was not a spell to be toyed with, he'd said. This was not a spell they were likely to need in the whole of their lifespan nor their children's nor their children's children. It was a spell to demonstrate in a lecture and then to promptly forget. Speaking it would make nothing happen unless the situation demanded it. Beyond that situation, it was completely safe. If one of the students had decided, after one too many Bombdropper's ales, to shout it from the rooftop of a pub, he may have been struck by a stray twig sucked up from the pavement, but the ground beneath his feet would not shatter.

But Bobby had not forgotten. She had not forgotten because the word had sent a thrill through her. And here and now, with the necromancer's mercenary power defiling nature in front of her eyes, she was sure, one hundred per cent sure, that this was the time. She reached the bank and stopped. Spray from the boiling river caressed her face in an icy kiss. She could see the air at the fringes of the great tear knitting and unknitting as the opposing forces vied.

Not good. None of this was good.

The warlock lecturer's name was Bolshoi. She pictured him, remembered how he sounded. She leaned down and picked up a pebble, thought of the word and the forma, squeezed her hand and let the spell out without a word.

The pebble in her hand melted.

So did the stones in the riverbed.

Then they erupted, flowing with the water, but separate from it, rising like liquid granite. From the outside in, the molten rock spread like sliding wax to fill the tear in the air. The flow of water hesitated and then stopped, falling back like some giant whale into the riverbed as its exit was blocked, leaving in the sky a huge wall of coalesced stone that rumbled and bulged but held firm. This was the moment to use the banishment spell. She didn't need a name, as with exorcisms; she simply needed the angry necromancer to be here and seething and off guard. Then she reached into a different part of her mind for another word.

Gwrach.

Bobby smiled. This word, a scream from a mad woman, had taken Bobby years to learn the truth about. The madwoman, her grandmother, had not been mad. And the guttural scream had not been so much insane nonsense. It had meant something. An old word from an ancient language. It had given Bobby, a witch's granddaughter, the three most powerful things: consent, confirmation, completion.

Gwrach.

Now whenever she thought it, help, belief and power came with it.

Gwrach meant Witch.

Bobby, as she had been taught, opened her mind, saw a wraith-like thing screaming and pounding in anger at a stone prison and imagined the wall falling. In front of her, the river stone, impossibly massive and immeasurably heavy, did just that. Only its fall was not back towards the earth, its fall was at right angles, defying gravity to pick up a stranger gravity that dragged and accelerated it into a different earth. Behind it, as it diminished, the air imploded with a pop to leave nothing but the grey sky and the last of the sea stench in its wake.

The silence buzzed.

Water lapped at her feet from the minor tidal wave the river's return had triggered. She danced back away from it, ignoring the absurdity of not wanting to get her feet wet. When she looked up, Morgana and Myrddin were looking at her with drawn, exhausted faces and an expression of wonder and relief.

'Mistress Miracle,' said Myrddin, breathless with astonishment, 'you exhibit a truly wondrous power.'

'I'm just a diligent student,' said Bobby. 'Following in my grandmother's footsteps.'

'Your grandmother? She must have been a truly powerful sorcerer.' Morgana was smiling.

'She was.'

'One of the best,' said Kylah, joining them with Bedwyr, who was looking about him with a puzzled expression.

'What is it?' Myrddin asked.

'Can you not feel it?' Morgana grinned. 'The air is lighter and purer. The necromancer's miasma has gone.'

They all looked up. The sky was indeed getting brighter. They all took in a lungful of pine-infused air.

'Does that mean it is gone?' Bedwyr asked. 'The ghoulish warrior thing?'

Bobby shrugged. 'I did use a banishment curse on top of the infringement reversal as we were taught to do. Hopefully, I've sealed him in. For a while, at least.'

'If it has truly gone, this a great blow against the Saicson,' said Myrddin, who seemed to have suddenly become ten years younger. 'From whom did you learn such wonderworking, child?'

'Chap called Bolshoi,' Bobby said. 'Funny thing is that he is actually our provenance teacher. You know, history of certain incantations. In fact, I've just remembered he said that the one I used came from the dark ages itself at around about this time.' Bobby frowned. 'I'm sure he said fifth century, though I can't recall the exact date…I…' Her words grew slower and the gaps between lengthened as her brain did the algebra and seized. She saw a similar perplexity in Kylah's eyes. 'You don't think that…'

'No, not possible. I mean how could it?' Kylah shook her head.

'You speak in riddles,' Bedwyr said, with a castigating smile.

'I was just wondering if in fact this…what I just did…was the first example ever of using this spell.'

'But how could that be?' Morgana asked. 'Surely if you are from another time, you would not have known how to…'

'Krudian paradox,' said Kylah. 'On the wings of a boomerang.'

They all stared at her.

'Never seen it. But people say it's theoretically possible. Bobby may have just created her own history.' Kylah blinked.

'Now I've got a headache,' Bobby said. What Kylah was postulating was ridiculous and impossible and…she caught herself. She was standing on a riverbank after closing a dimensional rip in the fifth century. That was impossible squared.

Bobby sat down on a rock. When she looked up at the sky, the sun seemed to have shifted. 'What time is it?'

'Late afternoon.'

'But it was dawn when—'

'The necromancer steals time. A minute in its presence is an hour of what you would normally experience.' Morgana sighed.

'Time might not like that very much,' Kylah said.

It was a concrete bollard statement: guaranteed to stop everyone in their tracks. An equal opportunities frown followed it as people, Kylah included, tried to assimilate its meaning, failed and then carried on regardless.

Morgana obliged. 'Come, let's get some food. I am spent.'

Bobby didn't argue. She was too busy trying to get her thoughts arranged into some kind of order. The trouble was they'd turned into a basket full of wriggling puppies that would not sit still.

CHAPTER THIRTY-SEVEN

THEY ADJOURNED to the king's encampment.

There, Myrddin made them all a mint-flavoured potion that had them all feeling a great deal better within minutes. And just as well because Arthur, like everyone, aware of the change, met them and made Myrddin recount the whole episode.

When he'd finished, Arthur drew his sword and knelt in front of the two seated women. 'By your hands, the darkness is dispelled.'

'It might not last,' Bobby said.

Arthur smiled at her and shook his head. 'Great deeds you have wrought this day, Bobby and Kylah. For your bravery and steadfast hearts, all men owe you a debt beyond measure. Know that your names shall endure in legend, honoured by the bards and cherished by generations yet to come.'

Gwenhwyfar hugged them both.

'Rest now,' Arthur said. 'We will watch the caves.'

Morgana and Bedwyr stayed with them under orders from Myrddin. They, like Kylah, having been exposed to the Krudian time slip the wonderworking had induced, needed isolation in case of 'side effects', as Myrddin had so worryingly put it.

'Such as?' Kylah had asked.

'Suddenly ageing or getting younger, perhaps. Exhibiting strange behaviour that might indicate possession...like turning into a bat, loud giggling or uncontrollable laughter.'

'Bobby already ticks a couple of those boxes.'

'Rest assured, we will monitor you.'

Exhaustion, however, did not so much as overtake them, it lapped them twice and left them floundering in its wake. Neither Kylah nor Bobby wanted to give in to sleep but once they closed their eyes, the battle was lost without a shot being fired. Unless you counted the noises Bedwyr occasionally produced, which were equally as explosive and, thanks to a diet rich in pulses and fibre, had all sorts of special effects that went with them.

But they all slept.

Fitfully to begin with, primed by a subconscious expectation of the worst. And dreams did come, but they were nothing like what they'd experienced before. These were weird as opposed to harrowing. Full of the strange and surprising as opposed to the dreadful and mortifying. And, as the night wore on, even these phantasmagorias receded. When Kylah woke, dawn once again was breaking. Morgana and Bobby were deep in conversation, the occasional throaty giggle piercing their whispered exchanges. Kylah watched and wondered at the wisdom of getting too close to someone fifteen hundred years your senior, but then they were caught up in the mother of all temporal paradoxes and by now, given the amount of interaction that had already taken place, non-interactive wisdom had already packed its bags and left on the early flight.

She got up, made some excuses and found Myrddin already up and potion-making in his tent. She got straight to the point.

'Since when have you been waging this supernatural war?'

'Since the Saicsons came,' Myrddin answered. 'Before that there was little call for warfare. We had never experienced it on this scale.'

'There is a great battle coming, you know,' Kylah said. 'Whatever the outcome, you must ensure Arthur and Morgana find safety.'

'People say that there is safety in death, mistress.'

Kylah looked at the old sorcerer. Did he know already? Could he foresee the future enough to realise that in victory there would be pain? 'And they may be right,' Kylah said.

'I will ensure that the king and his sister, who is like a daughter to me now, stay safe. If there is a battle to be fought, then fight we will. For fight we all must against the dread and terror that evil wishes to unleash upon this world.'

'Funny that. We seem to be saying the exactly the same thing fifteen hundred years from now.'

'That is disappointing.'

'Anyway, I'm sure you'll do a fine job,' she said.

Myrddin smiled and then frowned in surprise, as if a new deposit had been made in his memory bank. 'How did you sleep?'

'Remarkably well,' Kylah said.

'Were you troubled?'

'Apart from some weirdness in the early part of the night, no. I slept well.'

'But this is excellent news. Have you asked the others?'

'No, I—'

Myrddin strode from the tent. Ten minutes later, the whole encampment was awake…and well rested.

'Could be luck, I suppose,' Bobby said when both Cei and Bedwyr reported that the other knights had all been untroubled by horrifying dreams.

'Less luck than understanding,' Myrddin said, his eyes gleaming.

'Natural science,' said Morgana, grinning from ear to ear.

'I think now would be a good time to apply a little pressure to the situation,' Myrddin said. 'Tell the king that we need to adjourn to the cave.'

They left the tent, Bobby and Kylah walking together.

'What's going on?' Bobby asked, sounding anxious.

'Medal ceremony,' Kylah replied. 'I think you've made the podium, mistress Miracle.'

At the cave entrance, King Arthur stood with his men watching the last of bats return in the thin light of dawn. One or two of them hit the wall and fell to the floor before launching themselves again into the welcoming darkness.

'Oh dear,' said Kylah. 'Looks like their navigation is a bit off. Could be one or two too many mushroom-laced flies, you reckon?'

King Arthur greeted the women. 'As you foretold, our men and the villagers report less darkness in their dreams.'

'Best night we've had in an age,' echoed Cei.

'That could be a fluke,' Bobby said.

'Let us find out.' Myrddin led the way into the dank cave.

Inside, the air was redolent with fresh bat excrement. With a start, Kylah realised that this ammoniacal stench was the same as she'd experienced at the bottom of the sinkhole. The engineers had assumed the fractured sewer pipe was to blame. They had obviously been wrong.

Arthur walked in flanked by half a dozen knights, Myrddin right behind him. They halted at the spot where Kylah and Bobby had manifested and Arthur ordered the lights to be extinguished. The cave was plunged into almost complete darkness. As Kylah stared, she could make out the others only as grey shapes against an even darker background. The temperature dropped rapidly as Kylah's pulse accelerated. Vague lighter shapes appeared in the walls. Ghostly movements flitting here and there. But Kylah's mind stayed alert and orientated and no images of Matt came to her.

Suddenly, out of the darkness Myrddin's voice boomed. 'I summon thee, chieftain of the Nosdrwg.'

A fixed glow began to appear in the cavern wall. Within it a new shape appeared. Human, long hair, flowing cape.

'Who it is that summons me?'

'I, Myrddin, as mage to his liege, Arthur. I summon you.'

'What right do you have to disturb my rest?'

'Rest?' Myrddin said. 'What rest should the damned enjoy?'

'What rest indeed? But rest it is we have for the first time in an age. A peace has come upon us. Begone before I rip your soul to shreds.'

'What if I were to tell you that this peace you are so enjoying has been granted as a boon by us?'

'I would consider you a fool.'

'Then it is a fool who has fed you through the creatures to whom you are tied. A fool who has found a way to calm your wretched souls.'

'Speak, fool.'

'We have given the stlym a taste of good Celtic shrooms. They contain great magic. It is that magic that gives you solace.'

'And such sweet solace it is,' croaked the Nosdrwg chief. Everyone who heard his words heard, too, the unspoken relief they carried.

'But as we have given so we can take away. You have come to prey on us.'

'We go where our master bids. He who has cursed us.'

'What if we tell you that your master is banished, and you are free?'

'How can we be free when we exist only to feed on the stlym's foul soil?'

'But is not that soil a little sweeter with our recipe?'

'It is. I grant you that it is.'

'Then let me assure you of peace. I will send the stlym to a different place where you will not be disturbed by men. There they will feed according to our recipe and I will set beasts to guard them. Pale beasts of the night that no man would dare tame. What say you to a bargain?'

'We do not bargain with men. We rip their souls apart.'

'Then we will change the recipe back to the bitter harvest you have enjoyed for an age.'

'NO!' roared the chief.

Silence rang through the cave.

Kylah risked a smile. This wasn't a fair fight. Muscles were being flexed, but only one team had the ball and if the other side weren't careful, they'd take it home with them and there'd be no one to play with.

After what seemed like an age, the Nosdrwg chieftain spoke again. 'We agree to your terms. But if you break your word, our vengeance will be swift and terrible.'

That's it, let them blow off a little steam. Threats were always good for the ego.

But then Myrddin turned and addressed Kylah and Bobby in an urgent whisper. 'I fear my plan now falters. I had no idea they would agree so readily. I have not thought of a safe haven other than the great mountains of the north. Yet our people work the land there. Where can we send them where they will not pose a threat?'

'I think I know a place,' said Bobby. 'Somewhere I've been reliably informed is the back of beyond and in a different world to boot. Does that matter?'

'No, all we need is a name. So long as it is far from here.'

Bobby leaned forward and whispered something in Myrddin's ear.

The sorcerer moved towards the glowing shape in the cave wall and put his hand upon it. A deep rumble grew until it shook the cave. Small pockets of dim light glowed and then faded. Myrddin wasted no time. He drew a circle around his feet in salt except for a small gap through which Morgana stepped before closing it behind her.

'Leave us,' Myrddin ordered.

Kylah, Bobby, Arthur and the knights all left to stand outside in the cold dawn. The rumbling in the cave grew even louder until, with a great noise of squealing, the bats emerged as a dark, fluttering cloud and sped east. Kylah thought she could feel movement in the rocks beneath her feet too. It lasted for a brief minute and then was over. The first rays of light were kissing the tops of the trees when Myrddin and Morgana emerged.

'It is done,' said Myrddin. 'They have gone to a place of which I have no knowledge other than a name.'

'Then let us prepare for war,' said the king and his smile was bittersweet.

CHAPTER THIRTY-EIGHT

SPIV

AN HOUR BEFORE DAWN, Asher roused the others. The dying embers of the fire that had kept them warm through the night provided a dim orange light by which they dressed quickly and gathered up their belongings. Several times Wimbush cursed as he stubbed his toe or tripped over something.

'Why can't we have the lamp on?' he said after banging his knee on a chair.

'Because we didn't want to disturb anyone, though from the racket you're making we might as well set the bloody place on fire,' Matt hissed.

As if on cue, the door opened. Matt wasn't sure which was the chillier, the look on Dalibor's face or the brisk wind that whistled in before the door shut.

'We wanted an early start,' Asher explained.

'I cannot decide if you are brave or foolhardy to venture into the woods in the darkness. It is said that the vilest creatures roam at this hour.'

'You've been to Dublin on a stag do then?'

'What kind of vilest creatures?' Wimbush asked, ignoring Matt's aside and still massaging his knee.

'In the darkness, if the branch of a tree brushes your face, the banshee will take you. If you break a twig, it summons the capcaun. If you look at the moon with both eyes, Babramic Jaggr,' he shut his eyes and mouthed an incantation before adding, 'will strike you blind.'

Wimbush, wide-eyed, said, 'Perhaps we should wait—'

'We will take our chances.' Asher shook his head and hoisted his pack onto his shoulders.

Dalibor frowned. 'I would advise—'

'We have intruded on your hospitality for too long already. Thank you.' Asher walked towards Dalibor and stood toe to toe with the man. Finally, the alderman stood aside to allow everyone to leave.

The tail end of night was sharp and cool, but mercifully the rain had stayed away. Dalibor led them to the side of the village opposite the one where Nadia had taken them over the wooden fence. It was marked, as were the other cardinal compass points, by a flickering torch.

'This leads north. May good fortune speed your way.' Dalibor's words sounded polite enough but they oozed a contradictory subtext. *You're all idiots and the witch is going to tear you to pieces.* He turned on his heel and was gone.

Asher waited near the fence until he was out of earshot and said, 'Nadia, we need to find some flat ground for you and Wimbush.'

Nadia nodded and began to scale the barrier.

'Stay close, Wimbush. The capcaun love strays,' Asher said with a straight face.

'What is a capcaun?' asked Matt.

'I have no idea, but Wimbush clearly does.'

They watched the alchemist trot forwards to within a few yards of Nadia, who seemed as sure-footed in the dark as she was in daytime.

'Must be those blue sclerae,' Matt said, commenting on his own unvoiced thoughts.

'Or she has mountain goat genes,' answered Asher.

They walked for twenty minutes until the faint glow of light from the village was out of sight.

'This clearing looks to be as good a place as any,' Asher said.

'For what?' Wimbush asked.

'For waiting,' Matt said. 'I estimate it'll be dawn in twenty minutes. I suggest you try and keep warm.'

Even in the predawn grey, Wimbush's expression bordered on belligerent, but he didn't speak. Instead he started walking up and down, arms clasped about his torso. Nadia watched him as if he was some kind of large exotic bird.

Matt drew Asher to one side. 'I've been meaning to ask you this for ages. What exactly is lava juice? Is it some kind of potion?'

Asher shook his head. 'If it was, it would be easy to protect against. No, this is what you might term "old school". Our apothecaries term it a droge. There is no thaumaturgy attached. It exerts its effect purely on its own.'

'Droge? So, by that you mean drug.'

'We prefer the original etymology.'

'Okay, but is it plant-based? A chemical?'

'Ah, that is where things become a little less clear. It is sold as a laced tobacco. The "juice" refers to the droge itself which is infused into the tobacco. But as to its origin, all we know is that it comes from the north.'

'As in this north?' Matt glanced around.

'Yes. Rumours abound, obviously. Some say that it is the boiled venom of the poisonous pin-striped toad. Some that it is the squeezed juice of the flesh-eating Nando plant. Others suggest that it might be the distilled urine of a monstrous bat. As you can imagine, because of its nature, the more lurid the explanation, the more street credibility the droge attains.'

'So, there's no misanthropic alchemy teacher cooking it up in a secret lab under the stables in New Thameswick, then?' Matt accompanied this with a jovial laugh.

Asher shot him a glance. 'How did you know about Barnabus Blanc?'

Matt's laugh died. He blinked three times. 'You're kidding, right? There isn't…is there? Barnabus Blanc? Really?'

'Disappeared last year after illegally manufacturing rocky sheep-dip, also known as Meh. Made a fortune. Meh sent the dwarves crazy. It was a significant problem in the city for a while. Sparked a droge war between the gang Haggis Len works for, the snakes, and the bakers.'

'Oh, we have them too. Hell's Angels, they call themselves though the Americans call them just "bikers".'

'Not bikers, bakers. In New Thameswick, it is the bakers who deal. They bake speciality breads for various ethnic groups. Highly specialised. A troll, for example, would never dream of eating dwarf bread, partly because it would taste like a dog's doings and very likely put them into a coma. And vice versa.'

'I feel the same about the Kentish huffkin.' 'Queasy' best described Matt's expression.

'But you can understand the opportunities it offers the illicit baker to manufacture and distribute illegal and potentially mind-altering substances in their bread.'

'A bit like a chocolate croissant?'

'Exactly. Only a hundred times more potent and much less flaky.' Asher tilted his head. 'But why are you so interested in Barnabus Blanc?'

'Because we have this TV show about a chemistry teacher who learns he's dying and decides to start making…' Matt let the words run out. 'Was this widely reported in your press?'

'There was the usual column in the *Daily Scrawl*.'

'No chance of the story having leaked across, is there?'

'There is always a possibility.'

'Hmm,' Matt said. 'We ought to chat more often. See what other juicy storylines you can come up with.'

They watched the eastern sky bloom a faint pink and Asher spoke quietly to Nadia who led them along a difficult, ascending path to a promontory where they could look down on the village and the road.

A few minutes later, a group of figures emerged and began to walk along the track.

'This is it,' Asher said to Matt. He turned to Wimbush. 'You know what to do. If anyone challenges you, say what you're building is for observing birds.'

Wimbush gave no sign of having heard. But Asher took the lack of objection as his usual truculent acquiescence. Clever and misguidedly dedicated to his beloved plants he might well be, but when it came to personality, he really was, to quote one of Matt's flowery colloquialisms, a proper berk.

CHAPTER THIRTY-NINE

THE NORTHERN SARMATIC FOREST OF STEPPEINIT

As QUIETLY AS POSSIBLE, Asher and Matt negotiated the hill and hung back at the edge of the forest until the last of the trudging villagers had gone by. Quickly, they stepped onto the track and followed.

They slipped in behind without any trouble. The group of hunched figures spoke little. Asher realised that security was not an issue here because no one took this route willingly and a spontaneous rendition of 'Hi-Ho'—another of Matt's favourite quips —seemed unlikely. After a quarter of a mile, they came to a well-trodden path that led down into a wide ravine. Lamps hung from the branches and were still lit despite the improving light. A man dressed in a dark cassock wearing an expressionless mask watched the figures troop past into a cave entrance. He was taller than most of the workers. No, they were smaller than he was. Smaller…because they were younger. Many of these figures, Asher realised with horror, were children. He grabbed Matt's arm and they slipped off the road into the trees.

'If this is a party, I don't think much of the host,' Matt said.

'I doubt very much he is employed to meet and greet. I suspect his job is to stop them from running away once they're inside.'

'But we're going inside, aren't we?'

'Yes. But he will know we are not from the village since we are not aged between eight and fourteen.'

'They're kids?'

'From what I could see.'

Matt didn't speak for a while. When he did, his voice was drum tight. 'Shall I provide a distraction?'

Asher's eyes narrowed. Matt Danmor was a singularly unusual person. He was a *Homo sapiens* for a start. Well, mostly *Homo sapiens* with a pinch of something that made him skilled in a way that was difficult to define. He could make things happen by juggling the odds such that the unusual—in the sense of something being highly improbable yet imaginable—became manifest. Some called it the manipulation of chance, but whatever the label, it was usually worth watching when it happened. Trouble was, Matt had grown up in the late twentieth century where films and TV were the canon that moulded his imagination. And just like a canon, things that went bang and made a lot of fire were high on his list of distractions. His tendency towards the grandiose always got him into trouble with Kylah. And that was never a good idea. Matt, to his credit, had worked hard on his skill set. Even so, it was well worth watching.

'Don't worry. I'll keep it natural,' Matt said, noting the way Asher was looking at him.

'You don't mean a volcano, now do you?'

Matt sent him a hurt look. 'Oh, ye of little faith. No, I meant natural as in tusks and trotters.' He grinned.

From the forest to the left of where the masked guard stood came an unearthly meld of screech and grunt; a combination that hardly ever bode well and rendered spoonerism quixotic. The guard started and turned. The screech came again. The guard picked up a stout staff and braced himself just as a huge and angry-looking wild boar shot out of the undergrowth. There followed at least three short-succession events in the running away from a feral pig pentathlon. The throwing-the-staff-aimlessly, followed by the leaping-over-a-gorse-bush and ending with the running-away-at-full-speed-while-holding-a-cassock-up-around-the-waist.

Asher watched him go, boar in hot pursuit. 'May I ask…?'

Matt shrugged. 'It's what happens when a randy boar gets a

whiff of alderman parfum. Especially worn by one who might have not bathed for a couple of weeks.'

Asher didn't look round. The sprinting alderman was too engrossing. 'Yes, I suppose, as Roberta Miracle might say, "That will do it."'

They hurried towards a cold dark entrance that lay beyond where the guard stood. The path was beaten flat where it entered a crack in the rocks and the stench hit them after only a few yards. Pungent and ammoniacal, it caught instantly in Asher's throat. He fetched a couple of handkerchiefs from his pocket and applied some droplets from a small vial. The smell of fresh laundry enveloped them. He handed a handkerchief to Matt.

'Why is it always that I end up descending into the earth?' Asher muttered.

'Because that's generally where the bad things are,' said Matt, tying the handkerchief around his face.

They crept forwards for a hundred yards, descending steeply along a rocky path, the way poorly lit by flickering lamps. Ahead, noises drew them on. Mechanical clanking, the squeal of something wheeled that desperately needed oiling. The light grew brighter until they emerged into a large cavern, lit by numerous lamps, and a sight that would stay with both men until they died. They lay on their stomachs, hidden behind a couple of boulders. In front of them was one of the strangest scenes either of them had encountered. Above, the roof of the huge cavern was just about visible in the flickering light and it was moving. But then Asher saw that the movements were isolated. The dark roof was made up of thousands of tiny dark quivering dots.

'Bats,' Matt said.

Asher's eyes fell to the walls strung with ropes and lines criss-crossing the stone and running the length of the huge space thirty, forty, fifty feet off the floor. But it was what hung from these lines that was the most remarkable thing. People sat on wooden batons tied onto the ropes. They all had buckets dangling from their waists and, like Asher and Matt, wore scarves tied over their noses and mouths. There were perhaps twenty or more of them, and each worked at a point on the walls. And then Asher truly saw what they were doing.

'They're not whitewashing the walls, are they?'

'No. They're collecting the guano. They're *gathering*,' whispered Matt.

Asher nodded, frowning. 'But why such an elaborate arrangement? Why not use ladders and—'

The answer to his question appeared as a shadow moving in the darkness across the floor of the cavern. It was swift; a pale shape in the boulder-strewn space. Asher pointed, and Matt followed his finger to track the movement. Between the rocks, something white and feral stared back at them, baring its teeth and hissing. Asher felt something cold uncoil in his gut. If this was an animal, it was like nothing he had ever seen before.

'What is that?' Matt asked.

'Rjepers,' said a voice from the darkness.

Both men struggled onto their backs to find the tips of three sharp swords a foot away from their chests.

'Wouldn't it be easier to keep rabbits?' said Matt.

'They exist nowhere else. Voracious predators, white as milk, big as dogs. Some say they were placed here by a sorcerer to protect the bats.'

'Who are you?' Asher said.

'They call me Riggon. But who I am is of no concern to you. The villagers here consider this a sacred place. Appeasing the witch, they call it.'

Behind Riggon another man laughed. He was tall, and hatchet-faced.

Riggon went on. 'You are trespassing. The quick thing to do would be to throw you to the rjepers, but we know there are others. So why don't you take us to them, eh? At least that way you'll have a clean death, not be ripped apart like a piece of meat.'

'We are officers of the BOD,' said Asher. 'Know who you are threatening.'

'We could throw one of them in,' said Hatchet Face. 'It's been a slow morning.'

'Shut up, Kebbers,' said Riggon. 'You can throw the bitch in, if you want. Once we find her.'

'Nah,' Kebbers said through a tight mouth. 'She helped that alchemist get away, so we had to feed Ozil to the mabocawl to keep it happy. I've got other plans for her.'

Asher felt Matt tense next to him but held him back with a hand on his arm. There was another way to play this out.

'Please,' said Asher, holding up both hands to show he had no weapons, 'we'll do what you want. We'll take you to them.'

'Ah, thank the gods,' Riggon said. 'Someone with a lily liver who doesn't want to play the hero. Must be my lucky day.'

Asher caught sight of a few of the young gatherers' faces sitting on their precarious perches high above. They were watching with expressions of utter desolation. Working for the constabulary as he had done and now the BOD, he was quite used to opening cans of worms. But this was on a different scale. This was like opening a trapdoor on a cellar full of snakes. And nasty ones too. A quiet rage began to build in his core.

'Move it,' said Riggon and poked his sword into Asher's chest. 'Someone wants to ask you a few questions first.'

'All right,' said Asher. 'We do not want any trouble.'

Quietly, and under his breath so that only Asher could hear as they pushed themselves up from where they were lying, Matt said, 'Yeah, right.'

CHAPTER FORTY

Back in the forest, Nadia was busy collecting materials, using a handsaw to trim branches for walling material. Wimbush watched her, half-heartedly gathering his own pile of branches without enthusiasm.

'Why don't we just lean some larger branches against a tree? That'll do as a bivouac—'

Nadia cut him off. 'Asher says it has to be permanent structure.'

Wimbush looked around. 'But these aren't exactly permanent materials, are they? Bits of branch and twig.'

'We make hide. Like Asher wants.'

'Oh, yes. It's always what Asher wants, isn't it? What about what I want?'

Nadia snapped upright and swung around, the saw still in her hand, eyes blazing. 'What you want? What *you* want? Tell me, what *you* want? To go back to your little plants? To hide in laboratory? To see no one? To speak to no one?'

'My work is important. You wouldn't understand.'

'No one understands!'

Wimbush took a step back, unnerved by this small female who had suddenly turned into an angry wasp.

'It's…difficult to explain,' he said. 'It's really complicated—'

'Difficult? Complicated? How do you know? Have you ever tried explaining?'

Wimbush shook his head. There were years of aborted

conversational engagement in that shake. 'Not recently. There was never much reward for the effort.'

Nadia nodded. 'But if you try explaining, you will talk to other people. Perhaps you will begin to think of other people.'

Wimbush blinked, unsure if what he'd heard was pure gibberish or quite profound. 'Talking isn't my strong point.'

Nadia shook her head, turned away and started sawing again.

A rare pang of guilt twanged through Wimbush. 'Look, I know I've been somewhat remiss in not contacting you.'

Nadia paused again, but this time she didn't turn around.

'Time just seems to slip by when I'm working. I admit to being frustrated by the fact that and I am not one inch further forward with the cultivation of the *aconitum*. I can't help thinking that I'm missing something—'

'You saved my life,' Nadia said, still with her back turned. 'For that I will forever be in your debt. But you took me away from here and say you will help me but then do nothing. For weeks you do nothing and then you do not call or speak to me.'

'As I say,' said Wimbush, trying to swallow and failing badly, 'my work…' he let the words dribble away, for once realising how full of tepid air they were. There was nowhere to hide here. No library to bury his head in. No glasshouses to duck into. There was just Nadia, the woods and him. Panic threatened. This was new territory for him. He was being forced to reflect on his actions and, damn it all, his feelings. When he did swallow, it was as if he'd eaten a piece of Mr Tipling's sawdust doughnuts —'for display purposes only'—which were sold for breadcrumb-making on Popdy Street in New Thameswick. 'I'm sorry,' he said.

Nadia turned. If Wimbush was hoping to find forgiveness in her face, he was sadly disappointed. She shrugged. 'You owe me nothing. I owe you my life. Is unfair…equation.'

Wimbush wanted desperately to let his eyes slide away and look at the sky, the trees, the bushes, anywhere. But Nadia's gaze in those astonishing blue, blue eyes were full of unspoken challenge. Something else he didn't recognise in his head held him and wouldn't let him go. Another lump of sawdust doughnut slid down past his epiglottis. 'The truth is,' he began, 'I've been avoiding you because I didn't want…I was worried that…I haven't had much luck with girls and I thought that if you knew what I was really like, you'd end up washing your hair every night like all the others seemed to do.'

'Washing my hair?' Nadia frowned.

Wimbush nodded. 'Yes. You know, instead of wanting to perhaps…go out. All the girls I've known, well the three I actually talked to, were always having to wash their hair an awful lot.'

Birds were singing in the trees above their heads. It was a beautiful morning. If they had trekked back to the village and looked out over the meadow, they might even have seen the beginnings of a bright golden haze.

'Tell me about silver wolfsbane,' said Nadia.

'Family of *aconitum*—'

Nadia shook her head. 'It will not grow? Why?'

'That's precisely the point. I don't know,' said Wimbush. 'I've replicated the conditions exactly, or so I thought.'

'You have reekatsh?'

'Who?'

Nadia stomped across the gap between them, grabbed Wimbush's sleeve and dragged him thirty yards off the track to a shaded area. She pointed to a patch of flowering silver wolfsbane.

Wimbush gasped. 'How do you do that?'

Nadia knelt and pointed to some ferns growing adjacent to the silver flowers. 'Reekatsh.' She plucked a frond and sniffed it before holding it up to Wimbush, who took it and did the same.

'It smells of aniseed.'

Nadia shrugged and got up.

'So you're saying that this grows where the wolfsbane grows?' he asked, still staring at the ferns.

'Always.' Nadia nodded as she walked away.

'Symbiosis,' Wimbush whispered, staring at the plants. 'They're symbiotes. No wonder…' He got up and followed Nadia, catching her before she reached the place they'd been building the hide. He stared at her face, his own now transformed by wonder. 'That's amazing. You are amazing.' Laughing, Wimbush grabbed Nadia in a hug and whirled her around. The birds above them took off in fright. 'Symbiotes, who'd have thought it,' yelled Wimbush.

After at least half a dozen full circles, Wimbush remembered himself and let Nadia down with a jolt. 'I am so sorry,' he said, flustered. 'I don't know what came over me. I do apologise.'

'There is no need,' Nadia said. 'This is what comes from talking with people. With me.'

'Yes, absolutely. You're right, I…' He was standing close to her. Very close. Staring into those amazing blue, blue eyes.

'Come, we must finish hide and light fire.' Nadia turned away.

'Extraordinary,' whispered Wimbush. 'Truly extraordinary.' He began collecting materials for the hide with renewed vigour.

CHAPTER FORTY-ONE

KEBBERS LED the way after Asher and Matt's hands had been tied. They followed with Riggon at the rear. The path ran parallel to some narrow gauge rails. When they'd walked just a hundred yards, Riggon called a halt and stood to one side as a low rumble grew gradually louder. From around a bend, a figure approached. It wore a strap across its forehead to which were harnessed leather ropes leading back to a rusting metal tram. The figure leaned forward at an angle, straining against the weight of the fully laden tram. As it pulled opposite where Asher stood, he could see that the tram-puller was a girl, no more than eleven years old, sweat streaking her face. As she passed the men, she glanced at Asher. There was fear in her eyes as she reached a wooden barrier across the rail. There she struggled out of the harness, which was taken by two guards who hooked it up to a horse. The girl, having reached the point at which further access for her was prohibited, stood recovering, her hand on her knees.

Asher turned to Riggon. 'What sort of monstrous operation is this?'

Riggon smiled. 'A very profitable one. But then, why don't you ask the boss? He's dying to meet you.'

They set off again. The tramway stretched another quarter of a mile, ending in a clutch of drystone buildings, the biggest of which was a round tower built in to the hill behind. Smoke drifted up from the top of the tower, curling away over the trees.

'It's a kiln,' said Matt.

The tramway led to a stone shed full to the brim with bat droppings.

'Go to the top of the class,' Riggon said and poked Matt with his sword. 'Now, get a move on.'

Kebbers crossed the tramway and took them to a bigger stone building. This one with an archway leading to a wooden-framed interior office. Silhouetted against a window was a tall, angular figure who rose as they entered, though he never quite managed to get totally upright because of his immense height.

'Gentlemen, we meet again.'

'Oslo Elkson,' said Asher. 'I might have known.'

'Come, come, Mr Asher. If I were that predictable, surely you would have arrested me in New Thameswick?'

'I wouldn't have bothered with the arrest,' said Matt. 'I would have gone straight to hanging without passing go.'

'Ah, the enigmatic Mr Danmor. Still your lapdog, I see.' Elkson grinned at Asher.

'What sort of hell have you created here?' Matt demanded.

'I am a businessman, Mr Danmor, surely you understand that.'

'But those are lime kilns, aren't they?'

'Similar, but not exactly.' Elkson perched on the window sill, folding his long limbs beneath him so that his head didn't hit the ceiling. 'It isn't lime we are processing, it is glasstone. Unique to this area.' He picked up a nugget from his desk. It was shot through with blue crystal. 'It is what gives the villagers here their unique appearance. Their blue sclerae. It leeches into the water, you see. But by refining it and heating it, then extracting its compounds, it gets transformed into something truly remarkable. Capable of inducing the most astounding imagery in those willing to expose themselves to its power.'

'Corrupted lava juice,' Asher said.

'Precisely. It's laborious and complex work. However, our alchemists have recently discovered that by adding the waste products of the many bats that live in the caves, it speeds the process up to a fraction of the time.'

'But it changed the end product.' Asher pointed out. 'What you were peddling was bad enough before. Now it's—'

'Potent? Agreed. But time is money, Mr Asher. Our new

improved lava juice gets to the customers three times more quickly this way.'

'It's lethal, you sod,' Matt said.

'It is also illegal,' Elkson pointed out cheerfully. 'No one is compelled to buy. You pay your money and take your chance, eh?'

'What about the villagers? This is slave labour.'

'Oh, come now. They are only too pleased to take part in the Gathering.' He smiled. 'We keep them away from the furnace. Better they do not learn what we truly do. Let them do the donkey work. That way they can be certain of keeping the wolf from the door and the witch from the chimney.' The smile turned into an unpleasant laugh.

Behind him, Kebbers howled quietly.

Matt shook his head. 'It's all a sham. You're hoodwinking these poor people into believing a load of superstitious nonsense.'

'It's what poor people do, Mr Danmor. They need superstition so that their miserable existence has meaning. Better to believe that there is a witch or a wizard or a god doing the orchestration than not believe. That way lies free will and we all know what sort of trouble that causes. But enough talk.' Elkson put two big hands on the table. 'I know that you came here with the girl and the alchemist. He should have been collateral damage but the girl should not have left the forest. Those blue eyes of hers are what have brought you here, am I correct?'

Neither Asher nor Matt responded.

'No matter. It will be forgotten. The forest is a dangerous place. We need to arrange a little accident and it needs to involve all four of you.'

'Like what was meant to have happened on the barrel run?' Asher said.

'Ah yes, you met my feral cousins. May I say, you did well to get away from them. Hardly anyone ever does. Using the barrel line was a stroke of genius. Local knowledge? Let me guess, the girl? Pity it will all be for nothing. Now, where is she and where is that bumbling alchemist?'

'They've gone home,' Asher said.

'Really?' Elkson sighed. 'Then why are we not overrun with

BOD agents? You're lying, and I have no time for games. Kebbers, kill Danmor.'

Kebbers stepped forward, sword in hand. 'This will be a pleasure.'

Matt didn't move. He was staring out of the window at the kiln tower. Had been for some time. 'I know it's none of my business, but is smoke meant to be belching out of that crack in the side of that big tower thing?'

Kebbers frowned. Elkson, irritated, swivelled his neck to see. There was indeed smoke belching out and even as they watched, a fissure appeared and began to spread with a sound like snapping ice.

Elkson stood, or rather hunched, staring out of the window. 'What wizardry is this?' he hissed.

'Lousy maintenance, more like,' said Matt.

Elkson shot him a hateful glance but before he could move or say anything, Riggon shouted, 'It's going to explode!'

Elkson stumbled forward. 'Get out of my way!' He sent Matt and Asher tumbling with one huge hand and lumbered out, Kebbers and Riggon right behind him.

Asher started to struggle upright but Matt put his foot out to hold him back. 'I think we'll be okay. I've got a feeling we'll be better off lying still.'

With a loud crack, the tower split and the furnace erupted. Stones rained down, some of them red hot, most of them lethally heavy. A sizeable chunk fell on the facing wall, taking out the stonework to leave an equally sizeable gap. When the dust and smoke settled, Asher and Matt were still lying low while all around them the devastation looked like the apocalypse had been and left its calling card.

Matt cleared his throat. 'I suspect that's the end of operations for today. But, as luck would have it, no villagers were harmed in the making of this programme. And no point hanging round any longer, is there?'

'None whatsoever,' agreed Asher, coughing.

They scrambled out and over the rubble into the forest, hands still tied.

'Any direction?' Matt asked.

'Nadia has left us a signal.' Asher nodded upwards towards a thin curl of white smoke rising above the trees a mile to their left.

Matt grinned. 'I really like that girl.'

CHAPTER FORTY-TWO

MERTHYR, WALES, 500 AD

THE CELTIC ENCAMPMENT was a very different place that morning, largely because there'd been no skirmishes overnight and no one had suffered any nightmares. The Nosdrwg had been too stoned to bother.

By the afternoon, men were arriving to bolster Arthur's army and the noise of hammered iron echoed through the air as blacksmiths forged new weapons for the troops. Kylah watched the preparations from their quarters with growing impatience. Finally, she shook her head. 'This is so not our time.'

Behind her, Bobby was conjuring some cloth knights into doing a Morris dance with sticks, giggling to herself.

'Bobby!' Kylah said.

The knights collapsed into a handkerchief pile. Bobby rolled her eyes. 'Can't help it. Wonderworking feels so fresh here. It's really easy. And not having any technology is kind of liberating, isn't it? It's a bit like being a kid again.'

'I have noticed. That's another good reason for getting back as soon as possible. Whatever it is that's making you unendingly cheerful and mischievous is getting right up my nose.'

'Sorry.' Bobby made one of the cloth knights turn into a cloth maiden, spring up and curtsy. It then folded in a heap and she played with it between her fingers for a while before eventually asking, 'When we were fighting the necromancer, and the afternoon disappeared, you said something.'

'Did I?'

'Yes, you said Time wouldn't like it. Is Time a thing then?'

'Yes and no. I can only tell you what Uncle Ernest told me, and he should know because they are related. She is my Aunty Anke. And she does exist and is busy making sure everything's fresh from second to second. She's big on inevitability and fate. That's why she discourages time travel. That would mean her having to go into the dressing-up cupboard and recreating something for the traveller, which is a bugger because the person travelling into the past, the real past like we have, has no memory of it. And history's no help because the people with the pencils are generally the ones with the spears and the swords, too. They tend not to be that big on accuracy. So, she has to "provide" the past for a traveller and, that way, mistakes can happen. That's why she has a zero-tolerance approach. Usually. No one has yet gone back and returned successfully. Basically, because they forgot to apply for permission from Aunty Anke.'

'So when did we apply?'

Kylah shook her head. 'We didn't. But seeing what that necromancer did, making his own time co-exist with ours and eating it up like he did, that's not good. Anke wouldn't like that at all.'

'So, do you think Time—erm, your aunty—knows we're here?'

'Oh yes, she knows. I don't think we're here by accident. The question is, does she care?'

'Maybe she did know and has forgotten. Maybe she's too busy preparing for the equinox. That's probably like a huge spring-cleaning operation.'

'Maybe. So perhaps we ought to give her a nudge.' Kylah stood up. 'Come on. Enough is enough.'

They found the sorcerers foraging in a grove of trees.

'Love the outdoors, don't they?' Kylah said as they squelched along the path.

'It's their Druid blood. Plus, the fact that there's a lot more outdoors than indoors.'

'There is that.'

'Afternoon,' said Morgana as they approached.

'You look busy.'

'We're collecting herbs and plants in preparation for a potion that will give heart to Arthur and his knights.'

'Ooh, sounds good,' Bobby said, grinning. 'Want some help?'

Kylah yanked her back and stepped in front of her to address Morgana. 'We know how busy you are, but we need to talk about—'

'Kevin?' said Bobby and earned a withering over-the-shoulder look from Kylah that swiped the grin from her face like a wet mop.

'About getting back,' continued Kylah in measured tones.

Myrddin, intently studying some lichen on the bark of a wizened oak, swivelled his head towards them and then turned away, coughing as he did so.

'Perhaps if you could help us collect the herbs, we will get this task done and—' began Morgana brightly, but she didn't finish as Kylah cut across her.

'You don't know how, do you?'

The silence that followed was pierced by a raucous crow cawing out a territorial warning. It sounded like the wild laugh of some mocking hag.

'It was a very difficult spell,' said Morgana at last.

Kylah persisted. 'Myrddin, look at me. Do you, or don't you?'

Myrddin straightened, his expression drawn. 'Your arrival was fortuitous, a gift from the gods. The spell was not difficult since our only intervention was to offer a knight's sword, one that was successful in battle, and cast a preservation spell. It was meant to summon reinforcements. Contact our brethren in Cernew, but something else intervened. It was completely out of our control, and I have never truly experienced anything like it. I know of no spell that causes metal swords to plunge into solid rock and fuse with it such that it cannot be removed. We had no idea that it would lead to your presence here. And so…we have no knowledge of how to send you back.'

'I knew it,' Kylah said, the brightness in her voice the thin crust above a boiling saucepan of tinkling despair.

'But…' Bobby looked from Morgana's anxious face to Myrddin's pitying expression. 'You brought us here. Surely…'

'We hoped for succour.'

'That's exactly what I feel like,' Kylah muttered. 'Suckered.'

'We would welcome your tutelage,' Morgana said, with an attempt at an appeasing smile. 'You have powerful cunning.'

'Aw, that's the nicest thing anyone's said to me. Thanks, Morgana,' Bobby tilted her head and grinned. 'Maybe I could show you one or two little things.'

'Bobby,' Kylah warned.

'We would look after you both,' Morgana persisted.

'I know you would,' Bobby said, her smile faltering under Kylah's glare. 'But I actually hate those dresses you wear. I don't have the waist for it.'

'We need to think,' Kylah said. 'Think hard.'

Bobby nodded. 'Maybe if you did exactly what you did before, and we bury another sword, someone else would find it?'

Kylah shook her head. 'And drag some other poor sod back across the centuries?'

'I am truly sorry,' Myrddin said. 'We did not want to mislead you, but we have been powerless to prevent this.'

'Okay, okay,' said Bobby, beginning to pace. 'Concentrate, Bobby. Who do we know who could get us out of this?'

Kylah shrugged. 'What does it matter? Everyone we know is fifteen hundred years in the future.'

'I know, I know. But who?'

'Someone from the Academy?'

'Possibly, but then they're not going to be looking for us.'

'You're right. The only people who might be looking for us are Matt, Asher, Keemoch and Birrik.'

Bobby stopped pacing and pivoted. 'What about your uncle?'

Kylah blinked. 'Of all the people I can think of, Uncle Ernest is the one to have a word with Aunty Anke. But how is that going to help if no one knows where we are?'

Bobby started pacing again. 'Let me run with this for a minute. Geographically, we can assume that the sinkhole and here are one and the same place, right?'

'Can we?'

Bobby pointed to the east. 'Sort of. We've gone back in time, but not necessarily changed space. See that hill over there? It is the same as the one on the edge of the estate where the sink-hole…sank. I should know. I spent enough time staring at the damned thing in the rain.'

'It would make sense.' Kylah nodded.

'That, at least, is a physical link. Assume someone there knows we've disappeared by now, too. What we need to do is tell them what's happened.'

'Agreed.'

Bobby turned to the sorcerers. 'When did you offer the sword?''

'Six days ago.'

'Right. Kylah, can I borrow your phone?'

'Bobby, texting in the hope that the ether might hang on to your message for a millennium and a half is a bit of a—'

'Also, I need something sharp to scratch on metal and a way to preserve it. Do you have any amber?'

'Yes, we have amber,' Myrddin said, frowning.

Bobby nodded. 'Okay, since I can't think of anything else and I really, really do not want to be anyone's lady-in-waiting, let's do this.' She held out her hand.

Kylah, her frown now a smile of realisation, handed over the iPhone.

Myrddin nodded, glancing at the bac. 'I see you like apples. Now, go back to your quarters. Morgana will join you there shortly with what you have asked for.'

Pulling their cloaks about them, they headed back to the tents in a strained silence until finally Bobby commented, 'You're not saying much.'

'No,' Kylah replied. 'Not because of your idea. It's because my head is spinning with all the ramifications.'

'Any one in particular? There are so many, I've lost count.''

'The sinkhole.'

'What about it?'

'What I and those engineers experienced down there, it must be the Nosdrwg.'

'Obviously.'

'But they were meant to have been banished for all eternity. We saw and heard Myrddin's bargain.'

Bobby was nodding slowly. 'Something must have broken that spell to bring them back to haunt the place.'

It was Kylah's turn to nod. 'Something, or someone, has an awful lot to answer for.'

CHAPTER FORTY-THREE

THE NORTHERN SARMATIC FOREST OF
STEPPEINIT

Matt and Asher, hands still tied, jogged through the forest,
twisting their faces against the slapping branches, pausing occasionally to check direction. This was no time for stealth. They
needed to find Wimbush and Nadia, and quickly. They could
hear shouts behind them. The collapse of the kiln had thrown
the operation into disarray. Sheer luck for it to happen just as
they were being threatened. But Asher knew that luck had
nothing to do with it. Or rather had everything to do with it,
since Matt somehow managed to cajole luck into doing things
that might not otherwise have crossed its mind.

'Tell me about the kiln tower?'

'The tower?' Matt's question was all innocence.

'Yes. The one that conveniently collapsed a moment ago.'

'Oh, my guess is that water got into the brickwork. It froze
last night. Water acts just like a wedge in those conditions.
Expands and splits and causes all sorts of damage. Once they lit
the kiln, heat might cause expansion in the stone and that little
crack could become a big one very quickly. I suspect that's what's
happened.'

'Yes. I suspect so, too.' Asher grinned.

'And a buckled rail meant that all transport to the kiln had stopped. Fortunately, there were no young villagers anywhere near at the time.'

Asher nodded this time. This was how Matt worked. Imagining things that were all too feasible, even if highly unlikely, and somehow making them happen. He was a good man to have in a tight spot.

They followed animal paths in the general direction of the smoke. Soon the shouts receded. Once, Asher was sure he heard the snap of a branch behind them. He hissed a warning to Matt and they both ducked low, waiting and listening, but there was no further noise. Fifteen minutes later, they skirted the bottom of the rise they'd first scrambled down to join the path to the Gathering and began to wind upwards, the wispy smoke clearly visible now.

There was no sign of anyone when they finally got to the tiny clearing and the fire hissing against the wet leaves Nadia had used to signal with.

'Nadia?'

The girl appeared, brandishing a saw in one hand and a small knife in the other.

'Good to see you,' said Matt, grinning. He turned to let Nadia use the knife on the ropes binding his hands.

'Where's Wimbush?' Matt asked.

'Collecting specimens.'

Matt shook his head as he rubbed life back into his sore wrists. 'I might have known.'

'We had finished so I saw no harm.'

Asher looked around, frowning.

'Here,' said Nadia, walking across the clearing

Asher followed. The hide was five foot by six and large enough for one person to sit inside.

'The door works,' Nadia said and proceeded to demonstrate. She pulled on the rickety frame and the makeshift door opened with a squeak.

'Will it do?' Matt asked.

'It'll do nicely,' said Asher.

'Shame you're not going to be able to use it, then.' They all knew the voice. Behind them, Kebbers stepped out from behind a tree with crossbow raised. 'Don't try anything stupid 'cos this has a speed loader and it's ready to fire. You'd all be dead before you could pull out your knife. And, speakin' of knives, let's have that one, girl, before you do someone an injury.'

Nadia threw down the knife and the saw.

'That's it,' Kebbers said. 'You and me are goin' to be good friends, I can see that.'

Matt twitched and Kebbers shifted the crossbow sight to his chest.

'Uh-uh. Riggon wants to see you about a kiln. Otherwise, you'd be dead already. But don't be disappointed. You're still on my to-do list.' Kebbers grinned and let out a wolf howl.

Asher knew he was calling the others. 'You can do yourself a large favour by letting us go. I can put in a good word.'

'A good book, more like. I have a lot of history. A word ain't goin' to do it.' Kebbers grinned and howled again.

'Must you make that infernal racket?'

Kebbers had time enough to twist his head and take in the figure that appeared slightly to the left and behind him before a three-foot-long branch of thick Steppeinit pine hit him squarely on the temple. He collapsed in a passable impression of a sack of turnips. Ones that had gone off a very long time ago.

'Never thought I'd say this, but am I glad to see you, Wimbush,' Matt said.

The alchemist dropped the branch, walked back across the clearing and came back with an armful of ferns, complete with roots. 'Think nothing of it. Now, would it be too much to ask if we could leave?'

Matt turned to Asher, who in turn inspected the hide and its door. 'There is only one way to find out.'

From somewhere off to their left, they heard another howl.

'Wolves?' Wimbush asked.

'Yes,' Matt said, 'but not the four-legged kind.'

As if on cue, an arrow thudded into the tree three feet to the left of Matt's head. They all ducked.

Asher reached into his pocket and took out the Aperio, and, still on his haunches, attached it to the hinge side of the door.

'They're coming,' Matt yelled. 'Now would be a good time.'

Off to their left, the rustling of branches told them that Kebber's cronies were making little or no effort to disguise themselves.

Asher tugged on the Aperio, testing its adhesion to the door.

'We must hope that the Aperio recognises this as a permanent structure.'

He pulled. After a moment's resistance, the door opened, hinge side first.

'Go!' Asher yelled and propelled Nadia forward. Wimbush followed, then Matt and finally Asher, who grabbed for the Aperio as he crawled through. He heard the thunk of a steel-tipped crossbow arrow and saw the sharp tip punch through the thin door and stay wedged there just as he tumbled forwards into his dingy but ever so welcome office at the BOD in New Thameswick.

PART 5

CHAPTER FORTY-FOUR

NEW THAMESWICK

Over the next two hours, several remarkable things happened.

Crouch arrived within ten minutes. Within half an hour, all of Blechern Holdings' assets had been frozen and a clean-up squad of BOD and constabulary volunteers under Crouch's leadership were geared up and ready to go back to Spiv. Matt and Asher were all set to accompany them until Birrik arrived. The look on his face told both men something was very wrong.

'It's Captain Porter and Miss Miracle. They've gone missing.'

'Missing? What do mean, missing?' Matt demanded.

Birrik obliged with an explanation that was as disturbing as it was unsatisfying.

'We have to go to that sinkhole,' Asher said when he'd finished. He turned to Crouch.

'Of course, you do,' said the hawkshaw. 'Both of you.'

'But that leaves the clean-up squad without a guide,' Matt said.

'No, it does not. I will lead them.'

Crouch turned towards the source of this bold statement and found Nadia. He took one look at her frail form and started to say, 'No, I don't think—'

'Exactly, Crouch,' said Asher. 'Don't think. Nadia is more

than capable. Every one of us will vouch for that. And if that is not enough vouchers, having listened to what we have learned from that monster, Elkson, I think you will now have a great deal of trouble keeping her away.'

'Even so, this sounds like it might be messy work,' Crouch murmured so that only Asher could hear. 'Think she's up to it?'

'My village is living a lie,' said Nadia. There was a fire in her blue eyes. 'My brother died because of that lie. I also have excellent hearing, Mr Crouch. Give me a knife.'

Crouch's expression was suitably owl-like when he turned back. But he handed over a constabulary issue dagger regardless.

'Hang on.' Wimbush had remained seated in the corner this whole time, fussing like a mother hen over his wolfsbane and ferns, and ensuring they were wrapped and watered. Now he stood and addressed the group. 'Nadia, you don't have to go. These men are dangerous. You don't have to—'

'Is my village.' Just three words, but delivered with enough feeling to inspire an army.

Wimbush looked at the reekatsh and then at Nadia. He removed a bit of moss from one of the fern's leaves, and pulled himself up straight. 'Then I will go too. I know these men. Some of them might try and hide amongst the villagers. I can help root them out.'

Crouch grinned. 'Blimey, easiest recruitment drive we've ever had. Offer accepted.'

Matt blinked. Asher smiled. Nadia's face split into a grin that threatened to set the Bureau of Demonology alight as she ran across the room and jumped into Wimbush's arms.

'Am I missing something here?' Crouch whispered to Asher and Matt.

Matt shrugged. 'Loads. Much of which I don't pretend to understand myself and never will. But the gist of it is you'll be able to tell your kids you just witnessed a genuine, five-star epiphany.'

———

CROUCH ARRANGED for a Portway to be set up through the hide door but neither Matt nor Asher stayed. They grabbed Birrik and went directly to Mackeson's portacabin in Merthyr, where it was spitting rain yet again. The twelve-hour difference meant that it was almost 2.00 am when they arrived. Birrik, as Dwayne, went through the whole story again. At the portacabin, Mackeson filled them in on what progress—or lack of it—the police had made.

'Still no sign of them.' Mackeson shook his head. 'Current theories are that there was some kind of seismic slip that's closed up again. We've had heat-sensitive equipment down there, even tried sniffer dogs, but that didn't last. Whatever that stink is drives them mad. We had to abandon that.'

Both Matt and Asher were on edge, picking up on every word.

'But there was no noise or tremor when it happened?' Matt asked.

Dwayne shook his head. 'Nothing. They were simply there one minute, gone the next.'

'I want to see for myself,' Asher said.

'Fair enough,' Mackeson nodded. 'Dwayne will show you the drill since he's already been down. We've got no one down there at the moment apart from your man, Alf. Truth is we've run out of ideas.'

They suited up. The sinkhole looked as strange and unwelcoming as ever as they descended. The lights faded into a khaki murk and once they passed through the curious mist that hung like a horizontal curtain, the gloom was dense and almost palpable. Birrik showed them where Kylah and Bobby had been working.

'What are the weird lights?' Matt asked.

'We don't know,' Keemoch said. 'Except that they are in the walls.'

Asher spoke, and his voice was thick. 'I know. This is a repository for souls.'

'Souls? You mean, like a cemetery?'

'No. These entities are not here voluntarily. I sense that.'

'Imprisoned? You can speak to them?'

'No. They are no longer human. I sense an echo only. Whatever they are, they're ancient.'

These were enigmatic words. The knot that had tightened in Matt's stomach on hearing Birrik's report cinched itself again. Kylah could look after herself, but this place...this place was about as wrong a place as he had ever encountered, and his anxiety ratcheted upwards on hearing Asher's words.

'Let us examine the area they were working in,' Asher said.

The fetched lights and set them in position, guided by Birrik and Keemoch. Others had already done this, gone over every inch of ground and yet both men felt compelled to repeat the exercise.

'Were they digging?' Matt asked.

'They were leaning over as if they had found something on the ground,' Keemoch explained.

'Let us assume that to be the case,' mused Asher.

His hopeful words sank into the rubble-strewn mess that both men stared into as they surveyed the area. It was featureless; a haphazard jumble of rock and clay, some of which had already started to flow down as muddy rivulets now that rain was eroding the surface.

'I think we are going to need some help here,' Asher said.

Matt picked up a pick and swung it lazily at the wall. A chunk of clay come away and fell to the floor. 'It's going to take forever to search this.'

'I agree. I do not think that any seismic event would leave so little evidence. I suspect that wonderworking of some kind is involved. The truth may be hidden in these walls.'

'Gives me the creeps,' said Matt and stepped back as a trickle of water began to flow over his boots. It had already pooled around the chunk of clay he'd dislodged, turning the water a murky brown. But as Matt's eyes fell, something in the chunk of mud glistened in his helmet light. Curiosity aroused, he reached down and picked up the heavy lump. The clay was thick and sticky, and it took him a moment to peel it away. Inside was some kind of grey material. Grey like their hazmat suits, long and sausage-shaped. The material had been compressed and squashed, but inside it was something considerably more solid.

'Knife,' Matt said.

Keemoch obliged with a blade of some blue metal that split the material open with nothing more than a brush stroke. And there, inside, wet and glistening from the water on Matt's hands was, incredibly, a mobile phone. A modern mobile phone encased in a thick see-through block of jagged yellow material.

Matt rotated it, staring at it in astonishment. 'Is that amber?'

Keemoch frowned. 'What does that mean?'

'Amber was once used to preserve items,' Asher said.

'What, mobile phones?' Keemoch scoffed.

'Okay, that's weird,' Matt muttered. 'It's down here in the ground, in amber. Who the hell could dropped this—' And then his light fell on the letters scratched on the surface of the phone's silvery back. He rubbed furiously at the mud and peered at the scribbles.

Stuck in 500 AD

Contact EP @ Hipposync

HELP K & B

Matt read it again. With some difficulty, as his hands were shaking so badly.

'What is it?' Asher asked.

'It's Kylah's phone,' Matt croaked. There was more to say but he didn't say it. He could barely speak. He could hardly breathe. He held out the phone and let Asher read it himself.

'But that is not possible,' Asher whispered before handing the phone to Birrik. 'How could that be?'

'More to the point, how is it that you managed to find the right place with just one swing of that pick…' Birrik's words tailed off. He'd forgotten whom he was talking to.

But Matt was shaking his head, his breathing ragged.

'EP?' asked Asher. 'Who is EP?'

With a huge effort of will, Matt looked into his friend's face. 'Ernest Porter. Kylah's uncle.'

Birrik picked up a piece of fractured plastic pipe and hammered it into the soft clay next to where Matt's fortuitous gouge had dislodged the phone. 'A marker,' said the Sith Fand.

'Good idea,' Asher said.

But Matt didn't hear him. He was already scrambling up the ladder.

CHAPTER FORTY-FIVE

OXFORD, ENGLAND

GETTING in touch with Ernest Porter, proprietor and founder of Hipposync Enterprises, was never easy at the best of times. No one, except Kylah, knew where he really lived. There was, of course, an address on Crick Road, one of Oxford's leafy streets, but this was nothing more than a fetching red-brick garage in the grounds of a six-bedroom house owned by the university. Royal Mail were happy to leave post under the potted poinsettia outside the door, and it was, as boltholes went, most convenient. Matt had, of course, wondered why Ernest Porter and his wife lived in a double-fronted garage, but he had never questioned the situation since, where Hipposync was concerned, like a gung-ho skier atop a double black run, once you started, there was nowhere to stop. Any answers only ever led to more questions. What he did know was that Kylah kept a spare key to the lock-up in her office. And it was that key he now had in his hand as he, Asher and Dwayne hurried up Banbury Road.

No one spoke much. The gusting wind drove a thin and bitter drizzle into their eyes and there were few, if any, lights on in the big houses they passed. Given the circumstances, it was not a night that invited conversation.

They did not bother to knock. Dwayne did the honours with the key and undid the padlock. The door swung open with a jarring scrape against the concrete floor. He waited until they were all inside before shutting the door again and turning on the light.

What the single naked bulb revealed was a completely empty space that smelled of damp leaves and spilled oil.

'Well?' Matt said.

Dwayne shrugged off the camocharm and became Birrik before he spoke. They were words but not in any language Matt recognised. A door appeared in the back wall. Black and glossy with a large dragon's head knocker. Birrik motioned Matt forward. He stepped up to the door and rapped twice with the knocker.

Two minutes later it opened to reveal the housekeeper herself.

'Mrs Hoblip,' said Matt, 'we have a bit of a problem.'

The gurgled response would have made the top ten in any Hollywood studio's death rattle audio library. The smile that came with it curdled most of the milk in the neighbouring houses.

Ten minutes later, he and Asher were sitting in a warm and cosy library in a couple of far-too-comfortable leather wing chairs drinking hot tea and chewing on some of Mrs Hoblip's homemade biscuits. A bespectacled Ernest Porter, his ample stomach covered by an elaborately embroidered dressing gown, sat at his desk peering closely at the amber-encased phone as Birrik leaned over the back of the chair to point out the scratched lettering.

'And we are confident that this is indeed fifth century, eh, Sergeant?' he asked.

'We've run diagnostics, sir. The encasement spell was the last wonderworking we could measure. It has been confirmed as having been cast in 487 AD, as per the common parlance.'

'Buggery,' said Mr Porter, using even commoner parlance. He sat back in the chair, nibbling a biscuit. 'Remarkable. Truly remarkable.' He glanced up at Matt and Asher, both of whom were sitting forward on the edge of their chairs. 'Have you tried one of Mrs Hoblip's turmeric digestives?'

'Very nice,' said Matt, glancing with momentary confusion at the tray. 'So, what do you think?'

'Personally,' said Mr Porter, 'I prefer her cardamom variety.

Sources all the spices herself, you know. Wonderful cook, Mrs Hoblip.'

'Not the biscuits, I meant the phone.'

'Ah yes, the, um, ambulator phone, isn't that what you call it?'

'Mobile. It's called a mobile.'

Mr Porter smiled and shook his snowy head. 'Curious name for an item that paralyses young people into staring at it for hours on end.'

'Sir,' said Asher, once again sensing that Matt was on the point of exploding, 'have you any idea of what might have happened to Kylah and Bob…Miss Miracle?'

'A good question, Mr Lodge. If this is genuine, it would appear that both my niece and the delightful Miss Miracle have managed to transport themselves back in time by some fifteen hundred years.'

'But how is that possible?'

'Alchemists have tried manipulating time, but their experiments often end with only smoking slippers and stale tea left behind. Confirmation of time travel is elusive because the alchemist's interference typically erases their own existence. When they vanish, there's no worried relatives around to inform. If an alchemist does travel back in time, their meddling usually negates their presence altogether.'

'Oh, God.' Matt's head dropped, and he ran trembling fingers through his hair.

Asher was frowning. 'But surely, dabbling in any sense would change the world completely, would it not? If one person ceases to exist, it would affect everything and everyone connected to that person from that point on.'

'The butterfly effect,' Matt whispered. 'The flapping of an insect's wings on one side of the world can result in a hurricane ten thousand miles away.'

'Really?' Asher asked. 'And I always thought the things completely harmless.'

'It's a theory whereby any small change might have massive repercussions further down the time line. People in the film industry have made careers out of it.'

Mr Porter chuckled. 'It is curious how butterflies have an almost mystical connotation whenever they are mentioned.

Whereas their cousins, moths, are often considered nothing more than nuisances that one wants to swat away.'

'Is there such a thing as a moth effect?' Asher asked.

'Who knows?' Mr Porter shrugged. 'Though, in general, attempting to meddle with time is considered a risky thing to do,' he added with a sanguine look over the top of his glasses.

'But…'

Mr Porter smiled. 'I do not believe for one moment such an activity would have crossed Kylah and Bobby's minds. And let us not forget the fact that we are here, fifteen hundred years later, discussing them. It poses an interesting conundrum, does it not?'

Asher let this sink in. 'I see. Yes, if they had come to some harm then they would not exist and we would have no knowledge of them.'

'Exactly. And so, I think here we have the opposite scenario. One where time herself has decided to play a part and involve Kylah and Bobby as innocent—or perhaps not-so-innocent—players.'

'What's the difference?' Matt was beginning to look hopeful.

'The difference, my dear Mathew, is immensely significant. In this scenario, Anke, also known as Time, is an old and dear friend. Kylah even calls her Aunty. Anke may have a role for them both to play here. That is the point. I do not believe that they are where they are as interlopers. I would suggest they are there neither as butterflies nor as moths, but as guests. If this were not the case, I suspect they would have flown unheeding into the flames of a very large candle and been incinerated by now.'

'Is that what happens to the experimental alchemists?'

'Indeed, it is. Many make the mistake of believing that time is an abstract entity that flows like a great river from source to sea. She is that, but she also a great deal more. Unfortunately, she is also very forgetful, having been forced to live in the moment and only worry about the future, since that is her role. Even so, rivers have eddies and bends where the flow is much slower. It also has a ferryman whose job is to "sweat the small stuff", as they say. It is he that tends to do the mopping up when someone or something upsets the flow. Nice chap. Doesn't say much. But has an excellent memory.'

'Is it him who lights the candles?'

'Indeed, it is.'

Matt had gone pale again. 'But for the phone to be where it was means that it's been there for fifteen hundred years. That *they've* been there fifteen hundred years. They'll be long dead by now.'

'Very true.' Mr Porter knitted his fingers together. 'And yet possibly not true. That is the nature of a paradox. They have sent us a message, have they not? Would it not be reasonable to assume that they have completed their task and now wish to return?'

Matt's next words were a desperate whisper. 'If there is a way, any way, I think we should do it now.'

Mr Porter stood up. 'Let me have a quick word with Anke.' He left the others staring at one another. But half a minute later, he returned. 'Sorry about that, she does go on a bit.'

'You've been away for half a minute, sir,' Birrik said.

Mr Porter smiled. 'Really?' He tutted. 'Anke. Always the joker. Right, are we all ready?'

'Where are we going?' Matt jumped to his feet.

'To the source of the problem.' Mr Porter walked to the door, but then had a second thought as he looked down at his dressing gown. 'Sergeant Birrik, would you ask Mrs Hoblip for my mackintosh and sou'wester?' He somehow managed to make the order both apologetic and endearing. 'Oh, and Sergeant Birrik, ask Mrs Hoblip to fetch that ball of string she keeps under the sink.' He turned back to Matt and Asher, his eyes crinkling with amusement. 'It's been there for years. No idea why. Never needed it or used it. Until now. But first, let me have another word with Anke.'

CHAPTER FORTY-SIX

MERTHYR, WALES, PRESENT DAY

It was still drizzling in the sinkhole. Matt, Asher and Birrik—as Dwayne—suited up, but Mr Porter eschewed all attempts at convincing him it was necessary. 'I have my mackintosh and sou'wester,' he said, tapping his yellow plastic hat.

His descent of the ladders was slow but steady. On reaching the bottom, he frowned.

'My, this is a most disagreeable place.'

'It saps all your energy,' Keemoch—as Alf—said, with feeling. He'd been down the hole the longest and was looking decidedly under the weather.

'My dear fellow,' Mr Porter said, reaching a hand up to the Sith Fand's shoulder. 'This is not a place to linger.' He reached into his pocket and took out a bundle wrapped in a kitchen towel. He peeled the paper apart to reveal half a dozen biscuits. 'Have one of these. I had Mrs Hoblip prepare some before we left. Her own recipe, of course.'

Alf shook his head. 'No thank you, sir, I'm not hungry.'

'Hunger, my dear chap, has nothing at all to do with it. Here, I insist.' He snapped a biscuit in half and held it up.

Alf lifted up his mask and popped it into his mouth.

'Good lad,' said Mr Porter. 'Now, Mathew. Where exactly did you find the telephonic device?'

Matt led the way. The strange grey shapes in the walls followed their progress. Mr Porter stopped to stare, nodded and then continued his slow walk across the base of the sinkhole to where the plastic pipe protruded from the wall.

'It was a lucky blow,' Matt said.

Mr Porter chuckled. 'Indeed. However, we both know that there is no other type when it applies to you. Now, let me put on my glasses.'

From behind them, they heard a whistle.

Everyone except Mr Porter turned. Alf was striding along. To say that there was a spring in his step would be like saying that a whale is a large mammal: true but somewhat understated.

'Shut up,' hissed Dwayne.

The whistling stopped. 'Sorry,' said Alf.

'Mrs Hoblip's Bourbon peps,' said Mr Porter. 'Very potent. I suggest we all have a munch before we go any further.'

They all complied. The biscuits tasted faintly of mint and Matt felt the oppressive gloom of the sinkhole lift from his eyes, leaving his mind lighter.

'She'd make a fortune at a rave,' he said.

'She frequently has.' Mr Porter grinned. He moved forward to inspect the pipe and, without warning, thrust an arm deep into the clay, shut his eyes and stood stock still. In the sinkhole, the very air seemed to freeze. The strange and unnatural grey shapes in the walls froze too. It was as if all the molecules in the dank hole had been ordered to pose for a photograph. Finally, after several long minutes, Mr Porter withdrew his arm. There was no mud on it, and his expression was grave.

'This is an old curse. A promise made that has been broken.'

'What do you mean?' Matt asked.

'It would be easier to show you.' Mr Porter held out the hand that had been pushed into the sinkhole wall. It was still balled into a fist. He turned it so that his palm faced upwards and slowly opened his fingers. A tiny flame flickered on the skin. A flame that blossomed suddenly and without warning into an orange ball of dancing light. Inside it, Matt saw and heard and knew all at once as a visual story unfolded before him. No one narrated. No one spoke. Somehow, the meaning of what was being shown appeared simultaneously inside their heads.

It told of an ancient people. A violent tribe who defied the new conventions of clearing of lands and farming, preferring to raid and kill. It told of the sorcerers, the mages whose power was used to defeat these marauders. The battles were bloody with spear and axe and terrible deeds. The marauders, facing defeat, committed one final heinous act in stealing and murdering the young and innocent. Death, it was decided, was too easy a punishment on its own. And so after their executions, the mages captured their souls and condemned them to an unending existence within the rocks and mud of the earth. Forced to interminably contemplate the lives they had destroyed, to covet the sounds of birds and the laughter of men, existing only through the sustenance of those creatures reviled by men, the stlym, the bats of the caves wherein the tribe was banished in perpetual darkness, in purgatory. Banished until a necromancer revived them to do his bidding under the aegis of a Saxon chieftain whose bloody aspirations included subduing the celts. The tribe, given the name Nosdrwg by their victims, were dragged to this very place to wage war through nightmare and terror.

A immense elemental battle between the necromancer and the great mage Myrddin ensued. Within the dancing ball of light, the terrible power of that fight roared and hissed as water and fire and stone became weapons. But the necromancer's fate was sealed by the two witch-queens that joined the fight. Together, the triumvirate overpowered the usurper, leaving Myrddin to deal with the nomadic Nosdrwg. His vow was to ease their existence through the power of the penrudd, a mushroom to which the stlym, and in turn the tortured souls of the damned, became addicted. For millennia the dead Nosdrwg tribe existed in a peaceful limbo until, fifteen hundred years later, men interfered and broke the promise. With the stlym's produce removed from the caves, the tribe grew angry and thirsted once more for revenge. They returned across worlds to the place and time where the bargain was struck to seek vengeance and recompense.

The crackling ball of orange light faded, leaving the sinkhole as dark as before.

'As bedtime stories go, I think I prefer the one about Busty and Thrusty,' Birrik said.

'Don't you mean Flopsy and Mopsy?' asked Matt.

'Different sort of book. Not much text, mainly pictures.'

'Was it her?' said Asher, his voice almost breaking. 'On the river bank with Myrddin. Was it her?'

'It looked like her,' said Matt. 'It looked like Bobby. The boots gave her away. Not many witches wore what looked like DMs in the fifth century.'

'But how could that be?' Birrik asked in a terrible whisper.

No one answered. They all looked at Mr Porter.

'Do they have the girls? These Nosdrwg?' Matt asked.

Mr Porter shook his head. 'They are entities of misery, but they are incapable of any such action. Though time is irrelevant to these things.'

'So they've been stuck here since 487?' Birrik said.

Ernest Porter shook his head. 'No. Their presence here is recent.'

'But what is it they want?' a distraught Asher asked.

'Something that may be beyond our power to give them. But while they haunt this cavern, we have no chance to help Kylah or Bobby. I'm sorry. But this is old magic. The kind that grows stronger with time.'

'Can we communicate with them?' Keemoch asked.

'Their story is in the earth and easily extracted. We can see that they are aware of us. It might be possible.' Mr Porter sounded confident.

Matt turned away and strode to the other side of the cavern. Asher followed him.

'Matt, we will find another way—'

But Matt shrugged off Asher's hand before turning back to Mr Porter with a look of dawning realisation. 'I need to know one thing. Just one thing. Where was it they were banished to?'

Mr Porter frowned but then thrust his arm once more into the cavern wall. This time it took only a few seconds. 'Of course, there are no modern references. Suffice to say that it is in the north, and not in this world.'

'Steppeinit?' Matt asked.

'Possibly. There are memories of harsh winters and long nights of darkness.'

'Then I know what has disturbed them,' Matt said, excitement making him pace again. 'It's the village, and Nadia, and—'

'Mathew,' said Mr Porter, 'calm yourself.'

'It's Elkson and those bloody miners. They've made all of

this happen. Can we make them a promise?' Matt's expression was almost feverish. ' Can we broker a deal?'

'What exactly do you mean by that, Mathew?' Mr Porter asked.

'I mean, can we promise these Nosdrwg to make things as they were? Return them to their eased existence, as Myrddin promised? Bats, penrudd mushrooms, the works.'

'How?' Birrik said.

But Mr Porter was looking at Matt in that special knowing way he had and smiling. 'It is dangerous to make promises you cannot keep with these wraiths. But if you wish to talk, I suggest you use the pipe.'

'Matt, this is madness. You're not making any sense,' Asher pleaded.

But Matt had already turned to the muddy black wall where the grey shapes came and went. He knelt and began talking into the plastic pipe. 'Right, listen to me. If we ensure that your exis-tence is reinstated, ensure the stlym provide you with whatever it is you need, including penrudd mushrooms. If we do that, will you leave this place?'

The grey shapes stopped moving and coalesced into one single vaguely human shape. In front of it, the rock and earth extruded slowly with a sound like sliding mud and became a long bony hand. Matt stared at it and then reached out his own. He felt the cold damp of graveyard bones inside that slick excres-cence. Mr Porter put his own hand over them both. Matt let go and the hand disappeared.

'I hope you know what you're doing,' said Keemoch.

But Matt was already pulling Birrik away, issuing instruc-tions. Birrik hesitated only long enough to pass something to Keemoch, and within seconds was up the ladder. In the sinkhole, the atmosphere was changing. The damp fog was lifting. The Nosdrwg were leaving.

'Well done, Mathew, well done,' said Mr Porter.

'What about the girls?' Asher said.

'Oh, bother.' Mr Porter looked up at where Birrik was disap-pearing over the rim of the hole. 'Birrik has the string.'

'Do you mean this ball he shoved into my hands before he jumped on the ladder?' Keemoch held out the twine.

Mr Porter clapped his hands. 'Excellent. Now, Mathew, I

think it's about time we applied a little Krudian physics to the situation.'

'Should I get them to evacuate the neighbourhood, sir?' Keemoch asked.

'No need, Sergeant. I am sure this will be completely safe.'

Keemoch tied the twine around Matt's waist, bearing the look of someone who'd been forced to swallow a tablespoon of cod liver oil, while Mr Porter added, in a worryingly airy way, 'Do you know anything about the theory of twine, Mathew?'

CHAPTER FORTY-SEVEN

MERTHYR, WALES, 500 AD

'AND TOOTHPASTE?' Bobby asked.

'Powdered ash of ox hooves?' Kylah said. 'Eggshells and chalk?'

'Tell me you're joking, please?'

'It's what people used to use. With the frayed end of a stick as a brush.'

'And floss. What am I supposed to use as floss?'

'There's always catgut…' Kylah decided not to go any further. Judging from her expression, Bobby was getting less and less amused. They'd decided to draw up a list of essentials, given that they'd already been there for several days without a shower or a real change of clothes. Underwear had been rinsed and dried, but their clothes stank of woodsmoke.

'And let's not even mention shampoo,' Bobby wailed.

'Okay, we won't. Not even powdered sage, rosemary and egg white.'

'I think I bought one of those last month from Wonderdrug.'

'Or we could go native. Wear a cap and wash our hair once every month.'

'Have they got universities here, then?'

'Nice one, Roberta.' Kylah grinned. 'Though it's an invitation for mites and lice.'

Bobby's smile, already forced, segued into downturned horror. Despite the fooling about, the possibility, real and huge and gut-cramping, was becoming a reality for both women. What if they were stuck here? What if there was no way back? What if they were going to live out their lives in a period of history appropriately named the dark ages? A time when the Romans had gone and left Britain to its own devices. Devices usually designed for splitting, piercing, cleaving and chopping flesh, and which hardly ever involved a clean death. The life expectancy of a peasant was less than thirty years. The barbarians were, literally, at the gate.

It was not a jolly prospect.

Morgana stuck her head through the tent entrance. She, on the other hand, seemed delighted by their continued presence and was fascinated by their tales of what life might be like in the future.

'No news,' Morgana said. 'We've got a couple of knights in the cave. If anything happens, we'll know.'

'Good,' said Bobby.

'So, is there really a school named after me, or are you joshin'?'

'I am not joshing,' Bobby said, once again helplessly amused by the God of Krudian quirkiness who'd decided to give Morgana a Valleys accent with accompanying twenty-first-century lexicon.

'They decided to set it up in 1611 and it's an amazing building.'

'And there really is water that comes into your house in a pipe?'

'Yes.'

'And a way of seeing and talking to someone in another village even though you are miles away?'

'Yes.'

'Oh, I wish I could see these wonders. It sounds like magic is available to every man in your time.'

'It's called science and technology, and isn't always all it's cracked up to be. But you are a hero and your time is definitely now. Besides, there's always Cei—'

'Don't talk to me about Cei. He's gone off on one because I had a ride in Sir Jerome of Clarkson's new cart.'

Kylah crossed her arms. 'Please tell me you just made that up.'

'Made what up?'

'Sir Jerome of Clarkson. There isn't…can't be…'

Morgana's expression remained innocence personified. It was Bobby's guffaw that gave it all away. Kylah rounded on her. 'Very funny.'

Morgana grinned. Bobby laughed. 'We thought we ought to do something to get you out of the dumps.'

'It worked.' Bobby grabbed Morgana. 'Come on, then. Come and show me your herb collection. Might as well make the most of it.'

'Really?' said Morgana, her face lighting up. 'And you can tell me about horseless carts and *Top Queer*.'

Bobby shot Kylah a glance and got a raised-eyebrow tilt of the head in response.

Kylah watched them leave, glad of a moment to herself. In a way it was a relief to have Bobby with her. At least it was someone else to talk to and to share her predicament with. She tried her best to keep Bobby's spirits up, but the truth was, things could not be much worse. Time slippage was a very rare event. No one really knew how it happened, though modern alchemists felt that there were ways to explain it. Their explanations were so convoluted and full of holes—often supposedly made by worms —that Kylah had given up. It simply wasn't something she'd expected to come across, let alone experience herself. And yet here they were.

Bobby's theory and rescue plan seemed like hunting for a pin in a sack of straw. What were the chances of anyone finding their phone in fifteen hundred years' time? And even then, the chance of anyone understanding the message and acting upon it were infinitesimal. It would take an incredible amount of luck.

A shudder ran through her and she squeezed her eyes shut. That was the one and only thing that had allowed her to remain calm in the circumstances.

Luck. Not everyone got their fair share of it. Others had it by the bucketful. No one, with very few and notable exceptions, could call upon it when it was needed. She couldn't, Bobby couldn't, Myrddin couldn't.

But she knew a man who just might.

CHAPTER FORTY-EIGHT

MERTHYR, WALES, PRESENT DAY

'Twine theory?' Matt said as Mr Porter began to unwind a length of the green string. 'If it's like string theory, then a little. I do have a couple of nerd friends, so I know it's supposed to be mathematical glue that sticks Einstein's theory of relativity to quantum mechanics and—'

'Twine is good at holding things together, is it not?' Mr Porter asked, casually but determinedly ignoring Matt's reply.

'As in two pieces of rope, or a parcel?' Asher volunteered.

'Very good, Mr Lodge.' Mr Porter beamed. He took a tiny hurricane lantern out of his mac pocket, opened the glass door and lit the candle inside, before placing the little flickering light on the floor a few paces behind. The flame danced shyly for a few moments before surging up to burn brightly.

'—and that supersymmetry connects fermions and bosons and that the hadron experiments seem to support their existence —' Matt continued.

'The very best thing about twine is that it is strong,' Mr Porter added, ignoring Matt once again. 'Mr Lodge, if you could take this end and walk across to extend the length. Five yards should be sufficient.'

'—and then there was the addition of membrane to string

and the possibility of extra dimensions extending off the end of the membranes—'

'Now, if I cut it here…' Mr Porter held out the twine stretched between both hands. Birrik duly obliged with a knife. '…and then I apply a little wonderworking of my own.' He scrunched the cut twine into a ball and held it in one fist before clamping his other hand over the top. When he let go and opened his fist, the light from the hurricane lantern bobbed upwards and flowed in a straight line from the flame into the twine, where it glowed a cheerful bright yellow.

'—adding the potential presence of parallel universes and a multiverse utilising the extra-dimensional possibilities of a super-position ——'

Mr Porter cut in. 'Yes, yes, Mathew, I understand that your physicists have to find something to occupy their time, but this is not the place for fanciful theorising. As you have so succinctly put it, we need to do something, and we need to do it now. Twine theory states that if you tie twine to anything, it makes itself a damned nuisance and it is a tinker to loosen.'

'Right,' Matt said, suitably deflated.

'It is also the case that light, as we know, travels quite easily through space and time, does it not?'

'Does it?' Matt asked, wary now of agreeing.

'If it wasn't for this rain and the low cloud, you would have evidence enough. The light from the stars shows us what a star looked like eons ago.'

Matt nodded, clearly confused by this sudden switch from Porteresque logic, which at the best of times was a tortuous oxymoron of Saturnian proportions, to established scientific knowledge. He should, of course, have known better.

'Therefore, twine theory says that if you make twine glow and then tie it to something, whatever it is attached to should also be able to travel through time since it, too, is full of light. Simple, really.'

Matt stared with the expression of a pious man who has just learned the real meaning of the word 'berk', having used it with ignorant impunity for many years. 'But, that's not physics?'

'It is Krudian physics, which is the same only different. Now, Mathew, I want you to tie this around your waist.'

Matt, having long ago decided that one had to carefully pick one's battles when it came to Hipposync, said nothing and complied.

'Sergeant Birrik, we need a nematode of some description.'

Birrik scoured the ground and came back with a fat earthworm.

'Excellent.' Mr Porter beamed. He took the wriggling creature, tied the free end of the twine to it and carefully threaded it down the plastic pipe still protruding from the wall where Birrik had inserted it earlier.

'Dare I ask?' Matt said pointing at the disappearing earthworm.

'It will burrow into the wall, thus creating a—'

'Wormhole.' Matt grinned weakly.

'Excellent.' Mr Porter nodded. 'I see you are beginning to grasp the principle. In a moment, when I give the word, you will become the end of the string and a point of light. You will travel down the tube, through the hole made by the worm—'

'I prefer wormhole,' Matt whispered to Asher.

'—light will emerge on the other side. You will have a very short period of time to act before I pull the twine and yank you back. Do you understand?'

'Clear as…New Thameswick water,' Matt said, valiantly substituting an appropriate antonym for the word 'mud' which had been the one on the tip of his tongue.

'Excellent. So, shall we?'

Matt took the free end of the glowing twine, tied it around his waist and then stood in front of the protruding plastic pipe.

'Ready?' Mr Porter asked.

'As I'll ever be,' replied Matt, lining himself in front of the protruding plastic pipe. There was no sign of the worm.

Mr Porter smiled and said, '*Tempus Fugit.*'

Matt's world dissolved, and he was plunged into a whirling stream of brown water that roared about him. He fought to stay upright and keep his head clear. He was aware at some impish level, that all that was missing was some iconic BBC radiophonic workshop music of the *doof doof doof, doof-doof doof-doof-doof-doof* variety. That would have made the whole thing sublime-ish.

Above him, the world swirled a dull, featureless grey. Spluttering, Matt searched desperately for something, anything to focus on. Even so, the thud of the oar came as a sphincter-clenching surprise. It was just there, above the water—long and wooden and waving at him. He grabbed for it and felt himself dragged unceremoniously sideways. He had time to hear some-one, or something say, 'Hold tight,' before the oar did a reverse thrust and he was pushed, without warning, backwards, deep under the raging waters.

CHAPTER FORTY-NINE

SPIV

It should have been a time for the villagers to rejoice. There should have been bunting and fairy cakes, well…cakes, anyway, given that they were understandably scared of anything made by those capricious Fae bakers. They could easily turn you into a dung beetle, or indeed contain the by-products of said beetles as sprinkles. If you ate one, somewhere on an arm of the windmill of your mind, you'd likely hear high-pitched uproarious laughter and, looking around, see a spark disappearing out the corner of your eye at a rate of knots. Yet even knowing that the harrowing ritual of the Gathering was no more and never would be, there was no party, and no cakes. Nor singing, nor dancing, nor laughter, nor jollity.

The people of Spiv had forgotten how all that worked.

Nadia led Crouch and his clear-up squad through the forest. There were, of course, all sorts of issues surrounding jurisdiction and the constabulary's validity on foreign soil. But the fact was that lava juice deaths had all taken place in New Thameswick and generally, if there is an infestation of rats, no one objects to clearing out the nest, so long as someone is prepared to do it. And so long as it doesn't involve a magic pipe.

Crouch had taken the pragmatic approach of all good

policemen: sort the bastards out and fiddle with the paperwork later.

Nadia was a terrier in her thoroughness. Wimbush, too, proved to be a surprisingly ruthless and enthusiastic recruit. Blessed with an excellent memory, he had picked out several of Elkhorn's thugs trying to disguise themselves as villagers.

But after the initial search, Nadia had defaulted to helping the sick and injured, of which there were many. Sensing that the Gathering was no longer supervised, the young villagers had fled the caves. Elkhorn's men had lashed out in response. As a result, there were arrow wounds to dress, cuts to suture, bones to splint and bruises to inspect, and with each new injury, Nadia's mouth grew tighter. The tipping point came when an alderman's wife made a wicked accusation. She had been helping by supplying fresh laundry, carefully avoiding getting her own hands dirty. Sensing that the privileged, entitled lifestyle once enjoyed by aldermen and their families was gone forever, she whispered that someone had brought a curse upon the village. She deliberately said this within earshot of the person she was implying to be the source of the curse.

Nadia, chin down, turned her head to consider the woman with a look normally reserved for fresh roadkill. 'The only curse here is you and your kind's ignorant gossipmongering and super-stition that has blighted this village for years.'

Any thought the alderman's wife had of entering into an argument evaporated on seeing the expression on Nadia's face. An expression shared by all the other women there wearing blood-streaked aprons as their badge. The alderman's wife, not renowned for her speed in doing anything useful like weeding the crops, or peeling potatoes or providing encouragement, suddenly found a hidden talent for backing out of the room at Olympic-qualifying speed. If her bovine brain had registered any thought, it would have been that you did not throw pitch on a fire to put it out.

By the afternoon, Crouch's constables had cleared the processing plant with its still-steaming kiln of any remaining stragglers and locked them away in a pigsty. Elkson's body lay crushed and broken under tons of rubble. A displaced brick from the exploding kiln had bounced three times off adjacent struc-tures only to strike Elkson a terminal blow as the Wight bellowed at his men not to be cowards. It was a one-in-a-million piece of very bad luck.

Crouch ordered the corpse to be left. His men had better things to do with their time than uncover that piece of filth. Yet not all of Elkson's men were accounted for, including, worryingly for Wimbush, Kebbers.

'Maybe he's made a run for it,' Crouch said when Wimbush pointed it out. Beyond the village, the huge wall of trees and the unwelcoming shadows between made for a foreboding escape route. 'Coward's way. Best of luck to them is what I say. Still, let's make sure no one else is hiding, eh?'

They met with Nadia at a packed meeting house. She'd insisted on providing the constabulary with some hot soup and bread. Crouch posted constables front and rear and made everyone, men and women, remove hats, caps and bonnets. Two 'bearded' women tried to make a run for it, but were clobbered before they'd gone ten yards. One of them was Riggon, the other the guide, Steffan. Finally satisfied that there were no more stowaways, Crouch addressed the audience. They stared blankly back at him, exchanging whispered fears, and he read nothing but bewilderment and anxiety etched on every single pale browbeaten visage.

Well, not every visage, because Nadia sat there, too. And her expression was about as browbeaten as a fizzing firework. She was not troubled by Crouch or his words. She welcomed them. It was exactly what the rest of this little lot needed. A wake-up call. They'd been used and abused. Oppressed into believing a load of pigswill about an evil witch while their kids, their own young people, had been nothing better than slave labour for a drug baron who'd treated them worse than paper towels. The kind you discarded in the water closet. It was hard to believe and yet Elkson had done such a good job with propaganda it was ingrained into this lot's psyche. They needed something to get animated about. The Gods knew they had enough ammunition, but it looked like it was going to take someone or something to cock the hammer and fire the gun. Who or what, that was the question.

Crouch raised his hand and the whispering died away. 'Ladies and gentlemen, thank you for your cooperation. I know you have homes to get to and so I will try not to keep you too long. You all deserve an explanation as to what exactly has been going on here, and I'll be happy to provide that for you in the shape of Mr Wimbush here and your own Nadia Komangetme.'

Wimbush, who'd been sitting on a chair at the side of the dais, looked up in total surprise. He found Nadia staring at him from a row of seats halfway down the aisle with an identical expression.

'But…' protested Wimbush.

Crouch was having none of it. He crossed the stage and leaned in towards the alchemist 'You said you knew the place.'

'I said I knew the miners,' Wimbush hissed, but got up anyway.

Crouch shrugged. He turned to Nadia and beckoned her with a finger. She got up reluctantly. Crouch spoke to her in a low voice. 'If you've got something to tell them, you'll never have a better chance,' he said.

Nadia took some hesitant steps and joined Wimbush on the stage, staring out.

The alchemist cleared his throat. 'Good people of Spiv. Once upon a time in a place far, far away…'

CHAPTER FIFTY

MERTHYR, WALES, 500 AD

THE KNIGHT on guard duty inside the Nosdrwg's cave was thinking about his dinner and a flagon of ale and recalling a tale told by the resident bard about a bishop and a serving wench. The one with the 'you mitre told me it was a wimple' punchline that had sent him and his colleagues into fits of laughter. The bard had known his audience.

He yawned. It was dark and cold in the cave, but nowhere near as dark and as cold as it had been before the Nosdrwg had decided to leave. Another couple of hours and…he paused, squinting into the shadows. A glow had appeared on the wall off to his left. Just a small pinprick of light that seemed to wriggle and shift. He stared at it for several minutes before deciding that it wasn't his imagination and the light had become a definite gleaming protrusion. He approached carefully. This cave could play tricks with your head.

When he got to within a yard of the thing, he confirmed it had substance and was not just a trick of the light. It writhed like a tiny snake, arching and probing the air.

The knight drew his sword. Was this just another Nosdrwg falsehood? The easy thing to do would be to slice the thing off in one clean sweep. That was the one sure way of knowing if it was alive or not, even if Myrddin's orders were to employ caution.

He was a knight, after all. And caution for someone who walked about in chain mail usually meant stabbing the bloke in front of you cautiously before he had a chance to stab you. The knight raised his sword to strike.

That was when he heard the thing say, 'Kylah? Are you there?'

The sound of rapidly running spurred feet echoed through the cave as the knight exited at speed.

CHAPTER FIFTY-ONE

SPIV

Wɪᴍʙᴜsʜ sᴛᴀʀᴛᴇᴅ ᴛᴇʟʟɪɴɢ them about his quest to find the silver wolfsbane. He told them about how he'd heard about its medicinal properties, about how his research had brought him to the remote mountains of Steppeinit and the forest and of how, though he had come as part of the prospecting expedition, he was not one of them.

He explained how he'd encountered Nadia and of how she'd helped him find his plants, about how the constabulary had enlisted their help to root out the evil that was causing the suicides in his own city state, and, finally, about how Elkson had used and abused them all in pursuit of his criminal scheming. He told them how he and Asher and Matt had come back to the village and of how Nadia had volunteered to come back and help the constabulary.

There was not one slide or text book reference. Everyone stayed awake. It was probably, he thought, the best lecture he'd ever given.

'This girl,' he turned to Nadia, 'has done you all proud. She's brave and steadfast and bright and—'

'Your left bootlace is undone,' said a voice from the front row.

Wimbush frowned and shook his head, 'What?'

'Your left bootlace. Sign of very bad luck to leave your left bootlace undone.'

Nadia sighed. Wimbush stared at the man in the front row, flabbergasted.

He looked up at them all sitting there as if he was seeing them for the first time. All of them dumb, their faces blank. All through his speech they'd sat there, listening. No one shifted, or coughed, or cried. For a while he'd let himself believe there was hope. That his explanation for what had been done to them had cut through the thick blanket of ignorance and superstition. But no. They'd all sat there in trepidation because his left bloody bootlace was undone.

Anger flared in Wimbush. 'What is wrong with you people? It's not unlucky. It's just a bootlace.'

'Dirk Trotter's bootlace was undone when he tripped on the way to feed the pigs. Broke his leg in the pen, he did. Didn't have to feed the pigs for a good month after that,' said another voice.

'That's cause and effect,' Wimbush said, the exasperation not only showing but beaming out in waves from a slowly reddening face.

'Still unlucky,' said the voice.

'Well, it's not unlucky now, is it? It's just loose, that's all.' Wimbush raised up his booted foot and waved it around so that the laces jumped and darted. The audience watched, mesmerised. He waved both arms and the leg, precariously balancing on one limb like a mad dancer. 'Look, no breaks, both inta—'

He didn't finish because something heavy landed on his back and sent him sprawling.

Several people in the crowd screamed.

Crouch yelled, 'No, he's armed!'

Wimbush, half winded and on his belly, tried to turn over. But something sharp was pressing into his cheek, preventing him from doing exactly that.

'They're right and you're wrong, Wimbush. This is definitely not your lucky day.'

Wimbush stopped trying to turn the minute he heard the voice. He knew it well. Too well.

'Kebbers.' The words oozed out of the side of his mouth. 'I might have known.'

'You bushwhacked me, you shit. I couldn't go without returning the compliment,' Kebbers growled through what few teeth he had.

Someone shuffled over to their left. 'Call them off or I'll run this through his eye,' Kebbers warned loudly.

'Keep still, lads,' Crouch ordered.

'What's the point of all of this?' Wimbush said. 'Do what you like to me, you won't get three steps before the constabulary get you.'

'Really?' said Kebbers. Wimbush could hear the calculation in his voice. 'We'll see about that. Come here, girl.'

CHAPTER FIFTY-TWO

MERTHYR, WALES, 500 AD

THE KNIGHT'S explanation as to what was going on seemed totally nonsensical.

'A glow-worm?' Bobby demanded, trying, and failing, to keep the disdain out of her voice.

'A worm that glows, yes. That glows and speaks your name.' With a clank, the knight nodded towards Kylah.

'Speaks my n—?' Kylah left the sentence in mid-air and tore out of the room. As she ran, screaming for Bobby to follow, she swore she heard a swishing sound somewhere in the air above her, like the noise a curved piece of stick makes during flight.

They got to the cave in record time, Morgana in hot pursuit. It was indeed a glowing worm that greeted them. One with a vaguely human-looking face if you got really, really close.

'Kylah? Bobby? Is that you?' The voice was tinny, but instantly recognisable.

'Matt?' Kylah gasped, which was about all the rest of her could manage since her head had decided to reel. 'It's us, yes! It's us.'

'Thank God,' the worm said. 'I've come to get you.'

Morgana said what they were all thinking. 'Are you like, the advanced guard?'

The worm pivoted, 'Who are you?'

'That's Morgana,' explained Kylah. 'Morgana Le Fey.'

'They're going to name an academy after you,' said the worm.

'Already told her that,' Bobby said.

'I don't think we have much time.' The worm started wriggling a bit more.

'What do you want us to do?'

'If it's got anything to do with swallowing, I'm out,' Bobby said. 'James Bladderwrack swallowed one in Year Three and he was ill for the rest of the term.'

Kylah threw her a paint-stripping glance. 'James Bladderwrack was not stuck fifteen hundred years in the past and I doubt that was his real name.'

'We all had to sign an NDA.'

'You were fourteen?'

'Like I said, we do not have much time,' the worm insisted. 'You need to grab hold.'

'Okay, okay,' Bobby said. She turned to Morgana. 'You are going to be great.'

Behind Morgana, the noise of clanking metal got louder and Arthur, Myrddin and a company of knights appeared.

'What is this wonder?' Myrddin asked.

'Wormhole,' Bobby said.

'Twine theory,' Matt the worm said.

Both responses got the blank looks they deserved from the assembly.

Kylah managed to hold it together long enough to mutter a few words to Arthur. 'It's been…interesting, Your Majesty.'

'Songs will be sung of your deeds,' Arthur said, his voice tinged with a mix of awe and sadness. 'Both of yours and Mistress Porter's. Though time may forget about us, you will not be forgotten.'

Bobby tilted her head, a hint of mischief in her eyes. 'You don't need to worry about being forgotten, Your Majesty. Everyone knows about you. In fact, you're kind of a big deal.'

'I…I am?'

'Kind words indeed,' Myrddin said. 'It seems the future holds many wonders…and perhaps some burdens of knowledge. I wonder, do the ages treat magic kindly?'

Kylah and Bobby exchanged a glance, unsure how to

respond. Kylah finally offered, 'Let's just say, you leave quite an impression, Myrddin.'

'I will miss you, Roberta Miracle,' Morgana said, her voice thick with emotion. She grabbed first Bobby and then Kylah in a hug. 'And you too, Kylah Porter. You have shown me a glimpse of how strong we women can be. How strong I can be. I will not forget you.'

'And we won't forget you. You are going to be amazing, Morgana Le Fey.' Bobby hugged the sorceress with tear-filled eyes. Kylah followed suit.

'In your own time, ladies,' the worm said loudly.

Kylah and Bobby shared a look that mixed relief and wistfulness in equal measure. 'Ready to leave the Dark Ages?' Bobby quipped, but her voice lacked its usual snark.

Kylah nodded, her eyes scanning the faces watching them one last time. 'Dark it might have been, but—'

'Yeah, I know, it wasn't all that bad.'

Kylah addressed the worm. 'Tell us what we need to do.'

'Pull me out and there should be some twine.'

Kylah reached up and pulled the worm free of the wall. Attached to it was a piece of glowing twine.

'You need to tie the twine around yours and Bobby's waists.'

Kylah pulled more twine through and did as she was asked. 'Now what?'

'Close your eyes and say *Tempus Fugit*.'

The women held hands. '*Tempus Fugit*,' they spoke together.

Their world began to dissolve into a flowing brown river and through a swirling blur they caught one last glimpse of Arthur, Myrddin and Morgana. Legendary figures standing tall, their expressions a mixture of wonder, sadness and hope for the future they would shape.

The last thing Bobby and Kylah heard as they faded away was Arthur's voice, strong and clear: 'Farewell, friends. May your journey home be as wondrous as the tales we will tell of you.'

CHAPTER FIFTY-THREE

SPIV

Everything had gone very quiet in the meeting hall.

Sprawled on the floor with the sharpened point of a wicked machete pricking the skin at the corner of his eye, Wimbush could see Nadia staring at the scene, her face white with shock. At least it might have been shock.

'I said come here, or you're going to see an eye kebab.' Kebbers jabbed his sword into soft flesh.

Slowly, Nadia began advancing across the dais until she was within arm's reach of Kebbers, who grabbed her around her waist and pulled her to him before deftly dropping his machete and removing a long dagger in one practised movement. It was at Nadia's throat within two seconds. With the sword tip gone from his face, Wimbush scrambled away and got up, his eyes glaring into Kebbers'.

'It's me you want. Take me, not her.'

Kebbers sneered. 'Very touching. But we both know that's bullshit, Wimbush. You don't give a tinker's about anything but your bloody plants, so don't give me that. I reckon maiming is too good for you, anyway. Me and the girl here are going to walk out, find us a horse and leave. I reckon that'll be worse for you than losing an eye.'

'You'll never—'

'Get away with it? Let's see, shall we?' Kebbers began dragging Nadia with him as he backed up towards the steps leading off the dais to the aisle. He threw Crouch a venomous look. 'One move and I'll stick her. You know I will.'

Nadia started to cry.

'Shut up,' Kebbers said. 'Stop snivelling or I'll stick this knife through your windpipe for the thrill of hearing you squeal.'

'Please,' she gurgled in a strange and liquid voice, 'please don't hurt me. Please.'

A gasp went up from the room as Nadia's eyes rolled up and her torso flopped. It would have been a collective gasp were it not for Crouch, who had to look away because he didn't want Kebbers to see the little smile that twitched the corners of his mouth and crinkled the muscles under his eyes.

'She's dead,' said a voice from the crowd.

'She's fainted,' said another.

Nadia, diminutive and weighing no more than 100lbs dripping wet, nonetheless became a formless lump in Kebbers' arms. But he was a tall, rangy man with forearms knotted from prospecting the icy rivers. He simply yanked her up so that she folded face down over one knotted forearm, keeping the dagger point in touch with her rag-doll ribs.

'She weighs no more than a bird. And birds usually need a good stuffing.' He sneered, inching his way backwards, eyes darting left and right in case one of the villagers had a sudden, though unlikely, pang of heroism.

Fat chance of that, Crouch thought. His men stood poised. None of them wanted this piece of filth to get away with this. One nod from him and they would attack. But all of them saw the tiny shake of his head and mentally stood down. He read disappointment and anger, but they were disciplined and a good bunch of lads. When Crouch folded his arms and leaned back against the wall, there was a rapid exchange of glances between them. Crouch allowed himself a smile this time, sensing what they must be thinking, but was careful to let it flow into a kind of grimace.

What was this all about? Was Hawkshaw Crouch bottling it? He looked like a man settling down to enjoy a bloody show, not endure the harrowing sight of a psychopath abducting a girl. What did he know that they didn't?

Well, though he'd only met her a few hours before, he already knew Nadia. Better than his men did, obviously. She was the real deal. An angry, feisty, retribution-seeking missile. Crouch had watched her, that very morning, chase down a six-foot-two bruiser hiding in a tree and jump on his back until help arrived. And by the time help had arrived, it had been completely unnecessary from Crouch's point of view. Though the bruiser was quite glad to accept it.

The clue to what was really going on here was her starting to cry and beg for mercy, which was about as believable, in Crouch's estimation, as Thai Me Down Bundit winning a Firestone asteroid: New Thameswick's equivalent of a Michelin star.

The constables in the room knew their boss and trusted him. If he was relaxed, then they should be too. If there was going to be a show, and from the look of him Crouch believed there was, why not sit back and enjoy it?

Kebbers, believing he had them all in the palm of his big knobbly hand, had made it ten feet along the aisle when Nadia suddenly convulsed and threw up.

Now there are many things a human can tolerate. Darkness, solitude, the spun-out chronicles of a fictitious Abbey in Downton to name just three. But we are hardwired to react to some things. Charging rhinos, for instance, the sight of blood, a child's scream and the sound and smell of someone vomiting within one's personal space. Kebbers' immediate response to the spattering stomach contents that sent the crowd into a moan of disgust was to hold Nadia, still draped over his forearm, at arm's length until the exhibition was over.

And that was exactly what she'd been banking on. In one slick movement, Nadia arched her back and threw her head back. Momentum brought her feet to the ground and her head, travelling at speed, into direct contact with Kebbers' nose. A noise like someone crunching a nugget of gravel under their heel sent a moan of horror rippling through the crowd.

Kebbers, still holding the dagger, staggered back, blood spurting from both nostrils.

Nadia pivoted to face him. The constables pushed off the wall, ready to pounce, but Crouch raised a hand and they froze.

Kebbers was still armed, but the savvier and more experienced amongst the constables saw a glint in Crouch's eye that suggested, almost telepathically, that to interfere now would be an awful shame because they hadn't seen the best bits yet.

'You little bitch,' roared Kebbers and lunged forward.

Nadia watched his arm, let it come forward, grabbed the wrist and pulled at the same time as half turning and thrusting out a leg to let Kebbers' height and weight do the business. He stood no chance. Within less than three seconds, he was on his back, rolling in the puddle of cold soup Nadia had managed to conceal in her cheeks the minute Kebbers had landed on the stage. The knife clattered away.

Kebbers was winded but he was quick. He got to his feet and was about to charge at Nadia when a voice said, 'You were wrong about me and the plants, Mr Kebbers.'

Kebbers froze at the same time as something very cold and very sharp touched the skin of his neck. He turned his face towards the voice. Wimbush stood next to him holding the dagger against his jugular, a wild and dangerous smile on his face.

'You don't say,' said Kebbers, licking his lips, still crouching.

'I do say. Understandable mistake, since I think at the time we first met I probably did care more about silver wolfsbane than anything else in the world. But things change.' Wimbush threw Nadia a glance.

She smiled.

'But you wouldn't slice an unarmed man's throat now, would you Wimbush?' Kebbers' voice was wheedling. 'Not in your nature, is it?'

'Perhaps not. But there are, I believe, other ways to render a man harmless.'

Nadia stepped forward before Kebbers could react and her knee moved up swiftly and accurately, finding its soft target— well, two soft targets if truth be told—and the sudden and excru-ciating high-pitched yelp that escaped Kebbers' mouth told everyone that she'd hit a bullseye. Some people watching, but mainly Crouch, had already decided to substitute the 'u' in bull with an 'a' when it came to the retelling.

Crouch nodded, and his men were on Kebbers in a flash, though he was already doing a passable impression of a foetus by the time they got to him. They dragged him away, his shirt front red with his own blood, his face contorted with rage.

'I will get my revenge,' he screamed. Though it came out as a croaked and muffled, 'Ah weee gii ma vennnche.'

'No, you won't. Not where you're going.' Crouch said and stuffed a dirty rag into the killer's mouth as a coup de grace. Grinning, the constabulary man walked up to Nadia and shook her hand. 'Wonderful bit of misdirection, Miss. Made this whole trip worthwhile. You are a class act, and no mistake. I'll take the knife, Mr Wimbush. Oh, and you're a very lucky man, if I may say so. I'm usually in The Empty Vessel around nine most nights if you're ever both in town. And it's my round.' He turned back to his men, who were looking on with mouths open in a way that suggested they'd just heard something very rare and very precious being said. 'You lot, forget you ever heard that. Right, let's get this piece of effluent's mates from the pigsty and ferry the lot back to New Thameswick. I feel a celebration is in order.'

———

NADIA AND WIMBUSH stood at the top of the aisle watching the constabulary leave. Wimbush looked at Nadia and shook his head. 'Is there any point in me asking where you learned to do that?'

Nadia shrugged. 'Miss Nigishi. I had much time to spend in Dun Roomin, and Miss Nigishi is good teacher. She calls it "scumbag defence".'

All Wimbush could do was shake his head in admiration.

'I heard what you said,' Nadia added.

'Really?' Wimbush blushed.

'You were willing to sacrifice yourself for me.'

'Yes,' he said. 'I was.'

Wimbush had made progress. Yet still what his oppressed and emotionally anorexic brain wanted to do was to avoid at all costs an overt display of affection.

'I only wash my hair on Thursdays, and always in the morning,' said Nadia.

Wimbush grinned, and to the watching villagers' whoops of delight, mentally told his inhibitions to take a long hike, took Nadia by the shoulders and kissed her full on the lips.

In public.

They paused only when, to their astonishment, the villagers started to applaud. To stand up and applaud. And they weren't applauding Crouch. They people of Spiv had eyes only for the couple on the stage.

CHAPTER FIFTY-FOUR

OXFORD, ENGLAND

THEY THREW a party at Hipposync to celebrate the spring equinox. Bobby added, *Up the revolution*, *Girl power* and *liberation of Spiv* in invisible ink and *sealing of the spooky sinkhole* in bold black to the handwritten invitations. It was a two-stage affair, beginning in Mr Porter's office at Hipposync, where Mrs Hoblip had made two types of tea and a variety of sandwiches as well as a decent selection of biscuits, including Joyful Dodgers, with a raspberry jam centre and a guarantee to get everyone laughing; Welcome Waffles, that ensured a welling of tears during the speeches; and, at Kylah's request, Headache Hobledenobs, that were pre-emptive hangover cures since Mrs Hoblip's absinthe tea could leave the drinker well oiled.

Present were Keemoch and Birrik, Bobby, Kylah, Matt and Asher, and Crouch had cadged a special day-ticket from the BOD since he had significant intelligence to offer.

Mr Porter, two half-empty plates resting on his chair armrests and a cup of steaming Darjeeling balanced on his stomach—the absinthe would come later—did the honours.

'It falls upon me to simply say a big thank you to everyone concerned on completion of this difficult task and to celebrate the resurfacing of the Tripoli Road after the successful filling in of the sinkhole. All of you here played a significant part and you should all be very proud of yourselves. A special welcome is extended to our guests,' he nodded towards Crouch, who seemed to be enjoying himself immensely, having sampled Mrs Hoblip's baking. To the uninitiated, it felt like the first day in Neverland with each bite.

Mr Porter continued, surrounded by happy, mildly stunned from the hallucinogenic effect of the Hoblip bakery, and contented faces. 'It is not often we have the opportunity to cooperate on such a public issue. Our work is usually a much more clandestine affair. Nevertheless, the discovery of the pre-existing cave system, thanks to some sterling archaeological work by our team, led to a most satisfactory outcome. I look forward to further collaboration in the future. And, if you have not done so, please make sure you sample one of Mrs Hoblip's miniature corned beef pasties.'

'Had three,' said Sergeant Mackeson. 'Bloody lovely, they are.'

'Indeed,' said Mr Porter. 'And your dreams tonight will be all the sweeter for them.'

'This Mrs Hoblip of yours, she should go on *Bake Off*,' said the engineer, staring in unfettered delight at his biscuit.

'She should, but TV channels have this thing about maintaining viewing figures, so I think we'll hold off on that one.' Mr Porter beamed. 'Have a Joyful Dodger.'

There was polite conversation, a few war stories of time spent in the trenches, aka sinkhole, more tea and after an hour or two, the guests departed replete and happy in the firm lack of knowledge that they would remember not much about any of this meeting by the following morning. Or that their sclerae, still a little bluish from their prolonged exposure to Nosdrwg and bat guano, would be back to normal by the weekend. Mr Porter took his leave shortly afterwards with the promise of a late supper with Mrs Porter awaiting him. He got a kiss on the cheek and a thank you hug from both women as he left.

'What I still don't understand,' said Bobby afterwards, 'and what is still making my head spin whenever I think about it, is why we were made part of history.'

'You are not a moth and it's Krudian,' Matt said.

'Obviously,' Kylah agreed. 'And though that distilled and

enigmatic reply does go some way to explaining what happened, it is not particularly satisfying.'

Asher narrowed his eyes. 'I think that Anke's ferryman, or a combination of the two, monitors the time stream. Perhaps it is within their remit that any demonic interference that disrupts the stream allows, or even demands, a bending of those same rules to allow corrections.'

'And dragging the Nosdrwg back from our time meant that we had to go back to fix it?' Bobby asked.

'Exactly,' Asher replied.

'Blue sclerae,' Matt said. 'As in the engineers', Nadia's and everyone's in Spiv. And that poor girl that swung from the rafters. I still don't fully understand it.'

Asher turned to Crouch. 'Will you do the needful?'

Crouch swallowed what was in his mouth, surprised at suddenly being put on the spot. 'Lava juice. Used to be a nuisance. People cooked up their own. It's an old recipe that uses bottled-up pigeon guano and a few herbs. Fell out of favour with the current generation.'

He got a full house of distasteful looks for that one.

'I appreciate you using the correct terminology, Hawkshaw Crouch,' Mr Porter said.

'My pleasure. Anyways, then this new variety appeared. It's a free world, but when people started to top themselves, we had to step in. 'Course, the giveaway with this new stuff was them blue sclerae. Now we know that it comes from the glasstone in Spiv. The stuff that made it even more lethal was also the stuff that made everybody in Spiv's eyes blue.'

'Except babies,' Matt corrected him.

'Except babies. Because it's in the water and babies don't drink much of that to start with, do they?' Crouch. 'It leeches into the water in Spiv and is harmless. But combine it with the chemicals in bat poo, and people start jumpin' out of windows, thinkin' they've got wings.'

'So Elkson was desperate to keep everyone away from Spiv,' Asher said. 'To protect the illegal production of lava juice. Hence the prospector guides like Kebbers and Riggon always managing to ensure people found no silver ore on their trips.'

'Or getting rid of anyone who did find anything,' Matt added grimly.

'Like plants that grow near ore,' Bobby added. 'Plants like Wimbush's silver wolfsbane.'

'And,' Crouch added, 'as well as keeping everybody from Spiv, he wanted to keep Spiv from everybody else.'

Matt nodded. 'That's why he wanted to get rid of Nadia. Because of her blue sclerae, which would link the lava juice to Spiv.' His eyes narrowed as it all fell into place.

'Full marks, that man.' Crouch grinned.

'And the Nosdrwg, could they have been affected by the lava juice?' Kylah asked.

'I doubt it. Their dreamworld was mushroom-induced, though they may have been tainted by it since manufacture was now taking place in the caves and places they occupied.'

'That might be one explanation for our good friends in the sinkhole being similarly tainted.' Mr Porter beamed at the engineers, who were blissfully unaware of the meaning of any of this thanks to Mrs Hoblip. They were simply having a great time at the party.

'It's possible, too, that the Nosdrwg exude their own penrudd mushroom effect,' Asher added.

'Of course.' Kylah glanced at Bobby who caught it and raised one eyebrow. Kylah let it slide, though it went a long way towards explaining Bobby's irritating cheerfulness in Merthyr. What was done, was done.

'I'm still confused about how we were able to do things back then without changing everything now.' Bobby shook her head.

Mr Porter sent her a knowing look. 'Perhaps you did, and this is the now that is the result.'

'I quite like that. It has a certain…resonance,' Matt agreed.

'Except that it was my suggestion that sent them back to this time and Spiv in the first place,' Bobby protested.

'No, don't,' said Kylah clutching her head. 'It's too painful.'

'That is the nature of paradox,' Asher said. 'I did ask Zenk, one of our BOD consultants. He's doing Philistosophy at the Polyalchemy. He tried to explain, but then I got lost when the tortoise overtook the hare, and the algebra he was writing on the window turned into letters that started moving on their own at different speeds.'

'Of course, I have seen this world and a version of Fae world where Kylah and Miss Miracle did not confront the necromancer.' Mr Porter beamed at Kylah. 'Your Aunty Anke keeps them in a snow globe on her mantelpiece, along with many others. Suffice to say that version gives a completely new meaning to the term "Dark Ages".'

A silence peopled by collective frowns and the faint noise of boggling minds followed.

Bobby got up and left the room. At the door, she gave Kylah an over-the-shoulder look, followed by a tilt of the head, commonly acknowledged by almost all women in social situations as, 'I want a word.'

Bobby led Kylah not to the loo, but to the blue room. A spot where they were guaranteed privacy. She leaned against a wall, arms crossed, eyeing her erstwhile boss-turned-friend, with a mixture of concern and exasperation.

'All right, out with it,' Bobby said with her best schoolteacher expression. 'What's going on between you and Matt?'

Kylah blinked, caught off guard. 'What do you mean?'

'Oh, come off it. You've been about as warm as a penguin's backside since we got back. The man literally pulled us out of the past, and you've barely thanked him.'

Kylah's shoulders tensed. 'I did thank him.'

Bobby dropped her chin. 'Yeah, with all the enthusiasm of thanking the postman for junk mail.' She sighed and her eyes softened. 'Look, I know you. We spent fifteen hundred years in a tent together. Something is not right in Kylahville.'

Kylah shuddered, feeling her carefully constructed walls beginning to crumble. 'It's…complicated.'

'Isn't it always?' Bobby rolled her eyes. 'Come on, spill. What's really bothering you?'

Kylah hesitated, then the words tumbled out. 'He's reckless, Bobby. I saw what happened in that vision. In the cave with the Nosdrwg. He nearly got himself killed! And for what? Some hare-brained adventure?'

Bobby raised an eyebrow. 'You mean the hare-brained adventure where he was working with Asher and Nadia? Saving her and her people? Doing his job?'

'Exactly!' Kylah threw up her hands. 'He's always rushing into danger without a thought. How can I rely on someone like that?'

'Oh, I don't know,' Bobby said dryly. 'Maybe the same way he relies on you when you're facing down eldritch horrors from the dawn of time?'

Kylah faltered. 'That's poetic…and that's also different.'

'Is it?' Bobby pushed off from the wall, her voice gentle but firm. 'Captain Kylah Porter, I have news for you. You're scared for him and for yourself. I get it. But you can't protect him by pushing him away.'

'I'm not—'

'You are,' Bobby cut her off. 'And worse, you're not giving him credit for who he is. Yeah, he's a bit of a loose cannon sometimes. But he's also brave, loyal and damn good at what he does. Just like you. Plus he thinks you are the knees of bees. And together, you two are…'

'What?' Kylah's voice had become small.

Bobby shrugged. 'Like enchanted tea leaves and a possessed kettle. Chaotically harmonious and steeping in serendipity.'

'You're an idiot,' Kylah said, but her defences were falling apart.

'A truth-speaking idiot.'

Kylah felt a lump forming in her throat. 'But what if something happens to him because I've introduced him to this madhouse?'

'Then you'll face it together,' Bobby said simply. 'Just like you always have. Just like he did when he came to rescue us.'

The truth of Bobby's words hit Kylah like a ton of bricks. She'd been so focused on protecting herself from the pain of potentially losing Matt that she'd lost sight of what made their relationship special in the first place. She crossed the room and hugged Bobby. After fifteen seconds of hugging, she whispered, 'Oh, bollocks. I've been a right prat, haven't I?' She stood back, blinking back the tears.

Bobby grinned. 'Well, I wasn't going to say it, but…'

Kylah laughed wetly, wiping at her eyes. 'What do I do now?'

'Well, for starters, you could try actually talking to the man,' Bobby suggested. 'And maybe, I don't know, show a bit of appreciation for the fact that he literally traversed time and space to save your arse?'

Kylah nodded, feeling a weight lift from her shoulders.

'You're right. Of course, you're right.' She took a deep breath. 'Thanks, Bobby. I needed that kick up the backside.'

'Penguin backside,' Bobby said with a wink. 'Now can we go back before they snaffle all the biscuits? And please, go snog your man before he starts thinking you've been replaced by a particularly frosty doppelganger.'

With a grateful smile, Kylah turned and headed back to the others, her heart lighter and her mind clearer than it had been in weeks.

When they returned, Crouch was on his feet. 'Right, now that everyone's metaphysical balls have all dropped, I've booked a room at the Botherer. I'm meeting my team there at eighty-thirty. Everyone is welcome.'

'Excellent plan,' said Kylah, looping her arm in Matt's as they stood.

Matt's gaze met Kylah's gold-flecked eyes, a hint of curiosity mixed with mild concern in his expression. 'One question,' he said, gesturing towards her office. 'Why is there a boomerang hanging on your wall?'

'As a reminder.'

'Of what?'

'Of how amazingly lucky I am that I've had another chance. I thought I'd lost everything, but everything was only whizzing through existence waiting to be grabbed again, with a little help from a worm and some twine, and a witch we all know and love.'

On the other side of the room, Bobby curtsied.

Matt sent Asher a look. He could only respond with a shoulder shrug.

'Now let's go and get merry because afterwards, I have some ethically sourced furs I want you to inspect,' Kylah said.

'Well, we'd better get a move on, then.' Bobby glanced at her watch. 'Before you two spontaneously ignite.'

'It appears that you have become more assertive with old age,' Asher commented as Bobby grabbed his hand. 'This last fifteen hundred years has clearly taken its toll, milady.'

'Very droll.' Bobby offered him a plastic smile. 'Where's the Aperio?'

Matt fetched his and attached it to Mr Porter's office door.

'I do hope that Wimbush and Nadia come, though. I worry about them,' Asher said.

'They'll be fine,' Matt said, and opened the door to a waft of beer and warm pies drifting across the threshold, accompanied by the buzz of conversation. 'Asher, I do believe it's your round.'

CHAPTER FIFTY-FIVE

NEW THAMESWICK

As it turned out, Wimbush and Nadia did not attend the celebrations at the Botherer, though they did go and meet Crouch at The Empty Vessel a few weeks later, having been advised by Matt that Crouch's offer of buying a round was a never-to-be-repeated, once-in-a-lifetime offer they should not pass up lightly. But they gave the Ancient Dog Botherer a miss because that same evening they were heading towards a corner table in Withersporks, where Jac Logsdon and Wimbush's sister Selma were waiting, having been summoned by Hawkshaw Crouch on 'constabulary business' and to 'dress smartly'. Crouch had been more than willing to do Wimbush a small favour with this little white lie.

'They look scared,' Nadia said as Wimbush and she approached. 'And so do you,' she added when she glanced at Wimbush.

'I've got a lot to be scared about,' Wimbush answered. 'She's refused to answer any of my letters.'

Jac and Selma said nothing when Wimbush and Nadia approached. They seemed dumbfounded and hostile.

'Before you say anything,' Wimbush said, 'I apologise in advance for the subterfuge. The constabulary do not want to see you. I do. I'd understand completely if you stood up and left and did not want to listen after the way I treated you both. But I wanted to say I'm sorry and I wanted you to meet someone very special.'

Still Jac and Selma said nothing.

'This is Nadia. She's from Spiv and she's the best thing that's ever happened to me. Which makes what I did to you two all the worse because I know, now, what a complete and utter prat I've been. I was selfish, self-absorbed—'

'Misguided, unfeeling and cold,' Nadia added, reiterating the litany she had taught him to recite.

Wimbush sent her a slightly surprised look, but all Nadia did was smile sweetly.

'All of those things and more. I did not know what was important in my life and I should have. There's no real way to make amends for what I did, but I've been away and had time to reflect and…'

His words petered out as Selma got up abruptly, her expression unreadable. 'You are a prat, Kenwyn Wimbush. But you're my brother. Apology accepted. Come here.' The last two words came out in a sob as she threw her arms around him.

There were tears. Lots of them. But there was even more laughter. The landlord brought sparkly wine from Froag. But it took a pointed look from Nadia and jab from her elbow for Wimbush to remember the best bit. The most important reason he'd arranged all of this.

'Oh, I almost forgot. While I was away, I made some friends in high places. Some *very* high places. So, though it might not be what you'd planned for this evening and it is against all sorts of city rules in that it isn't a Saturday and before three o'clock, there's a notary waiting in a little office on Bell Street. And I've taken the liberty of inviting some of your friends to attend. So, if you're both up for it, I'd be honoured if you'd accompany me to the registry office where, Jac, I'd be even more honoured to give my sister away to you in marriage.'

It turned out to be a belter of a wedding. Wimbush and Nadia even danced to Wimbush's favourite song, *Troll Lotta Love*.

———

Over the following weeks, Wimbush and Nadia spent considerable time inspecting premises for their new venture: Laboritoire Nadier.

Wimbush decided on the name because it sounded a bit Froag and people liked that sort of thing. It added a degree of sophistication that was distinctly lacking in their first suggestion, K Wimbush And N Komangetme's Embrocational Rejuvenator.

Amazingly, it took them a whole day and a guffaw from Matt to work out how wrong that was, even after he'd suggested they take another long, cool look at the acronym.

Within three months they'd set up some glasshouses with carefully controlled environments and shady spots where the wolfsbane and reekatsh could thrive. Along with a dozen other products. Laboritoire Nadier's line quickly gained popularity among the city's fashionable elite. Their bestsellers included the shimmering Moonlit Glade Illuminator, infused with biolumines-cent petals from Spiv's nocturnal blooms, and the age-defying Whispering Willow Wrinkle Reducer, crafted from the bark of Spiv's ancient sentient trees. The Sprite's Dew Hydrating Mist promised to imbue skin with an otherworldly glow, while the Enchanted Thistle Balm soothed even the most stubborn burns and rashes almost magically. For those seeking a more dramatic look, the Crimson Wyvern Scale Lipstick offered long-lasting colour with a hint of fire resistance, and the Gossamer Wing Eyeshadow Palette allowed wearers to change its hues with a mere thought. All from the preparation and labelling plant in a small village called Spiv.

Every Friday in the village they had a 'left bootlace undone day' and, apart from the odd slip and scraped knee, nobody died.

Of course, the cosmetics paid the bills, allowing Wimbush to develop the pharmaceutical arm of Laboritoire Nadier, and fulfilling his lifelong ambition of successfully cultivating silver wolfsbane. From that came a breakthrough and an elixir that, in three doses, made people immune from the red death. The Sultan of Rainever even bestowed upon him the Order of the Triumphant Dromedary. The back of the medal was proudly engraved with the phrase: For turning the tide of disease faster than a camel can spit. Wimbush took to wearing it to breakfast.

As part of an environmental initiative, the aldermen of the village of Spiv, headed by the portreeve Dalibor, were tasked with ensuring the wellbeing of the stlym in their caves. They 'employed' a full-time keeper for the rjepers in the form of Haggis Len, who'd decided, quite sensibly, that fifteen years in a cave full of bat guano was infinitely preferable to spending one day in a prison where several bereaved friends of lava juice victims languished, just waiting for someone to blame and punish for what had happened.

The truce between the present and the past prevailed. The stlym fed on dung-infused with magic mushrooms. The Nosdrwg were being looked after as promised, and, in New Thameswick, no one else died from tainted lava juice.

Once a year, Kylah, Bobby, Matt and Asher inspected the caves and had a cheeky mushroom omelette for lunch. Kylah insisted they wrote up their report before lunch because ten minutes after it, no one remembered anything, including how to spell their own names.

———

A FEW YEARS, three factories and two (hers and his) doctorates later, Nadia and Wimbush had their first child and named him Arne. Young Kasimir followed and then Poppy, Briony and Violet. The alchemical herbologist, it turned out, did know a thing or two about propagation after all.

But Nadia Komangetme never forgot her passion. Early mornings, sometimes late at night, she would sit at her writing desk, a gift from Wimbush to celebrate her first published novel, marvelling at the journey that had brought her here. The simple crow's feather quill and blackberry ink of her youth had given way to a sleek self-inking pen, but the magic of words remained unchanged. She thought of the little girl who once hid her stories within *The Chronicles of Spiv*, terrified of discovery yet unable to quell the burning need to create. That same fire still flickered within her, but now it blazed openly, warming her family and illuminating the world with tales of wonder.

This evening, her fingers traced the spine of her latest book, a collection of reimagined folktales from Spiv. Inside, Lilith still wandered through sun-dappled forests, but now she was joined by brave hunters, misunderstood witches and villages learning to embrace the unknown rather than fear it. Nadia's eyes misted as she thought of Kasimir, hoping that somewhere, somehow, he could see how far she'd come. The scent of masoma dust no longer cloyed the air, replaced by the sweet aroma of Laboritoire Nadier's latest creation. As she put pen to paper, beginning a new story, Nadia smiled. She had escaped the shadows of superstition, but she would never stop believing in magic: the kind found in imagination, in love, and in the power of a single voice to change the world, one tale at a time. Even the fearsome Babramic Jaggr, once the source of nightmares, was transformed into a complex character with depth and nuance. Nadia smiled, thinking again of how far she'd come from the girl who once hid her writings in *The Chronicles of Spiv*.

Wimbush appeared at her elbows, smelling of the baby lotion he'd used on their youngest after her bath.

'You writing about that witch again? What was her name… Babramic Jaggr?' he asked, his eyes twinkling with mischief.

Nadia shook her head. 'There is no witch, Wimbush. That's just an old folktale used to frighten ignorant people.'

'Oh, come on,' Wimbush said with exaggerated disappointment. 'I was hoping to read about her turning a few geological guides into frogs or the odd newt. Ah, well.'

With a wry smile, Nadia turned to face her husband. 'I am willing to listen to any suggestions you have. The fact that we now have five children is evidence enough of that. But, when it comes to Babramic Jaggr, Wimbush, I am afraid you can't always get what you want.'

ACKNOWLEDGMENTS

As with all writing endeavours, the existence of this novel depends upon me, the author, and a small army of 'others' who turn an idea into a reality. The Hipposync Archives are a work in progress. Special mention goes to Ela the dog who drags me away from the writing cave and the computer for walks, rain or shine. Actually, she's a bit of a princess so the rain is a no-no. Good dog!

But my biggest thanks goes to you, lovely reader, for being there and actually reading this. It's great to have you along and I do appreciate you spending your time in joining and the team at Hipposync and in New Thameswick where anything is possible.

CAN YOU HELP?

With that in mind, and if you enjoyed it, I do have a favour to ask. Could you spare a moment to **leave a review or a rating**? A few words will do, but it's really the only way to help others like you discover the books. Probably the best way to help authors you like. Just visit the book's page on Amazon and leave a few words, or a rating, if you have the time. Thank you!

FREE BOOK FOR YOU

Visit my website and join up to the Hipposync Archives Readers Club and get a FREE novella, ***Every Little Evil,*** by visiting:

https://dcfarmer.com/

When a prominent politician vanishes amidst chilling symbols etched in blood, the police are baffled. Enter Captain Kylah Porter, an enigmatic guardian against otherworldly threats. With her penchant for the paranormal and battling against cynical skeptics, she dives into a realm where reality blurs. Her toxic colleague from the Met is convinced it's just another tawdry urban crime. But Kylah suspects someone's paying a terrible price for dipping a toe, or something even less savoury, in the murky depths of the dark arts.

She knows her career and the missing man's life are on the line. Now time is running out for the both of them…

Pour yourself a cuppa and prepare for a spellbinding mystery.

By signing up, you will be amongst the first to hear about new releases via the few but fun emails I'll send you. This includes a no spam promise from me and you can unsubscribe at any time.

AUTHOR'S NOTE

Once upon a time, in the swirling mists of the last century, my journey into the fantastical began. A devotee of the greats like Tolkien, I found myself drawn deeper into Terry Pratchett's Discworld and Tom Holt's tilt at the modern—the holy trinity of the Ts, if you will.

Two decades ago, I embarked on what I now affectionately call "the archives." But alas, life's currents swept me into real world. I found myself scribbling away in different genres. Don't get me wrong, I still do that. But those archives? They never stopped whispering my name.

Fast forward to now, with a bit more time on my hands and with newfound vigour and fresh releases on the horizon. We have new covers, new titles—everything's getting a makeover to match their quirky, satirical souls.

A Troll Lotta Love is the latest fantastical, time slip, Arthurian adventure for the Dept of Fimmigration which allows me to delve into ideas and genres that I love. I can highly recommend writing one of these. It really is a lot of fun. I hope you enjoyed the ride as much as I did.

All the best, and see you all soon, DCF.

READY FOR MORE

Somewhere Ogre the Rainbow

Probation officer Trevor Reeves wants to escape his chaotic life for good—but fate has other plans.

Rescued at death's door, he's drafted by the Department of Fimmigration (DOF) a secret agency overseeing supernatural borders. Teaming up with agents Matt and Kylah. Reeves soon realises he's in a different kind of nightmare. A world of collapsing bridges, cruel conspiracies, and power-hungry megalomaniacs from beyond

As the trio investigates these attacks, Reeves must reckon with his strange new role and unpredictable allies in a mission to save two worlds.

But does he have it in him to face the challenge, or will he simply give up (or become) the ghost??

Printed in Great Britain
by Amazon